Mark Urban graduated from the London School of Economics and served as a regular and territorial officer in the Royal Tank Regiment. He was Defence Correspondent of the *Independent* for more than three years before joining BBC2's *Newsnight* where he reported on the Gulf War, the collapse of Soviet communism and Bosnia. He spent a year as the BBC's Middle East Correspondent before being made *Newsnight*'s Diplomatic and Defence Correspondent. He is the author of several non-fiction books including the bestselling *Big boys' Rules: the Secret Struggle Against the IRA*. He has written one previous novel, *The Illegal*.

Also by Mark Urban and available from Headline Feature

The Illegal

The Linguist

Mark Urban

HEADLINE
FEATURE

First published in 1998
by HEADLINE BOOK PUBLISHING

First published in paperback in 1998
by HEADLINE BOOK PUBLISHING

A HEADLING FEATURE paperback

10 9 8 7 6 5 4 3 2 1

ISBN 0 7472 5471 0

Typeset by Avon Dataset Ltd, Bidford-on-Avon, Warks

Printed and bound in Great Britain by
Mackays of Chatham plc, Chatham, Kent

HEADLINE BOOK PUBLISHING
A division of Hodder Headline PLC
338 Euston Road
London NW1 3BH

For my beloved Isabelle

Chapter One

Lofting heard the distant thumping of the Chinook's approach and tried to gather his papers, vu-foils, pens, pointer and coffee together. In his hurry, he tipped over the plastic cup, sending a brown foaming wave across the presentation he had spent the last eight days preparing. 'Buggeration!'

The uncharacteristic eruption of bad language from inside the windowless office brought his secretary Brenda in at the run. As the pounding of huge rotors became louder, rattling the cheaply built office block, she mopped his notes with tissues. Both of them lunged for the phone as it sounded.

'Yes, I know they're almost here, I can hear them,' Lofting was shouting to make himself heard, 'I'll be right over.'

As he slammed the receiver down, she presented him with a cleaned-up stack of papers. 'Good luck, Mr Lofting. We know there's a lot riding on it.'

'Yes, thank you,' he said, although she hardly heard the 'you' as he was already through the door. As he raced along the path, Lofting felt the downwash of the massive helicopter as it dropped down towards the helipad. He was racing towards the squat three-storey building at Benhall where the Director and the other bigwigs had their offices. As the head of a newly formed and largely experimental division, he was lodged in one of the old Portakabins at the bottom of the slope below the office block, close to the triple fence which seals GCHQ from the unknowing world beyond.

Two firemen in silver suits stood by the side of the pad with an absurdly small fire extinguisher. Lofting wondered how much good it would do if the great machine with its two sets of whirring rotors were to strike a building or plough into the ground with all its VIPs on board. It was hardly a fanciful notion – it had happened at the Mull of Kintyre a couple of years earlier.

Lofting sent the door flying as he bounded into the main conference room where a phalanx of GCHQ high-ups awaited their distinguished guests. He made his way to the front of the hall, nodding at colleagues and muttering things none of them could quite make out. He heard a 'Good luck!' from Bill Jenkins, the head of K Division.

As Lofting struggled to organise his vu-foils, he remembered the Director's words again and again: 'Keep it simple, Ted, for heaven's sake.' He looked up to see the guests were already filing in.

He could not put a face to all of them, but he knew from the names in the Director's memo that they were the most senior audience he had ever addressed. Sir Peter Scarlett, the Cabinet Secretary, was there. Even if Lofting hadn't known his face, he would have detected the man who runs Whitehall from the nervous body language and brittle smiles of those around him: the permanent secretaries from Defence, the Foreign Office; one senior RAF officer; the Vice Chief of the Defence Staff.

Then Lofting recognised two people who had not been on his list: the Chief of MI6 and the Director

General of MI5. His heart began to pound madly. He wanted to loosen his collar and tie but couldn't. He had cautioned the Director that the labs had not yet produced a final working model, but the Director had insisted: 'No point keeping this magic to ourselves, Ted, we've got an iffy spending round coming up.' Now the Head of B Division was gripped with anxiety that the device codenamed OREGANO might not work as planned. Quickly Lofting checked his panic, telling himself that it would. It must.

As Bill Jenkins took his seat, he gave Lofting a nervous smile. Jenkins had never seen his old colleague look so overwrought. Lofting was a top-grade officer. His care in measuring his words, his rigorous methods, his professionalism were all well known at Cheltenham. Ted was a rarity here: having joined as an engineer he had so impressed his bosses that he had been able to switch into the fast-track management stream, the master race which ran the place. He had become one of the few divisional heads who had not joined GCHQ through the elite Graduate Management Training Scheme. Jenkins always thought Lofting looked like something of a relic from the heyday of the scientific civil service in the 1950s, when great legions of the best and brightest marched from Cambridge or Imperial straight into the labs at GCHQ, Aldermaston and Fort Halstead. Physically, there was something of Clem Attlee about Lofting: a largely bald pate, bushy moustache and a vaguely mischievous half-smile. As the boss of K Division watched his friend and colleague silently fussing with his notes and heard the guests fall silent in anticipation, he willed him on.

The Director mounted the podium and began the presentation. 'Ladies and gentlemen, we've invited you

3

here because we believe we have found a solution to the biggest problem facing the signals intelligence community in the world today . . .' He then held aloft what looked to most people like a small piece of electrical flex and said: 'This! The fibre optic cable.'

Scarlett sipped from a coffee cup as he listened. Nobody was taking notes. To make jottings at a presentation as highly classified as this one would have been the surest sign of the ingenu, and this audience consisted of the scions of the secret state.

'This section of cable was dug up by our British special forces sixty miles south of Baghdad during the Gulf War; it was called Operation MAUDE.' The Director came to the front of the stage and handed his trophy to somebody in the first row who nodded appreciatively and passed it on to another guest. He continued, 'It was the main link between GHQ in Baghdad and Southern Theatre HQ in Basra. Before we dug it up on January 23rd 1991 we had very little of Saddam's strategic traffic. After that . . . well,' the Director smirked knowingly at Scarlett, 'our results were most impressive, he was forced to use the good old-fashioned wireless set. In the next war we may not be able to pull off a coup like that. Short of war, we can hardly go landing the SBS in countries whose signals we can no longer intercept. Our problem today is that the volume of world telecommunications traffic moving through fibre optics has multiplied tenfold since 1991.'

The Director continued his presentation, showing graphs of the trends in GCHQ's target countries, noting that the Americans had no answer to the problem and speculating on what the Russians might be doing. Lofting recognised the words which signalled his ordeal was about to begin: 'What we have come up with is something codenamed OREGANO. We're so convinced of its effectiveness that we've formed a new division to prepare our discovery for operational use. I'd like to ask Ted Lofting, who heads that new division and is one of our most distinguished senior officers, to tell you what it does. Ted . . .'

Lofting rose to his feet and, as he was about to speak, felt a sudden inspiration. Ignoring the 'No Smoking' signs, he drew his pipe from the pocket of his tweed jacket, pressed down some Old Holborn in its bowl and lit up. Savouring the impatience of his audience like some summer season comic, he took a good long draw and blew out a cloud of smoke before he began.

'Thank you, Director. I won't keep you on tenterhooks any longer.' Lofting's voice was completely composed; his panicked run to the admin block apparently belonged to another time. 'OREGANO is a device we have designed which allows us to tap the signals passing down a fibre optic line. To our knowledge, nobody else in the world has anything like it.'

As he spoke, a curtain drew back behind him revealing several technicians sitting at computer terminals.

'The problem with fibre optic cable is that, if you cut it, the user will detect the interruption in his signal. This is why all of our defence communications network trunk lines have random streams of data sent down them when they are not in use – any break in the signal would be noticed. So what we had to do was come up with something which would allow us to intercept the signals going along the cable without cutting the cable or reducing the strength of those signals in any detectable way.'

Lofting walked over to one of his teams: 'Right, Jennifer, please start sending the test signal.' He walked the few feet to the other side of the stage, tracing a fibre optic cable with his finger as he went, then pointing to a monitor, on which the test message was appearing. He walked back to about halfway along the cable and showed his audience a matt-black device about the size of a small drum of motor oil which was attached to the cable. 'This is OREGANO. It's very small, as you see, although it does consume quite a bit of power, so it needs a healthy supply. That's one area where we would like to make improvements.' He smiled pleasantly at his audience, the people expected to find the money. 'If you look onto that wall you will see a display connected to OREGANO. We haven't started the interception yet, so of course the display has nothing on it. Sir Peter, may I ask you to step onto the stage?'

The Cabinet Secretary stood a little self-consciously, surprised to find himself in the role of magician's assistant.

'Now if you will just join me at this display.' Lofting took his station next to a powerful desktop. The Cabinet Secretary looked at the screen, a little surprised to find it looked much like any other computer application:

INTERCEPTION PROTOCOL START [Y]
TYPE N TO HALT

'If I may just ask you to press "enter", Sir Peter . . .' As he finished the words, Lofting's nerves finally showed themselves: he sucked vigorously on his pipe. The Cabinet Secretary tapped the key with a small flourish and both men looked up at the wall-mounted display. The words 'Welcome Sir Peter Scarlett and other distinguished guests' raced along the display, repeating themselves every few seconds.

There was an audible 'Bravo, Ted!' from Bill Jenkins. The Director smiled benignly; his Whitehall invitees murmured, apparently impressed.

Lofting savoured his moment of triumph. 'Of course, I can't tell you exactly how it works but . . .' he looked down at his audience over the top of his half-moon glasses, 'it is done with mirrors! And some laser light.'

The Director mounted the stage and told the guests it was time for lunch. People had begun to stand when the Chief of MI6 cleared his throat: 'I think we've got one or two questions before we move on.'

The Director shot a nervous glance at Lofting. 'Certainly.'

'Obviously you still have to plant OREGANO somewhere on the line. Yes?'

'Indeed,' Lofting replied.

'So there will always be a risk of discovery.'

'We're planning to make all of the components untraceable – as you know the components are made either by us or sourced in a particular way, as you'll remember from Operation CATALYST in Moscow,' the Director chipped in, wondering why the boss of MI6 had been brought along at all.

'It's just a matter of a little more funding,' said Lofting, much to the annoyance of the Director, who had hoped to stay off the subject of money.

'How much?'

'Well—'

'We can discuss that later, Chief,' the Director interrupted Lofting.

The guests repaired to the Director's dining room, where the Cabinet Secretary had been seated to the GCHQ head's right. Lofting was the only other GCHQ officer present: all of the remaining places at the table had been taken by the visitors from London. On the walls of the dining room were a GCHQ crest, some slightly faded photographs of listening posts around the world and a somewhat overspecified wall clock – bewildering in the number and complexity of the cogs and springs which whirred in full view – with a plaque underneath saying 'Presented to the Director by R Division Apprentices, 11th February 1978.'

'We're lucky enough to have a most creative chef,' the Director boasted, as his guests surveyed the chicken breast with a peach coulis.

'This is really ghastly,' Sir Terence Jennings, the Foreign Office Permanent Secretary, murmured to the Air Chief Marshal.

Throughout the meal, the Director succeeded in keeping his guests off the subject of money. He sensed, however, that Lofting's presentation had gone down well. Sir Peter Scarlett had said something about how good it was to see it was still a world-class organisation. Jennings argued that the invention of OREGANO confounded those who claimed the spending cuts of the mid-1990s had emasculated the establishment's research and development capability.

As the guests filed out towards the waiting Chinook, the Director gave Lofting a benign smile and allowed himself the unheard of intimacy of patting his new division head on the back: 'I think we've done it, Ted, excellent presentation!'

'Thank you. Do you think perhaps we might do a similar turn for the Foreign Secretary?' Lofting asked, already keen to try his spiel on another audience.

'Heavens no!' the Director recoiled, startled and at the same time vaguely comforted by Lofting's lack of savvy about Whitehall protocol. 'We couldn't possibly show this to politicians without Sir Peter's say-so; he'd cut me off at the knees if I tried that. "Direct lobbying to ministers," that's what he'd say. No, no. We couldn't possibly. We'll have to carry this through the PSIS machinery to get the proper funding, then perhaps at some future time . . .'

Lofting set off towards his office, composing his report of the event to Brenda as he went. Phrases like 'I think it did the trick' and 'they seemed to take on board the magnitude of our discovery' were going through his mind as he spotted Cord Cortland heading towards him along the same path. Lofting wondered whether he might take evasive action, but resigned himself to having to walk straight past the senior American official based at Cheltenham, since veering off onto the grass would be too obvious a ploy.

Cortland was known to all at GCHQ as Suslo, which meant Senior US Liaison Officer. There were some who argued that he was the second most powerful man in the organisation after their own director. Others disagreed: they said Cortland was the bigger fish. While the Americans knew about British research into fibre optic interception, the success of OREGANO had been concealed from them. There were very few areas in which GCHQ could offer their cousins in the eavesdropping business anything of real value any more, so OREGANO was being kept under wraps until it could be used to get the maximum possible leverage.

The Suslo had one of those extremely short haircuts favoured by American military types. He was a big man; his frame belied his New York Dutch origins. Cortland had been a high-flyer at NSA, GCHQ's American sister organisation, until Iranian Revolutionary Guards seized the embassy in Tehran. Cortland and the CIA Station Chief were not personally responsible for the fact that the shredded contents of their registries had been pieced together by squads of veiled Persian women, but somehow blame had attached itself to them. It had happened, as Cortland himself put it when drawn onto the subject, 'on my watch'. Lofting hoped against hope that his 'good afternoon' would suffice to get him past the American, but it did not.

'Hi, Ted, I see you've had some bigshots to visit.' Cortland knew this was about as far as he could go. Under the unwritten rules of intelligence community etiquette, any more direct enquiry would be bad form.

'Oh yes, indeed,' said Lofting a little nervously. 'Just trying to impress them for the upcoming spending round.' He knew that he might well have to brief Cortland on OREGANO at some point and consoled himself that this answer was not a lie, since it was part of the reason for his presentation.

'I hope you did the trick!' the Suslo replied as he resumed his journey towards the Director's office.

Cortland knew he had been given flannel, but that it was impossible for him to push the point. Lofting felt no guilt about it because on this occasion the high security classifications and compartmentalisation of knowledge which surrounded their daily work was justified: OREGANO really was an invention which could change the whole nature of espionage.

Chapter Two

Phil Keitel enjoyed his reputation as one of the Agency's old school. He was known as a *bon viveur* who subsidised his pleasures from his own pocket in these cash-strapped times at CIA. Phil's greatest pleasure was his food, and he did not intend to let his casework in Lyon pass without enjoying the delights of Paul Bocuse's celebrated restaurant. The fifty-three-year-old Pennsylvanian had a large frame, but the fact that he was pushing twenty stone meant he was rotund in anybody's book. While his appearance occasionaly earned him looks of contempt from the thrusters padding the corridors at Langley, in Lyon, France's gastronomic city, and at Paul Bocuse, the holy of holies of Lyonnais cooking, Phil's florid cheeks, jowls and ample frontage helped him fit in nicely.

Phil dined alone because his partner, a reedy man in his early thirties with high cheekbones and narrow eyes, had insisted that he was not going to spend $100 of his own money getting lunch on the job. At first, Phil had tried to persuade his colleague, James MacTernan, to come with him, saying 'You will never truly understand this country unless you allow me to rally your palate to a few of its gastronomic summits.' MacTernan had replied deadpan, 'Phil, I'll get a sandwich.' The younger CIA man did not hold Phil's lofty Ivy League tone against him. He knew Keitel had been in Vietnam, Iran

11

and other places and that his prickly wit had long ago cost the chance of promotion. He also knew there was much that Keitel could teach him.

Keitel consumed a last mouthful of soufflé and asked for the bill. He saw with satisfaction that his feast had only cost the equivalent of $90. It was true, of course, that he had limited himself to a single glass of Brouilly rather than the bottle he craved, but this was work after all. In flawless French, he recounted highlights of the meal to the waiter, who greeted his remarks with suitable expressions of delight. He then signed the American Express bill with the name 'Mike Samuels', picked up the aluminium briefcase beside his chair and left. Keitel and MacTernan met on the street not far from the Gare de Perrache.

'I trust your sandwich was pleasant?'

'Fine, fine I got a *croque monsieur* at a bar up the street there – and a coffee.'

'James, when my retirement comes around, which is not too long now, I shall always remember you as the man who was offered the culinary equivalent of an orgy with the world's supermodels and chose instead to give himself a handjob in the corner.'

MacTernan smiled weakly. He might resent Keitel's humour but he remained the junior officer on this case.

The two men parted on the street and Keitel headed for the Hotel Laconte, a sad place a couple of notches up from those which rented rooms by the hour. He signed in and handed over a Canadian passport in the name of Frederick Stephens for registration. Armed with his key, Keitel proceeded to the third floor.

Meanwhile, a few hundred metres up the street, MacTernan had taken up position in a café and sipped his seventh espresso of the day.

12

* * *

Fourteen minutes later, the man described in Agency records as WE/KITE but known to his case officers as Thierry Dupré appeared. MacTernan looked around, checking for surveillance as he left his seat, went out onto the street and fell in about twenty metres behind the Frenchman. In more hostile environments, there might be seven or eight operatives conducting counter-surveillance. The head of the Clandestine Service's Western Europe Division did not feel that Dupré merited such attention, so instead the task fell solely to MacTernan.

As he drew level with the entrance to the hotel, the Frenchman stopped and pretended to tie his laces. MacTernan walked past him, checked the road ahead and drew a mobile phone from his pocket, dialling Phil Keitel's number from memory.

'Jerry?' MacTernan began, 'Just to tell you I can't make the meeting. Too bad, huh?' As he spoke, MacTernan made eye contact with the moustachioed Frenchman, who stood about fifteen feet away from him. The subtlest glimmer of recognition and complicity passed between them. This was their third meeting. Without saying a word, MacTernan put the phone back in his pocket and made a note in a diary. This was his prearranged signal to Dupré that it was safe for him to proceed into the hotel. Keitel had already checked the lobby, corridors and room.

Keitel had prepared two chilled beers as Dupré rapped on the door. The CIA man intended simply to take a few sips of his, but had noticed during previous meetings that Dupré liked a drink while he was talking.

'Jack!' Dupré said as the door opened and he recognised his handler. 'Come in, my friend.' The conversation proceeded in French.

Keitel did not mention his fine lunch to Dupré, he believed doing so might annoy a middle-ranking executive in France Telecom. 'How was Morocco?'

'Very pleasant, thank you. Sylvie couldn't believe how we could afford another holiday so soon after Flaine, but it didn't seem to worry her too much.'

'Perhaps we should work out something to say to her – could you say that you're doing some freelance work for a German firm or something?' Keitel prompted.

'*Peut-être, peut-être*,' maybe, maybe.

They chatted about Thierry's children. As the agent lamented the lack of a home computer, Keitel wondered if this was a hint. He made a mental note, while the conversation progressed into Pentiums, Windows 95 and educational software. Keitel fought the instinct to move onto subjects which he would have found more interesting, instead thinking up different ways to allow Dupré to talk about the bewildering variety of topics which shared one common denominator: money and how he needed more of it.

Phil had run many sources who he called 'givers', people who felt the need to spill their thoughts without mentioning reward or even needing to be complimented as they did so. It was sometimes quite difficult to hand money to 'givers' – they found it painfully embarrassing. Often he would have to resort to gifts or 'loans' in order to overcome their sense of guilt at being rewarded for their treachery. Some of them, a small number of course, really didn't want anything for their services, but a comfortable democracy like France was not the place to find such people. The real 'givers' existed only in odious dictatorships.

Thierry was very definitely a 'taker'. He peppered

the conversation with references to the cost of kids' clothes, the electricity bill, the car, the whole nine yards. Keitel began to play a game as his informant rattled on: he counted the number of words between Thierry's mentions of French francs or '*balles*', which was slang for the same thing. The Frenchman's longest interval between these words had reached thirty-eight (only Keitel had cheated a bit: he had added '*liquide*' as he went) when he realised he was being asked directly for money. The CIA man moved to the bed, popped the locks on his briefcase and brought out four bricks of 500-franc notes, $30,000 dollars' worth in all.

Dupré was then silent as he spent the best part of twelve minutes counting the notes. It was only then that their conversation began in earnest.

'You asked me about the Jubayl-Riyadh trunk modernisation contract.'

Keitel nodded: he had received details of the French bid during their last encounter, in Abu Dhabi.

'Our bid is seven hundred and two million US for option one in the paper I gave you last time, four hundred and sixty-eight million US for option two.'

'What can you tell me about the Shantung project?' Keitel enquired about France Telecom's plans to build a plant in southern China through a front company – a plant which would produce the hardware to modernise China's entire telecommunications system.

'We've still got a couple of meetings to go before the contracts will be ready for signing. Nobody thinks the deal will be closed before next Easter. There's some concern in Paris that the British might be onto it – maybe trying to block our deal.'

The two men spent a few minutes reviewing various aspects of the French company's export business –

aspects which Dupré as number two in the overseas contracts setup was well placed to know about – when a mischievous look crossed the Frenchman's face. He leaned forward and handed Keitel a floppy disk.

'There are some interesting files on here. Let's call it a present from me.'

'Oh?' Keitel replied; his surprise at the idea of a gift from Thierry left him momentarily speechless.

'It's nothing to do with my department but my work on foreign contracts means I have the highest level of access to our network. It's about *TONNANT*.'

'*TONNANT?*' Keitel chipped in. The word meant something like Thundery or Thunderer – but that was hardly a clue.

'It's a French government project. Very secret. You have never heard about it?'

'No I haven't. What's it about?'

'You can read the files when you get home. It is about the most secure communications system in France. It's just finished. It connects all of the special places,' Thierry reeled them off: '*Elysée, Matignon, Intérieur, DST* – they are all being connected by *TONNANT* – voice, data, video, everything.'

'Excellent, I don't know what we'd do without you!' Keitel placed the disk into a concealed pocket inside the briefcase as the Frenchman stood and began to move towards the door.

'Goodbye, Thierry,' the American took his informant by the hand, 'keep well. You can treat yourself to that new Peugeot now. Until the next time!'

Chapter Three

As Margaret Reynolds took the first Kirwandan inter-cept tape from the combination-locked drawer under her desk she could not concentrate. Her thoughts ran like a torrent, swirling and eddying feelings of betrayal and bile as she placed the cassette into the player and slapped down its lid. She hoped the daily ritual would soon carry her off, distract her from the full horror of what that spineless turd Peter had done to her.

'Morning, Mags!' A cheerful voice from behind her broke the trance.

'Hello there, Edward,' she replied, and asked dutifully, 'Good weekend?'

'Yes, pretty good really,' the other linguist answered. 'We went water skiing again with the kids.'

She did not listen as Edward droned on about the prodigious sporting abilities of his six-year-old son; instead she just made occasional interested noises. It was Reynolds's section – she led the team of a dozen linguists – but it was informally run and most of them called her Mags or Magsie. The task of the section was to cover Africa but, like Reynolds herself, its members had mastered a bewildering variety of tongues.

She put the headphones on and fired up her computer, ready to begin transcription. Margaret's hair was blonde, but streaks of grey were gaining a grip, so the combination looked a little mousy. Her eyes were clear blue and complexion fair but her English-rose looks were not flawless. Margaret's brow had taken on almost permanent furrows, as if she couldn't get over life's iniquities. Her nose was rather bulbous at the end – not enough to spoil her face, but to deny her real beauty.

Reynolds was GCHQ's primary translator for Kirwanda, the language used extensively in Rwanda and Burundi; another member of her section was studying it. She had learned the language several years earlier, but now of course it was in vogue as there was the prospect of British troops being sent there and the bosses had decided more people needed to know it. Her first language was French, very useful in Africa of course, and she had also mastered Spanish, Romanian and Swahili. She had been fluent in French and Spanish when she joined, some seventeen years earlier, but the other three languages had been learned while working for the government, and each of them was worth another £12 per month on her pay packet. She had plans to study Thai and Bahasa although she wondered whether she would ever achieve any kind of proficiency.

Margaret was not exceptionally gifted at languages, but she applied herself singlemindedly. She had not graduated with first-class honours or anything like that, but had built her proficiency in each language over years. When learning a new one, she immersed herself in it completely, reading its literature, travelling to places where it was spoken and even raiding world music shops in London for its pop records. Her methodical approach and humility meant she fitted in very well with others at Cheltenham.

The intercept in front of her was a signal fished out

of the ether by an American satellite called MAGNUM
4B. It consisted of a conversation between the
commander of a Rwandan army brigade and his headquarters in Kigali. The signal was not encrypted and the
two people talking were very sloppy in their voice
procedure and attention to security.

'Will Claude come?' one voice asked. She imagined
its owner sitting sweating in some tin-roofed shack.

'Who knows with him?'

'But we need his car for Uncle Joe.'

Slowly it dawned on Margaret that the conversation
seemed mainly to concern the organisation of a wedding
party. This annoyed her intensely since it prevented her
using work to smother thoughts about Peter.

Six weeks ago he had told her it was over. It had
happened before but this time it was completely different. A mutual friend had let slip at a party the
previous day that Peter was getting married. Married!
Seven years she had been with him and now six bloody
weeks after he calls it quits he's engaged to someone
else. When had it started? It couldn't have started five
and a half weeks ago; she couldn't believe that. And
then she felt close to crying as she remembered all of
the stupid excuses he had used when she asked why
they didn't get married, all of the ways she had fooled
herself that he might still come good, all of the times
she had believed that her father might still walk her
down the aisle.

She put the intercept tape back into its secure
container and fished out another one. It sounded more
promising, a Rwandan minister talking on his carphone.

'Our friend from Mulenge says he needs more
assistance militaire.' The reference in French to military
help was a little odd, but she had grown used to people

19

in that part of the world dropping French or English phrases into their vernacular.

'Mzee's always scrounging – tell him to dig up more gold!'

The two men laughed in complicity. Yes, this was more promising: they were obviously talking about Laurent Kabila, the newly-installed Zairean president. She began a new intercept report page on her computer.

Instead of heading to the canteen for lunch, Margaret Reynolds left the base. It took quite a while to walk to the back gate, across the fields where the bigwigs landed in their helicopters around to the phonebox in Springbank Road on the estate with her pile of change. She spent the best part of an hour there. As she was coming back, feeling painfully exposed as she crossed the open ground behind the Benhall buildings, Ray Skinner caught sight of her and waved. She did not respond.

Skinner was an earthy ex-Royal Navy chief petty officer who had been working at Cheltenham for a few years. Ray had long lusted after Margaret Reynolds from afar. He was single; his wife had moved out fifteen years ago, when he was on a nine-month round-the-world deployment on *Invincible*. They did not have children and he did not particularly regret her passing, as he had been coming to the conclusion that she was a shrew. But as the years had gone by and he had failed to find someone else, Skinner had abandoned his dreams of starting a family, consoling himself instead with a series of flings with the wives of shipmates.

As he watched Reynolds stride back towards the main gate he admired her long, athletic legs. She had looked after herself well – did aerobics a couple of times a week, played tennis and cycled to work in summer.

Although thirty-nine, she had been able to keep the sort of figure which women admire because it is the perfect Size 10 of the clothes horse and men fancy because it suggests the power and self confidence of a superior lover. Her dress sense, though, like many of her attitudes, was definitely Cheltenham and a little out of date. Ray looked at her sensible court shoes, navy pleated skirt and guernsey sweater and daydreamed about her in something racier.

On the way back to her desk, Reynolds bumped into Brenda Skuse, a busy-body who considered herself one of Margaret's close friends. Brenda was Ted Lofting's secretary and, although Margaret was happy enough to be friendly, she didn't want it developing into anything that went outside work. Brenda was aware of the breakup of the relationship with Peter so she began gently by her standards: 'Hello, my dear! You're looking super.'

'Do you think so?'

'Yes, lovely, but then you'd look good in anything! Was the weekend bearable?'

Margaret knew the grilling was starting but kept her fixed smile: 'Oh yes, it went quickly enough,' she replied. 'I went to see Dad of course on Saturday, as usual.'

'How was he?'

'Oh, you know, it's settled into a bit of a pattern these days, just the occasional burst of him being his old self. He spent most of the time singing this song; I suppose it must be a 1950s song that he remembers from his youth; he must have sung it for an hour and a half while I was there.'

'I'm sure he benefits from your visits though. Mags . . . you will come around to dinner soon, won't you?'

'Of course. You know my routine well enough. There's Keep Fit tomorrow of course; I'll probably stop in and work on my Thai course Wednesday; Thursdays I'm usually free!'

'Well, I'll be in touch,' said Brenda, apparently backing away from a firm date.

'That would be super!' Margaret said, grateful that nothing specific was arranged.

As they parted, Brenda decided that Magsie must be a very balanced person to remain so positive in the face of her twin personal disasters.

That evening when Peter returned to his flat, the indicator on his answerphone showed there were twenty-three messages waiting for him. Under normal circumstances three or four would have been the cause for mild excitement. He pressed the 'play' button with trepidation.

'It's me,' Margaret's voice. 'I'm sorry about all the things I said,' she let out a great sigh, 'I suppose we might as well be civilised about this; it just doesn't work out sometimes between people. Timings . . . you know . . . everything else. Anyway, I suppose it's goodbye then.'

The answerphone beeped, the figure '2' flashed up in the message indicator and it began to play, 'I can't just say goodbye I'm afraid,' her voice was exasperated now. 'How can I wish you luck when I hear you're going off to get married. How do you think that makes me feel? Why couldn't you tell me what was going on? I trusted you. Well, you've really screwed up the last seven years of my life,' her tone had reached despair. 'You promised me you would never leave me, you promised.' Peter knew this was true. He had said that, albeit two years ago, staring up at the bedroom ceiling at 3 a.m. when he had reached the end of his tether during one of her anxiety attacks. Margaret's message finished, 'So I'm not sorry at all that you're out of my life.'

By message 14, there were no words. There was just a scary howling cry like the noise of a mortally wounded beast going to ground in the forest. Peter thought of wiping the remaining messages; he had already spent a quarter of an hour standing by the answerphone. He gazed towards his mantelpiece, where the heavily embossed invitation to his wedding was propped up. He did feel guilty about leaving her this way. He owed her this last favour of hearing through her pain. Anyway, he thought absentmindedly, someone else might have left a message too. So he fixed himself a large Scotch and sat through.

As the indicator showed message 19 her tone was completely normal, almost as if she was talking across her desk in the office: 'I'll survive I suppose. Perhaps you've done me a favour. I just wish you could have done me the same favour a few years ago.'

Beep, number 20, more agitated again: 'I hope you haven't been too bored listening to these messages, but I couldn't be bothered to sit down and write it all down for you. Anyway, goodbye.'

Number 21: 'I hate what you've done to me; I hate you, Peter.'

Number 22: 'Anyway, don't worry about me. I'll find someone else. There's still a few here that fancy me even if I am an old maid, so piss off!'

Peter took a long draw of whisky as the last message began: 'All I wanted was to marry you, that's all I wanted. For me to wear a white dress. For my father to give me away in the church at Milton. For us to walk back from church across the fields to Ascot holding

hands. And I never will now. My father never will now,
you bastard!'

Chapter Four

Ted Lofting's home was in Charlton Park, one of the smarter areas on the fringes of Cheltenham. He had bought the house twenty years earlier with a large mortgage. Once the eighties boom sent prices beyond the reach of someone pulling in a civil service Grade 5 salary, the house became their nest-egg for retirement, a promise of comfort for him and Sara. About the only promise of comfort Ted had.

The Loftings' union had produced a single child, Emma. She had arrived in their mid-thirties after years of fruitless trying and late enough to ensure that she would remain their only issue. This year Ted had reached fifty and Emma fifteen. To him, both of these milestones seemed ominous. He had come to recognise that he would not make it to the top at work, and in the inner sanctum of his mind he still hankered after the directorship. Emma's fifteenth year seemed to have brought her to some sort of crisis of adolescent awkwardness and surliness. The contradictions of her past as a child – she still insisted on going horseriding on Sunday mornings – sat uneasily with the seismic forces of her emerging adulthood. Her fixations with the callow youths at her school drove her through extreme mood swings. Ted knew this was all part of being a teenager – he had compared notes with the parents of enough of her schoolfriends – but he was worried about the intensity of her darker moods.

As he sat at breakfast, Lofting was even less communicative than usual. His occasional grunts in response to Sara's readings from the *Daily Mail* did not in themselves constitute evidence that he was listening to a word she said. Emma remained silent. She did not respond to either of her parents' 'Good Mornings'.

'I see the Duchess of York is pushing her tawdry autobiography...'

'Mmm.' Lofting's head remained arched over his *Telegraph*.

'She's lost weight. I suppose that's one thing. I don't know why she thinks these outpourings of self-pity are worthwhile. Stupid girl!' Sara's harangue continued with her characteristic cut-glass vowels.

Emma stood up and raced upstairs without saying anything.

'I might be home a little later than usual tonight,' Lofting said as he folded his paper neatly and stood up. 'An important meeting in London.'

'I'm sure it is,' his wife remarked sourly. At the time they married, Sara's parents – her father, Sir Percy Higginbotham, reached lieutenant general before retiring from the Army – had considered the match beneath her. Although she had defied them in the spirit of young love, their two decades of marriage had apparently brought her round to the view that her parents were right all along.

Lofting had left his usual tweed jacket in the wardrobe and donned a clapped-out navy-blue pinstripe suit for his trip to the Cabinet Office. As he made his way to the door, he tucked the tupperware box containing his sandwiches into his briefcase, which was empty apart from some crossword puzzles cut out of the *Telegraph*, and called out, 'I should be home by six thirty,' as he banged the front door.

Lofting and the Director passed the journey in the Daimler to London by exchanging vague pleasantries. It was their habit not to discuss the detail of their work outside the office, even if this car did receive the most comprehensive annual de-bugging inspection of any automobile in the country, bar the Prime Minister's. So the two men in the Daimler switched uneasily between perusal of their briefing papers and desultory conversation about the state of English cricket, BSE and the social unacceptability of mobile phones. The atmosphere was not helped by the fact that Lofting knew the Director was relying on OREGANO to try to save the agency from heavy cuts.

On arrival at the Cabinet Office in Whitehall, they passed through the glass tubes at the entrance which sniffed them for explosives and headed up to the second floor. A uniformed guard of the government's Custody Service examined their passes before unlocking a heavy iron grille gate which controlled access to the floor. They passed into the ante-room of the Intelligence Coordinator where they found a number of other officials waiting with the tense expectation of dental patients expecting a full extraction. Although Lofting often considered his Director to be a master of meaningless phrasemaking, he found himself admiring the old man's *sang froid* as he stood their turn in front of the Permanent Secretaries' committee, which handed out the money to the intelligence services and was known in their world as PSIS which insiders pronounced as 'P.Sis'.

Once inside the meeting room they surveyed a dozen faces – the significant ones had all been at the OREGANO demonstration the previous week. There was Air Chief Marshal Atkinson, the Vice Chief of the Defence Staff, this time resplendent in his uniform with its single medal ribbon, Sir Terence Jennings from the Foreign Office and a number of others.

The committee's task was to marshal the different requests for money from MI6, MI5 and GCHQ, allowing them and the mandarins who represented the customers for their information to slug it out. The Director of GCHQ already knew that MI5 had questioned the efficacy of OREGANO but he was not sure what kind of ride the others would give him.

As the two GCHQ men took their places at the table, they were handed cups of tepid coffee and a plate with three stale digestives on it.

'Well, we've had a chance to study your submission for Project OREGANO and I think there are still one or two points of concern.'

'I'm sure we can allay that,' the Director answered with a smile.

'The outturn on the project, since its inception has been . . .' The Chairman looked into his specs at a long printout of figures which clearly baffled him.

'At current prices, with the Treasury inflator, £78m,' the voice of the Coordinator's number two, a fearsome-looking MoD civil servant in her forties chipped in.

'There is a concern, Malcolm,' he addressed the GCHQ chief by his first name, 'that this technology remains . . . unready for operational use.'

'We are ready to use it operationally, Dickie, but we do need a little more funding just to develop a new power supply unit for OREGANO and to manufacture non-traceable components for the first three units and for £14m we believe—'

'It's £14m this year and another £11m next year, isn't it?' the man from the Home Office cut in.

'Well, the £11m next year covers a number of improvements we hope to make following its first operational use: that's right, isn't it, Ted?'

'Indeed, Director. Next year's heading covers training and establishment costs for staffing B Division too,' Lofting prompted.

'I'll be surprised if we see our first intercepts for under £100m,' Terence Jennings drawled while looking out of the window onto Whitehall to admire the auburn mane of hair on a young woman running across the street, and already savouring the idea of lunch at the Garrick.

'You do understand why it's hard for us to authorise such substantial additional expenditure in this year's public-spending climate?' the Chairman remarked.

'What we have here is world-beating British technology,' the GCHQ Director countered. 'We have the ability to make signal intelligence history!'

'You've certainly made spending history,' the Home Office man shot back.

'Couldn't the Americans chip in the extra?' the voice of the Treasury was heard at last.

'We believe that if we can use OREGANO operationally and deliver the first intercepts to the Americans then we can say, *voilà*! Show this to anyone who doubts the wisdom of the UK-USA partnership! If the Americans get involved in funding the first operations they will inevitably start to regard our invention as their property.'

'QV radar, the computer, the Harrier jumpjet *et al.*,'

the Air Chief Marshal added helpfully.

'It is really a question of whether we wish to remain in the first rank of sigint powers. If we do then this is the kind of investment we have to make.'

'Malcolm, everybody here, particularly those who were at your fascinating demonstration, understands the quality of research which has made this invention possible, so surely this is the moment to say to the Cousins, 'Look, this is what we can do, how about some funding?'

After a further fifteen minutes of skirmishing the committee members adjourned. The session would continue that afternoon without the GCHQ men present. The Director had already made an arrangement to have lunch with Terence Jennings at the Garrick Club. He parted from Lofting with an absentminded, 'Would three o'clock outside the Cabinet Office be all right, Ted?'

Lofting strode along Whitehall in the early autumn drizzle, protected from the elements by a Barbour and flatcap. At Charing Cross, he boarded a train to Greenwich. As it rattled along, he tucked into his salmon paste sandwiches and wondered whether he had said ten or eleven words in the meeting. He decided the 'B' in B Division did not count as a word and tried a number of times to remember the exact phrases he'd said.

As he strode up the Garrick stairs with Terence Jennings, the Director of GCHQ knew that this informal meeting with the Foreign Office Permanent Secretary was his last chance to lobby for an all-British OREGANO. The Garrick was a lawyers' and hacks' haunt, with very few Foreign Office men on its roll. The Head of the Diplomatic Service, Jennings also held that title, liked it for that very reason – it fitted with his self-image as a thoroughly modern mandarin who eschewed the Travellers' or Reform clubs in favour of keeping a toehold in the wider world. In fact, the visitor from Cheltenham knew enough about his host's career in the Foreign Office to know that his background was utterly traditional – down to having read Classics at Christ's – and that he had got the idea of joining the Garrick when he had heard that the previous Cabinet Secretary was a member. The PUS's looks fitted into the traditional mould of the British oligarchy too – he had matinée-idol features.

Jennings sipped a double Bloody Mary while the two men perused the menu.

'I must say, I appreciate the opportunity for this chat,' the Director began.

'I can really recommend the *Crotin de Chèvre*, Malcolm.'

'Indeed, well I'll go along with that then . . . So do you think the Committee was convinced?'

'The venison is rather middling . . . people speak highly of the monkfish here . . . and of course the rib of beef is usually *sans pareil*.'

Having been parried with such brutality, the head of GCHQ realised he had no alternative but to let the Foreign Office man set the pace for the conversation.

The main course plates had been cleared and it was almost 2 p.m. before Jennings began: 'In OREGANO, at least, we have a project which we can discuss over fine food without fear of someone hearing the name.'

'Quite!' the Director answered with relief.

'Malcolm, your people really have come up with something terrific. How soon do you think we could get it into action?'

The Director knew Lofting had told him the operational model would take another £10m and six months. 'There's no reason why we couldn't put it into action tomorrow – some of the improvements could be made along the way.'

'What about targets?'

'We've identified three possible links which we think might be particularly vulnerable to attack.' It would have gone against all the GCHQ man's instincts to list them in public.

'Ummm,' Jennings surveyed his dessert, 'do tell.'

'Here?'

'We should be all right if you keep your voice down.'

'I'm really not sure . . .' the Director bridled.

'Just tell me the target nations,' Jennings said in a slightly exasperated way.

'One is in . . .' the Director looked around with a schoolboyish air of conspiracy, 'Japan, one in Baghdad and . . . er . . . the other New York.'

'New York!'

'At the United Nations, yes.'

'I'm not sure what the Yanks would think of that,' he spooned some *Crême Brûlé* into his mouth. 'I suppose they might go for it.'

'If it was an all-UK project we wouldn't tell them. UN Missions have never counted as US territory as far as the usual allied rules of the game have gone.'

'We'll have to tell them, Malcolm,' Jennings shook his head like the school head boy reining in an over-zealous prefect. 'PSIS won't find you more than £7m to finish the project. You can't do it for that can you?'

'Well, obviously it would be far better to have more than that.'

'Malcolm, you know we'll have to give OREGANO

to the Americans eventually and you now have a working prototype; you've made your point most effectively already.'

'But just imagine their faces,' the GCHQ chief had become animated, 'if we could be feeding them reams of top quality intercepts from a target *they* really value with them going out of their minds trying to work out how we'd done it – our three potential targets have been selected with that in mind! The payoff to GCHQ would be that much higher than if we tell them now.'

'Oh, is *that* why you chose those three targets?' Jennings allowed his irritation to show: 'Listen, Malcolm, I can tell you it's time to get American funding into the programme. You know what they're like – you'll have unlimited resources to do the job properly and you'll have made your point *vis-à-vis* the quality of British research.'

The Director smiled weakly and agreed, understanding that Sir Terence's offer of lunch had never been more than a consolation prize.

Lofting had meandered through the galleries of the National Maritime Museum for over an hour without thinking of OREGANO, Sara or the journey home. He had been keen to see a special exhibition on the life of Admiral George Rodney while he was in London and it had not disappointed him. He studied the paintings of wooden-walled ships of the line with the eye of a true connoisseur, searching out little details to add to his fund of knowledge – a fine study of the capture of Admiral de Grasse aboard his flagship at the Saints, a sketch of Sir George as a young man aboard the *Eagle* and some of Rodney's personal letters. Lofting had failed his Admiralty Inspection Board as a nineteen-year-old on the grounds of poor eyesight, and this had put paid to his dreams of emulating the nautical heroes of his childhood. He remained though passionately interested in sail, consumed the seafaring novels of Patrick O'Brian with relish and had acquired his own miniature fleet for re-fighting the great actions of the time on his dining-room table.

Lofting was browsing in the museum bookshop when he realised how late it was. He rushed to the railway station so briskly that he was gasping for breath. During the fifteen-minute journey, he completed two *Telegraph* cryptic crosswords which he had been saving for just such a moment of stress.

The return journey to Cheltenham passed with the same banal conversation as the one down. Lofting had judged the mood of the PSIS meeting well enough to know there was little chance of keeping OREGANO to themselves for much longer. His feelings about this were not entirely negative. He knew the ways of Whitehall well enough to understand that if it remained an all-British project it would not be properly funded. The Director confirmed things were looking 'iffy', but insisted he might still appeal to the Cabinet Secretary in person.

Sara heated up some Marks and Spencer's meals for dinner. Lofting resented the expense of these but welcomed the fact that they tasted a good deal better than her rare attempts to cook. He thought that buying these triumphs of packaging which usually lasted no time whatsoever in the fridge was another of Sara's social affectations. During the meal they came close to a family conversation when he suggested they might go sailing in the Aegean for their next summer holidays. Sara said the Greek islands were 'terribly dreary', but Emma had agreed to the idea gracelessly while wondering to herself whether the places they might visit would boast any kind of club scene.

After dinner, Emma lay on her bed with headphones on listening to music, tears rolling down her cheeks, while her mother sat in front of the TV, drawing on her third stiff gin of the evening.

Lofting retired to the loft which he had converted into a refuge from family life. Its shelves were lined with books on nautical history, his beloved O'Brian novels (all from the fourth onwards were first editions) and his collection of ships for wargaming. Under the dormer window was an old kitchen table with an anglepoise lamp, strewn with small pots of paint, brushes and models. He was currently working on a scaled-down version of Toulon harbour to be used in a forthcoming game with his regular sparring partners at the Club. He reflected on the systems of semaphore and ciphers used in Nelson's age and how unimaginably different things would have been if they had communicated at the speed of light. And that brought OREGANO back to mind again. He wondered with awe when and where he might first put this extraordinary invention of theirs to the test.

Chapter Five

A week passed before the Director's next trip to London. The weather was turning colder and the state's secret servants found themselves profoundly uncertain. Normally they would have been considering their budgets for the coming three years but spending limits and the new government's foreign policy rethink had surrounded everything with question marks. Tough decisions were required by the Cabinet Office master race and they were awaited at Cheltenham with trepidation. The Director had addressed his staff in the main dining hall and told them he had every reason to believe their work would carry on as before. In the outbuildings and outstations, however, the pessimistic gossips who predicted staff cuts and the end of working patterns which had remained unchanged since the fifties were closer to the mark. Somehow GCHQ had remained true to the values of the scientific civil service. There were no 'cost centres' or 'internal markets', and 'contractorisation' was something people knew about only from newspapers or friends. Cheltenham remained a place free of the marketing buzzwords which had contaminated Whitehall, a palce where the dinner ladies still had the same pension rights as everyone else and where it still took weeks to get a lightbulb changed.

The Cabinet Secretary had made an appointment

with the Director to take place immediately after the Thursday JIC meeting. It was billed as 'an informal heads up'. Lunch at the Reform for the two of them without seconds or note-takers. Sir Peter Scarlett's style was very different from that of Terence Jennings, the Foreign Office man. Scarlett was almost incapable of smalltalk, his stature matched his charm – he looked like Lester Pigott only with finer features, twice the IQ and a newer camel coat. He had gone to the top of the civil service via Nottingham Grammar School and Oxford. Two days earlier Scarlett had reviewed the spending figures at a meeting with the PSIS committee Chairman. The GCHQ Director was unaware of the case MI5 and MI6 had made but he was confident that the Security Service, having found their anti-IRA casework dwindling, would be bleating about the need to switch their resources to the fight against organised crime. Whereas Jennings had consumed his main course before he could bring himself to business, Scarlett had not even opened his menu when he said gravely, 'Very bloody spending round this year, Malcolm, very bloody. New government. Everything up in the air.'

'Not too bloody for us, I hope.'

'New policies require funding – that's the problem! Reconciling apparently unreconcilable spending requests – that's what we're paid to do. But when so many new ideas are being thrown into the sums – all of them with unpredictable public expenditure consequences, well . . .'

'You know there's no fat left at Cheltenham,' the Director said, believing it for the moment.

They had ordered starters before Scarlett delivered the bad news: 'You're going to have to take a four per cent cut next year and four point two the year after.'

'That's unaccep—'

'You'll be expected to contract out your support services – after the usual study, of course – where you make the staff cuts is up to you, that goes without saying but having worked on your figures I expect you'll have to.'

'What are we going to say to the Americans?' the Director asked, staring ahead because he was unable to look Scarlett in the eye.

'They've made enough reductions themselves; we all know the name of the game. Your new invention should keep them sweet for a year or two – wouldn't you say?' Scarlett spread some pâté on the toast in front of him.

'Perhaps . . . we're bound to have a very difficult negotiation over the INTRUDER satellite.' The GCHQ man felt sick as he realised that, far from boosting his case for funds, Ted Lofting's invention had provided the Cabinet Office with their excuse to cut them.

During the main course, the Director made one or two futile attempts to counterattack, but these sallies were repulsed with ease by Sir Peter. There was one more piece of bad news to be imparted, and he waited until coffee in the lounge to relay it.

'Malcolm, you must judge for yourself of course how to apply these reductions, but we have endorsed a principle in all departments which the Chancellor is very keen on – one of "New Labour – equal misery", you might call it. Cuts have to been seen to be taken at the management level too, so we'd expect any reduction in your establishment to be matched near the top. You've got a tough job ahead of you during the next couple of years – we don't underestimate that and of course,' and then the pill was sugared, 'a Director who successfully put GCHQ on course for the next century would be entitled to expect some performance-related adjustment to their pay package – it's a big job, so we'd be talking about a commensurate enhancement.'

For a brief moment as he got in the Daimler to return to Cheltenham, the Director considered going to the Prime Minister. He had the right to under long-established Whitehall protocol. The measures required by the revised budget would mean making 700 or 800 people redundant, cancelling various research projects, bringing the NSA into OREGANO forthwith and of course restructuring the organisation to dispense with a number of heads of division. As the car crawled through west London towards the M4 he felt pangs of regret at the way he had played his cards during the past year – above all he wondered whether the OREGANO demonstration had helped or hindered their case.

Forty minutes up the M4 and he had convinced himself that things could have been much worse had they not demonstrated their ability to intercept fibre optic cables – that after all was the future of sigint. He was already beginning to wonder how he could sell the changes to his workforce – he began trying to formulate a slogan for his changes. 'Leaner and Meaner' – no, that struck the wrong tone. 'Smaller but Better' – a little flaccid but maybe.

As the Daimler passed through the front gate, the Director had settled in his mind many of the details of how he would brief his senior officers on the changes required. He had begun to wonder about just how big the promised performance-related pay increase might be. It could easily be another £15,000 or £20,000 a year. How would he spend it?

* * *

Margaret Reynolds came home from work the following day and slumped in an armchair. She had not turned the lights on, and being past 6 p.m. it was soon pitch black in the room. Her flat was in Oxford Parade, a Georgian terrace not far from the centre of town and from GCHQ's Oakley complex. Unfortunately for her, she worked across town at Benhall. The original name of the house was still visible on the front: Esperanza, which was Spanish for hope. The front of the building was an elegant sandstone, and the door which led to her first-floor apartment had a handsome fanlight above it. Her living space was the front room – in earlier times the drawing room – with windows which stretched almost from the floor to the high ceiling. The two alcoves on either side of the chimney breast had fitted bookcases which told the story of her adult life. The Voltaire, Balzac, Cervantes and García Márquez which she had deconstructed in her years reading Modern Languages at college; Rough Guides and Lonely Planets from her early years at Cheltenham, when she had backpacked her way around much of South America, Indonesia and parts of East Africa. During her mid-twenties to mid-thirties she had travelled for a month or two each summer, her supervisors often agreeing to a few weeks of unpaid extra leave in order to perfect her language skills. And while some people might have thought GCHQ should finance trips to acquire the knowledge of dialects and slang needed to listen to the secret conversations of Argentines or Rwandans it was in fact her employer's flexibility in allowing her the time to travel which had created a profound sense of loyalty in her towards them. There were plenty of modern novels too, ranging from historical sagas to worthier pieces of literary fiction. Almost all were written by women.

Margaret had laid the room out in the conservative manner one might expect from the daughter of a country accountant. Framed photographs decorated a round table in the corner. Her sofa and armchairs were covered with a Chinese floral chintz. As she surveyed these items in the murky darkness of that October evening she began to notice more and more signs of untidiness and disorder. Few people would have said there was anything out of place in the room, but she could see papers sloppily stacked, books placed out of sequence on her shelves (and she had thought she had eradicated the last signs of Peter's presence) and she felt sure that the place was too dusty. She got up from the armchair, dabbed her wet cheeks and began moving around the flat. That night when she had got home her spirits had reached rock bottom, and at last she felt a little *esperanza* return.

She tore a bin bag from the roll in the kitchen and moved purposefully around, filling it with things of Peter's she had hidden at the bottom of her drawers. She dusted, cleared up, scrubbed the kitchen floor and then started work on a drawerful of photographs, weeding each envelope of every picture of Peter. When she had finished that she thought about going through the negatives and eliminating those too, but before she could give effect to that idea she had another. She scuttled downstairs to the small back garden shared by the flats and burned the bag full of Peter's things.

It was nearly 3 a.m. before she went to bed. She could not drift off and so she found her hands, as so often these days, sliding down between her legs and stroking herself as she filled her mind with images of an anonymous stranger. Her fantasy ran along similar lines to that of the night before and the night before that. A

tall man, typically Latin-looking, pursuing her relent-
lessly by means of dinner dates, love letters, flowers and
phonecalls. A man so desperate to sleep with her, so
driven by desire, that he could no longer distinguish
between his real opinion of her qualities and the
compliments he garlanded her with. Sometimes, perhaps
after seeing someone during the day whose features
fitted well into her daydreams, she could not wait until
she got to bed and would stand in the bathroom with
her head arched back, slowly running her fingers back
and forth, prolonging her pleasure. At other times, when
she was tired and frazzled like that night, her fantasy ran
by numbers and she would not dwell on it, bringing
herself to a climax in a few minutes.

The following day, Margaret performed her weekly
pilgrimage to Clifton. She had a car, a beaten-up Fiat
Panda, which she kept for the purpose. Mags listened to
Radio 4 on the way down – the usual schedule of
Breakaway and *Loose Ends*. By the time Ned Sherrin
had almost finished his camp witticisms, her Panda
lumbered into the drive of the Bethlehem Home.

Margaret's mother had been killed in an accident years
before, her father had been in the home for more than
two years. It was a well-thought-of place, run by a
Catholic trust, but it cost £20,000 a year to keep him
there. Bills for Patrick Reynolds's care and sundry other
debts he had run up had already consumed most of the
value of the flat which had been sold when he could no
longer cope on his own. Margaret occasionally fell into
deep anxiety when she considered the choices she would
soon have to make. When the money from his flat ran
out, the local authority would never pay for care that cost
so much and she would either have to agree to having

him moved into some second-rate place or settling a big slice of the home's fees herself. Patrick Reynolds also had a son, but her brother had only visited the home twice and had rarely spoken to what remained of the family.

When she entered the dayroom her eyes met her father's and there was an electrifying moment of recognition. He had always been a handsome man – he was tall and had a full head of ash-white hair. His eyes though were his most attractive feature, a milky grey-blue which sparkled as if in defiance of the disease which blighted his intellect.

'Hello, my dear, how sweet of you to come and see your old Dad!'

She felt elated, overwhelmed, as she bent down to hug him.

'Don't go getting yourself upset, my lovely!' he said as she pulled up a high-backed chair beside his so that both of them could gaze out of the panoramic window and admire the Avon gorge.

'You seem full of the joys of autumn today, Pa.'

'Who wouldn't be, with a daughter like you?'

She looked down shyly, an unaffected reflex which she reserved only for him. It hadn't changed since she was three. Margaret remembered an occasion – she must have been about three at the time – when she had gone to the bottom of the garden and stepped into his shed. He'd been pottering about, doing nothing in particular, and she just wanted to watch him, but her feelings of self-consciousness about intruding into his private sanctuary had been so intense that it had taken an eternity to will herself across the threshold into the battered old place.

She spied one of the assistants and asked for coffee to be brought.

'How's that fella of yours?' he asked, sending her into a state. She did not want to spoil the most lucid moments she had enjoyed with her father for months.

'He's well enough.'

'Don't expect great things of him,' he said in a hushed, almost conspiratorial way. 'I wouldn't ever want to hurt your feelings but if he's kept a girl like you waiting for years, he might not be the most honourable of men.'

This sudden clarity, after so many visits in which no meaningful conversation had passed between them, left her speechless with happiness. Not only were there still signs of the old Patrick Reynolds, but he understood enough about that cretin Peter not to be disappointed by the failure of their relationship and, for a moment in the depth of her despair with men, she dared to hope that he might still be able to see her happy.

Almost as soon as he had spoken, he began to drift back into the fog of oblivion, looking around angrily and saying 'bloody flies!' to himself several times. By the time the coffee arrived, his mouth was gaping open and a stream of saliva poured over Patrick Reynolds's twitching lower lip.

During her journey home, Margaret remembered that her father had told her about the fly-infested camp in Gaza where he had done his National Service. The events of those times seemed to plague him like an endless stream of misaddressed E-mails returning to sender. Her thoughts switched to her childhood in north Oxfordshire: how often he had read her stories; how he had walked her around the room with her little feet standing on his and how desperate she had been during those games of hide and seek for the moment he would catch her and sweep her up in his arms. While she surrendered to these echoes of childhood she barely recalled his face as she had left, instead thinking over and over again of his wisdom about Peter and the love in his eyes. She switched the car radio to Radio 1, wound up the volume and for the first time in months felt happy, insanely happy.

Chapter Six

After the Director's meeting with Sir Peter Scarlett, Ted Lofting was given two and a half weeks to prepare his new invention for demonstration to the Americans. A meeting had already been set for the first week of November and it would present a convenient opportunity to show off OREGANO. The occasion was the annual UK/USA Treaty conference which this year was to be held at Fort Monkton on the south coast. The treaty between the English-speaking sigint powers had been drawn up in 1947, but in the decades since none of the governments had ever publicly discussed its existence or contents.

In the fifties and sixties Anglo-American eavesdropping activities had been surrounded which such secrecy that reference to them had been omitted even from the D Notices intended to muzzle the press. Neither GCHQ nor its huge US counterpart, the NSA, had been publicly acknowledged by their governments until the 1970s. Up to then, the American global network of listening posts and codebreakers had been known to Washington insiders as No Such Agency.

It was the practice for denizens of these secret empires to hold summits each year. One was restricted to the Brits and Americans, the other meeting, at which some super-sensitive matters would be withheld, included the

Canadians, Australians and New Zealanders too. The UK/US meeting was regarded as the best forum for the revelation of OREGANO and it was a happy coincidence that it was Britain's turn to host.

Delegates to the meeting were brought to Fort Monkton in four large helicopters. Two RAF Chinooks ferried the British – one flying from Cheltenham; the other picked up Whitehall brass from Chelsea barracks. The NSA party flew to Mildenhall in Suffolk before being ferried down by two US Marine CH-53s. Such sensitivity surrounded the meeting that all conference papers and reference materials were taken on board the helicopters in crash-proof steel lockers.

As the American helicopters approached the old nineteenth-century fortifications, the lead machine banked into a turn, giving its passengers a chance to survey MI6's training base two hundred feet below and the pilot a view of his landing zone.

The pilot lowered the collective control which looked like an overgrown handbrake beside his seat, the machine flattened its rotors, the swirling arms lost their purchase, and the CH-53 settled in the Fort's central courtyard. The tailgate at the back was lowered and junior members of the American delegation paired up to heft the secure steel containers out into the sea air.

Accommodation in the fort's thick-walled bastions was predictably spartan. Civil service armchairs covered with psychedelic nylon sat beside skinny single beds and utility drawers and desks. The rooms were designed for MI6 trainees. The Fort was where they learned the more dashing aspects of the 1990s intelligence officer's art: pistol shooting, scaling fences, breaking and entering. Shortly after arriving on the GCHQ Chinook,

Cord Cortland, the Senior US Liaison Officer, invited his boss, the Director of the NSA, for a stroll around the walls. The Director, a blunt USAF lieutenant general drafted in to propel his organisation into the new millennium, understood Cord wouldn't ask him outside unless it was a matter of great sensitivity.

'The Brits have put in a two-hour session tomorrow to discuss "UK research developments",' Cortland began as a bracing offshore breeze whistled about their ears.

'What's cooking, Cord?'

'Well, for the last three years they've only given an hour to that topic, so they obviously think they've got something to say.'

'Do you think it'll be the usual bullshit? Telling me something I knew nine months ago with the Brit "kiss my ass" face on?'

Cortland felt protective of his colleagues from Cheltenham, but tried not to let his resentment of the general's tone show: 'Well, they've still got a respectable R&D effort going; there have been a whole lot of comings and goings recently.'

'You told me their appropriations just got stomped on.'

'That's true, but they've got something to tell us. I've tried hard to find out what and I think it's connected with a guy called Ted Lofting who seems to have been given a new division.'

'What's his bag?'

The two men stopped, their way barred by a high-security fence, and turned around. Cortland answered, 'Knowing Ted's resumé I think he's been given the task of attacking fibre optic links.'

'OK,' the general tried not to sound too interested.

'There's a couple of options. It may be they just want to pitch us some new R&D effort, something untried. It may be they want us to pay for development of something. Or it could be that they've got something working; something important they really think they can share with us.'

'Something . . . effective?'

'Who the hell knows, General? But my gut instinct is that it's the last option.'

'Hot damn!' the general's excitement burst out. 'We've put hundreds of millions into that without a bean to show for it. Time we kicked ass with those research types at Meade. This could be the first UK/ USA Conference I ever attended that was worth the jawing time.'

The Americans kept their counsel until Ted Lofting's presentation the following day. Lofting performed much the same act as he had in the lecture theatre at Cheltenham. However his technical account of the way the success had been achieved was fuller than the one given to the British mandarins.

Afterwards the Director of GCHQ, his deputy, Lofting and three NSA officials retired to the Commandant's conference room for sandwiches and glasses of wine.

'Ted, your work certainly has considerable potential,' the NSA boss began.

'It's a breakthrough of the first importance,' the GCHQ Director said emphatically.

'There's still a considerable investment required to bring it to operational status,' the American number two said.

'I'm not sure I'd say "considerable", General – about

twenty per cent of what we've already put in would yield a couple of operational devices,' Lofting countered.

The general ignored Lofting's defence, adding, 'make no mistake, Malcolm, we're impressed by your work. Our own research was close to producing very similar solutions, of course . . .'

'Well it's clearly time to pool our knowledge then,' Ted Lofting said with unblinking sincerity.

'We all look forward to that, Ted.' The general marked Lofting down as a smartass for calling his bluff.

The meeting meandered around the issues of how much the Americans should invest and how soon, in return for their money, they might be able to start making OREGANO devices without British help. These issues had been resolved after a fashion when the GCHQ Director produced a piece of particularly highly classified paper, saying, 'General, we've prepared a list of potential targets for our first operational use, perhaps next summer.'

'Next summer?' the general growled. 'That's as much use to me as a bullhorn in a deafhome!'

The Americans conferred briefly, mostly to give their suggestion the appearance of spontaneity: 'There is a high-value target which we have become aware of recently.' The general's voice had gone from its usual boisterous roar almost to a hush. 'It's the French government's new secure trunk system in Paris. It's codenamed *TONNANT*,' which he pronounced as Toe-nant.

The GCHQ Director looked at Lofting, who raised an eyebrow in response. 'Someone sold us the plans,' the general added, smirking at his colleagues with self-satisfaction.

'Certainly a sensitive target,' Lofting answered.

'Highly sensitive,' his Director added.

'Political approval could be tricky,' the Deputy Director from Cheltenham said his piece.

'Toe-nant is used by the Elysée and all the key ministries. We could tap in to Mon-sewer le presid-ant on the can, video conferencing, foreign ministry messages prior to encryption – the whole nine yards!' The NSA man was speaking with almost missionary fervour.

The GCHQ Director began thinking of the consequences of being caught bugging the French government and found himself momentarily unable to speak. Ted Lofting broke the silence:

'I believe it's pronounced "T'nan": it means Thundery. It's a name used historically by French warships – for example by one of Admiral d'Estaing's squadron that went to help your chaps in 1778.'

The general gave Lofting a look of baffled contempt and ignored the history. 'Without risk, gentlemen, there is no reward. The rewards of tapping Toe-nant would be quite outstanding. We must be ready to do it in two months.'

At the end of the conference, while waiting for their Chinook back to Cheltenham, Lofting and Cord Cortland found themselves standing on one of Fort Monkton's walls surveying its solid defences.

'Sorry for not telling you about OREGANO sooner, Cord.'

'Nonsense, Ted, think nothing of it.'

'You'd obviously found out or guessed anyway.'

'Well . . .'

'That French target was too good to be an inspiration of the moment.'

'I'd kind of figured things out. Anyway, you've

obviously done some brilliant work.'

Lofting had drawn a pipe from his pocket and began stuffing its bowl with tobacco: 'Well, plenty of its technology is based on American academic work and I'll be most interested to see what your teams have come up with.' He struck a Swan Vesta, shielded the flame with his hand as he lit up. 'I'm not altogether sure about the target, I have to say.'

'Wasn't this place built to protect you against the French?' Cortland surveyed a large bastion where artillery had once been. 'You guys have a seven hundred-year history of hating one another.'

'I'd like to think that history had taught us something – the danger of untrammelled rivalry. Of course we intercept certain types of French communications and they try hard enough to get ours, but this proposed operation in Paris really would escalate things.'

'You have a close and complex relationship with the French – isn't that the kind of target you most need good intelligence on?'

'It may be that ministers will follow that argument, Cord, or they may not. The new lot say they're big on honesty and Europe and all that, but you never can tell of course, as those of us old enough to remember the last Labour government will testify. Our Director would rather avoid asking them – he hates to seek specific political approval for any operation or project. He considers it insecure, prefers to keep things vague.' Lofting blew out a cloud of smoke as two seagulls drifted over, riding the eddies of the wind. 'I'd be rather surprised, *entre nous*, if ministers knew, in any specific sort of way, about our little invention.'

Lofting and Cortland's conversation had to end when

the Chinook finally arrived and drowned out their voices. They went back to Cheltenham tense with the knowledge that the approval of Whitehall could soon send them into frenzied preparations to tap into the synapses of the French state.

Chapter Seven

'The French government secure trunk system in Paris?'
Sir Peter Scarlett repeated, with the barest hint of
incredulity, as he stared across the table at the GCHQ
Director and Ted Lofting.

'I say! How . . . adventurous!' Terence Jennings added,
sounding like an aristocratic cricket commentator
applauding an unlikely six.

The two Cheltenham men had travelled down without explaining beforehand exactly why they needed an
urgent meeting with the Cabinet Secretary and the chief
Foreign Office mandarin.

'Go on,' Scarlett said, closing his eyes and dipping
his head into his hands which were joined as if in prayer.

The Director had been hoping to adjust the tone of
his presentation to fit Sir Peter's mood, but as the
Cabinet Secretary was giving away nothing, a balanced
'on the one hand – on the other' presentation in the
best traditions of the British civil service followed. It set
out the intelligence prizes which could be won, as well
as the keenness of the Americans for the target, before
adding weighty caveats about the fallout which might
result from discovery. Scarlett allowed the Director to
finish and then asked, 'Mr Lofting, what do you think of
this target?'

'Well, Sir Peter. There's no doubt that it's a rare thing

indeed to get information about trunk systems which would carry quite such a rich flow of information. If, as the Americans suggested to us, the French are so confident of its security that they are only going to employ the weakest encryption, the results could be most impressive – there would barely be any high-level secrets the French could keep from us. On the other hand . . . I'm not sure quite how the Foreign Secretary would feel if I or some of my colleagues had to be collected by an embassy car from a French police station . . .'

'You know why the Yanks want it running by the end of January?' Jennings asked rhetorically. 'There's another round of trade talks scheduled for the thirty-first in Tokyo – they want to get the European position – and that'll just be the start of it for them.' They were all aware that the American interest in the planned operation was not identical to their own.

'Terence,' Scarlett raised his head and opened his eyes for the first time in several minutes, 'how would you balance the quality of this intelligence with the fallout of being discovered?'

'Well, it's the usual story. The Foreign Secretary would be falling over himself with gratitude if we could pre-empt French diplomacy on everything from beef to Saudi arms sales. He'd be less happy explaining to the House why the kind of scenario Ted has just hinted at might have come about. I have to say, if I was going to give this my backing I think we would need to be sure that everything that could possibly be done to disguise the origin of the tapping device and the people placing it should be done.'

'We would envisage an operation of maximum deniability,' the Director replied.

'How feasible is that? I mean, ultimately the device is going to be made in Cheltenham and the people who place it are going to be British and American,' the Cabinet Secretary said, moving from his contemplation into cross-examination.

'Everything in OREGANO is non-traceable,' Lofting began. 'The chips are specially made by the NSA for covert uses, no identifying markers whatsoever, the power unit ditto. The circuit boards and wiring are made by us at Oakley, once again completely untraceable. Where certain metals are used which might be identifiable, we blend the product of different countries—'

'It's the human factor though, isn't it,' Scarlett interrupted. 'You're not going to subcontract an operation like this to Ruritanian Intelligence, are you? It'll be our chaps running the risk.'

'Yes and there are certain factors you need to be aware of.' Lofting seemed to be qualifying his earlier enthusiasm. 'OREGANO's power requirements mean we can't just leave a battery-powered unit and walk away from it. There has to be a continuous supply . . . from somewhere.'

'We could use a very long extension flex and plug it in at the embassy I suppose,' Jennings chipped in caustically.

'There's another important factor. *TONNANT* will be carrying so much traffic – hundreds of calls as well as broadband items like pictures and certain datastreams – that we will have to make the initial selection about what we intercept in er . . . in er Paris.'

'This gets better by the minute,' Jennings's hostility was now clear.

Lofting answered with the sensitivity and patience of a doctor giving a nasty diagnosis: 'There's simply no other secure way, no other deniable way – if we tried to relay that quantity of information back to the UK by microwave or satellite, there's every chance the French would detect it – and if we encrypted our relay signal, that would simply make them even more curious. We will have to have linguists and analysts *in situ* to grade the material. The really valuable stuff can then be sent back for translation and in-depth study. In time, as our intelligence improves, software tools could be developed to lock on to the worthwhile parts of the traffic and then we could take all of our people out.'

'How long and how many people in Paris until such things are developed?' Sir Peter Scarlett still betrayed nothing by his tone.

'Not many, I'm sure,' the Director tried to reassert his authority.

'Well, it's very early days . . .' Lofting added, 'but we could manage with a couple of dozen for up to three months.'

'Christ!' Jennings was in like a shot: 'Engineers, banks of copy typists, a few management types – very low-profile!'

'We would envisage the setting up of front companies,' Lofting explained. 'Everyone working on the project would have identification as employees of that company from – well, you name it. Canada, Belgium, Ireland, wherever. The companies themselves would be offshore and untraceable.'

'There's still a risk of arrest and trial,' Jennings objected.

'There is,' Lofting confirmed flatly.

A chime from Big Ben accentuated the silence as the officials digested this truth.

'We have a new PM who is not a great believer in the

intelligence services,' Sir Peter began. 'He may express his admiration for Mrs T. on various matters, but in this respect he's very unlike the Blessed Margaret. We have an opportunity here to feed him top-grade intelligence. I can't think of any coup you could get which would be more interesting to him than the inner thoughts of *Monsieur le Président*. Impressive by any service's standards. Likely to make him change his attitude to secret activities and how much we spend on them,' he nodded slightly at the Director for emphasis. 'Being in with the Americans is an asset if we do get discovered. Since the risks of discovery worry us so much, it's an asset which outweighs the negative aspects of working with them – we know their agenda with France is quite different to ours. Would you take exception to that, Terence?'

'Well I suppose working with the Americans might mitigate the nightmare scenario somewhat . . .'

'My view is that we should do it on two conditions which must be made absolutely clear to our cousins: that deniability is paramount and I don't give a stuff if that means taking longer and them missing the trade talks; the other is that we must work out some sort of agreement about certain European Union matters which are out of bounds – if collected, they will not be disseminated by the American side.'

'All of that sounds eminently sensible,' the Director answered. Lofting began mulling over the problems of imperfect deniability and of pervious Chinese Walls between GCHQ and the Americans. To him it all seemed eminently unworkable. Lost in thought, he took his pipe out and began to fish around in his pocket for a packet of tobacco.

'Do you mind?' the Cabinet Secretary broke Lofting's spell. 'There is a no smoking policy on this floor.'

Margaret Reynolds had allowed all but one of her college friendships to slip away. The exception was Bella Crewe, another languages student who had ended up running a marketing company in Bath. Reynolds dressed herself cheerfully in anticipation of seeing Bella and realised that one of the principal reasons why the friendship had survived was because Bella never asked about her work. Other friends, particularly the men, had teased her or been boringly persistent in trying to prise out of her exactly what she had been doing. Right from her induction course, the bosses at work had stressed that any details given to those outside her world could compromise GCHQ's operations. Any disclosures, even about the languages she had mastered, could endanger a particular operation. The problem with college friends was that they already knew about her French and Spanish as well as her interest in certain regions of the world. Bella seemed able to accept that Mags would never reveal certain things – including details of some of her long holidays – and that made it far easier to keep things cordial. There was another thing about Bella, of course: she was single too. Margaret had grown tired of the endless baby and kiddie-talk of her married friends, even though she always managed a suitable display of fascination. Bella was the only one left who knew how much of an effort being single in your late thirties was.

They met at '81', a bistro on the Promenade, with smart décor, well-designed menus and a suitably nineties commitment to balsamic vinegar, meat-free recipes and cappuccino. Bella had got there already and she rose to meet Margaret with her head tilted slightly to one side and one of those 'you poor puppy' looks in her eyes. To look at, they were chalk and cheese. Margaret: tall, fair-haired and sensibly dressed. Bella: dark, five-foot three inches in heels, her Rubensesque proportions covered by a stylish Ghost crushed black silk creation. There were plenty of differences in attitudes too, but it never seemed to disrupt their rapport.

'I just wonder how I could have wasted so much time with such a loser,' said Margaret with a suitable serving of self-disgust.

'Look, Mags, we've all wasted years of our lives with jerks.' Bella's voice was raspy from cigarettes, her accent south Yorkshire.

'Are all men shits? There's still a part of me that wants to believe I'm wrong, that I might find someone.' Margaret sipped her Chardonnay.

'The last thing you need to do is go looking for Mr Right now. Why don't you have some fun? Take yourself a toyboy? Christ, you should have no trouble finding someone! I've always said I'd die for legs like yours – you're so pretty!'

Margaret smiled dutifully at the compliment. 'I wish I could. I really wish I could. You always seem to have been able not to take the . . . physical side of it too seriously.'

'Ultimately, we all need a decent bonk from time to time, love.'

'Tell me about it,' Margaret replied, moving a piece of dry fish around the plate with her fork.

'Well, you always hinted Peter wasn't great in that department.' Bella seemed siezed by a sudden inspiration and flushed a small diary from her handbag. 'I know! Why don't you give Mike Redman a call?'

'I suppose his velvet flares are back in now,' Margaret replied flippantly. 'Anyway, he's married.'

'Not any more. Messy divorce. Needs TLC.'

'Two emotional cripples together, you mean? Not a good idea.'

'OK. Sorry.' Bella was momentarily deflated. She caught the waiter's eye and ordered a second bottle. 'Anyone nice at work?'

'No. I couldn't face them the morning after anyway.'

'Any nice pubs or clubs locally?'

'Bella, I'm just not cut out to sit on some meat rack waiting to be picked up. I just worry that I'd sleep with someone from work or who knew Dad or something – God that sounds stupid!'

Bella decided to take the opportunity to change the subject before Mags got too ratty. 'How is your dad?'

'Oh you know, all right as far as someone with that bloody disease can be. There was a really lovely moment of talking together on Saturday when he seemed like his old self. The whole thing just scares me so much though.'

'You wouldn't be human if it didn't.'

'Not just the disease – I mean that scares all of us – it's everyone's nightmare to lose their mind, isn't it? No, not just that: there's the whole financial side of it; I don't know how I'm going to pay for his care.'

'Have another drink, you poor love.' Bella poured another glass and tried to move the conversation on to easier subjects. She wondered how Margaret kept it all together. In the same situation she'd be sitting there screaming. As they ordered a couple of fruit teas Bella had another inspiration on the man front. 'Have you thought of putting an ad in somewhere?'

'Lonely Hearts? I'm not that desperate, am I?' Margaret sounded sour. Her friend decided attack was the best form of defence.

'Listen! nobody ever finds out except the men you

want to. You screen out the nerds by insisting on a photo. You don't even have to use your own name.'

For a brief moment the idea of meeting men in complete secrecy appealed to Margaret – but she kept the thought to herself and replied teasingly instead, 'You seem very knowledgeable about all this.'

'Ummm, well, you know about John who I was seeing a couple of years back?'

'The married one?'

'Well, that's how I met him. He wanted sex. I found him dishy. No complications. It was fun while it lasted,' Bella drew deeply from her glass, 'and boy was he good with his tongue!'

Margaret had known Bella long enough to enjoy the indiscretion rather than be embarrassed. She smiled and shook her head slowly. 'I really wish at times when I'm longing for the physical side of it that I could do that but I just can't. I'd be thinking about his wife. I'd be thinking about how it wasn't going anywhere.' She worried for a moment that this might sound to judge-mental, so she added quickly: 'You're right about one thing though. I've got to get away from seeing every date as an audition for Mr Right. I'm never going to find someone like that. I should just play it footloose and fancyfree for a bit.'

'Attagirl!'

They clinked their glasses together as if these musings had been a toast. Bella was impressed. She and Margaret went back long enough for her to know more clearly than Margaret herself could that this was the closest her friend could come to declaring she would jump on the next passing able-bodied male.

Chapter Eight

The task of seeking political authorisation for the Paris operation fell to one of those least convinced of its wisdom, Terence Jennings. On a Friday morning in mid-December his car brought him from home in Wimbledon to the King Charles Street entrance of the Foreign and Commonwealth Office. In his briefcase was a draft of the authorisation which he would ask the Foreign Secretary to sign. It read:

Operation POLYP

1. An opportunity has arisen to obtain information of the highest value on the French political decision-making process. It is believed that possession of this information would significantly assist HM Foreign Policy formulation and the pursual of UK national interests. Operation POLYP is therefore approved under the terms of the 1993 Intelligence Services Act.
2. A joint Anglo-American operation to obtain the information has been prepared. The operation carries certain risks of discovery by the French authorities. Given the closeness of our relationship with France, Operation POLYP has been planned with a high degree of deniability. It would be unwise for the UK government ever to acknowledge it had taken place.
3. The operation is expected to make a significant

contribution to the UK/US intelligence relationship.

Below the text was a space for the Foreign Secretary to sign. During his car ride, Jennings decided to strike out the codename, since what a minister did not know he could not accidentally reveal. Instead the memo, which he would ask his secretary to re-type, would simply be headed 'Foreign Intelligence Operation' and refer throughout to 'the operation'.

Sir Peter Scarlett had decided that the Foreign Secretary should authorise the operation. Jennings believed the Cabinet Secretary had made this decision because the operation needed to be authorised by a senior government figure but that an operation so potentially embarrassing should not be acknowledged by the Prime Minister himself. Since there was no intention to share the secrets of POLYP with any other ministers, there was only one person fitted to the task of signing it off. Scarlett had told Jennings to 'massage it through as gently as you can', a measure of his anxiety about a Foreign Secretary who had already attained a fearsome reputation in Whitehall for his eye for detail and prickliness.

It was 11 a.m. before Jennings drifted through the Secretary of State's front office into the inner sanctum and dropped effortlessly into one of the chesterfield chairs placed in front of the minister's huge mahogany desk.

'Did you see that policeman on Whitehall posing for snaps with a Father Christmas hat on?' the Secretary of State asked irascibly.

'I don't believe I did, Secretary of State.'

'The problem today is that people are afraid of being

thought of as bad sports. It seems to be a national crime not to be happy to be sent up.'

Jennings studied the gingery hair scraped over his boss's rounded head and briefly examined the angry mouth surrounded by its frame of bristles. The idea of anyone trying to get this man to pose in a Father Christmas hat struck the Permanent Secretary as comical but he said, 'It's part of the general coarsening of society.'

'So, what have we got?' The Foreign Secretary eyed the Permanent Secretary's folder of letters, the eye of a macho minister who measures his success in the yards of paper he can consume each week. He didn't want to hang around, he liked to head west to Chevening by lunchtime on Fridays, but often found himself in the office until 4 or 5 p.m. Jennings had calculated carefully.

'Well, there's a farewell letter to our Ambassador in Rome – leaving at short notice because of wife's terminal illness.' Jennings handed the letter across.

'Perhaps I should add a little note – something like "your devotion to the ambassadorship at such a difficult time was in the finest traditions of the Diplomatic Service".'

'I'm sure that would be appreciated,' said Jennings as he eyed the minister signing. 'We've got one here to the new Malaysian Foreign Minister – congratulations on your appointment, the usual form.'

The Foreign Secretary made his swirling mark without comment and continued to do so as Jennings worked his way to the nineteenth letter, the one authorising POLYP.

'This is one from the hush-hush boys.' He passed the paper across with a studied insouciance. 'And girls, I suppose I should add.'

The minister mouthed the words 'unwise ever to acknowledge' and then he gave voice to his thoughts: 'What does "maximum deniability" mean?'

'I felt it wise to insist on that,' Jennings answered with a certain smugness, 'given the need to balance the great potential benefits of this operation with the potential costs of discovery.'

The Foreign Secretary glanced at his watch. 'Is this going to be some "burn before read" operation or are we going to get a decent readout from it?'

'I'm informed that, if successful, the operation will produce information of the highest quality.'

The Foreign Secretary signed and they moved on to a letter to the Nigerian High Commissioner concerning £73,000-worth of unpaid parking tickets.

Ted Lofting and his wife chose the following day to go Christmas shopping in the middle of Cheltenham. They parked in what Ted noted with satisfaction was called Rodney Street and made their way through to the Promenade. The thoroughfare which represented the zenith of the town's Regency splendour also contained some additions by a fiercely patriotic but tasteless Victorian corporation. There was the monument to locals killed in the South African wars, which Lofting found tolerable; a statue of Edward Wilson – one of Captain Scott's unfortunate colleagues, mildly eccentric – and a scaled-down imitation of the Trevi fountain, copied from its Roman original in 1893, which he thought pretentious and cheap. Ted knew that Sara loved the fountain and could not pass it without making comment.

'I wonder whether they'll ever get the fountain going again?' she asked as they walked by Neptune and his prancing concrete dolphins.

'I heard they've got a European Commission grant to demolish it.'

'No! How awful, bloody Eurocrats!'

'They're going to replace it with a sculpture called "Greek Love" apparently.'

The coin dropped: 'Don't be tiresome, Ted.'

They had decided to avoid buying Emma clothes, since she invariably rejected anything they tried to dress her in. Instead, Ted bought her a CD (Pulp, which she had chosen) and a book on the Grand Tour of the eighteenth century, which struck him as the sort of thing she ought to be interested in but which of course would lie unopened in her bedroom for years. Sara bought her daughter a new hairbrush, which was intended as a heavy hint. It was part of the ritual of the Loftings' annual Christmas shopping expedition that, having bought everyone else's presents, they would separate to search out something for each other. Ted could not understand why they persisted in this charade since his wife only bought him handkerchiefs or socks and he usually got her the same bottle of Chanel scent.

As he made his way through the throng he toyed with buying her something outrageous. Lofting snickered to himself as he thought of getting her some flared trousers or, better still, a dildo, before settling on the usual small bottle of Chanel.

That evening Ted found himself on fetching and carrying duty, taking Emma to a party beyond the racecourse on the Evesham road. She was wearing a microscopically small orange skirt, a lime green top which bared her midriff, and thick platform soles. Her mother had only allowed her through the door on condition she agreed to cover the ensemble with a long school coat. Given that she would soon be sixteen, Lofting had resolved to make Emma's future birthday and Christmas presents contributions to the cost of an old banger to drive herself around in when she was old enough.

'So what kind of party is this then, Emma?' he asked as they sped along.

'It's a rave, Dad.' Lips clamped tightly in contempt. 'You wouldn't understand.'

'Oh, it's not that difficult, is it? Boys and girls get together, have a few drinks, let their hair down – I'm not that old-fashioned.'

'They don't sell booze – just mineral water and fruit juice,' she answered in a superior way.

Lofting had many anxieties about what might happen to her at these events, ranging from the 3 a.m. phonecall following her arrest to nightmare visions of gang rape. On this occasion his anxieties triggered a different line of questioning: 'Are you offered drugs at these parties, Emma?'

She rolled her eyes, looked out of the window and flushed slightly. 'Well, of course *some* people take them.'

'Don't you though, darling: you saw what happened to that girl on the news.'

'Oh yeah! I suppose you'd rather I got pissed all the time like Mum!' Emma almost spat the last bit.

Lofting did not rise to her anger, but answered calmly instead, 'I'd rather you did neither, my love.'

'It's here! Just beyond the corner, drop me here!'

Lofting pulled the car over and saw a group of youngsters milling around outside what seemed to be a disused Scout hall. Several burly men were unloading sound system speakers the size of front doors from a luton van outside. He put his arm around her shoulder, pulled her straining body towards him and kissed her on the top of the head. 'You're very precious to me, so you take care of yourself.'

'I *will* – I'm very precious to *me* too!' She unbuckled her seatbelt and fled towards a group of friends standing around outside the hall. He watched as one of them handed Emma a cigarette. His daughter looked daggers at the friend, nodded towards him and attempted with touching ineptitude to hide it.

When Lofting got home, Sara was champing at the bit, standing in the hallway in her coat. 'I wish you hadn't taken so long, I'm going to be late.' She took the car keys.

'Sorry, but I've forgotten, where are you playing bridge tonight?' he asked as she scurried towards the car.

'Why?'

'Oh, just in case I need to get in touch – Emma's party looked a bit rough to me.'

'At . . . Oscar and Monica's,' she replied with what he considered to be an incriminating moment of hesitation.

Lofting fixed himself a Scotch, put Bach on the CD player and sat down with a lavishly illustrated book on Nelson's victories. He was annoyed with himself for showing Sara that he was suspicious of her. He really preferred not to know if she was having an affair. Certainly he recognised that their own occasional couplings had become as dutiful as well as predictable as their Christmas shopping trips. And about as frequent.

He read a passage about Nelson's victory at the battle of Aboukir Bay. It was very familiar to him – he knew the story all too well, but however many times he read it, it humbled him. The Battle of the Nile was celebrated by jingoistic historians, but it had followed weeks of panic in the Royal Navy after the French had given Nelson the slip. He marvelled at the courage of the French Admiral de Brueys, who had remained in command despite having both legs shot off. He had had himself propped up on deck in a chair as the British hero sailed his fleet into the French line and demolished it with salvo after salvo from his big guns. This orgy of violence culminated in the explosion of the French flagship *Foudroyant* and the marooning of Napoleon's army in Egypt. He considered the selectivity of much of British history, how it usually denied Albion's enemies any credit for their heroism or victories, how it brushed over the incompetence of much of the Royal Navy leadership. What a great mistake it is to underestimate one's enemy, he thought. What a great mistake it is to underestimate the French in particular.

Chapter Nine

Margaret found herself in the usual morning funk that Monday. In her heart of hearts she knew that setting the alarm fifteen minutes earlier would solve the problem, but whenever she had tried this remedy she had lain in bed because she knew she didn't have to get up quite so early. Instead she would rush around throwing on clothes while nibbling a lightly buttered piece of toast and drawing on her mug of Earl Grey. As she gave her watch the fifth nervous glance of the morning she remembered the envelope on the mantelpiece, walked across, and took it in her hand. It was addressed to the personal ads section of *Private Eye*. After her dinner with Bella she had rung a dating agency in Gloucester. It had seemed reasonably upmarket and everything had been going well until they mentioned the issue of money. They wanted £1,000 for six introductions. Margaret had hung up; she simply couldn't spend that sort of money on herself when her father's nursing home bills were so far in arrears. Her mind moved to Bella's suggestion of personal ads. She had thought about various magazines but opted in the end for the *Eye* in the hope that it might produce men with a sense of humour. The text inside read:

YOU TARZAN, ME JANE: youngish (39) free and

single woman barely hanging on creeper needs rescue
by fit, tall, solvent and amusing gentleman swinging
through trees in Gloucester/SWest area. Let's meet
up and maybe build treehouse together. Send photo
and letter to: . . .

It was Margaret's penchant for neatness rather than the
cost per word of the ad which had led her to keep it as
short as this. She did not want to say much about herself
since she was loath to describe herself as a 'babe',
'stunning blonde' or anything else. She had thought it
best to be upfront about her age though. Her pre-
scriptive male was the shortest way she could think of
saying that fat, short losers need not apply. And the
'treehouse' bit? Well, there had to be some filter against
psychos. She had decided not to put something like
'unattached' since she didn't really care. Margaret had
enclosed a cheque for the ad to appear three times.

The moment of truth did not come until she reached
the pillar box near work. Having tucked the letter into
her handbag without a moment's thought, she stood in
front of the red column's gaping slot feeling rooted to
the ground. She glanced at the envelope. God, it made
her feel like a tart. Surely she wasn't this desperate?
Margaret wondered whether to tear it up. Put it back in
her bag, think about it and maybe post it tomorrow?

The quandary seemed to torment her for minutes.
She was suddenly aware of people walking behind her
and felt so dumb just standing there with this envelope
in her gloved hands. And then, with a thought of 'I
don't have to reply to any of them', she sealed her fate
and tapped it in. She heard it drop into the pile of
innocent and mundane communications behind the iron
door.

As she walked away, Margaret remembered the last time she had felt so awkward and hesitant about posting a letter. It was about 1973 or 1974. It was a letter to Marc Bolan's fan club. She had been about seventeen at the time and she had agonised about whether sending it would make her seem like a kid of twelve or thirteen. Anyway, she had strong feelings for Marc and these outweighed her sense of being an ageing teeny-bopper. She remembered that the reply, complete with poster and scrapbook, had arrived in a pink package with yellow flowers on it. Post addressed to her was still sufficiently rare to arouse comment and her Dad had brought it to the breakfast table with the words 'another of your male admirers writing to you, Margaret?' She remembered his wry smile and her momentary embarrassment giving way to a warm complicity which, typically, her mother failed to detect.

Lofting had received a call that morning from his technical team, asking him to pop over. He took his car and left Benhall, crossing town until he reached Oakley, and drove through one of the security gates. About halfway up the hill on which the site is laid out, he parked in a bay outside P Block, a shapeless, almost window-free building clad in metal sheeting. He walked through the doors and into an airlock area where he changed into white overalls, white Wellingtons and a rather effeminate cap. He placed his watch, and other metallic objects, into a plastic bag which took its place inside a row of lockers. Having donned this anaemic garb, he pressed a button on the intercom box beside the door into the core of the block. As the buzzer sounded to open it, Lofting climbed two steps to enter the place known in GCHQ as Special Facilities

Research. SFR was a building within P Block, suspended three feet off the floor, its walls eighteen inches inside those visible to the outside world. The cavity between the outer shell and the interior was filled with an insulating material designed to protect super-sensitive components from any form of electromagnetic interference. The great majority of the surveillance equipment used by the British Government was put together by industry in nondescript warehouses on trading estates from Bracknell to Cambridge. SFR served two purposes: it was the place where prototypes of new devices using exotic technologies too secret to be let outside GCHQ were built and it could assemble those pieces of bugging equipment which were to be used in circumstances so sensitive that even a technician's fingerprint or hair could not be allowed to get inside them. SFR could not therefore have asked for a better job to justify its continued existence than the assembly of the first operational OREGANO pack.

Lofting walked past a series of cubicles where technicians were working in a somewhat relaxed way on some deniable video equipment to be installed in a Saudi Prince's house in Windsor and into an open-plan workshop about thirty feet square where ten people had lovingly crafted OREGANO/Mk3/1.

'Morning, Ted!' Megan Trelawney, the team leader greeted him, barely looking up from some microcircuitry she was examining under a desktop magnifier. 'Just looking at this signal amplifier for number two,' she added. Trelawney was in her fifties, a PhD in electrical engineering who had apparently reached the top of her own exotic specialism.

'No hurry, no hurry!' Lofting said. But the last four weeks had been a blur for most of the team, who eyed him with proud satisfaction. Most had worked eighteen-hour days without weekends. An American technician had been grafted on to the team about halfway through this process, simply as a courtesy since nobody had really had time to explain to him all of the secrets of the magic box they were building. The technician had brought with him a host of components which represented an early Christmas for SFR. There were untraceable chips, boards and connectors from the NSA's stockpile on a scale that the impoverished GCHQ boffins dreamt about.

Megan Trelawney stood up at last and summoned Lofting to a self-contained area which took up one of the room's corners. It was a kind of glovebox, much like those used to work fissile materials or the most lethal toxins. An over-pressure inside the box prevented any dust from entering the components.

Lofting peered through the large glass window at its front and smiled with paternal satisfaction as he saw the OREGANO pod's black casing. He would have liked nothing more than to have a good smoke, but it wasn't allowed of course and his pipe lay in the plastic bag at P Block's entrance.

The housing was about eighteen inches long and it lay open in its two halves like some exotic shellfish. It was designed to wrap around the bared fibre optic wire, so there was a groove down the centre line of each half. When the two pieces were assembled around the cable they formed a pod of around eight inches in diameter. In the centre of the grooves into which the target line would be clamped and in the core of the device itself were apertures about two inches long which were covered with an adhesive plastic film which would be removed seconds before the two halves of OREGANO were clamped together. Through this protective packaging, Lofting spied the gallium optics which were the heart of this invention. When the two halves of the pod were perfectly aligned, these devices mated into a single device which would spin around the bared fibre optic like a bearing. The extraordinary precautions taken at P Block were designed to keep even the tiniest speck of dust from entering this fibre optic reading device as well as to disguise its makers' identity. The outside of the case was of smooth black polythene except for two plug points. Power supply went into one, intercepted traffic came out of ethe other.

'Do you like the look of our baby?' Megan Trelawney cooed, as if reading his mind.

'Very nice, Megan. You've worked wonders.' He turned around to the other technicians: 'You've all worked wonders. It's . . . it's,' Lofting felt momentarily awkward about voicing his thoughts, 'a brilliant British achievement!'

The boffins exchanged sheepish grins.

Lofting and their section head chatted for a while about the progress of the second device. A backup would be needed in case there was any fault with the first one. Dr Trelawney assured Lofting it would be ready by the 20th January. She prolonged the conversation with Cheltenham smalltalk until she could contain herself no longer. Having ensured they were standing far enough away from her underlings not to be heard she said, 'Look, Ted, I know there are certain things we're not in the habit of asking here, but . . . well, can you tell me where it's going?'

They both understood that she had transgressed a fundamental rule of intelligence etiquette. All of them knew the embarrassment of having to brush off a highly cleared colleague with an 'I can't tell you', or worse still some dishonest operational cover-story. Lofting looked at his feet: 'My dear, I—'

'Sorry, Ted, I'm a fool for asking, I'm sorry.'

'No no no!' he pleaded, although they both knew she had created precisely the sort of embarrassment they all preferred to avoid. 'I will be able to tell you quite soon, because it's almost certain that you'll be going out to provide technical support – obviously you'll be the only person on the section who does know, initially at least.' This last assurance was a respectable consolation prize, since it reaffirmed her closeness to the heart of the operation. 'I'm expecting that there will be a briefing on the forthcoming operation just after Christmas, and of course you'll be there, Megan.'

'Thank you, thanks.'

'I owe you the thanks, Megan. And your whole section.'

'I know, they've all put their heart and soul into her.'

'You've really done brilliantly.' Lofting went to put his arm around her shoulder but suddenly lost his nerve and let it fall back beside him. 'I look forward to the second of the twins!'

In the Suslo's office at Benhall, Cord Cortland greeted the man NSA had sent from Fort Meade, its HQ in Maryland, to run the American side of the forthcoming Paris operation. Even though he was little over thirty years old, Dan Birnbaum was highly respected at the agency as a sort of super-nerd able to crack the toughest computer-related problems. His thick black-framed glasses, unruly black curls and scruffy tweed jacket all compounded that image. Birnbaum's accent betrayed his origins in Brooklyn. He had grown up in a stinking project where they were the only white family left. His father had persevered with his local electrical store until they were robbed for the fourteenth time – then he and his wife had moved down to Miami Beach. The son had risen entirely by ability, winning a series of scholarships which had taken him to MIT before he finally became jaundiced with the world of pure research and, declining offers from the computer industry which might have made him rich, decided to enter the Puzzle Palace.

Cortland was able to sail through most situations with his patrician Ivy League charm, but he found Birnbaum's presence profoundly unsettling. His youth was alarming given that he would be NSA's point man on Operation POLYP, but he was the Director's personal choice. As Cortland briefed him, the young man seemed to grow bored as soon as the Suslo had moved from each new fact to the background information which surrounded it.

'The exact operational technology of this OREGANO pod is, I confess—'

'It's OK, I was indoctrinated before I left Meade.' Birnbaum glanced nervously out of the window.

'Yes,' Cortland seemed a little deflated. 'Well, anyway, let's always remember that the Brits invented it and as such we owe them a certain courtesy.'

'All sorts of people in history threw away good inventions because they didn't have the savvy or money to exploit them.'

'Yeah, well be that as it may this is a delicate relationship, as I'm sure you know. Now, this guy Lofting will run the operation on the British side.'

'I read his resumé at Meade,' Birnbaum added blankly.

'Well, there are things you should know that aren't in his resumé,' Cortland said a little tersely, worrying about how the Brits would react to this upstart. 'He's old-school – modest, a little shy, very good on the technology; he has a very dry sense of humour – all in all he's a regular guy if you get to know him.'

'The Director doesn't like him.'

Cortland had picked up the bad karma at Fort Monkton but had preferred to ignore it. 'Well you know, Ted does his own thing and I think the Director doubted his commitment to the operation.'

'Does he believe in it?'

'He's a professional, Dan. I think he had some misgivings, but now it's green-lighted he's giving it 110 per cent.'

'Someone told me he likes lecturing us on our history.'

Cortland felt a pang of intense protectiveness towards Lofting: 'No, no! That's his hobby. He just loves history, particularly naval history.'

'Does he play with ships in the tub?' Birnbaum nibbled the tip of one of his fingers, apparently un-interested in the answer.

'Almost – he does do wargames.'

'Yeah?'

'Well, Dan, you know how it goes. I play golf, Ted plays the Battle of Trafalgar.'

'Yeah sure. Whatever. Let's go through this timetable.'

As Cortland talked he worried about how the two men running the operation would get on. He had a sense though that Lofting's character had aroused Birnbaum's interest in a way that none of the operational details had. Cortland hoped they would get on, as any conflict would derail an operation which already had a budget of $110m and which daily was sucking people and resources towards the point of no return.

Chapter Ten

An NSA man named Jed Hawkins drove the dark blue Chevrolet with the legend 'US Air Force' stencilled on its doors up the Jersey Turnpike from Fort Meade past Trenton and Princeton to the area south of New York where an area of steel mills and chemical works the size of some European principality stretches back from the Atlantic coast. Jed had an appointment with EZ Hydraulics, a relatively small firm which nestles among the industrial giants south of New York and which had done a good deal of business with the Federal Government over the years.

As the car drove through the main gate, Jane O'Connor, the firm's VP Marketing, appeared from a small door in the side of a warehouse and allowed a welcoming smile to flicker across her hard face. Hawkins locked his car door and they shook hands purposefully against a backdrop of flaming towers and petroleum crackers covered with lights in the Exxon refinery behind the lot.

'Colonel Hardy! Nice to put a face to the name.'

Hawkins returned the courtesy, 'Roger that, ma'am.'

As she led the way into the storage area, Hawkins noted the confident gait and flat-soled shoes that propelled her strong frame towards a series of office cubicles. Forklift trucks wheeled and pirouetted around them as they went, fetching and carrying the sturdy metal components of O'Connor's trade.

'So,' she said purposefully, looking at a fax from the US Air Force Procurement Agency, 'we've got the props ready to go, likewise cement pump. The air compression ventilation unit is also outloading today or tommorrow . . .'

'Uh-huh,' Hawkins scanned his copy of the order.

'The track sections are all crated up – all but one, which we got airfreighting out of Fort Worth tonight.'

'When will you'all have the track to us?'

'OK, Colonel, let me check that.' O'Connor's hand moved swiftly to the phone, which she put on speaker as she dialled the supplier in Fort Worth. It was bad news. The Texan on the other end of the line declared a problem 'at this time' which would mean the vital components wouldn't get to New Jersey for at least three days. 'Maybe we could arrange delivery direct to site?' O'Connor asked.

'No,' Hawkins said a little too firmly, adding, 'Hell, I'd be rearranging transportation for the next seven days nonstop if we did that. No, we'll get a truck down to you Tuesday.'

'Some rush job, huh?'

'Yeah,' said Hawkins. 'Well, they got an inspection on the base in February and the CO wants to get the new storm drains in before the general comes: says his butt's on the line – pardon my French, ma'am – so the word's getting passed all the way down the chain of command on this one.'

'We'll get it here for you for Tuesday, don't worry, Colonel – those guys in Fort Worth know we play for keeps.'

After checking the remaining inventory items, worth

a total of $912,000, Hawkins and O'Connor inspected the pallets of heavy equipment which were ready to go.

As he drove back to Meade, Hawkins was satisfied that things were going to plan. He had bought the equipment for the Moscow tunnel and the Damascus one but he had no idea where the equipment which he had spent the best part of a million dollars on that day was going.

By the time Hawkins was back at the headquarters of the NSA, across the Atlantic, Ray Skinner was arriving by GCHQ car at Vauxhall Cross on the south bank of the Thames. Skinner was not sentimental about his naval service, but had chosen a tie with the crest of HMS *Bulwark*, one of several ships in which he had served, to wear with his dark blue blazer. The ex-service attire gave him confidence when entering uncharted waters.

'Just here, Mr Skinner?' his driver asked as she steered towards the kerb. She was formal out of habit, despite the fact that Skinner was sitting next to her instead of in the back.

'Tie her up here! Ceausescu Towers.' He surveyed the soaring front of ochre cladding and bottle-green glass: 'You can pick me up at noon, my lovely!'

Skinner made his way through the opening in the slablike bronze-coloured gates which guarded the mouth of MI6's HQ and up the short flight of stairs into the foyer. He presented his Cheltenham security pass to a woman behind armoured glass at the visitor's reception and announced himself: 'Ray Skinner, GCHQ, to see Mike McPhee in COS, I believe he's on extension 3476.'

McPhee's department, Controller Operational Support, had been set up in 1994. Its main task was to furnish the increasingly complex cover businesses, activities and identities needed to protect intelligence operations around the world. GCHQ had no equivalent, since the great majority of its work was done in the UK or in its own listening stations overseas. MI6, the Secret Intelligence Service, had therefore become involved in Operation POLYP.

As Skinner waited for McPhee he inspected the pass which had been passed through a security drawer. It was simply a white 'V' on a pink background, laminated and hanging from a chain. He turned it over and noticed the writing on the back: 'This Visitor is to be Escorted at All Times'.

Skinner was ushered through one of the glass tubes which opened into the building and shook hands with McPhee. The two men had met before and got on well enough since McPhee's Army service as a warrant officer in the Scots Dragoon Guards in some ways mirrored Skinner's as a petty officer afloat. Although the men shared a similar background they were very different to look at. Skinner had acquired a thick gut through the consumption of large amounts of Flowers bitter. He was also ten years older than McPhee and somewhat shorter. The ex-Army man therefore looked considerably fitter and more dynamic as he strode down the corridors.

'You blokes are obviously planning a rather fancy works outing,' McPhee said. His accent was cockney, perversely, given his old regimental assignment.

'Well, it's nice to get the staff out and about – and the travel's good for morale and retention,' Skinner countered gamely.

'No jabs needed I take it?'

'No, nowhere that exotic.'

As they entered McPhee's office, which overlooked the busy Vauxhall Cross road interchange, the Londoner was able to drop the pretence that he was ignorant of the GCHQ team's destination. McPhee was 'need to know' – the preparations of his team required them to tailor things to the French environment. He produced a large box file from a combination-locked cabinet. 'Right, Ray, we've got forty-seven passports here – the Yanks are providing their own I take it?'

'Yep.'

'We've got eight Canadian, seven Australian, seven NZ,' McPhee continued to sort them as Skinner checked against a list he had plucked from his pocket, 'and one each Serbian, Belgian and Russian. We have four British, since it was agreed by COS and your bloke Lofting that it might be suspicious if none of the people working for this company were Brits. I take it they'll all be low-ranking bods?'

'Oh yes, at the lowest level.' Skinner thought of the four tunnellers and was pleased with his private joke. Since the digging experts could speak no language but their own, it was as well to give them the British ones.

Skinner looked down at the neat stacks set out on the table in front of them. 'I'd better check a few at random – nothing wrong, I'm sure, Mike, just going through the motions.'

'Be my guest, old kid. Shall I lively us up some coffee?'

'Cracking! Milk-one-sugar please, matey.'

McPhee sauntered out with the casual aplomb of a man whose stock in trade was providing false identities for spies. To Skinner though, this was all uncharted territory. He plucked Lofting's passport from the Australian pile. It identified his Head of Division as one Humphrey Barclay – Humphrey seemed to suit a man with a pipe like Lofting. Skinner's own document was Canadian. He could not resist a peek. Richard Simpkins

– like many of the names it was deliberately similar to his in order to make it easier to remember. Skinner felt vaguely insulted that a birthdate nearly three years older than his own had been inserted. He examined his reflection in the triple-glazed window somewhat indignantly before dipping at random into one of the other piles. It was Margaret Reynolds's. She had been equipped with a Spanish paper and whereas many of those going to Paris spoke the language of their fake passports well enough only to fool a French passport officer or policeman, Margaret could deceive even a Castilian with her Spanish – for a short time at least. Mags's *alter ego* was Pilar Carrizosa from Bilbao in the Basque country.

McPhee reappeared: 'You dirty old matelot! I knew you'd find the classy skirt!'

'What? Oh yeah, I should say!' Ray replied with more than a hint of embarrassment.

'Once you've got those squared away, we need to talk about the company business.'

'It's fine, let's do that now,' Skinner finished putting passports back into the box folder.

'*Hamsin* – it means hot wind in Arabic. We've used a company set up for an Op last year which never came off. So it's been around for a while and the names registered as its original management team are all among those ID's I've just given you – that way if Froggie checks up on it, it doesn't look like something born yesterday.'

'Very good, yes.'

'Business cards, letterheads, all that clobber will get to you in the next couple of days. The idea is that the business exports quality cars to the Middle East and eastern Europe – you know, flash jobs; big Mercs with smoky windows and low-profile tyres. Clearly someone is going to have to buy some tart carts and ship them out for this cover to work. You may even have to sell some, you lazy bastards!'

'It's easy for you to wind me up,' Skinner replied, his mind reeling with the amount of effort which would be required to make the cover work. 'Tell me, Mike, do you think this business is the right kind for an operation that could involve seventy people?'

'Well, you're never going to have more than a few visible to the Frogs at any point, are you? The overall staff represents a global force – the cover story for an individual who, say, gets arrested for drunk driving—' Skinner rolled his eyes at the thought of such a cockup. 'Well, don't rule it out, these things happen on a big op like this – the cover story is that he's some buyer or salesman who happens to be in France for a couple of days. As I understand it the cover is only required for a few months – which is as long as it takes for the company to realise that owning a prestigious showroom in the centre of Paris is an uneconomic proposition.'

'I suppose so,' Skinner still sounded a little dubious. 'Christ, Mike, 'I've been booked in with one of the linguists for five hours' coaching in a Canadian accent!'

'It'll be fine, mate, no worries. Is there any news yet on where you're going to set up shop? We need that address for all the documents.'

'No, the boss is going over tomorrow; I'll give him this passport this afternoon. I think they've found somewhere promising.'

The following day Ted Lofting and Dan Birnbaum were using their new identities, strolling the streets of Paris. Someone from COS had lined them up with a property on the Rue Boissy d'Anglas and, by their rough calculation, this put them less than fifty metres from the *TONNANT* cable running down the Faubourg St Honoré from the *Elysée* before it turned towards an Interior Ministry on the Rue Surène which ran behind and parallel to Rue Boissy d'Anglas. The property which had been selected was on three levels: a ground floor with shopfront which would be suitable as a car showroom; first-floor offices where about twenty-five or thirty people could work in comfort and, most importantly, a basement garage big enough for about eight vehicles which was reached by a carlift from street level. The only other possible property available to them was well outside central Paris, where the fibre optic trunk ran towards the headquarters of the DRM, French military intelligence. Since this location was unlikely to yield the same high-level political traffic, there was no real contest. The only drawback with the Rue Boissy d'Anglas site was its cost. This was the smartest part of the city; there'd be little change from £1m for one year's rent. Lofting and Birnbaum did not want to show themselves to the estate agents leasing the property, so they had to restrict their visit to peering through the window and walking the ground towards the line of the target cable.

'I'll say one thing,' Birnbaum remarked as he looked into the window of the big Hermès shop on the corner of their street and the Faubourg St Honoré: 'we're a darn sight less conspicuous in this city than our folks were in Damascus.'

'One of the advantages to spying on your friends,' Lofting replied ironically.

Birnbaum didn't get it: 'Do you still have a problem with this mission?'

'Heavens no, my dear fellow! I was merely struck by the irony of our situation.'

'Yeah, well I always say, if you've got a low weirdness tolerance, don't tap your neighbour's phone.'

'Yes, quite,' Lofting replied, stretching out the 'yes' to indicate 'up to a point'.

'If we're agreed on this, we'll get Zeke to do the survey,' Birnbaum pressed on impatiently.

'No doubt about it. This is our property.'

Ted had not met Zeke yet, but he was clearly something of a legendary figure in NSA. Whereas GCHQ or MI6 would have to have found a trusted outsider to do an engineering survey for them, the Americans seemed to have such a person in-house. Lofting wondered how many interception tunnels or other secret excavations the NSA must conduct in an average year in order to retain the services of such an individual. Birnbaum and Cortland had referred obliquely to Zeke's achievements. The Moscow tunnels, three of which had been dug from inside the US Embassy compound in the early 1990s in order to tap into old-style underground communications landlines, were known about at GCHQ. Even though the operation was an all-American one, its rich take of Russian secrets had been shared under the UK/USA arrangements. People at Cheltenham also knew a good deal about the Damascus tunnel, which had been dug in 1994. Polish intelligence had helpfully provided the cover business needed to secure a property for digging a 200m-long interception shaft on that operation. There were, however, other operations which the NSA had not specifically told GCHQ about. Lofting could read the intercepts which the Americans had gathered from the Japanese embassy in Bonn or the North Korean UN delegation in Geneva, but the compartmentalisation of secrets meant he was not party to the means used to obtain them: he suspected though that Zeke had had a hand in both operations. Lofting did not know Zeke's name, only that Birnbaum used this nickname and that the famed tunneller was already in Paris, ready to begin his survey as soon as Hamsin signed the lease on its new showroom.

Chapter Eleven

Margaret was surprised when Brenda Skuse phoned her and told her that the Head of B Division wished to see her. To all but the initiated few at Cheltenham, B Division was something which, even in the closed world of their work, was unknown and mysterious. For something to be so secret within an organisation in which even the rotuine work is so highly classified gave the new organisation a special cachet. Margaret made her way over to Benhall, to the windowless cabin with the security-locked door which was her friend's workplace. She had never met Ted Lofting before, but knew from colleagues he had a reputation as thoroughly decent – by the standards of management.

'He's just on to the Director,' Brenda explained, smiling, as Margaret entered Lofting's outer office. 'Honestly, it's been a madhouse here for the last month – I feel lucky being allowed off for Christmas.'

'Oh really!' Reynolds replied. One did not enquire further.

'I've more than a hunch that you're about to be invited on board!' Brenda said with almost schoolgirl excitement.

'Really?'

'Foreign travel, Mags, that's all I'll say, foreign travel!' Brenda was beside herself. 'Anyway lovey, you're looking marvellous.'

Margaret smiled demurely: 'One has to try, as an old maid!'

'Nonsense, nonsense! You look super.' Brenda looked around and then mouthed the words, 'Any new fella?'

'One or two prospects,' Margaret replied, thinking of the pile of mail forwarded to her by *Private Eye* and of the first letter to which she had replied.

'Do tell!'

Before Margaret could reply, Lofting appeared from his office, and asked shyly, 'Miss Reynolds?'

'That's me!' She extended her hand confidently to shake Lofting's.

'Come in, do come in. Well . . . marvellous! Do come in!'

Reynolds placed her folded coat over one of the armchairs in Lofting's office and sat on the other.

'Miss Reynolds – would you mind if I call you Margaret?'

'Of course, no problem,' she was already touched by his formality.

'Margaret, I'd like to ask you whether you would be interested in taking part in an overseas operation. If you're agreeable, I would like you to head a group of translators and analysts – your post would be quite pivotal.'

'That sounds quite a challenge.'

Lofting became more relaxed as he continued his spiel: 'You would have to be willing to work overseas for as much as three months – there might be the possibility of one or two weekends off.'

'When would I start?' She knew it was pointless to ask where the job would be or what exactly it involved.

'After Christmas, but it would probably be two or three weeks into the New Year before you'd go abroad.

It's a joint Anglo–US operation and it has the potential to change the whole future of sigint – I don't think it would be immodest to say it's the most exciting operation that's likely to happen here in many a year.'

Margaret felt a little panicked by the thought. What if something happened to Dad? What about her personal plans? She put these ideas to the back of her mind. The offer was a vote of confidence in her – clearly very important work. It would take her away from crummy Cheltenham for a bit, away from the nagging reminders of Peter. 'OK, I'd love to do it,' she cracked a radiant smile.

'Marvellous, marvellous! Margaret, there's just one more thing I need to do before you get fully signed up.' Lofting fiddled nervously with a combination-locked drawer on his desk. 'All a bit embarrassing, this! I've got to ask you to sign something – I know you're as highly Comint-cleared as anyone could be, but the sensitive nature of this operation requires certain special measures, in the Director's view.' He handed across a sheet of paper and placed a biro on top.

OPERATION POLYP

1. The Operation involves technology of such sensitivity that its details may not be discussed with any non-indoctrinated personnel.
2. Although the Operation is being jointly conducted with the US, certain restrictions are to be placed on the exchange of information. UK personnel are not to intercept material relating to certain US government policies. US personnel are not to intercept any signals relating to UK/European Union matters.
3. Because of the sensitivity of the Operation it is to be afforded maximum deniability. Under certain

circumstances your status as a member of GCHQ or even the Civil Service may not be acknowledged by HM Government.

Margaret was disturbed by what she read. She wondered how Chinese walls could be maintained with the Americans and why she was being asked to acknowledge her own dispensability.

'It's all very dramatic I know, Margaret.' Lofting sensed her hesitation.

'Do you think this UK/US restriction is workable?'

'Well, you know, it's meant to be the same principle as when we inadvertently intercept personal conversations here – as soon as we establish the nature of the conversation we're meant to switch it to the Americans, or vice versa.'

'And this third point – it's a bit, well . . . you know.'

'It's a bit blunt, I know. Many of us have done jobs in the past where that might conceivably have happened in a *sauve qui peût*, but seeing it spelled out is a bit disconcerting.'

Margaret knew there was little point having a big discussion about it. It was there in black and white and she'd been at GCHQ long enough to understand they wouldn't change it on her account. She took the pen and signed the declaration.

'Well done! There's a briefing for key members of the team at 14.00 in conference room eight at Oakley.'

Reynolds picked up her coat and reached out to shake Lofting's hand: 'Thank you for choosing me – it's clearly going to be a fascinating operation.'

'Yes, one never to tell the grandchildren about!'

They laughed and parted.

* * *

Reynolds was one of the first in the conference room. It was her habit to get so nervous about being late that she would arrive twenty or thirty minutes early and end up marching up and down corridors or sitting in the canteen. The others filed in. There were a number of people whom she recognised, but most were strangers to her. She heard a couple of the Americans speaking in hushed tones about their jetlag. Ray Skinner then appeared carrying a stack of vu-foils. 'Well hello, Margaret!' His face lit up as if he were surprised to see her.

'Hello, Ray.'

'So you've joined the POLYP crowd – things are brightening up by the minute!' He gave her a stagey wink. She looked down because she was embarrassed for him. Ray took it as shyness.

'What's your role in this great venture?' she asked politely.

'Mr Lofting's IC admin really – fixer, security officer, jack of all trades, ship's cat, you know!' He deposited the foils by the projector and then began greeting the others. At 1.56, Lofting entered with Dan Birnbaum.

'Welcome ladies and gentlemen, please take your seats and we'll begin.'

Reynolds was struck by the difference between the shy alone-in-his-office Lofting and the leader of this operation.

'I'm Ted Lofting, Head of B Division. This is Dr Daniel Birnbaum from NSA. We are jointly in charge of Operation POLYP and you are the only people who will be indoctrinated into all aspects of the operation.' A frisson of self-satisfied whispers from the audience greeted this news.

Lofting proceeded to brief them on the OREGANO

breakthrough and how it worked. Except for Birnbaum, the audience were spellbound: there was no fidgeting or looking out of the large window which surveyed the Oakley site from its fifth-floor vantage point. The NSA team leader bit his fingers and looked around distractedly since he already knew the secrets of Lofting's invention. Once or twice he made eye contact with Margaret, which she quickly broke.

'Which brings us to Operation POLYP,' said Lofting as he helpfully placed a vu-foil with 'Operation POLYP' on the projector. Unlike the previous ones this had the words 'TOP SECRET – POLYP' at the top and bottom in red. 'You will notice the new codename compartment. All papers relating to the op and all take resulting from it will be classified in that way, please. The aim of Operation POLYP,' Lofting removed the foil and then his glasses, allowing the pause to build the tension in his listeners, 'is to intercept France's highest security fibre optic trunk system in Paris.'

Lofting heard one American say 'Holy Shit!' under his breath, another 'Way to Go!' The British said nothing.

'To intercept France's highest security fibre optic trunk system in Paris,' Lofting repeated the mission objective, which was standard practice in such briefings. Then he began to pace like some admiral on his poop deck as he spoke. 'The trunk link in question carries most of the key traffic between the *Elysée*, *Matignon*, *Quai D'Orsay*, interior, defence ministries and so on. It runs under some of the smartest parts of Paris. Fitting the OREGANO pod will require us to tunnel under the Faubourg St Honoré. I would hesitate to speak for NSA – but I don't think it would be exaggerating to say it will be one of the most daring operations ever mounted by GCHQ.'

Margaret Reynolds greeted this news with mixed emotions. She was a Francophile – she loved their culture, their food, their sense of romance – but she also found something breathtaking about the audacity of it all.

'I'm going to hand over to Dr Birnbaum now, who will brief you on Phase One of the operation.'

Birnbaum stood up. 'Outstanding, Ted! Outstanding!' Lofting's brief had genuinely impressed him. 'Phase One,' Birnbaum cleared his throat, 'will last from December twenty-six thru when we throw the switch and get our first live intercepts, which should be January twenty-one, to late February or early March when the Paris team will be withdrawn and a second cover business will begin relaying the intercepts back here and stateside automatically. Which means we got a hell of a lot to do.'

There were further murmurs from the NSA contingent.

'At the point where we will intercept it, the cable runs about thirty feet underground.' As Birnbaum spoke his left hand lifted unconsciously to his head and he began to wind a black curl around his index finger. 'Our starting point will be an underground garage at this point,' he pointed on a sketch map, projected onto the wall, 'which means we got to go about one hundred and fifty feet along. The tunnel will be at quite a slope because it's got to go down about twenty-one feet from its starting point. Zeke is over there at the moment surveying the site. He'll run the dig, but we got some British folks coming in to do the spadework. Most will have to be done without the use of any power tools – we can't have the vibration and noise. We hope to break into the tunnel heading – that's what the diggers call those underground channels – around January fifteen.'

Ray Skinner's thoughts flitted from how he would get rid of the spoil from the digging to whether he would be able to fix his accommodation next door to Margaret's.

'A British team headed by Ted himself, backed up by Dr Megan Trelawney – who built these babies, stand up, Megan . . .' she duly obliged and took her bow, 'will then place two OREGANO pods on the cable. The idea is that there's redundancy if we get a point failure on one.' Birnbaum borrowed the term used when one of NSA's satellites went wrong. 'Once one of the pods goes live, we'll have a period of analysis to work out exactly what we got in that cable – which will be a hell of a lot, maybe four hundred channels of voice – and how we harvest it. There will be two groups of analysts and translators: group one, UK, headed by Margaret Reynolds – show yourself please . . .' She stood up, clasping her arms across her stomach with the self-consciousness of it all. 'Group two, the US group, will be run by Max Kampfner . . .' A reedy and ridiculously tall man showed himself and smiled politely at Margaret. Birnbaum continued his briefing: 'We will develop some software tools to screen out the trash – about 90 per cent of what's going through that cable – I'll be taking responsibility for that myself. The aim is to produce a package that can push out the really good stuff, for relay back to the UK. That will lead to Phase Two of the operation – when all of the personnel forward deployed in Paris will be pulled out. When we're ready for Phase Two, the cables carrying the power in and the signal out of the two pods will then be connected to a relay point, where we'll also have data processing. The tunnel will then be pumped full of concrete, the cover company at Rue Boissy d'Anglas will be wound up, and some unsuspecting sucker will move into that property.'

During the question and answer session after the briefing, most of the points were of narrow relevance to particular aspects of the operation. Margaret did not speak: she wondered whether she was the only one thinking about the bigger picture – was the operation right? What exactly would happen to them if a squad of Gendarmes broke down the doors and found them all sitting there eavesdropping on *Monsieur le Président*? Slowly she began to realise that her feeling of unease was balanced by one of excitement and that what thrilled her was the cloak and dagger nature of the whole enterprise – it was exactly the kind of thing she thought she might be letting herself in for when she had joined years before but which all of her experience had led to doubt would ever happen. It was the kind of mission her dad might have imagined she meant all those years ago when she told him she'd joined and he said, 'Secret work! Hush, hush! Don't say another word.'

Chapter Twelve

On Christmas Eve Margaret drove down to Clifton to see her father. It was a miserable visit: miserable because she had to drive through pouring rain to get there; miserable because he seemed barely aware of her presence throughout the two hours she spent by his side, and most of all miserable because she felt guilty that she would not be with him on Christmas Day.

The year before she had picked him up from the Bethlehem Home on Christmas morning and driven him to her flat in Cheltenham. Her brother Marcus, his wife Penny and their two snotty children had also come. While he and Marcus were doing the washing up, and Penny was strolling the kids around the block trying to tire them out, Dad had gone wandering off into the darkness of that December teatime. It took almost thirty-six hours for the police to find him. He had gone ten miles down the London road towards his old home in Ascot. In the process he was soaked through by rain, splattered with mud by passing cars and generally ignored by hundreds of passers-by returning from their festive visits. It was only when Johnny Farrell, a builder from Burford, had recognised the man who used to audit his accounts, that help had come.

This year Margaret had been told by a nurse that her father's condition had deteriorated sufficiently to make a Christmas outing a 'hazardous proposition'. They had not told her she couldn't take him away for the day, but they had made it clear she would be taking on an awesome responsibility if she did.

So Margaret and her father celebrated Christmas on Christmas Eve. She spoonfed him chopped-up turkey, brussels and roast potatoes and afterwards pulled a cracker. One of the nurses snapped Margaret with her arm around her father and them both wearing paper hats. When she got the prints she couldn't bear to look at the picture because she and the nurse had forgotten to remove his bib before taking it. Margaret had bought him a yellow cashmere scarf and tied it around his neck before she left. The only good thing about the visit was that her present remained in place and unstained.

Christmas Day was better than she had imagined it could be, under the circumstances. Marcus had made one or two comments on the lines of, 'Dad's far better off where he is, receiving expert care.' It had not even irked her too much that he always claimed to be too hard up to contribute to that care. She had knocked back two large glasses of South African Shiraz within half an hour of arriving, which numbed her enough to get through the proceedings. They bought her rather a nice gift, chosen by Penny presumably: a trendy blue velvet shirt. Margaret even found the children a pleasure, sharing in the delight of their present opening. The conversation ran its pre-dictable course, meandering to and fro across the familiar plain of Reynolds family experience: how difficult Christmas had been for years after Mum's death in a car crash – it happened when Margaret was still a teenager; Dad's worsening condition; hopes and aspirations for Marcus and Penny's children.

Surrounded by this hubbub, Margaret's mind wandered to the forthcoming operation. She did not think about the many practical issues of how she would pick her team or the complexity of sorting the wheat from the chaff in all those hundreds of conversations which could travel down a single fibre optic wire. Instead she found the whole concept staggering: tunnelling under the Faubourg St Honoré; tapping the President and his most senior officials; stealing the most precious secrets France had. This was an operation of such aggression and daring. It was one thing tapping the Chinese embassy or bugging cables in Moscow – those people expected the Brits and Americans to get up to that sort of thing, but what if they got caught by the French? There was a good chance they would find the whole thing too embarrassing to admit to. Was that what the bosses at Cheltenham were gambling on? But what if Paris used it in some way to denounce *perfide Albion* – the untrustworthy British; to show that old man De Gaulle had been right all along: there was no place in Europe for those who would always put English-speaking solidarity ahead of the great dream of unity. Reynolds realised the stakes in Operation POLYP could hardly be higher.

Zeke spent Christmas in a camper van in Paris. He and his partner Ron found the break speeded up their survey – the streets were almost empty for three days. Under some circumstances this might have been a problem, since the spy is always more comfortable in a crowd, but Zeke and Ron had a whole tourist routine worked out.

Zeke was a big man – large-framed and overweight. He had a chubby face, drooping moustache and hair which had thinned on top but grew far too long at the back. The NSA's engineer habitually wore jeans, sweatshirts and squished around in trainers. When he stood next to Ron, a dapper little Texan, the effect was predictably comic. Ted Lofting's assumptions about Zeke were not quite accurate in that he was not employed fulltime by NSA. Instead Zeke worked freelance in the civil engineering business but spent most of his time in a log cabin in a beautiful part of Colorado where he lived alone, hunted, fished and fiddled with a collection of old Apple Mac computers picked up in junk sales. His work for the government was charged at $20,000 per month and a few jobs each year were enough to keep him in rifle shells, tackle and chips. Zeke was just a nickname – a *nom de guerre* known only to his colleagues in the black world. It had been given to him by a Company type on his first covert operation years back and had stuck. The CIA man had got it from a Larsen cartoon featuring a dog of that name who bore more than a passing resemblance to the engineer. On Christmas Eve, Zeke had taken a walk around the Faubourg and Hamsin's new office building lugging a large black Samsonite suitcase. The tunnel required some very exact measurements to be taken from a dozen different places. Those measurements needed a theodolite – a tripod-mounted surveying instrument which revealed the relationship in angle and elevation of those different spots. Each measuring point had to be precisely fixed using a steel disc of about one centimetre diameter implanted in the ground – which is where the Samsonite suitcase came in.

Zeke's bag looked weighty because it was: it contained a magazine of steel plates and a gas piston firing device linked to a button in the carrying handle. Each time the

American rested his heavy load in the right place, he pressed the switch, firing a plate into the ground below. It worked well and almost silently.

The day after Christmas, Zeke and Ron took a drive around Paris. Inside the rear of Zeke's camper van, a theodolite stood mounted on its legs. As he neared the measuring points in turn, Zeke flicked on a small TV screen which he had secured to the dashboard. It was linked to a camera on the underside of the vehicle. He parked roughly over each steel plate before ducking back through the curtains obscuring the saloon of the vehicle. Once inside, he lifted a plate in the vehicle's floor and located the theodolite precisely over it. He would then aim the viewing part of the device, much like a camera, through one of the windows and call Ron on his CB radio. The second vehicle then parked at a point where it was directed to by Zeke. On the back of Ron's van was a ladder up to the roofrack. It had been remade so that its rungs were the precise distance apart required for the elevation measurements. A touch of Day-Glo yellow paint had been added to each step to assist Zeke.

As he worked, Zeke switched his radio to the police frequency in case some of the many *agents* who guarded this neighbourhood of ministries and embassies grew suspicious of the two foreign-registered vehicles. Zeke and Ron did a little acting too, one or the other stepping out of their vehicles to take a photo, theatrically examine a street map or check their tyres at each location.

There was only one tricky moment during the triangulation of these measuring points, which occurred on the Faubourg, as Zeke parked over the suspected location of the *TONNANT* cable itself, just outside the Japanese embassy. The engineer knew this might be tricky since the parking bays in that part of the street had all been suspended for some inexplicable reason and the measuring point required him to stop the van about eighteen inches out from the kerb. As he stood behind the tripod, which was extended to full height so the optic of the theodolite could be aimed through a window at the front of the van, over its cab, there was a banging on the vehicle's side which made Zeke jump.

The thumping was repeated, '*Monsieur, c'est défendu, vous ne pouvez pas stationer ici!*'

Zeke shot back through the curtain into the front before opening the driver's door and coming face to face with the policeman. 'Understand! Si, si, no parking!' The American smiled apologetically.

'*Vas-y!*' the officer said rather rudely, waving his hand aggressively.

Zeke made a show of discovering that the keys were not in the ignition: 'Oh! Keys in the back, sir! I will get the keys.'

The policeman nodded, clearly having understood, turned and began walking back towards the British Embassy, which was back beyond the Japanese and American missions. Ron's vehicle passed him as he went. It took about ninety seconds for it to get into place before Zeke completed the measurements, jumped into the cab and drove the van away. He listened to the police frequency for almost an hour before resuming his work.

Two days later an MI6 officer attached to the POLYP team checked the British Embassy security log in case the policeman had noted any details of Zeke's vehicle. It was always possible that the *flic* might have been worried that the van was part of some IRA plan to blow up Britain's splendid diplomatic premises. Zeke and Ron were relieved to hear that they had not aroused such suspicions. By the time MI6 came back with the all-clear, the surveyors had finished their measurements and had already removed seven of the twelve metal plates. Zeke would soon be finished with the work needed to plot the route for the interception tunnel.

Ted Lofting's Christmas, like Margaret Reynolds's, departed from its usual script that year. His mother-in-law did not make her annual appearance – she had gone instead to Sara's brother's. Lofting's brother Vincent, a confirmed bachelor of forty-seven who worked in a merchant bank, had made alternative arrangements, so another regular attender missed the Lofting's fixture.

About an hour before lunch Lofting helped himself to a generous glass of sherry and wondered if Sara's mother and Vincent might have made their excuses because the marital tension had been so palpable last year. Christmas dinner was one of Sara's unusual sorties into the kitchen – to cook a proper meal in any case – and it made her unbearably nervous.

The doorbell sounded and Lofting stood up.

'Get the door!' Sara boomed from the kitchen.

'Getting it, dear!' Ted replied.

Dan Birnbaum's intense features greeted him as he opened it. The American proffered a bottle of wine which Lofting took with alacrity.

'Perfect timing!' said Lofting, as he helped his guest out of his Brooks Brothers mac.

'It's really good of you to ask me,' Birnbaum responded in a display of social grace even his friends would have found pleasantly out of character.

'Nonsense, nonsense! We weren't going to have you sit in that dreary hotel on Christmas.'

'Well, I really appreciate home cooking.'

'I can't make any promises, but Sara usually rustles up something pretty decent.'

Birnbaum had already given some thought to how he might pass the time at this lunch, since talking about their project was out of the question. His American colleague at Cheltenham, Cord Cortland, had primed him with suitable topics. After a hefty whisky had been thrust into his hand, he began to cross-examine Lofting about his interest in naval history. Since the GCHQ man had enough self-awareness not to advertise his interest in naval wargames, it took a little while before the conversation reached the point where he asked his guest, 'Would you like to see them?'

'Sure,' Birnbaum replied, already mellowing with the intake of spirits.

They climbed the stairs to the loft. Birnbaum inspected the intricate rigging and painting of the small model ships. 'You did all this yourself?'

'It passes the time, dear chap, takes my mind off things.'

'It's very impressive.' In truth Birnbaum was more puzzled than impressed but he felt he couldn't express his scepticism that such long hours of labour could ever be justified. 'So how do you fight these things?'

'Well,' Lofting replied, taking down a pamphlet from one of his bookshelves, 'you have these rules which determine everything from how far a ship can move during a set period of time, to how much damage their cannons can do against different targets. It's all very compromised of course – it's hard to represent the confusion and terror of battle—'

At that point, Ted's explanation was interrupted by a cry from below. 'One tick – She Who Must Be Obeyed might need a hand!'

Lofting found Sara standing with one hand on each of her tartan-clad hips.

'What are you doing up there? I need your help getting the turkey out! You haven't even introduced me to our guest and you're up there showing him those stupid ships!'

Lofting realised it was not the time to run out his guns: 'I'm sorry, dear, you're right of course. Let me give you a hand with the turkey and then I'll go and get Dan.'

As was often the case in their arguments, this admission of full liability by Ted simply launched Sara into a higher level of indignation. 'Honestly! This happens every time we have someone round, you've just got no idea about helping me, have you?'

'I'm sorry, dear, I've said I'm sorry.'

'Some husbands make the whole Christmas spread, you know!'

Ted could smell the gin on her breath: 'Come on, Sara, let's get on with it,' he said, opening the oven door.

'Two days I've been preparing this meal and then you disappear to the loft when I'm just about to serve it.'

Her husband had endured enough. 'I was searching the house for you – I forgot it was the one day of the year you're in the kitchen.' Ted's ultimate resort to sarcasm was another feature of their rows.

The American was still in the loft studying the wargames rules when Ted ushered him downstairs. 'Have I got this right? For one ship to fire at another you have to get its "Gunnery factor" from this table, throw a dice, then multiply it by the number of batteries firing,' he flicked through several pages of the pamphlet, 'which you get from this page, which then gives you Total Damage Points Inflicted, which you then check against this table of Hull Defence Values?'

'Well, with practice . . .'

'I'll write you a spreadsheet that'll do that for you in half a second.' Birnbaum was not being boastful, he had just spotted an application for his considerable talents.

'No need really,' Lofting was embarrassed. 'We've both got much more important things to do – maybe we'll talk about it after the operation.'

'I can do this in a couple of hours,' Birnbaum countered confidently. 'Let me borrow these rules, I'll do this tonight – nothing else planned.'

'Very kind,' said Lofting, bowing to Birnbaum's vigour and his own interest.

As the adults sat down to eat, Ted finally noticed Emma's absence and had to go upstairs and bang on her door to get her to emerge. Once at the table she behaved reasonably well. There was something about Birnbaum's intensity which fascinated her. He had not made the flabby compromises her parents had. Ted and Sara continued their spat in a coded language which Emma understood but which Birnbaum hardly noticed. For most of the meal it seemed like two different conversations going on. Presents were opened afterwards, including a pictorial history of Cheltenham which Lofting had bought Birnbaum, and dutiful thanks exchanged.

Afterwards, the American volunteered to do the washing up. Ted tried to dissuade him and they ended up doing it together. Sara sat in front of the TV drinking brandy and Emma fled to a friend's house.

As Dan moved on to the tough stuff – the fat-encrusted baking pans – Ted peered next door into the lounge and registered that his wife had gone to sleep. He rejoined Dan in the kitchen.

'She's nodded off,' he said, with an affection surprising given the circumstances.

'Does she know anything about this operation?' Birnbaum asked.

'Heavens no! She's from a Service family. She'd be shocked if I ever confided in her.'

'Very secure,' the American said earnestly.

'I suppose so,' Lofting replied while taking a dishcloth to a dripping pan he'd been handed, 'although sometimes I wish I could share a burden with her.'

'It can be a lonely job, stealing other people's secrets.'

They worked in silence for a few moments before Lofting asked, 'Do you see yourself making a lifetime's career out of NSA, Dan?'

'Sure,' he replied swiftly, 'I like it. I'm moving onwards and upwards.' Then his brow arched a little: 'Shouldn't I want to?'

'I don't know – for people of my generation it all seemed to be so clear: the worldwide battle against communism. Now it's all so muddied and I would have thought a chap with your skills could command a thumping salary in the commercial sector.'

'My skills, Ted? What can I ever put on my resumé about my skills? That I devised a programme which could filter out phonecalls going to Syrian Air Force HQ even though the dialling code is the same as that for the Ministry of Construction? I couldn't tell Bill Gates about that, and if I could I'm not sure he'd understand what it meant.'

'I see your point.'

'Does the fire still burn for you, Ted?'

'Well of course I want OREGANO to be proved a success – I've invested the last five years of my life in that technology so it's desperately important to me. After that though? Well, I suspect things will be a bit of an anticlimax. I expect I'd be happy enough to shuffle off into retirement.'

When Birnbaum had left, Sara awoke from her slumber. The brandy had put her in a foul mood. She laid into Ted with a mercilessness he would never forget.

Chapter Thirteen

At the end of the first week of January, Operation POLYP went into a higher gear. Paris was suffering one of its periodic cold snaps: the canals in La Villette had frozen over, police stopped hassling the vagrants sleeping in department store doorways in Les Halles and the wealthy women of the city walked the Faubourg in their full-length fur coats.

The shopfitters had kitted out the premises at 26 Rue Boissy d'Anglas in the style which the largely Middle Eastern clientèle for Hamsin's special cars might expect. There was a good deal of polished brass, mirrored walls and halogen lighting. A team from Controller Operational Support at MI6 had gone in to get the business started from offices on the first floor. They had already bought some vehicles which were to be delivered soon. Their stock was a mixture of new cars with flash modifications like special wheels and entertainment systems as well as some classics. A Ferrari Daytona, a thrusting creation of the early 1970s with a huge bonnet and a squat, aggressive mien would take pride of place in the front window. Ads had already been placed in the *Herald Tribune* and several Arab papers offering the Daytona and some of the other vehicles for sale.

Ted Lofting took the Eurostar over on January 6th,

accompanied by Ray Skinner. It was to be the first of a large number of journeys they would make, trips complicated by the needs of security. Ted spoke little, something which the ex-Navy man put down to security-consciousness but which actually stemmed from an inner turmoil. After their American guest had left on Christmas evening, Sara had dropped her bombshell.

'I want a divorce,' she had said. He had been too shocked to reply so she followed up with, 'I've met someone who's very fond of me.'

Eventually Ted had replied, 'You're drunk, shut up before you cause us both a great deal of pain.'

Little more had been said during the days between Christmas and New Year's Eve, which they had spent with old GCHQ friends. On New Year's Day she had announced, 'I wasn't drunk the other night. I want you to arrange an appointment with our solicitors when you get back to work.' That evening she had gone out 'to play cards' again.

Ted had not made the appointment: he had decided they might benefit from a cooling-off period. On the train, he tried to decide what there was to be saved in his marriage. In his heart of hearts he knew it was years since he had treated her with real love. They had fallen into a routine which alternated between friendly co-existence and bitter sparring. There had been times when he had fantasised about how he'd feel if she died in an accident, but now there was a real possibility his marriage might end he had mixed feelings. As he watched the liveried steward waddling up the aisle pushing his refreshments trolley, Ted remembered what had originally bound them together – shared jokes, an indefinable sense of fitting well together. Given the kind of hours he would have to devote to the operation, it all seemed impossible.

Dan Birnbaum had gone back to the US for a few days, to Fort Meade, to work on the computers which would be used to handle the intercepted traffic. Lofting and his Director understood perfectly well that the Americans would hold all sorts of aces if they were given sole charge of this area, but did not see any alternative. Ever since the first communications intelligence birds, the RHYOLITEs, had been put in space in the early 1970s, Fort Meade had been building up its experience in handling eavesdropping which could produce hundreds, sometimes even thousands of conversations or data exchanges simultaneously. It was something they had spent billions of dollars and thousands of man–years of effort on: GCHQ had no similar expertise.

Lofting and Skinner arrived by taxi from the Gare du Nord at lunchtime. They were cordially greeted by Mike McPhee from COS.

'Morning gents, welcome to Hamsin motors, purveyors of bespoke tart carts and passion wagons to the sheikhs of Araby!'

'Impressive progress, well done.' Lofting was friendly but businesslike.

'We're all set for our opening party next Tuesday,' McPhee added.

Lofting looked at him in a way which betrayed his thought of 'is that really necessary?'

'All part of the cover, Mr Lofting,' Ray Skinner chipped in.

'Yes I suppose so.'

'Your presence definitely not required, Mr L.' McPhee explained: 'Always best if you and Mr Birnbaum maintain a low profile. You're not missing anything I can assure you!'

At the back of the showroom was a partition wall behind which was a kind of kitchenette – useful for preparing drinks for clients – and a spiral staircase down to the garage below.

'Not too handy for getting gear up and down,' Lofting noted as they descended.

'You'd be surprised what you can do if you put your mind to it,' Skinner said in a sort of 'I served on ships far more cramped than this' way.

The garage seemed very small to Lofting. It would take great skill to park eight cars in it, let alone to conduct a major excavation. On two of the four walls were marks made with spray paint which related to Zeke's survey points. Beneath one of these groups of arrows and figures, the American had sprayed a one-metre square area, the bottom of which touched the floor.

'This is where it will all happen,' McPhee said.

As they stood admiring Zeke's hieroglyphs, the engineer himself came thumping down the spiral staircase. He seemed almost to ignore them as he walked over to one of his survey points and checked some figures on a notepad. Then he looked up at them and said, 'Hi guys.'

'Ted Lofting,' the British team leader extended his hand.

Zeke wiped his big paw in his jeans and grasped it firmly. 'All righty, I guess you want a brief?'

'That would be nice,' Lofting replied politely. Skinner and McPhee withdrew gracefully, leaving Lofting and Zeke alone in the cold garage.

'OK,' Zeke said, walking over to the painted square

on the concrete wall, 'this here is where this heading's starting out.' A 'heading' was engineer-speak for a small tunnel of the type they would dig. 'Ron and me done the survey. Everything's cool. We're gonna push this sucker fast as we can. Just as soon as your diggers are here, we'll take off this concrete. I'll get some final readings.'

Lofting noticed that Zeke rarely looked him in the eye as he paced up and down. Although there was a radiator in the garage, nobody had worked out how to switch it on yet, so the American's breath could be seen billowing out in the harsh neon light.

'If we gonna make Jan fifteen as a deadline, we gotta stay lucky. So far we been lucky. You never can tell when you're pushing a heading.'

'What can go wrong, Zeke?' Lofting drew out his pipe as the engineer composed his answer.

'Unexpected obstacles for one. Folks who have structures registered as two floors deep, but actually they go down three – maybe they were trying to save on their taxes!'

Lofting realised this was a stab at a joke and smiled obligingly.

'Flooding. We had plenty of flooding in Moscow. Then there's gas – natural methane – shouldn't be no problem here. But you get other shit. You get buildups in a heading this long. That's why we brought the ventilator plant over from Jersey. Once we hit the target heading then there could be other problems.'

'Oh?' Lofting had already been briefed on some of these, but wanted to give Zeke his head.

'When Frenchie built his heading – we think it was back in the fifties – he went down thirty feet. He didn't do that for no single trunk. Frenchie put twelve cable

116

channels into that heading, then filled all the space around it with concrete. Your *TONNANT* –' Zeke said Toe-nant just like the NSA Director had at Fort Monkton – 'it's just one of those twelve channels. When we take out the concrete in Frenchie's heading we gotta be real careful.'

'Quite,' said Lofting, imagining some powerful drill careening through the fibre optic and wrecking the whole operation. The Englishman lit up his pipe and began puffing away. 'Anything else I should bear in mind?'

'Don't ever leave nothing in our heading. In Madrid some asshole left a wrench in our heading. We lost one week, one whole lousy week looking for it—' Abruptly, Zeke stopped himself.

Lofting of course had noted the reference to Madrid – not an American operation which GCHQ knew about – but couldn't tell whether that or a notion of professional pride had halted the engineer. 'Did you find it?'

Zeke looked as pained as if he was remembering the most awful bereavement, bit his lower lip and shook his head.

Lofting, Skinner and McPhee ate baguette sandwiches packed with salami and lettuce for lunch. Zeke declined an invitation to join them on the first floor, saying he was too busy. Skinner noticed him half an hour later eating alone in the garage. The British had already worked out certain procedures for eating and travelling to and from Hamsin's premises. They could not become regulars in the surrounding restaurants and cafés – on the other hand they had to patronise them occasionally in case they did come under surveillance: a workforce which prepared all its meals in the office would be rather suspicious. Sometimes personnel would journey to Paris by Eurostar, sometimes by plane, by car and via various other destinations such as Lyon and Geneva. Hamsin had rented an entire floor of an apartment building across the Seine and to the west near La Défense – this would be the dormitory for up to forty people engaged in Operation POLYP.

Two highlights were scheduled for the afternoon. The first was the delivery of some of the tunnelling equipment, the second the arrival of the four men who would dig it.

At about 3.30 p.m. a Belgian-registered van appeared in the street outside. It had come from Mildenhall, the USAF base in Suffolk to which the first consignment of props, pumps and stays had been consigned. The van had then been driven to Paris via Antwerp.

Lofting tried to demonstrate indifference to the arrival – such details were best left to Skinner. He heard a loud beeping as the driver engaged reverse, beginning to back the vehicle gingerly into the narrow opening to the vehicle lift. Once the driver, some old Walloon who had been on the MI6 payroll for forty years as a chauffeur in Germany, was confident he had lined up properly, he raised the clutch and began moving backwards at several miles per hour. That was when the almighty crunch came.

A middle-aged Frenchman walking a poodle along the opposite pavement shouted, 'Bravo!'

Lofting abandoned his attempts to look detached and rushed to the window. The van was too high. It had stuck fast against the roof of the lift. Skinner and McPhee were in the street fussing around. The old Walloon meanwhile simply raised both hands and thrust out his lower lip as if disclaiming all responsibility.

It took no more than five minutes to extricate the van, which was driven off hurriedly with McPhee in the passenger seat. The equipment would have to be transferred to something smaller.

Skinner climbed the stairs to the office and faced Lofting. 'I can't figure it out! I'd checked the height of the van and it was four inches less than the garage entrance,' he shook his head in disbelief.

Lofting said nothing. He was thinking that Skinner should have considered the height of the kerb too. Ted bit his lip though – it was far too early for bollockings.

Late that afternoon, McPhee took a small Citroën van down into the garage and opened its rear doors to reveal the four men who would dig the tunnel. They stretched limbs which had been constricted for hours in the vehicle and then removed a few cardboard boxes of tools and other possessions. The men were called Tom, Fergus, John and Martin. They were all Protestant Ulstermen from two villages in Fermanagh. Tom – the eldest – wore a threadbare tweed jacket and crumpled flannel trousers. The other men were dressed in a combination of shellsuits, jeans and sweatshirts. Lofting approached Tom, shook his hand and asked him, 'Are you the foreman?'

'Not exactly, but I'll be supervising the lads, right enough.'

Lofting was puzzled but moved on: 'I'm Ted. I'm in overall charge of this operation. You'll meet Zeke a bit later. He's one of our American friends. He's done the surveys and will be in day-to-day charge of your work.'

'That's grand, so it is,' Tom said as he began rolling a cigarette.

'You'll probably be starting this evening,' Lofting said.

'For two hundred and fifty pound a day I wish I'd started yesterday!' Fergus, John and Martin laughed appreciatively.

'Any questions?' The GCHQ man asked.

'There is one – where can we get a brew on?' Tom held aloft a battered electric kettle.

A little later Lofting was in the office on the first floor when McPhee appeared. 'What was that business with Tom about not being the foreman?'

'Boss, that's their way of honouring the three foremen they used to work for who got slotted by the Provisionals.'

'Oh, I see.' Lofting felt embarrassed for asking.

'For six years those four blokes worked for the only firm in Ulster which would build for the security forces. They rebuilt accommodation blocks so they'd be less vulnerable to mortars after the Newry disaster in '85. You know the score.' McPhee walked over to the bright new plastic kettle in the corner of their office: 'Cup of Gipsy, Mr L.?'

'Yes, white with one sugar, please.'

'Anyway the PIRA didn't like it. So they gave Pat . . . Sheehy I think it was, they gave him the Armalite pension plan. Gunned him down when he opened the front door of his bungalow – he was the last Catholic working for them as a matter of fact. The next foreman lasted seven months. They gave him the Semy-send-off. One pound of Semtex under his car. I was on a tour in Armagh at the time – the Scene of Crime Officer showed me the pictures. It took them a week to find his head. It was on the roof of his garage – he'd been backing out when the bomb went off, see?'

Lofting nodded, not sure if he wanted to know what had happened to the last foreman, but felt he ought to ask, if only to allow McPhee to finish his saga. 'Then what happened?'

'Well, the last fella lasted the best part of three years. A nasty shite of an IRA player called Liam Duffy walked up behind him when he was walking in Enniskillen, doing the Saturday shop, like, and shot him through the head four times. That's the IRA for you, Mr L.' McPhee looked down into his brew and shook his head in disgust: 'And to think that these days those cunts get asked for tea at the White House! Anyway, those four fellas downstairs were redoing the security fence at Rosslea RUC Station at the time and their firm told them to forget it – they were abandoning the job. But Tom and the others kept turning up for work, even though the boss stopped paying them. They turned up for about two weeks until the job was finished. Now they work for us . . . well, for us and Five. They do all the "no questions asked" building jobs. It might be making good a wall we've chiselled into to put up a pinhole camera. It might be something this big. In a way we're all they've got left. They always do what they're asked. They never complain. They never ask questions. Diamond blokes!'

McPhee's story was brought to a halt by a thump from downstairs. Lofting and the MI6 man arrived to see Fergus crouched by what would be the opening to the tunnel, battering away with a mallet. The other three men were standing around him, as if studying a great painter at work. Tom looked towards Lofting, nodded, smiled and then said proudly, 'Fergus is our demolition man, Ted!'

Lofting suddenly felt intensely fond of the four Ulstermen but was too reserved to convey his thoughts.

Instead he said, 'Excellent! Excellent!' and stood mesmerised as lumps of concrete began flying off the wall and Operation POLYP began in earnest.

Chapter Fourteen

Lofting took the RER, Paris's super-fast commuter line from La Défense, where he had spent the night in one of the Hamsin company flats, to Les Halles where he changed onto the Metro. He found the first section of the ride deeply impressive – the train whisked him into the centre in about ten minutes. As he travelled underground he daydreamed about all of the different secrets which lay beneath Paris's streets. He wondered about the nuclear bunkers, stocked with dried food, empty bunkbeds and inert computers, waiting for a holocaust which now seemed inconceivable. Then he thought about the information coursing through the trunk lines of a modern capital: every minute thousands of financial transactions and data exchanges. Lofting pondered why the *TONNANT* trunk was only thirty feet below street level. BOXER, the British equivalent, was 150 feet down under Whitehall: digging an interception tunnel in London would be a very different proposition. A vague twinge of suspicion crossed Lofting's mind and he made a mental note to talk to Zeke about it.

When Lofting arrived in the garage he was amazed with the digging team's progress. A canvass army tent had been put up around the mouth of the heading. Skinner periodically doused it with water: Hamsin's fine cars had to be protected as far as possible from the dust and mess of digging. As it was McPhee and Skinner found themselves washing the two big Mercs which now sat crammed in among the construction materials every day. Lofting could hear the roar of electric power tools from beneath the tent. Zeke had decided this was necessary to get through the foundations and that neighbours would assume it was simply a further instalment to the works which had been going on at the premises for the previous two weeks.

As Lofting stood wondering whether to poke his head inside the canvas, the digger named John emerged looking like a man dipped in flour. He hauled a big plastic bag of smashed concrete and bricks, dragged it across the floor to the back of the big Mercedes S600 and opened the boot. Lofting noticed the back of the car had been lined with heavy-duty plastic as well as canvas and that three other bags of spoil already sat neat and upright like soldiers awaiting inspection. The Ulsterman hefted his load in, winked at Lofting and said, 'Nice to be on a job with a half-decent dump truck.'

At that point Zeke emerged wearing a boilersuit and respirator and gathered an armful of planks from a pile of them in a corner of the garage. As he went back in, Lofting gave in to his curiosity at last and pushed his balding head inside the tent.

The concrete wall of the basement had been opened up like a gaping mouth. Fergus's legs could only just be seen as he battered away at the last few inches of foundation. After that they would be through to clay – they hoped. The downward slope of the heading was already apparent. The planks Zeke piled inside the tent were just over one metre long and would be used to line the shaft as it advanced – creating a box big enough to stoop or crawl in. As they pushed deeper under Paris, a small track would be laid on the bottom to carry truckfuls of spoil back up to the garage for removal by the upmarket site transport. The rail-mounted skip would be shuttling back and forth dozens of times in the coming days. The tunnel would be fifty metres long, but the excavated spoil about ninety cubic metres because clay which has been excavated fills out. They could get little more than one cubic metre into each car boot, so the dig would generate a good many journeys. As far as possible they were trying to plan these so that each Mercedes run out would bring back planks for the heading in the first phase and later bags of cement which would be needed to fill up the tunnel before they quit the property.

The POLYP team in Paris soon found they were running out of room. Zeke and the diggers had decided to work a shift system to keep digging going twenty-four hours a day. Since there was only room for one 'pony-man' or digger at the front of the heading, it was easy enough to split the small group into two teams who would work six hours on and six off. Those not working wanted to sleep and there was no room for beds, so they took to crashing out on the floor.

When Lofting went down to inspect the work during the afternoon, less than twenty-four hours after it was started, he was gratified to see the heading had progressed almost twelve feet. Having supervised the start of his campaign, he could do little but retire to Cheltenham for the time being. There was plenty to do there – checking on the progress of the second OREGANO pod for one thing.

* * *

That evening before boarding a redeye from Baltimore back to London, Dan Birnbaum was summoned to the Director's office at Fort Meade.

'Bourbon?' the general asked, standing at the bar, fixing himself a generous slug of Wild Turkey.

Birnbaum found spirits made his heart race, stopping him sleeping. 'I'll have a beer if you've got one, General.'

'Sure.' The Director handed him an open Budweiser without a glass. 'How's Paris working out?'

'It's looking A-OK. Tunnelling has started. We've got a basic signal-processing software package running on the workbench. I've also developed a system for relaying intercepts back to Cheltenham and Meade during Phase One of the operation through E-mail.'

'E-mail?' the general almost spat out a mouthful of bourbon.

'Yeah, I figured there's so much out there, it's the best way of hiding our traffic. It'll be encrypted of course – but with one of the strong algorithms the computer nerds use – nothing governmental.'

The general knew that amateurs now had codes strong enough to resist anything but the most deter-mined attack by the humming Crays which sat in Fort Meade's Cryptanalysis Centre. He shifted his attention to other matters. 'I suppose you got an answer to this Brit Chinese wall bullshit?'

'Of course, General,' Birnbaum seemed flush with pride.

'Outstanding, outstanding!' The general ruminated a little, while swirling the liquor around his mouth. 'Is this Lofting guy up to scratch?'

It was a tricky question. Birnbaum's feelings about Ted were mixed. Initially Dan had regarded Ted as a bit of a has-been – he still thought he lacked aggression.

The more he learnt about OREGANO, the more he realised the scale of GCHQ's achievement. On the personal level, he was grateful for Lofting's kindness to him over Christmas. He tried to resolve these feelings with a noncommittal, 'There's no arguing with what he's achieved, General.'

'The Brits have some shit-hot technology. It was a team effort. He didn't do the science, did he?'

'No, he led the team,' Birnbaum replied.

'I don't like him,' his boss anounced with finality.

Sara Lofting had dropped Emma off at another rave that Saturday and was sitting in front of the television, staring blankly at a gameshow when Ted got in from the office. He noticed an empty tumbler on the small table beside the settee. Force of habit seemed to take over as he said, 'Evening, darling.'

She looked up at him without reply.

'Sorry I'm so late.' Ted felt so weary he didn't know if he was being nice because he wanted his marriage to go on or because he was just too tired to face another argument.

'I'm used to it, don't worry.'

Ted poured himself a small sherry and sat down. He wondered whether their conversation marked some sort of ceasefire. For a moment he felt happy and, liberated by this flash of optimism, he said what was really on his mind. 'You know, darling, tonight there are people tunnelling under the streets of the capital of one of our allies in order that we can bug their government and I'm in charge.'

'I'm sorry?' Sara said, stunned by his indiscretion.

'That's why I've been working these wretched hours lately. If anything goes wrong and those people are arrested, we'll have to disown them.'

'Ted?'

'I just thought you deserved an explanation.' Suddenly he felt guilty: 'I won't say any more of course and I know you'll be discreet.'

She stared down for a moment, feeling his candour had come so late in the day as to be meaningless. 'Have you phoned the solicitor?' Ted felt crushed. He stood up and headed for the door. 'Don't drink too much, old girl. Emma'll want picking up at some stage.'

'You've had all week!' she said as he walked up the stairs.

It was 2 a.m. when Ted's sleep was interrupted by the phone. He fumbled for the light switch and his glasses, noticing Sara was not in the bed. As he picked up the receiver, he heard his wife lifting it a moment later.

'Hello, hello.' It was a young voice almost inaudible for the loud dance music thumping away in the background.

'Yes,' Lofting said.

'Is that Emma's Dad?'

'Yes—'

'It's her mother,' a slurred voice cut in.

'Sara, for heaven's sake!'

'She's been taken to the General Hospital. She passed out. There was an ambulance . . .' The voice trailed off and he could hear someone laughing loudly in the background.

He felt furious; he wanted to scream; but instead he asked, 'Was Emma conscious in the ambulance?'

'She's gone to hospital – it's going to be OK.'

'Who is it?' Lofting was close to bursting.

'Look man, I just said I'd call, right?' The girl who had phoned simply hung up.

Lofting struggled into trousers, pulling them on top of his pyjamas. He wrapped a navy blue blazer about himself, stepped sockless into his shoes and raced downstairs. He found Sara fumbling with the chain on the front door. 'What are you doing?'

'I'm going to get my daughter.'

'You're plastered, Sara! Give me the keys to the car, I've got to get to the hospital!'

'Hospital?' At that point Sara's face crumpled like the façade of a demolished building. She began to sob: 'I'm so sorry, I'm so sorry!'

Ted's anger subsided for a moment, 'I'll drive, you come too. Emma needs both of us now!'

Moments later the Loftings' Rover sped into the night.

Chapter Fifteen

Ted Lofting and his wife sat in one of the cold miserable corridors of Cheltenham General waiting for word from one of the nursing sisters. They had arrived while Emma was being stomach-pumped and checked out. It wasn't clear why she had collapsed, but her friends had told the ambulancemen that she had taken Ecstasy about two hours before she fell down on the dance floor.

For much of the time they waited Sara had actually fallen asleep. Ted was furious that she must have been so drunk, but did not wake her until one of the doctors appeared.

'Mr and Mrs Lofting?'

'That's right,' he said, looking at the young Asian woman with haunted eyes and a stethoscope dangling from the pocket of her white coat.

'You mustn't worry, your daughter's going to be all right.'

'Thank you, thank you,' Ted bit his lip. Sara's head pitched forward into her hands and she began to snuffle.

'She took Ecstasy – you know what that is?'

'Yes,' they said as one.

'It seems she became completely dehydrated. Normally kids know that they have to drink a lot of water if they're doing these kind of dance drugs, but she didn't. We try to tell kids about the risks of dehydration, so this doesn't happen . . .' The doctor's words trailed off.

'You tell them how to take drugs?' Sara was flabbergasted, dabbing her eyes with a tissue.

Before the doctor could answer, Ted cut in: 'Well, thank you for everything you've done for her, we really appreciate it. When can we see her?'

'She's gone to sleep now and we'll keep her in at least until tomorrow morning for observation, but we'll probably send her home about lunchtime.'

'Can we just see her for a moment?' Ted asked.

They made their way into one of the wards; there were few lights on as most patients were asleep. Behind a drawn curtain they found Emma, clutching her pillow, deep in her drugged slumber.

The Loftings reached the car without saying another word to each other.

On Monday, Ted Lofting was summoned by the Director's secretary and made his way up to the headquarters block at Benhall. His boss invited him in, stepped out from behind his desk and sat with Ted in the armchairs he reserved for less formal conversations with his senior officers. He cross-examined Lofting gently about the progress of Operation POLYP. This seemed unnecessary to Ted, since they were in frequent contact about it. It was only after the preliminaries that the head of GCHQ moved to his real topic.

'Ted, I'm sorry if this is embarrassing, but we've been notified by the local police of the incident involving you daughter.'

Lofting's mind raced. How on earth had they found out? 'Incident?' he asked to stall for time, as he struggled to contain a rising feeling within himself.

'Yes, well there are certain liaison procedures with the Gloucestershire force. It's all fairly commonsense. If they arrest someone for drink driving who they think is one of ours, they notify us – that sort of thing, you know, could become relevant to somebody's positive vetting status . . .'

'I understand the principle, Malcolm, but my daughter's . . . misadventure on Saturday night really is a family matter.' Ted had now recognised as anger the sensation building up within him. Why was he being grilled about something like this by the Director?

'Of course it is, Ted, and I think the police were being a little – well I suppose over-zealous in telling us about it. All I wanted to say, was that if we can do anything at all to help . . .'

'That's very kind, Malcolm,' Ted said while wondering what in hell GCHQ Welfare Branch could do to assist in his misery of a home life.

The Director smiled benignly and nodded to himself. Then he asked, 'How's Sara taken it? Not too badly I hope?'

Ted was really struggling to contain his annoyance: the bastard must have been told about Sara's drinking but didn't want to say he knew for fear of having to explain *how* exactly. Then a feeling close to panic gripped Lofting: were they trying to take him off the Paris operation? As these thoughts throbbed through his tired head, Ted tried to conceal them. 'Well, it's traumatic for any mother to think she might lose her only child – but that's only human. We spoke to Emma yesterday – it turned out she'd never taken one of these tablets before, that's why she keeled over. Maybe in a way it's all for the best.' Lofting looked down at his tightly clasped hands: 'I think she'll be terrified of ever doing it again.'

132

'Quite . . . Ted, I hope you'll think of me as a friend, if things are getting on top of you, at home.'

Lofting couldn't suppress his feelings any longer: a pang of emotion forced its way past his usual self-control and he asked, 'You're not trying to take me off the Paris operation, are you?'

'Perish the thought, Ted – no we'd really prefer you to take the laurels, it's your baby after all.'

As he left the Director's office, Lofting bitterly regretted the last exchange. He had been goaded into mentioning the possibility of his own removal from POLYP and the boss's answer 'we'd really prefer' had hardly been a ringing endorsement.

During Lofting's ordeal, Margaret Reynolds was in his office for an appointment he had failed to cancel when answering the Director's summons. She didn't mind, since it gave her a chance to chat to Brenda while they waited.

'So what about these prospects of yours?' Lofting's secretary asked with her usual bluntness.

Margaret had already decided that her earlier hint about possible male admirers was a mistake. She might meet a couple of the men who had answered her lonely hearts ad but had come to realise that she could only amuse herself with them as long as the two sides of her life remained completely seperate. In time she might meet someone special and then busybodies like Brenda would find out about them. 'There's nobody really,' she looked down at her hands. 'I'm better off without a man at the moment. It's going to take time to get over the Peter business.'

'Of course, dear.'

'I'm not going to rush into another big relationship.'

'No, well that would be silly . . . but a girl can still have fun.'

Margaret smiled. 'Oh you know me . . . I think I'll just grow old gracefully . . . I'd much rather remain on my own than get married to somebody who's second best and we both just end up being miserable.'

Before Brenda had a chance to agree, Lofting came bowling through the door.

'I'm terribly sorry, Margaret – quick chat with the Director. I think you'd already set off so Brenda couldn't—'

'It's fine don't—'

'No, it's really not on keeping people waiting. Anyway we're all here now so come on in.'

Margaret went into his office and presented her proposals for how they should sort the Paris intercepts once they began coming through. During the meeting Lofting told her about one of the targets in which Whitehall had a particular short-term interest. 'The Defence Export Sales bods say they have high hopes of bringing off another great slab of business with Saudi Arabia during the next few months. It could keep thousand of people in work for the next decade, so its importance can't really be overstated. I'd like you to do some thinking about it, Margaret – work out who might be the most valuable people to intercept in order to improve our chances of getting the order. Then when we discuss who's doing what with the Cousins, we'll make sure your group gets it.'

That Monday was a big day for Hamsin. A Saudi gentleman had walked in and put down $50,000 in cash for the Ferrari Daytona. The sale had been handled by a man called George – one of MI6's old Lebanese playmates. George was another of the Secret Intelligence Service's retainers who had been drafted in by Controller Operational Support to lend credibility to the Hamsin operation. The Lebanese was always immaculately dressed and as well as his native Arabic he spoke fluent French and English. There was only one problem with his polished performance as a salesman – George knew nothing about cars. After weeks of sitting him in front of enthusiasts' magazines and books, George could distinguish a Testarossa from a Mini Cooper. When no potential clients were in sight, the others would test George on his car knowledge. During the sale of the Daytona, Mike McPhee had to remain one step behind George in the role of his flunkey, in case the customer should want to know whether the engine was a flat twelve or a V twelve or, worse still, ask Hamsin's Chief Salesman to open the bonnet. After taking delivery of the cash, the MI6 men were beside themselves. McPhee raced down the spiral staircase to find Ray Skinner.

'Fuck me, Ray!'

'Not while there are dogs around.'

'We just sold the Daytona and we're not even officially open!'

'I suppose it'll help the petty cash.' Skinner wiped his dusty face against the sleeve of his boilersuit.

'Old Georgie did the business. A few minutes of Arab malarkey and this Saudi produces a case full of $100 bills. I've got to hand it to the old fella, he could charm the pants off a Mother Superior!'

Ray looked a little troubled.

'Problem?'

'No, not really . . . We're just going to have to go through all the hassle of buying a new car flash enough to put in the window.'

'Do behave, Ray! It's good cover – we've already got an immaculate left-hand drive Aston Martin Vantage coming over. We're in business!'

Skinner looked through the flaps of the tent. The heading had already progressed nearly forty feet. Rails had been put down so that the truck carrying spoil could be winched back up to the garage. At least now the digging was further away the Mercs in the basement didn't have to be cleaned all the time. Skinner turned to McPhee and smiled. 'We certainly are in business, matey, we certainly are!'

Every few hours one of the Mercs would come up in the car lift and speed off towards the west of the city with a bootful of spoil. The car – usually driven by McPhee, Skinner or Zeke – would speed off to a point near a sports centre on an island in the Seine where they were hidden from other traffic by trees and haul the bags out of the boot. The muck from Zeke's tunnel could then be tipped down the embankment into the river. By a happy coincidence this place was near enough the flats rented by the front company for it to be kept under periodic observation in case someone reported the frequent and puzzling trips by luxury cars to the river bank and the police became involved.

Chapter Sixteen

On three successive Thursday evenings Margaret Reynolds became someone else entirely. The first of her dates with men who had answered her ad in *Private Eye* took place during those dog days between Christmas and New Year.

Throughout the day of that first meeting she had been in a state of nervous tension. Again and again the phrase 'I can't believe I'm about to do this' had gone through her head as she worked through a great pile of files on current French governmental organisation. Once she had got home, she had poured herself a glass of wine and for a while paced up and down in her living room with her arms folded tightly across her chest. The clock kept reminding her she had less than an hour to decide whether she was going to get dressed, set off and meet Jonathan, the first man she had selected from the pile of letters. She had phoned him just before Christmas to arrange the date. That call had been easy enough, he was well spoken, polite, and went out of his way to be flexible. She had called herself Jane during the conversation – it seemed the obvious pseudonym after her 'You Tarzan Me Jane' advertisement.

Margaret decided to get dressed while what she thought of as her good and evil sides battled it out. She went to her wardrobe and pulled out a navy-blue wool dress. After two seconds' consideration it was thrown on the bed – too mumsy. Inside her head, an idea would not go away: it was more than a year since she had had good sex: why should she be so miserable and lonely? This thought eventually repeated itself with such frequency and power that it overwhelmed her reservations and she decided to wear a knee-length skirt with high black leather boots, a polo-neck sweater and dark blue jacket. The outfit showed off her long legs without being at all tarty. She retrieved her car keys from the copper Kenyan bowl near her front door and headed out of the flat. She drove towards the M5 and Bristol. With each little milestone of commitment, Margaret had told herself she was always free to pull out. Even at this late stage she knew she could always wait at a distance for Jonathan to arrive and leave if she didn't like the look of him. She had his photo – he only had her elliptical description of herself during their phone conversation to go on.

They had arranged to meet at the Sportsman, a pub just north of the city – close to the motorway and to a Holiday Inn place for commercial travellers which Margaret had decided would fit the bill if she liked Jonathan. She parked her Fiat in the hotel's lot and walked across to the pub. That way he might never see her car. Keeping men like Jonathan out of her real life was one of the only ways she could handle this. Throughout her journey she kept thinking about the packet of condoms in her handbag. She had bought them in a self-confident 'I'm old enough not to be embarrassed about this' sort of way before Christmas but now she felt as self-conscious about their presence there as would someone smuggling nuclear waste.

By a happy accident of timing, she noticed Jonathan

getting out of a Golf GTI in the pub car park as she walked across. A shiver wracked her whole body. He was three minutes early, over six foot, as he had said in his letter, and seemed conservatively dressed. She decided to follow him in.

He spotted her approach and held the door open.

'Thanks, Tarzan,' she said.

'Jane!' He laughed with embarrassment and looked down at his brogues.

'Yes! What are you drinking?'

It seemed inevitable that Margaret would take control. For one thing she was thirteen years older than Jonathan. He was a captain in the Army, stationed at Warminster. She found it vaguely ridiculous that a man who looked as young as he did could be a captain, but it soon became apparent in conversation that it was true enough.

Jonathan was most of the things that Margaret had hoped for when she placed the ad. He was tall, had a sportsman's broad shoulders and was conventionally handsome. His hair was almost black, his strong brow being underlined by thick eyebrows. He wore a blue and white gingham shirt, the collar of which protruded from a Guernsey sweater. Within minutes of sitting down he had announced, 'I must say I really am very pleasantly surprised that you're such a good-looking . . . woman.' Jonathan was very sweet.

Margaret's head flipped back – he could see the sinews of her neck – and she had a good loud guffaw. 'You'll embarrass me!' she had said, as her laughter subsided and she looked him in the eye. As one compliment had followed another it gave her a glow inside – like warmth returning to toes which have lost their feeling in some long arctic winter.

The pub had a good restaurant, one of the reasons why she had suggested it, and they quickly resolved to eat supper together.

Jonathan ordered rib of beef, Margaret had monkfish. He was gentlemanly enough to have white wine, insisting, 'I may be odd, Jane, but I love a glass of white wine with meat.'

Margaret decided during the meal that Jonathan was not the brightest of men. Many of his answers to her questions began with 'At the end of the day . . .' and they revealed precisely the attitudes she expected from a young infantry officer. Still, his heart seemed in the right place. As they tucked into dessert he had said, 'Why don't we go to the cinema one evening?' and she had been touched that he had thought of more than a one-night stand.

'When I saw your ad, I thought "what the heck!" I might as well answer it,' Jonathan felt the need to explain himself. 'I was just back from six months over the water, Belfast, and you've no idea what havoc that plays with your life. And I thought to myself, "At the end of the day, I just can't face the same drinks parties with the same couple of girls who've been passed around all the players in the mess: I just want something different." And I'm very glad I wrote to you.' She rewarded his candour with a big smile.

Margaret had gabbled on about her travels, sometimes truthfully. She had talked plausibly about her work for the Inland Revenue, spinning yarns from a tissue of fantasy. She insisted on paying her share of the bill, which she did with cash. It was at that point that she said, 'Jonathan, I've drunk far too much to drive home; perhaps we should get a room at that hotel over the road.'

'Right . . .' he said, evidently expecting to drive back to Warminster drunk and frustrated.

As they walked along the patches of light in the Holiday Inn corridor, Margaret said, 'You can't drive home, you silly boy!'

They stopped, Jonathan squeezed her hand and replied, 'No, I can't . . . I suppose I can't believe my luck really, being with you.'

For Margaret that moment seemed to make the whole exercise worthwhile. Inside her head, her good side put in its final argument for restraint: 'Why not go home now? That's all you wanted.' But by that point another force was driving her. She could feel it in the throbbing of her throat, the dryness of her mouth and the moistness of her palms. As he fumbled the key into the lock, Jonathan's step had taken on the lopsided awkwardness of a man walking with drum-tight trousers.

The room door banged behind them. He switched on the light, she turned it off. Margaret popped the fly buttons on his cords and freed his dick. Then she sank to her knees and took it in her mouth.

The booze and her need for release combined so that she completely abandoned the care with which she lived most of her life. Margaret and her man fucked until she hurt too much to go on.

Once his clothes were off, she could feel the lines of his stomach and the strength of his arms. For a moment she was frightened by the power of his body – Peter had been a Grade 1 couch potato and it was seven years since she had slept with anyone else. Even then, it was never with someone so fit. She had given in to her desire for it. At times when she heard her own gasps and moans they seemed to belong to someone else.

Jonathan was not the perfect lover. His passion came

on with all the tenderness of waves of fusiliers in the assault. Several times she had whispered into his ear 'Slowly', 'There's no rush', and at times when he was pleasuring her but seemed set to move on to something else, 'Don't stop, it's too nice to stop.'

As they thrashed across the bed, the sheets became tangled around one of her arms, a bedside light was knocked crashing to the ground and at one moment the unfortunate occupant of the neighbouring room had bashed on the wall and shouted, 'For fuck's sake, I'm trying to get some kip in here, you animals!' They were helpless with giggles after that.

A bit later they broke off for a while. Exhaustion had overtaken them and they were both parched so Jonathan searched the room for something to drink. There was no minibar so in the end he had brought her glass after glass of tap water from the bathroom. She had gone down on him again after that, and their struggle resumed for another half-hour.

Margaret slept so deeply that she was unaware of anything until he woke her at 6 a.m. with a kiss on the forehead. She opened her eyes to see a fully dressed Jonathan staring down at her.

'I've got to leg it back to Warminster for first parade, Janey. We must do this again,' he smirked.

'I'll call you,' she said smiling, but not at all sure she meant it.

'Jane, can I ask you something?'

'Sure.'

'You're not, I mean I know you *said* you weren't last night, but . . . I mean, I don't care if you are . . . but you're not . . . *married*, are you?'

'No, I'm not.'

'Neither am I,' he said earnestly.

'I'm very relieved to hear it,' she said and turned over.

As the door banged, Margaret wondered why it mattered.

The week after that first encounter had passed quickly enough. She had put her team for Paris together and was preparing their departure. At first she'd been bursting to tell someone what she'd done, but when her friend Bella Crewe had telephoned one evening Margaret had realised that she simply couldn't. Even though Bella had encouraged her to 'have fun' she couldn't own up to what she had done; she was terrified that she might be judged a slut. Margaret had also realised that the way to avoid any possible disapproval or expectations of the 'so when can we meet him?' type among her friends and colleagues was never to tell anyone about what she was doing.

Margaret considered ringing Jonathan and arranging to meet the following Thursday, but she had already lined up dates numbers two and three. Perhaps she could go back to the Tank, as she called him when she contemplated her soreness, after the third date, but she had embarked on an experiment and intended to complete it.

When she saw Terry James, the second of her dates, arrive at the Sportsman, she considered driving back to Cheltenham. He was around fifty and despite his height showed the unmistakable signs of a small paunch and after Jonathan she felt a little spoilt in the stomach department. She knew Terry was married, as he had made it clear in his letter but had decided to try to set aside all of her natural prejudice against unfaithful husbands given Bella and other friends' experiences. As they began to eat, Margaret decided that Terry had a rather charming smile: she would go with the flow.

'Have you done this kind of thing before, Terry?'

'No, no, perish the thought!' he answered in his soft West Midlands accent.

She didn't believe him. 'Don't worry, I wouldn't care if you had.'

Something she said seemed to have pricked his conscience and after taking a swill of red wine he said, 'She's probably getting it on the side. Makes no odds to me if she is. I've told her enough times things weren't coming up to par in the bedroom, but she doesn't seem to care.'

By dessert, Margaret was finding his repeated self-justifications a little boring – that and the presence of his hand on her thigh under the table. It had grown clammy as he had left it there and seemed to move it only slightly, up or down depending on his level of guilt. Margaret had come to this date more racily dressed than the last. She was wearing stockings and a shorter skirt.

'I suppose lots of people have told you you're a very attractive woman, Jane.'

She smiled demurely, disguising her impatience with him. Margaret had already downed three glasses of wine – she felt high, much more in control even than with Jonathan, so she dropped her hand below the table and placed it on his, dragged his fingers up her leg and pressed them against her crotch.

Terry pulled his hand back as if he had burnt it. 'Steady on!' he said, flushing.

Margaret felt suddenly sober and embarrassed.

He was tongue-tied for the next few minutes, before

finally standing and saying, 'I'll just go and settle up, love.'

'Let's go halves.'

'Don't be daft!'

She made for her purse.

'I won't hear of it, you put that away.' He turned and walked towards the cash desk at the front of the restaurant and then straight past it. Then she heard the shower of gravel as he sped away in his company Rover.

Terry was cheap as well as a coward. He had left her with a bill for £54.

And the last of her dates? It finished off her appetite for sleeping with strangers. It was obvious from his letter that the man who called himself Ron was not educated. She didn't mind because she was not thinking of spending much more than one evening with the men she met. Ron was quite a looker. Not much older than her with Celtic features and a powerful build. She had actually wanted to meet him first since his photo was the dishiest of the dozens she received, but Ron had made a variety of excuses as to why he couldn't. During their meal it had become apparent that nobody would meet Ron for his conversation. He had talked about his miserable childhood in Bristol being beaten by a drunken father. He was consistently vague about his work, implying that he had previously been in the building trade but was now running his own business. Margaret suspected he was a minicab driver. At one point as they ate he had asked her point blank, 'So what sort of thing are you into between the sheets, like?'

'Oh the usual boring sort of thing.'

'You look like the type who wants to be tied up to me.'

'No, not really,' was all she could think of saying to that, although in truth she did wonder whether she would enjoy a little low-impact bondage. It should have set the alarm bells ringing, as should his later remark that, 'Women only respect a man who shows them who's boss.' Why did she go any further? Perhaps it was the silly logic of her commitment to going through with her experiment; perhaps it was because she did not want to think too ill of Ron, and perhaps, after the letdown of Terry, she really wanted a good time in bed.

Ron suggested they go to the hotel over the road and she agreed. They got their key from the receptionist, whom she recognised from her stay with Jonathan. The pimply youth behind the desk said, 'Enjoy your stay,' and then added under his breath as they walked away, 'I'm sure you will.' For some reason this quip seemed to sober her up in a really unsettling way. She cursed her laziness at using the same venue for her encounters.

As they walked up the corridor, she said, 'Listen, Ron, I'm not feeling all that well . . .'

He responded with a sensitivity which sent her into real confusion, saying, 'All right, my lovely. No probs. If you want to turn around and walk away I'll understand.'

'It's not—'

'And if you want to go to the room and just rest, that's no probs either.'

'Yes, OK, I'll lie down for a bit and watch the telly or something . . .'

They went in and she lay down on the bed while Ron bumbled around the room looking for the non-existent minibar. He eyed the kettle and sachets on top of the dresser. 'Shall I make you up a cuppa?'

'Yes, thank you, Ron, I'd like that.'

By the time he brought it to her and sat on the end of

the bed, he had successfully put Margaret at her ease. As he slipped off her shoes and began to massage her feet with his big hands, she smiled and felt ready to go on, imagining for a moment that Ron might turn out to have Jonathan's physical power but with the advantage of greater experience.

In fact he came on with a vigour which made the captain seem insipid. As he slugged away on top of her, Margaret opened her eyes and looked into his grunting contorted face. She did not want to be there. She felt dirty. She had wanted to get even with Peter and all she had done was humiliate herself. Margaret did not try to stop him, even though it began to hurt more and more as he pounded away and sweat dripped off his brow into her eyes, stinging her however tightly she shut them. At one point he bit her neck hard enough to make her shout 'Stop!' but he went on. Then he tried to tie her hands with his belt. She wrestled them free each time and said 'no' with increasing firmness.

When at last he gasped and rolled over onto his back she left as little time as she decently could before going to the bathroom and washing herself. She looked at her reflection in the mirror. A red welt had already appeared on her neck. She fought back tears.

As she emerged, Margaret said, 'Listen, Ron love, I must get going.'

'Husband expecting you home?' he said with contempt.

'I'm not married, never have been, I told you.'

'Don't lecture me!'

'Sorry,' she was becoming frightened.

'Sod off then, see if I care.'

She dressed in silence as Ron treated her to more abuse.

147

'You're not a bad-looking bint, but you should lighten up before you become a bitter old maid.'

'Really,' was all she could think of saying – in truth she had become intensely frightened of him. She walked out briskly through the lobby, remembering as she went that she was leaving him to pay for the room and taking some small pleasure from it.

Margaret did not even say goodbye – not audibly at least. She scurried through the reception and out to her car. She cursed herself as she went. How desperate could she have been to have submitted herself to this?

The wheels of the Panda screeched as she pushed it towards the motorway and the sanctuary of Esperanza, her home. Margaret was determined not to cry as she sped along, shifting now and then in her seat to ease her discomfort. Stupidly though she pushed a Patsy Cline tape into the deck and as the words 'Crazy, for feeling this way since I met you' sounded around the Fiat she found herself laughing and crying at the same time. In the depth of her misery she hoped – even though she knew it was completely illogical given his condition – that nobody would ever tell her father what had happened. Once after she had come home late from a disco in Charlbury – she must have been about fourteen or fifteen – he had been pacing around. He had sat her down and told her, 'Don't ever give yourself away lightly, a woman's honour is her most sacred thing.' It was all very old-fashioned and she had resented it at the time, but God how she had betrayed that idea in the last few weeks. She joined Patsy Cline – 'Crazy for lying and crazy for trying'. As overhead lights flashed across her wet face she longed for something to deliver her from this mess.

Chapter Seventeen

For Tom, Fergus, John and Martin days and nights had merged. They were working a shift pattern which usually meant they could not be bothered to go back to the Hamsin flat for proper rest. Instead they would emerge from the heading caked in clay and dust and crash out on a camp bed in the garage. Skinner and McPhee kept up a stream of takeaway pizzas, baguettes and other fast food. At night Tom would sometimes use the single cooking ring in the kitchenette behind the showroom to serve up bacon and eggs for the boys. They so loved these midnight tastes of proper food that the man going onto rest time would happily spend an hour or two afterwards airing out the showroom and spraying deodorant in case some Arab customer should catch a whiff of streaky the following day.

Skinner and McPhee occasionally lent a hand with the digging. They did not take the role of ponyman at the head, but instead would load spoil into the small truck. The tunnel itself had progressed to within a few yards of the estimated breakthrough position. Along its floor there was the track for the rail cart. The floor, walls and ceilings were shored up with planks, giving the tunnellers the feeling of being inside a large box as they loped forward with their heads and shoulders tucked right down. There was a tube on the floor connected to a water pump in the garage – it kept the liquid which dripped from the roof from building up. The ventilation tube and power lines were held on side walls with metal brackets shaped like U's. Ray Skinner in particular kept bashing into these as he made his way up and down the heading – often his overalls got caught and on one occasion he gashed his arm. The Ulstermen often chuckled as they heard the ex-chief petty officer making his way towards them. 'Ya fucker! ... bastard fucking thing!'

Tom, Fergus, John and Martin had shared a number of private jokes about Ray's ungainliness underground. Early on Tom had said, 'I'm surprised an old submariner like you finds it so tricky down here.' Ray had exploded, 'I was never a fucking submariner – you've got to be mad to want to sit under water smelling your mates' arseholes for three months at a stretch.' Having seen how sensitive he was on the subject of submarines they had decided to make a point of teasing him regularly and although Ray knew they were doing it, it didn't stop him rising to their bait every time.

Ray took a stroll the evening before they were due to break into the *TONNANT* heading. They had all noticed the change in temperature in recent days and he felt sweaty in his down jacket as he strolled around La Madeleine. The huge church was like a copy of the Acropolis, with great columns surrounding a massive rectangular structure and a soaring triangular portico above its entrance. Ray decided he quite liked it. He dawdled a bit and then decided to head back. When he got to the garage he heard the communications intercom beep.

'Hello!' It was Fergus's voice – he was taking his turn

as ponyman. Tom was pottering about in the garage, John back at the flat and Martin asleep on the floor.

Skinner was the closest to the voice box so he leaned over. 'Yes?'

'Can you bring us up that large chisel, I think I might be getting near the concrete.'

'No worries, matey, I'll be with you in a tick.' Skinner went to the rack of tools against one of the cold walls. Each one had a number taped to its handle. Beside the rack there was a notebook with a hole punched in it through which a string of elastic bands connected to the rack and a biro. Skinner noted the chisel's number in the column headed 'Down'. This system had been introduced on Zeke's advice to keep a strict control on everything in the heading. Beside the tool rack were two sets of miners' emergency breathing apparatus.

Having donned his overalls, Ray began his passage down the heading. He hated the first bit most since it was on a fairly pronounced downward slope which resulted in him loping along uncomfortably like someone doing a bad Groucho Marx impersonation. After about fifty feet it levelled out. Ray was trying to keep his thoughts focused on a barmaid he knew in Gosport when he tripped on the rails and pitched forward onto the ground, bruising his hand badly on the chisel. 'Fuck it!' he shouted.

When he made it to the front, where Fergus was hacking at the clay with a stubby pick, the Ulsterman asked him deadpan, 'Did they not teach you about movement in confined spaces at submarine school?'

'Shut it! I've done my hand in now.'

Fergus did not even look around in sympathy. 'Close the bulkhead on your way back to sickbay then.'

'Yeah yeah,' Ray said, as he nursed his hand. 'You

reckon you're near their heading then?'

Fergus leaned forward and flicked away bits of dirt at the furthermost point of his digging to expose a small patch of dull grey. His smile of triumph revealed three missing teeth.

'Nice one!' Ray said, patting him on the shoulder before beginning his journey back.

About twenty feet before the uphill stretch, Ray felt a trickle of water go down the back of his neck. Taking a small maglite from his pocket he directed it at the roof. He could see a steady flow of liquid coming down where two of the planks joined. A puddle was collecting on the floor.

When he arrived back in the garage, Ray took a deep breath and examined his hand in the light.

'I'm away to get a fry on,' Tom said as he began climbing the spiral staircase.

'Brilliant idea! I'm so hungry I could eat a scabby horse between two pissy mattresses!' Skinner began to salivate in anticipation. Then something else occurred to him: 'There's a fair bit of water—'

Before he could finish, a crash from the tunnel interrupted him. Ray and Tom turned as one towards the heading entrance. A column of air forced its way through the canvas sides of the tent covering, which flapped about like washing in a gale. Tom jumped off the stairs and towards the emergency breathing apparatus.

As the water hit Fergus, he flailed in panic, knocking on the intercom.

In the garage Ray heard his 'Jesus Christ!' and the sound of rushing water.

Tom had already put one mask over his head and bounded into the tunnel entrance with the other.

The initial rush had only half-filled the lower part of the tunnel, but it was enough to slow Tom down as he pushed himself forward. Cursing and swearing, he reached the point where one of the roof planks had caved in. Water was still cascading down, and a pile of clay washed down onto the heading floor had created a letterbox about eighteen inches high through which Tom had to push himself.

Fergus had been knocked out when the initial torrent threw him against the raw earth he was excavating. Luckily for him, he was floating face up on the water when Tom reached him and struggled to put the spare breathing apparatus on him.

'Come on, Fergus,' he said as he fumbled with the straps, 'I'll not leave you down here, you've got to make it!'

Despite Tom's shouts, Fergus did not stir. Tom knew more water was pouring through the roof, so he set off, dragging the younger man along with a hand under his chin to keep his head above water.

The gap between the ceiling and floor was already narrower than when Tom had come up the tunnel and he clawed at the earth to try to make the space big enough to crawl through. 'Ray, get down here, you bastard!' he shouted, but wasn't sure if he'd been heard.

Eventually Tom pulled Fergus through the gap. He felt the water thumping down on his back from the hole in the roof. It was like clenched fists pounding on him. By that point there was no more than six inches of air at the top of the tunnel. Tom's eyes were still above it as he moved along, but his mouth was under it as it drew air from the breathing set. 'We're not going to die, son! We're not going to die!' he shouted into the mask.

When they reached the uphill part of the tunnel, Tom

knew they'd make it. Ray was waiting to help him manhandle Fergus's big body up the slope. The Englishman lifted Fergus's head and shoulders and began backing up the slope, while Tom carried his feet. Crouched over carrying the heavy weight, Skinner thought time and again his back would give out. He cursed and muttered as they hauled Fergus up the gradient.

Martin had leapt up from his camp bed in the commotion, but he knew there was no point him going into the tunnel since it was too small for him to be able to get a hand to Fergus. Instead he peered into its mouth and shone a torch onto the bobbing sodden shapes slowly making their way up towards him, occasionally shouting encouragement: 'Only fifteen more feet now, Ray!'

As his body struggled in the confines of the heading, Skinner's mind had been racing. How would they get a doctor? There were emergency procedures but it was the middle of the night and they were meant to cover routine fractures and cuts. What if Fergus needed emergency surgery? What if he died? His hands had gone stone cold, his lips bluish. Ray called across his shoulder to Martin: 'Get on the phone to Mike at the flats; tell him we need a doctor PDQ!'

When the huddled threesome came out of the tunnel mouth, there was an explosion of coughing and spluttering from Tom and Ray and then they fell on the floor in a soggy heap. They looked like trawlermen who'd gone overboard in the North Sea and been rescued against all expectation. They were soaked in freezing, grimy water.

Skinner tried to put Fergus into the recovery position. 'You've got to come right now,' Martin was on the phone to McPhee, 'and we need a doctor! We've a man badly hurt.' All security had gone out of the window.

It was then, with rising anxiety, that Ray realised Fergus had stopped breathing. His face was ashen.

'Oh Christ! He's fucking arresting – Tom, help me put him on his back.'

They ripped open Fergus's overalls, finding a blue Rangers shirt undereath. With a strength which surprised himself, Ray ripped it apart to reach the man's chest. Frantically he tried with his cold-numbed fingers to find any sign of a heartbeat.

Something seemed to occur to Tom and he quickly stood up, grabbed a torch and peered into the heading. 'Martin, get that fucking water pump working double speed, or we'll be standing about in water in five minutes, so we will!'

Martin ran over to the machine, his ginger hair still boyishly tousled from his sleep, and began fumbling with the controls. Tom ran over and helped – the whine of the electric pump reached a higher pitch.

Ray was kneeling beside Fergus and knew he had only a few minutes to revive him. Clasping both hands together, he raised them up like a hammer, bringing them down with an awesome thump on the Ulsterman's breastbone. Nothing. Tom looked over – it was as if Fergus was his child. Skinner raised his hands again and brought them heavily down. Fergus's back arched for a moment and then he began to cough and splutter.

'YES!' Tom shouted.

Ray put the injured man back into the recovery position. 'That's all I can do till the MO gets here.'

Mike McPhee arrived surprisingly quickly after that. He started briefing them on the emergency plan as he came thumping down the spiral staircase. 'OK boys, we've got to get him up the stairs and out into my van. I've got a doc lined up over in Neuilly. Listen carefully: the cover story is that he's been working over here doing building work on the lump – and he's had an accident on site.'

Martin, McPhee and Tom manhandled the injured man up the tricky curves of the spiral stairs up to the ground floor. Once Fergus was in the van, McPhee told the other Ulstermen to go back inside and see to the tunnel.

Moments later, Ray noticed Tom turning into one of the garage's dank corners. He walked over and as he heard the older man's dry sobs, put his arm around him. Tom looked around, his eyes watery and bloodshot: 'I just couldn't bear to lose another one, Ray, I just couldn't bear it.'

At 4 a.m., Zeke appeared. He informed them that the sudden thaw had caused a water main to fracture and that the authorities had switched off the mains supply. It was time to get back to work. Zeke walked over to the equipment rack and examined the notebook. 'Hey! Some gomer took those breathing sets without signing for them. And where's this chisel you logged going down, Ray?'

Without saying a word, Tom walked over to the big American and, in the manner of a John Wayne bar fight, dropped him with one awesome right hook.

'I'm sorry I had to do that,' Tom said, 'but you had it coming to you. The matter's closed as far as I'm concerned.'

'Too right, mate,' Skinner murmured.

By the time dawn came, the pump was already lowering the water level to the point where Martin could slosh along the tunnel and begin repairing the breach in its roof.

Shortly after daylight, a gang of workmen from *Général des Eaux* appeared in the Faubourg and began digging. Skinner arose from a couple of hours' sleep on the campbed and decided to go for a stroll. To his alarm, he saw that the workmen fixing the watermain had gone down seven or eight feet by lunchtime.

He scurried back to Hamsin, where MacPhee and Zeke were chewing absentmindedly on baguettes in the office.

'Those Frenchies are going down a long way to that fucking main.'

'It's OK, the water pipe is more than twenty feet above our heading,' said Zeke, who was now sporting a real shiner.

'You got another one of those sarnies?' Ray asked.

'Over there, cocker,' McPhee gestured at a littered table. 'There's a couple of cheese and one ham one left, I think.'

Skinner grabbed a sandwich and tore at it distractedly. He paced as he ate, meandering up and down the office. 'You don't think the Frenchies might have done this deliberately?'

'Bullshit!' Zeke said contemptuously.

'Yeah, yeah, thanks, Fat Boy!'

'Ray, for fuck's sake!' McPhee butted in: 'Cut it out, will you both?'

Skinner flopped down into an office chair and opened a can of coke.

'You mean a sort of disruptive action?' McPhee had been thinking about Ray's proposition: 'Trying to hinder us without letting us know they know?'

'Yeah, that's what I meant.'

'Bullshit!' Zeke repeated.

Skinner looked at him with contempt. 'I realise it's not likely – but I just thought it might be possible.'

'It can't be too likely, Ray old kid, but obviously the bods at HQ can factor it in – they'll have the full picture.'

'Bullshit!'

Skinner stood up and walked towards the door: 'I'm going downstairs, Mike – we're expecting a first shipment of computers this afternoon. While I'm down there, maybe you can improve this dopey cunt's vocabulary.'

Chapter Eighteen

It did not take long to get rid of the silt from the heading. Fergus had been declared free of major injury, although doctors were keeping him in hospital for forty-eight hours. They had accepted the building site explanation and the Ulsterman had duly been registered for treatment under his pseudonym.

Of course the flood set back the schedule and there was much grumbling among the Americans. Zeke was spending long hours at the digging face because the excavation had reached its most delicate stage. At the point where the interception tunnel met the French one, a small gallery had been dug to increase the space available for working. As Ted Lofting reached the head of the tunnel, he was able to straighten his complaining back and stand, gazing in awe at the wooden-wrapped shaft of concrete which encased *TONNANT* and several other cables. Inside the wooden planks, several inches of concrete and a plastic tube was a fibre optic line a couple of millimetres thick: the target of his operation. If it was severed in their rush to get the OREGANO pods in place, then the French government would know it and the whole effort and expense of developing the tapping device would be wasted. The work of removing this mass of packaging was to be done with chisels. A hacksaw would then be used to cut through the plastic

159

tubing carrying the cable and finally a scalpel wielded by Lofting himself to strip off the plastic around the glass fibre itself so that the OREGANO optics could spin around its surface. The CIA's French agent had provided them with a drawing of a section of the heading which showed the *TONNANT* wire had been run along the cable channel closest to the centre.

Lofting gazed on intently as John and Martin began bashing away. Zeke was also there, making it something of a crowd in an area about the volume of three phone boxes. Their bodies soon created a stifling, smelly heat. The wooden planks, which had originally held up the French constructors' tunnel just as theirs was now being supported by similar shoring, were rotten and came away almost immediately. The French heading had apparently been dug in the early 1950s and was intended only as protection against nearby conventional bombing or an atom bomb detonating half a kilometre away.

'Why didn't they put this thing deeper?' Lofting whispered into Zeke's chubby ear.

'They were worried about the metro,' Zeke answered without turning to face Lofting. 'They had a real deep trunk system planned in the sixties, kinda like the one you got in London, but I guess they must have run short of money.'

Martin was now bashing away at the concrete, and to his relief found it was rather brittle, flying apart in great lumps. Lofting knew there were many other things he ought to be doing but he stood mesmerised as they worked nearer and nearer to the target of his operation.

Within fifteen minutes the black bakelite casing of one of the cable-ways was partially exposed. Martin had donned plastic goggles and was battering away with zeal. Then there was an awesome crunch as his chisel glanced off a particularly unyielding horn of concrete and smashed into the side of a cable casing.

'Goddamn it!' Zeke cursed under his breath.

'Out of the way!' said Lofting, trying to push past the American's bulk. He extracted a small maglite from his overall pockets and peered into the broken cable pipe. As he leaned over it, sweat dripped off the end of his nose. Gingerly, he picked some flakes of bakelite out of the hole, knowing that if the cable inside had been damaged the entire operation could be scuppered. 'Remind me which cable this is, Zeke.'

'It's believed to be part of the Paris civil defence organisation.'

'It could be worse, I suppose,' Lofting said, imagining that a Cold War organisation like that would rarely test its communications these days. Eventually, peering through a break about two inches across in the plastic, the light of his torch picked out the cable, a thick, shielded thing almost an inch in diameter. 'It looks all right,' he announced.

'Thank fuck!' Martin's voice was louder than the required whisper.

'Indeed,' Lofting replied deadpan. 'Try to be careful. We don't want to end up in jail.'

Martin had flushed with the heat and embarrassment, and simply nodded.

Skinner was upstairs: he was giving Zeke a wide berth and there was plenty of work to do installing the ten PCs which would be hooked up to the interception software on the first floor. A pair of fibre optic lines had already been run through the floor to the showroom level, down the spiral staircase to the garage and along the heading to a point close to the digging. These would carry the intercepted traffic from the OREGANO pods to the analysts in the office. The central processing unit and big computer which went with it had not yet arrived from Fort Meade, where it was being loaded with the NSA's software.

'Is there anything you need, Ray?' Lofting asked as he watched Skinner trying to make sense of the plugs going into the back of one of the computers.

'I'll be happier when that bloody Yank is out of here!'

'He's not the most charming of men, I agree, Ray, but please tread softly – we can't afford to have any aggro with our cousins on this operation.'

'I'm not worried, boss: as soon as the pods go on he'll be out of the way for a week or two until we start filling in the tunnel.'

'Yes, that's true. Shall I lend a hand there?' Lofting went to work pulling the desktops out of their packing and getting them fired up.

'Have you seen the water board people?' Ray asked.

'Yes, Mike mentioned your concerns to me. They're a pain because the flood slowed us down and nearly did for Fergus, but I'm not unduly worried.'

'Right,' said Skinner, admiring Lofting's cool.

'You could argue that it works to our advantage – if people do hear something underground despite our best efforts, they may well think it's to do with the main being repaired.'

That evening, Margaret Reynolds arrived at the Hamsin flat at La Défense. She had come via Brussels on her fake Spanish passport lugging two large holdalls with everything she would need for a stay of up to six weeks in Paris. She had been cheerful on her journey because she had been able to forget about the nightmare of her last encounter in Bristol, instead passing the time reading her new Jane Atkinson novel and wondering about the challenges of the coming operation.

The flats were in a thirty-storey block overlooking the Seine. She had memorised the address and the digital code for the front-door lock before leaving Cheltenham. Reynolds rode the lift to the twenty-seventh floor. There were seven apartments on this level, all of which had been taken by Hamsin. They could each sleep from two to six people. Margaret rang the bell for flat 273.

A middle-aged woman with greying hair scraped back into a bun and beautiful hazel brown eyes answered the door.

'Hello,' Margaret smiled in embarrassment – she had not been briefed on whether there was some secret procedure for introducing herself to her flatmate – 'I'm Margaret.'

'Hi,' the American replied, 'Colette.' There seemed to be a trace of French in her accent. 'Let me give you a hand.' The two women heaved the bags into the warmth of the apartment.

Margaret glanced around – it had been furnished in a modern, corporate style. There were expensive-looking leather sofas, a thick glass coffee table and various fancy lamps. 'It's nicer than I expected,' Margaret said, instantly thinking she sounded like someone who hadn't been abroad before.

'Yep, it's comfortable, the kitchen's through there. The groceries get delivered so we don't even have to buy them. So far there's nothing to do except read and watch TV.'

'Are you a linguist?' Margaret asked.

'Yes I am – and you?'

'Yes, me too.' Margaret nodded and looked down '. . . Well, I'm running the British analytical and translation group actually.'

'Oh . . .' Colette seemed to stiffen a little as she realised Margaret was management.

'I'm Max's opposite number . . .' Margaret went into her bedroom. 'I'd better get unpacked, then maybe we could get some dinner.'

'Sure . . . I'm not sure whether we're allowed just to go out,' Colette seemed to defer to Margaret.

'I hadn't thought of that . . . I'll ask Ted. Perhaps we should cook in tonight – I'm tired anyway.'

Margaret was pleased to find a double bed and a cupboard well stocked with hangers. She had been ordered not to bring anything with her real name or address on it. There were a plethora of other rules too – no mobile phones, no fraternisation with the French, telling a colleague where you were going at all times. Her usually bulging purse was slack because of the absence of its stuffing. Instead she had been provided with a single Banco de Bilbao credit card, a Spanish driving licence and various other bits of tat which the covert operations specialists described as 'pocket litter': a street plan of Brussels; Hamsin company literature and an address book full of her non-existent friends and family in Spain. She had brought a framed family photo which she set up on her bedside table next to her alarm clock. She had decided there was nothing in the picture which really identified it as a picnic in Oxfordshire in 1973.

Margaret and Colette chatted in the kitchen. The older woman had been with NSA for over twenty years. Her mother was French and had met her father when he

164

had worked at Nato when it was based at Fontainebleu in the fifties. Margaret was slightly surprised that the Americans had selected somebody with potentially divided loyalties for such a sensitive mission. The NSA linguist was the only one of the dozens of people on the operation who had been provided with a fake French identity. There was something about the Americans' trust of employees like Colette which Margaret found deeply impressive. Then she thought that the American attitude made good sense given that the consumers of intelligence who ran foreign policy were often Kissingers and Albrights born in other countries.

The two women cooked some spaghetti with a mushroom sauce and a mixed salad. Margaret was delighted to find a bottle of white wine in the fridge. She did not find Colette the most sparkling of company, but after a couple of glasses of Chardonnay she felt lucky enough to have her as a flatmate. Think of the alternatives: Ray Skinner for example. At about ten, Margaret made her excuses and retired to her room. She was just unbuttoning her silk shirt when she heard the doorbell. There was an indistinguishable murmur – male voices.

'Sure, she's here. I don't think she's gone to sleep yet,' she heard Colette say, before drumming on her door.

Margaret said 'Coming', fumbling to do up her shirt again.

Lofting and Ray Skinner were standing in the living room. 'Welcome!' said Ted. 'Pleasant journey?'

Skinner simply smiled.

'Uneventful, pleasant enough.'

They sat down on the leather sofas. 'I thought I'd bring you up to speed. You won't actually start work until the day after tomorrow. We're expecting the key bits of hardware tomorrow – and Dr—,' he pulled himself up: 'My American opposite number. We're a bit behind on the digging because there was a flood – there have been one or two other dramas.'

'Oh dear.'

'But nothing to really worry us. I don't think we'll have anything for you to work on until Monday, as I said. It might take longer if we don't get a good clean hold on the cable. You might wish to drop in at the office tomorrow p.m. but just to familiarise yourself with the layout of things. Ray has provided for you very well – but just tell him if there's anything you need. Please don't just go wandering around the city, we have to be a little bit careful – we just want to minimise the chances of somebody being involved in an accident or getting badly lost, whatever.'

'I see,' said Margaret, abandoning her dreams of balmy spring strolls in the Luxembourg gardens.

'Please let your flatmates know when you're leaving for work and someone at work when you're coming back here – it doesn't have to be too formal, but just make sure people know where you're going. Well, I don't know about you, but I'm bushed.' Lofting stood up and left, but Skinner remained in his seat.

'Have you got a drink? I'm gagging.'

'There's some white wine in the fridge if that's OK?'

'Sure.'

Margaret fetched Ray some wine while wondering why he was staying.

'I'm in the next-door flat, by the way, if you need anything.'

'I see.'

As Margaret bent down to put the glass of

Chardonnay on the table, Ray noticed the bite on her neck.

'You're a sight for sore eyes, I have to say.' Ray sipped the wine.

She ignored the compliment: 'Has it been tricky? The operation so far?'

'We've had our moments. It has its stresses, I don't mind telling you. The thought that the Gendarmes might batter the door down at any moment.'

'I was thinking on the train today,' Margaret began to relax a little, 'our best protection is the very cheek of this operation – I mean even if the locals thought they'd discovered something, they probably wouldn't believe we'd do such a thing.'

'Perhaps.' Skinner seemed uninterested in this line of conversation.

'Listen, Ray, I'm really rather tired.'

'Oh! I get the hint.'

'There'll be other opportunities for a chat,' she said, not meaning it.

'I hope so,' Ray perked up and repeated, 'I'm in the flat next door by the way if you're feeling lonesome or whatever.'

'Well, I'm sure we'll both be very busy,' Margaret tried to make her position crystal clear.

'Oh come on, don't be so uptight – we can have some fun on this operation.'

Margaret usually hated confrontation, but she just wasn't in the mood for Ray's hopeless advances. 'Let's just keep it professional, shall we, Ray?'

He stood up and began heading for the door. 'I wasn't trying to come on strong or anything – I just thought as you were single now . . .'

'I'm not ready for anyone new, Ray.'

'You're not seeing anyone then?'

'No, no!' Her answer carried the tone of 'perish the thought'.

'Well goodnight anyway. I'll probably see you tomorrow.' Having spotted the bite on her neck, he wondered why she was lying. As he banged the front door to flat 273, though, he was already feeling strangely optimistic – to his mind Margaret was clearly putting it about but didn't feel committed to anyone new yet.

That evening in Cheltenham, Sara Lofting took the family Rover and parked it by the football fields just behind GCHQ's Oakley site. After she had been sitting listening to Radio 3 for a few minutes she was roused from her daydreams by a rap on the window. She leaned across and unlocked the door.

'Hello, darling,' a portly middle-aged man climbed into the seat beside her.

Sara leaned across to kiss him; there was something boyish about his excitement at being with her.

Oscar Phillips did not work at GCHQ – he did not even live particularly close to the football fields, but it was a spot where lovers often parked their cars. It did not worry Sara particularly that she had come here, so close to GCHQ premises in a car which some employees at least might recognise as Ted's. In fact, in her heart of hearts she had always wanted Ted to find out about her affair, so it rather appealed to her.

'I've had a beastly week at work,' he began.

'Poor thing!'

They kissed on the lips and as they separated he smiled: 'I don't deserve you, darling.'

'I've told Ted I want a divorce.'

'Good.'

'Everything's going to be all right now, isn't it?' Sara asked plaintively.

'I'm sure it is, darling; I'm sure it is.' He leaned across and started a new bout of kissing. As it became more intense their hands began to wander. While Ted lay in bed in Paris staring at the ceiling, wondering about how the next phase of his operation would go, his wife struggled with the belt on Oscar Perreira's cords.

Chapter Nineteen

There was much debate about delivering the OREGANO pods to Hamsin's offices on a Sunday. The two cases carrying them would fit easily into the small van which regularly zoomed in and out of the firm's undergound garage, but there were concerns about reminding any possible onlookers that the firm seemed to work all hours on all days. In the end Ted Lofting had said they had to 'take a view' about the delivery over Birnbaum's reservations. As a compromise it was decided that the computer which would channel the intercepted signals into the office on the first floor would not arrive until Monday morning.

The two interception units had been packed into foam inside aluminium flight cases at Oakley. The boxes were about three feet long and eighteen inches square in cross-section. They had been taken by an MI6 man masquerading as a photographer who had flown first to Basle and then, switching from his fake British passport to a fake New Zealand one, had rented a car with Swiss plates and driven to the Bois de Boulogne in Paris, where early that Sunday morning they were transferred into Hamsin's van. Having said, 'I suppose some coffee and croissants might be in order,' MI6's bagman had driven into the grey gloom of that January morning, leaving GCHQ's multi-million pound investment in Skinner and

McPhee's hands. Before heading for the office, they had picked up a third box – one made of cardboard and bound at the corners with black masking tape.

In the upstairs room of the POLYP HQ, Margaret sat beside Max Kampfner poring over printouts which had been brought from Cheltenham. All around them people moved about, plugging in equipment, moving furniture and generally looking purposeful. It was about the worst environment imaginable in which to hold a meeting but the technical bods could guarantee that it was clean, free from bugs. They could not be completely sure in the case of the flats they lived in and everywhere else they went in Paris. The pressure of time had been such that Margaret and Max had been unable to finish the I Plan, or Interception Plan, before leaving Britain. As they struggled to do so amid the crashing and banging of their office coming into being around them Kampfner insisted on talking in a whisper. His years at NSA had left him with the conviction that nowhere was safe from eavesdropping and after all, they were discussing the most sensitive of secrets.

Margaret had made an important discovery before leaving the UK. France was pursuing the Saudi arms contract with the same awesome vigour as Britain and she had found out from the defence sales types that the key person in their sales drive was working out of the *Elysée* itself. She had discovered his name, Bernard Bourrat, and that he had made a packet in the electronics industry before being invited into the presidential palace to act as a special adviser. Bourrat was rumoured to have his fingers in all sorts of other pies too and had therefore become GCHQ's prime target. It was taken as read, of course, that both the UK and US teams would be relaying the conversations of the top ministers back to their respective masters, but it was in the subsidiary work, which the shortage of analysts forced them to divide, where she and Max each hoped to gain the advantage. Margaret was confident because she had discovered Bourrat's private extension number.

Kampfner looked around furtively and whispered something which sounded like, 'If we done the fence let move on the spray.'

'I'm sorry, Max, what did you say?' She leant forward so that her ear was only inches from his mouth.

'I said, if we've done defence shall we move on to the *Elysée*?'

'Yes, of course.' They flicked their printouts to a long list of names and numbers.

Kampfner began going through them. 'Montmorency yours, Vital yours, Saint Pierre – the one in Francophone relations, ours—'

'Did you say Saint Pierre?'

Max nodded and Margaret drew a line through that listing on her printout. Nobody from GCHQ was going to argue with the Americans listening in to that adviser – he dealt mainly with French-speaking African countries and the Brits were happy to watch Washington and Paris fight it out for influence in central Africa.

'These unallocated numbers . . .' Margaret felt intensely self-conscious as she moved towards the moment of deception.

'Yep, extensions 7001 to 7100.' Kampfner scrolled through his huge printout.

'Since we've no idea what they'll yield,' she lied, knowing Bourrat's line was 7046, 'shall we just take 7001 to 7050? And we'll just exploit whatever we find? You take 7051 to 7100?' There was a great crash and a cry of 'Fuck it!' from downstairs. Ray Skinner had dropped something.

'Sure, whatever.' Max looked around nervously.

'OK, 7001 to 7050 ours, 7051 to 7100 yours,' she scribbled away and felt thrilled with her deception.

They carried on for about another twenty minutes and then suddenly Kampfner asked her, 'You get the hens for Bourrat?'

'Sorry, Max, I didn't hear you . . .'

Since this was about the twentieth time she had asked him to repeat himself, Kampfner lost his temper, 'I said, have you got an extension for Bourrat?'

'Oh! Bernard Bourrat, the special adviser?'

'Yes!'

'No, have you?' Margaret felt sure she blushed as she said this brazen lie.

'No, we got squat on him.'

She wanted to ask if she'd heard him right, but thought better of it as they moved on to the foreign ministry numbers.

When McPhee's van came down by lift into the under-gound garage, Lofting was waiting for it. Two other people were standing by him: Megan Trelawney and one of her boffins called Roger.

'Top of the morning to you,' McPhee said in an exaggerated Irish accent. He felt it was safe to make such jokes, as the Ulstermen had been sent back to their villages in Fermanagh for the most sensitive phase of the operation.

'Let's get on shall we, Mike?'

Megan and Ray went to the rear doors of the van and lifted out the first flight case. Lofting and McPhee manhandled the second.

'I'll take care of the other box,' Skinner said before Roger could get a hand to it.

'OK, let's get the first pod up to the front of the tunnel,' said Lofting, his voice dry with nerves.

At two places the plastic case carrying the *TONNANT* cable had been cut for a length of about two feet. In each section, the top of the duct had been sliced off with hacksaws leaving the bottom supporting the fibre optic cable a little like a section of guttering. Around each of these openings, a specially designed airtight plastic covering had been fitted. These had been designed with two fitted gloves to allow technicians to work and a zippered opening through which tools and the pods themselves could be passed. Roger and Megan has used blowers during the early hours of Sunday morning to get the area enclosed by these bags as close to dust-free as possible. A small air hose had then been run into each of the bags and a pump switched on so they had puffed out like the hood of a hairdryer. The aim was to create a slight over-pressure inside each so that no dirt would enter when the zips on the sides were opened. The gallery where the French cable had been intercepted had taken on the appearance of an underground intensive care ward, complete with tubes, power cables, humming generators and the strange incubators where Lofting and Trelawney would place their fragile invention.

An NSA technician called Miguel completed the crowd in the gallery at the front of the heading. All of those present had changed into disposable white paper coveralls. These had become smudged with dirt during the crouched approach down the heading. The American was there as a courtesy, as he had no idea how to install the devices himself. The Director had felt Cheltenham had to show willing given that the NSA now considered itself the joint owner of the OREGANO secret.

Lofting stood with his hands in the plastic gloves of one of the cable coverings. 'Miguel, you may wish to observe over my shoulder.' The American pushed between Megan and Roger.

'I'm going to remove the plastic sheath which covers the fibre optic.' Lofting had a scalpel in his hand. 'If I cut too deep, I could score the glass itself and that could cause us all sorts of problems.' With the same steady hand that had rigged his collection of warships, Lofting cut into the thin plastic and peeling it back with tweezers, revealed the *TONNANT* fibre itself underneath.

'Well done, Ted!' Megan Trelawney said when he had bared the required length of fibre. She and Roger then unbuckled the first aluminium flight case and revealed the black pod sitting in its foam cradle. They lifted it gingerly to the opening in the over-pressure bag and passed it through into Ted's gloved hands. Once he held it, he opened it like a large seashell and, balancing it on the palm of one hand, used the other to remove the plastic film covering the optical devices at its heart. He then rested the device on the cable ducting and closed small clamps held by screws onto the fibre optic to keep it firmly in place. Lofting folded the other half of the pod down and began the process of making the two sections which now sandwiched the fibre optic cable completely dust and water tight.

Back on the first floor, McPhee, Birnbaum and various others were sitting around pretending to be busy and relaxed. Margaret and Max's meeting had ended.

George, the silver-tongued Lebanese salesman, was padding up and down in the showroom, admiring the Aston Martin which had taken its place in the window a couple of days earlier. Since the Ferrari sale, he had added to his reputation by selling two of the tarted-up Mercedes. Skinner repeatedly teased George about his success creating extra work in acquiring more cars, and in fact he really resented it.

George noticed a young man in a dishevelled suit entering through the glass doors. He carried a huge briefcase, of the type used by commerical travellers to carry their bumf as well as their overnight kit.

'*Oui, monsieur?*' George asked with the disdain obligatory when addressing somebody who clearly could not afford an Aston Martin Vantage.

'I represent Alpha Com – we're opening a new printing centre soon and I'd like to familiarise you with our range,' the nervous salesman replied.

'One moment,' said George before ringing up to the office.

Colette, the NSA linguist, came down and introduced herself as the office manager. Birnbaum had told her not to bring the salesman up to the first floor. Instead she sat him at the smart table in the showroom used to close deals with clients. It had been placed just in front of the mirrored wall, behind which was the kitchenette and spiral staircase down into the garage.

He presented his business card: Pierre Moutet. His hair was curiously thin for a young man, scraped across his bulbous forehead. Moutet had the complexion of glue. Colette was in a flap at being sent down – it was her first day on the job. Birnbaum thought it was better for the salesman to talk to a native French speaker, but in truth she knew little about the cover business's activities. George meanwhile had popped upstairs to relieve himself.

'If I may talk you through our range.' He hoisted what appeared to be a laptop from his cavernous briefcase and popped open its top – where an Alpha Com logo popped up on the screen.

'I'm afraid, *Monsieur Moutet*, that we have an established relationsionship with a printer.'

Moutet ignored her and took a Hamsin brochure from the desk. 'How much per unit did they charge you for this?'

Of course Colette had no idea.

'I'd be surprised if it was less than five francs per unit on an order of ten thousand plus – we can do it for four-twenty.'

'Really, I am sorry,' she countered, 'but between us, our printing is handled by a firm owned by a friend of our managing director.'

The salesman seemed to sense defeat at last. 'I see, well perhaps I can add you to our list – we'll fax you details of our new promotions, you may find we can help you for some rush work.'

'Yes, why not,' she answered.

'Do you have a card?'

Colette kicked herself. She had left them upstairs in her handbag. 'One moment, I'll go and get one, excuse me.'

When she came back down, Moutet seemed to have left. Then her eye caught his case beside the table and then she saw him peering behind the partition and the back of the showroom, down towards the staircase.

'*Monsieur,*' she said, walking briskly towards him with the card in her hand.

'It's a really nicely designed place – who did you use?'

'If you'll excuse me, I have to finish the accounts for this month.' It was the first thing Colette could think of.

She wondered whether she should say anything when she got upstairs, but at length decided she had to.

'What?' Birnbaum had asked incredulously when she reported Mr Moutet had been peering behind the wall.

'How long do you think he might have been looking?' McPhee was trying to sound unfazed and failing. 'Do you think he might have actually looked down the stairs?'

'Impossible . . . it was just seconds . . .'

Birnbaum eyed the business card. 'OK, we'll do a full check on this company and this guy – let's E-mail Meade now.'

By late that afternoon, Megan Trelawney had fitted the second OREGANO device, the back-up one. After that, they had connected power to both. Since the computer required to handle the intercepted traffic was not due to arrive until the following day, the boffins rigged up a small test device, a sort of oscilloscope, at the other end of the relay cables in the first-floor offices.

Lofting, Trelawney, Skinner, Birnbaum, Colette, McPhee, Zeke and a couple of others were all crammed into the office as Roger prepared to switch on the two devices.

'I'll just check the power stability,' he muttered as the tense crowd looked on. While Roger tweaked and mumbled, Skinner disappeared for a moment, returning with the bound cardboard box which had been offloaded from the van with the interception devices.

And then he was satisfied – Roger turned and looked up at Lofting. 'Would you care to press the switch?'

Ted's excitement was enormous, but he also thought of the diplomatic factors and looked nervously at Birnbaum. 'Well, I don't know . . .'

'You do it, Ted,' Birnbaum said briskly and then began biting his fingers with the tension of it all.

Lofting leaned over, extended his finger towards the switch marked 'Power' and pressed it. Streams of digits began racing across the small green screen so fast as to be indistinguishable.

Skinner drew a bottle of champagne from the box he had carried in and popped the cork.

'It works,' said Lofting so quietly as to be almost inaudible.

'Of course it works,' said Trelawney, smiling as a single tear rolled down her face.

Lofting found a plastic cup of champagne thrust into his hand.

'To us!' Birnbaum proposed.

'To us!' they all replied, and although the liquid was not a cold as it should have been, Lofting thought it was the best drink of his life.

Chapter Twenty

With the arrival of Birnbaum's computer from the States, the operation had gone 'live'. By Wednesday the signal-processing technicians from NSA had set up their computer – an awesomely powerful machine called a Sun UltraSparc E10000. It could act as a server for the desktops, farming out data messages on screen and sound through headphones which had been attached to each workstation.

Birnbaum had called his computer Wasp, for reasons known only to him. As soon as it had been hefted up to the first floor of Hamsin it had been loaded with many gigabytes of software. The bulk of this dealt with signal processing and driving the workstations. A small number of these millions of lines of code consisted of facts which formed a sort of database of what might pass through the *TONNANT* cable. GCHQ and NSA research had already provided thousands of French governmental phone numbers and names of the *fonctionnaires* who might use them. Max and Margaret had finished the I Plan detailing who would do what. Each of the analysts who would be listening to a conversation could add to this knowledge. They could enter S\I or Station Identity records, as they figured out who each new number they heard belonged to. There were also T\I or Traffic Interception reports in which they were required to assess the quality of conversation which a particular line or individual might have on a scale of A for most interesting to F, not at all interesting. There was also K\E for Keyword Entry, which allowed them to update Wasp's ability to sort conversations of interest from the use of particular words or phrases, a relatively straightfoward task as all of the information came down the line in digital form. It was simply a question of how fast the NSA boffins' machine could sort digits, and of course it could do so at a mind-numbing speed.

Wasp was designed to 'learn' from all the data entries so that, in time, it would automatically route the conversations most likely to be of interest towards analysts or recording machines. Birnbaum boasted that, as the database expanded, it would calculate even for when a particularly well-placed or indiscreet official might be on holiday. He and Lofting had allowed the best part of a month for this process before the analysts would be withdrawn, the signals relayed elsewhere and Hamsin wound up. Even when the whole operation was being worked remotely, Wasp would still be learning from every entry.

During the first day of listening, Max Kampfner managed to raise some excitement when he flung his gangly arms above his head and shouted '*magnifique*'. In truth, all he had done was listen to a fairly mundane conversation between the Defence Minister, riding in his official Citroen, and a member of his private office. Kampfner's excitement arose from the fact that the Minister's carphone number was not already in the database and from a delight with the beauty of a system which allowed him to hear a conversation in which a heavily encoded signal had been decrypted as it entered the *TONNANT* system at some point upstream of their tapping pods.

Margaret so hated fuss and show that she had simply smiled a little patronisingly at her American opposite number and gone back to work. In truth, though, she also felt a childish excitement. Everything she had ever done at Cheltenham had involved listening to material which had already been through a number of technical and human filters. This was completely raw – there was no telling what she might find when she pressed the 'enter' on her keyboard over one of the conversations the computer offered up in a great rippling menu. She watched a line move up to the top of her screen which the computer had marked as a Ministry of Defence number and pressed 'enter'.

'It's straightforward enough, *Mon Colonel*: we won't meet the target date for the evaluation because we haven't been allowed enough time,' an angry male voice barked down the line. 'Tell the general he can have his *Pac deux mille* when he gives us a few more AMX's and a longer trial.'

Margaret was slightly puzzled. She turned in her seat and tapped Colette on the shoulder. American and British analysts sat in back-to-back rows. 'Colette?'

'Yes,' she removed her headphones.

'An AMX is a tank, right?'

'Yes, or sometimes some other kind of *véhicule blindée*.'

'So do you know what "*Pac deux mille*" is? I think it's some sort of new system?'

Kampfner had obviously been listening to his colleagues and he turned and said brusquely, 'It's probably *projectil anti-char* two thousand – their new anti-tank shell.'

'Thank you,' said Margaret, simultaneously struck by

Max's knowledge and lack of manners. She had noticed Ray Skinner appearing at the end of the cramped office and giving her a warm smile. Without being aware of it she adjusted the silk scarf she had put on that morning to make sure it covered the bruise, traces of which remained on her neck. After a few moments and to her relief, Skinner disappeared again.

After listening for a while she decided to give the conversation a T\I of 'C' – occasionally of interest. Part of her felt this was a real British middle-of-the-road cop out, but one thing she and Kampfner were absolutely agreed upon was that there was no point putting too many numbers into the top two categories simply because they contained something relevant to defence or foreign affairs.

Margaret selected another conversation and pressed 'enter'.

'Well he's not due to have the operation until April and mother's terribly worried . . .' A woman, clearly closely involved in the trials of her elderly parents, was talking to her brother – equally distant – and barely interested. 'She and I should get together and have a moan.'

After fifteen minutes of listening she had gleaned nothing which gave away either the identity of the speaker or who she worked for. With some reluctance she abandoned the call without categorising its value for the Wasp database. Margaret made another selection.

'I'm going to London at the end of the week – more liaison with the Roast-beefs about their naughty Irish,' the tone was a sort of laconic post-four-glasses-of-Bordeaux with lunch. The number did not match up with anything in the database.

'Last time we did it *Chez nous—*'

'At the Rue Marengo?' the other man asked.

'No at the swimming pool.'

Something clicked in Margaret's mind: swimming pool – *La Piscine* – it was longstanding slang for the headquarters of DGSE, France's overseas espionage service. So the caller worked for DGSE but not at the main HQ building, somewhere in the Rue Marengo. This turned out to be the best call of the day for Margaret. Subsequent inquiries at MI5 established the name of the French officer going over to London and what exactly went on at his office. It became an A-category line for interception: after all, if Paris wasn't playing a straight bat on counterterrorism, MI5 would be more than grateful to know about it.

Under the GCHQ/NSA I Plan, numbers were allocated according to the specialist skills of the different translators and the discreet Chinese walls that the two partners were trying to insert between themselves. It had been agreed, for example, that Margaret herself would listen to the African hands at the Foreign Ministry, whereas one of Max's people, a Spanish speaker, would do all of the calls related to Central and South America. In the case of the French secret policeman she had just been listening to, the plan would be modified in the light of the new information and the line added to those over which the Brits took the primary role.

Margaret looked down at her watch. It was eight o'clock in the evening and there were only three listeners left. She got up and fetched her coat. Dan Birnbaum was hunched over his machine in the corner – he hadn't left the Hamsin office in seventy-two hours. He looked up: 'Knocking off, Margaret?'

'Yes, if that's all right?' For some absurd reason

she felt guilty about her fifteen-hour day.

'No problem! You're going straight back to the apartment?'

'Yes, of course.' She resented his tone. She was older than him and only one grade below on this operation. What would be so wrong if she did some window-shopping on the way back to the flat? She buried her injured feelings, smiled and left him to his calculations.

It wasn't long before Lofting appeared from downstairs with two cups of coffee he'd made. 'I thought you might need some fuel!' he said to Birnbaum.

'Um? Sure,' the young American said a little absent-mindedly as his fingers clicked away on the keys. Then he seemed to come out of his trance and turned away from the monitor, towards Lofting's rumpled presence: 'Thanks, Ted, appreciate it – I was miles away then.'

'No problem.' Ted smiled benignly and began turning to go.

'Hang on, Ted! I need a break – if you want to talk, that is.'

Lofting smiled his agreement and the two men headed down to the back of the showroom.

Birnbaum sipped from his Styrofoam cup. 'It's amazing to see it all working.'

'Yes, it's been quite an experience.' Lofting had the dewy eyes of a new father emerging from a hard night in the labour room.

'I'll be back in Cheltenham this weekend, Ted – I've done that spreadsheet for you.'

'What? The naval gunfire thing? How kind of you, Dan – I'm really surprised you've found time. Will you come over for lunch on Sunday?'

'Sure, we'll try it out.'

A look of disquiet seemed to cross the young American's face. 'Call me dumb, but . . .'

'But what?'

'Well, I know it hasn't exactly been easy, but . . .' Birnbaum lifted his eyes to meet Lofting's: 'it just seems to have been a bit too easy.'

'Are you worried about the visit from that salesman?' Lofting tried to cut to the root of the American's anxiety.

'Sure. That was weird, don't you think?'

'I'm not sure. I wonder about the actual tunnelling bit sometimes – you know, why the French didn't bury something so valuable a little deeper. But I simply can't believe that we're the victims of some sort of sting.'

'I know, I know – if we were being suckered, why send in a salesman to arouse our suspicions?'

'Precisely! And the water main breaking – that couldn't be some sort of disruptive action on their part – I mean if the French wanted to make fools of us why not cut to the chase and let the fun begin? No messing about delaying us.'

'I'll say something else,' Birnbaum was now enthusiastic about knocking down his own anxiety: 'To fake the volume of traffic coming through that line would be such an enormous task in itself.'

'Well, of course the bulk of the traffic would be real in a deception operation – I'm sure it would if you or I were running it.' At this point Lofting's eyes met Birnbaum's once more, and as the smiles faltered the germ of uncertainty had found new life.

By the time Margaret was back at the flat, Colette had already finished her dinner and was sitting on one of the sumptuous leather sofas watching the news. Some shaky footage showed the aftermath of a bomb in Algiers which had killed thirteen people that morning.

'It's funny we see nothing of this ghastly war at all in Britain,' Margaret said as she poured herself a glass of wine from the fridge and sat beside her flatmate: 'Perhaps it's too dangerous even for Kate Adie.'

'Kate who?'

'Sorry, Colette, she's a British national institution – a fearless lady reporter.'

The story changed – an item showed a Saudi prince being received at the Elysée. He meandered along in front of the Republican Guard looking vaguely amused. Then they came to a 'bite' of an interview.

'Of course our relationship with the Kingdom has never been better,' the electronic type strapped the words 'Bernard Bourrat, Special Adviser' across a civil servant's Cerutti-suited, Hermès-tied chest, 'and we've every reason to hope for expanded trade ties.' Margaret felt suddenly excited and guilty, seeing her quarry on screen but knowing she couldn't reveal too much knowledge about him.

'He's very suave, don't you think?' Colette asked.

'He's all right.' In fact she thought him very dishy.

'A bit like Jean Paul Belmondo, don't you think?'

The man in question had already disappeared from the screen, so Margaret couldn't compare him to the actor. Then, for a moment, he could be glimpsed ushering the prince through a door as the reporter came to her breathless conclusion. He was tall and slim, which of course Margaret liked, but he was just a bit too smooth, too French, so she said, 'I expect he cheats on his wife.'

'Every man does, my dear.'

'Not in the house I grew up in,' said Margaret, instantly regretting her superior tone.

'No, I expect not.'

The two spoke little after that, retiring to their own rooms to suffer the fitful sleep of the overworked.

The following day brought the first real intelligence nugget of the operation. One of Margaret's linguists had been listening to the home telephone of a top foreign ministry official and had quickly put the recording machine which was part of each workstation into action. Seeing the excitement, Margaret had switched her own headset to monitoring the conversation. It related to a European Union foreign ministers' meeting due to take place in four days' time.

'I think we can count on German, Spanish and Italian support in blocking the British proposal on border controls – plus a few of the smaller members,' the oily voice of the number two in the ministry opined.

When Margaret and one of her political analysts had listened to the conversation again, they typed up a small report of its contents which was duly passed, via Birnbaum's E-mail system, to Meade and Cheltenham.

Ted Lofting was due to return to London later that day. He nursed the hope that he might be able to brief Terence Jennings, the urbane Foreign Office man who had been so sceptical about the operation in person. Surely this would prove OREGANO's potential beyond doubt?

Chapter Twenty-One

Lofting had received a terse message from his Director to meet him in London rather than proceeding to Cheltenham, so he got a cab from Waterloo to Palmer Street in Victoria where GCHQ had its main operation in the capital. By the time he arrived, most people had already gone home for the night and he had to rap on the door to get one of the Custody Service guards to answer it.

Ted felt so tired he could hardly trudge up the stairs to the first floor. The foreboding about going home to Sara which had been growing in him all day was beginning to overpower the work stuff which had dominated his waking thoughts since the previous weekend.

'Come in, grab a seat, Ted,' the Director said without warmth as Lofting went into one of the drab meeting rooms used by his boss when he was in the city. Lofting studied his boss. Glasses, greying hair, grey suit. He was the ultimate intelligence bureaucrat, the sort of person who you instinctively avoided if you saw them standing alone at a party because you suspected they would be so boring. In the Director's case of course, this wasn't entirely right. His grey exterior did conceal the intense ambition and ruthlessness which had carried him to the top of GCHQ.

'I've seen the foreign ministry intercept,' the Director announced joylessly.

'Yes, we're all very pleased, getting a result like that at such an early stage of the operation.'

'I'll be seeing Terence Jennings in about an hour,' the Director glanced at his watch, 'and I've suggested to him that I might brief the Foreign Secretary in person on this.'

'I see,' Lofting replied, trying not to betray any disappointment that rank was being pulled. In Nelson's time a captain bearing news of a famous victory to the King could expect rich rewards of cash and honour. He wondered what the Director was angling for? Ted reflected that he would not have the pleasure of delivering word of his personal Trafalgar. Then he checked himself: this was hardly a sigint Trafalgar. He had survived it for one thing.

'I must say I'll sleep a lot easier when we've got out of that blessed car showroom and moved on to Phase Two,' the Director interrupted his thoughts.

'You and me both, Malcolm.'

'Well, pass my congratulations on to your team – good effort.'

'They've been marvellous I must say,' said Lofting, without even noticing the absence of praise for his own role.

The Director glanced down at some papers in his lap in a rather self-conscious manner before changing tack. 'Ted, sorry to have to bring this up – but it's always better to nip a problem in the bud.'

'Yes?'

'Just that there's been a bit of negative feedback from our American cousins.'

'Really?' Lofting remembered his friendly conversation with Birnbaum over coffee the night before and was puzzled.

'One or two of the senior NSA people have been a bit critical of your handling of the operation.'

'Well that really suprises me, frankly. We've all been pulling together marvellously.'

'To be blunt, I'm afraid the General is not a great fan,' said the Director, allowing his reference to his opposite number at NSA to escape his lips without any apparent feeling. 'So Ted, please tread carefully with them.'

Suddenly, through his fatigue, Lofting was aware of the same anger that he had felt when his boss wanted to talk to him about his daughter's mishap. He didn't give voice to it though. Instead he thought of Trafalgar again and wondered whether some bureaucratic sniper was indeed about to cut him down at his moment of victory.

A little later the Director made his way over to the Foreign Office where Terence Jennings and the Secretary of State were both working late. He arrived to find Jennings in his dress shirt, with the two ends of a proper bow tie hanging from the open collar.

'Come in, Malcolm, we've got fifteen minutes before the Secretary of State and I have to go to this execrable banquet for the Bulgarian PM.'

'We've had something very significant from Operation POLYP, PUS and as it's the first take from our fantastic new invention I wanted the pleasure of delivering it personally.'

'Oh really?' said Jennings, expecting the usual GCHQ guff, the diplomatic significance of which was as low as the security classification was high.

The Director fiddled with the combination locks on

his briefcase. When he opened it, Jennings could see that, comically, it contained a wafer thin folder binding a single piece of paper. The GCHQ man donned his specs, checked the intercept boldly headed TOP SECRET POLYP in red ink and set it on Jennings's desk. Then, to underline the drama of the occasion, he said, 'The French are planning to ambush the Secretary of State in the Hague on Tuesday. They've got Germany, Spain and Italy lined up to block our proposal of border controls.'

It was apparent from the Permanent Under Secretary's face that he was barely aware of the Director's commentary as he read. 'Surprised to see the Spanish and Italians deserting us on this,' he murmured. 'We knew the Germans were going wobbly, but I must say I thought we had the others batting on our side . . . Most interesting!'

'I thought you'd want to know about it as soon as possible.' Remembering the mandarin's scepticism about the whole Paris operation, the Director intended to play his advantage to the full. 'As indeed would the Secretary of State if you think he could spare me a moment.'

Jennings felt horror at this idea – he didn't want the spooks running into the minister's private office every time they had something to say, and anyway he felt he needed a little more time to play his own cards. His face betrayed none of this, instead returning the Director a smile and the words, 'Wait one, I'll just pop over to his office and see if he's available.'

He walked through to the Secretary of State's outer office, where one stalwart secretary soldiered on and greeted him with, 'Good evening, Sir Terence.'

'Evening, Pat, is Secretary of State ready to leave within the next five?'

'Yes, I believe he is.'

'Could you get his car round?'

'It's already waiting downstairs.'

'Good, I'll pop back in a mo then.' Jennings returned to his own office. 'I'm terribly sorry, Malcolm, he's got to leave any moment but he sent his congratulations to all involved – it's just not going to be possible for you to see him though.'

'I see,' the Director knew defeat when he saw it.

'Anyway, this is impressive, I don't mind saying,' Jennings toyed with the folder. 'Well done!'

'I'll have that back, if you feel you've digested the contents, PUS.'

It was not the first time that Jennings had had a sensitive intelligence report snatched out of his hands the moment he had read it. He mumbled, 'Of course.'

As the Director replaced it in his briefcase he said, 'I suppose it goes without saying that you will remember the exceptional sensitivity of this—'

'Yes it does go without saying.'

'Excuse me, PUS – it's just that we have a good many people in Paris at the moment – please bear that in mind when working out how you'll respond to this information.'

'Point taken, Malcolm, point taken.' Jennings pulled the two tails of his tie into a smart bow with the practised ease of a lifelong diplomat. 'Well, if you'll excuse me, I'm most grateful to you for dropping in at this hour – it was well worth it,' he managed a smile.

By the time he was sitting beside the Foreign Secretary on their way to the Savoy, Jennings was ready to pass on the intelligence.

'I had a visit from the hush-hush boys this evening,'

he said, looking out of the bulletproof glass at the heavy traffic.

'Oh yes?' The minister's pale head did not rise as he studied his Bulgarian briefing book.

'It seems the French are planning to block your proposal at the Hague for delays in the border controls relaxation.'

'We thought they wouldn't like it.'

'Yes, well we have sensitive intelligence that it's more than that – they've already lobbied the Germans, Spanish and Italians and lined them all up against us.'

The Foreign Secretary's head snapped around: 'The bloody French! Their behaviour is just ludicrous sometimes!'

'What I suggest is that we circulate a draft resolution on lamb quotas – I've got Dominic drafting one right now – that will get the French panicking like mad because they know they're on a sticky wicket, and they know there's a lot of support for our position. We can then agree to drop the lamb resolution on Tuesday if they drop their opposition to our border controls resolution – a counter-ambush if you like.'

'Good – yes!' The Foreign Secretary appeared almost childishly grateful. 'Well done!'

'I can't guarantee it'll work, of course, but at least it means we won't go naked into that rather chilly Dutch conference chamber.'

'Bloody French!' The Foreign Secretary repeated to himself. Then he turned to Jennings again: 'Is this connected with that paper you slipped into my book a few weeks ago?'

'Paper?'

'Yes, you know, the one authorising a foreign intelligence operation. You put it in when you thought I'd be itching to get off for the weekend – in among a lot of rubbish.'

'Oh yes.' Jennings made something of a pantomime of regaining his memory. 'Pressure of time, Secretary of State, pressure of time . . .'

The Foreign Secretary smiled and nodded as he returned to the study of the Bulgarian Prime Minister's CV.

It was almost midnight when Ted turned the key in his front door. There were no lights on. He called out, 'Sara!' They hadn't spoken by phone all week and there was no answer now. He went into the kitchen and found himself a can of beer.

Emma had appeared in the doorway, dressed in clingy cotton pyjamas.

'Hello, darling.'

'Hi, Dad.'

'What about a kiss for the returning matelot?'

She walked across the cold lino in her bare feet and obliged. 'Have you been in France?'

Lofting was shocked but managed to say, 'Why on earth do you think that?'

'You just seem to use a lot of French words these days.'

He felt a pang of pride at her intuition.

'Mum's not here – don't ask me where she is.' Emma poured herself a glass of water from the tap. 'Are you getting divorced?'

'I don't know.' He felt suddenly weary. 'Only your mother knows.'

'Something's got to change, because she's just going to pieces.'

'I know, you're right. Shall we go and sit in the lounge,

you must be cold in here?' They flopped into the worn armchairs. 'Your mum is having a sort of mid-life crisis I think – I'd like us to stay together, if we can get life a bit more sorted out. I'm sorry, I think I'm just too tired to make much sense.'

'Yeah, well I'm going to bed,' she announced, signalling that the first proper family conversation Ted could recall for months was over.

'Sorry, I didn't mean to—'

'It's all right, Dad, don't worry about it. I'm really tired too. Anyway, I hope you . . . sort things out.'

'So do I, darling, so do I.'

When Ted went upstairs he saw there was no sign of Sara clearing out her things. She would be back later that evening presumably.

Ted and Sara said little to one another the following day. She had been too hungover to make much sense during the morning and he had dashed off to the supermarket in the afternoon to replenish the empty shelves in their kitchen. He presumed poor Emma had been scavenging for herself the previous week among the tins of tuna and beans which were all that seemed to remain.

Lofting was not a great cook. His talents did not run beyond doing the Sunday roast; he had grown up before that generation of men transported to the kitchen for a lifetime of penal servitude because of the sins of their fathers. Since Dan Birnbaum was coming over for lunch and he knew there was little chance of Sara making an effort, he was sure it was down to him.

Given that she had moaned despairingly, 'Don't you see enough of these dreary people at work?' Ted was pleasantly surprised that Sara put a brave face on for the occasion. After a slightly strained conversation in which they had managed to make only sporadic small-talk, Dan and Ted retired to the study, where a card table spread with a sea blue cloth, two model frigates and a computer awaited.

'I thought we might try out your programme in a small engagement?' said Ted.

'Sure.' Dan somehow suppressed the last pangs of his embarrassment. He had been reading a book about nineteenth-century naval battles and now considered himself better informed. 'Why don't we do USS *Wasp* against a comparable British frigate?'

Lofting smiled back his surprise: 'Yes, excellent. I'll take HMS *Frolic* and, to even things up a bit, given I'm the more experienced captain, I'll put you on the windward side.'

The game began. Birnbaum's natural aggression soon revealed itself, as the *Wasp* came bearing down on *Frolic*. Lofting turned the stern of his vessel to the bow of Birnbaum's and then began a series of tacks or turns which allowed him to fire one broadside and then the other. Since he was turning onto the front of Dan's ship, the American was unable to return fire before Lofting tacked back the other way each time.

As soon as Lofting had tapped the variables into the computer for each broadside, the results appeared from Birnbaum's spreadsheet. 'This is really excellent, I must say, Dan – by the way, you've lost three men, and one cannon from my last broadside.'

Birnbaum screwed his face up in in concentration: 'OK, you're turning back and forward, keeping yourself in the best aspect to the wind and at the same time, kicking hell out of me. If I turn and stay on a new course so I can hit you back next time you turn, I'm running the risk that you'll stay on your current course, and soon you'll be out of range and you'll get away . . .'

Lofting smiled back at him: 'You could always do something to slow me down . . .'

'You mean fire at your rigging?'

'Um hmm.'

'I've loaded roundshot though, not barshot. It'll take me a long time to reload my guns.'

'Look, you're new to this, let's just say you've got barshot loaded in your guns.'

'I don't know.' Birnbaum hated the idea of being given a handicap.

'All right, fire the roundshot at my rigging – it could still do quite a bit of damage – and then reload barshot.'

The game progressed with *Wasp* landing some heavy punches on the British ship – though Lofting kept up the broadsides so both vessels were taking damage.

As the action slowly progressed on the tabletop, Lofting remembered the Director's words on Friday night about problems with NSA. Ted was not naturally one of life's worriers, but he was unable to get it out of his mind. 'Dan, old chap?'

The American was measuring the movement of *Wasp* with a small ruler. 'Um hmm.'

'If there was a problem between us, on the project, I'd like to think you'd broach it with me.'

Dan looked up, concerned: 'What do you mean?'

'I had a word with the Director on Friday night – says your people are – how should I put it? – not entirely . . . happy with my handling of things.'

'Well, beats me,' Birnbaum looked deep in thought. 'You know the General wasn't exactly thrilled with the presentation back at the Fort.'

'Yes, but there hasn't been anything since then has there?'

'I don't recall hearing anything bad at Meade.'

Lofting tapped some more figures into the computer. 'You would tell me if you personally had a problem, wouldn't you?'

'Sure – I mean get outa here! There's no problem from my side – I mean it's been a great experience so far.'

'You've got twenty-four casualties, by the way.'

'Twenty-four?' There was a hint of incredulity.

'Yes, sorry, I've just turned across your bow and raked you with grape I'm afraid.' Lofting's *Frolic* had just cut down half the *Wasp*'s crew.

'I'm afraid you've got to take a morale test.'

'Morale test?'

'Yes, to see if your chaps fight on.'

'Of course they'll fight on!' Birnbaum replied with almost childish outrage.

'That often wasn't up to the captain . . .' Lofting begun to consult the tables before finally handing the American a dice. 'You really want to throw four or over.'

Birnbaum threw the dice down. A single spot blinked up at them.

'I'm afraid *Wasp* strikes its colours.'

'Surrenders?'

'Yes. Not everybody wants to fight to the death for their captain you know! Still you fought very well – an honourable battle.'

'Better than being shot in the back by my own admiral, I suppose.' Birnbaum eyes met his host's.

Lofting returned the glance for a moment and then looked out through the window: 'Indeed my friend, indeed.'

Chapter Twenty-Two

On Monday, Margaret Reynolds checked that Bernard Bourrat's phone numbers would be routed to her by the Wasp database. If he made a call, a window would open on her screen and allow her the option of discarding or recording the one she was already listening to. She had told Lofting that his extension was part of the GCHQ workload and he had congratulated her. Matters on the Saudi contract were hotting up. London was pleading for information since it had discovered that a Saudi royal was in Paris as the guest of the French. With the prince remaining in Paris for several days, Margaret knew that Bourrat would be discussing the order for new fighter planes with others in government. Margaret took to this new mission with relish since it marked a change from sampling the enormous traffic which ran down that thin fibre optic to hunting aggressively for useful intelligence. The defence export people had told her that ten thousand British jobs depended on the order. If she could tap into the right conversation, the secrets of the French bid would be theirs, and Britain could secure the work.

She had fixed herself a coffee, sat at her PC and logged herself in. She ran a hand through her fair mane before putting on her headset. A series of possible calls raced up her screen. To her satisfaction she saw that about one-third of them already had a letter from A to F reflecting an analyst's assessment of the traffic. She chose one from a number known to be on the French Foreign Ministry European relations side. Following the previous week's tip on the Hague negotiations, London had asked for anything more they could supply.

'We're not going to discuss green issues in Ankara,' said a tired Parisian voice.

'But I thought we were free to table any business we wanted?' The other party was apparently an Italian speaking French.

Margaret was adjusting to the fact that the call would probably yield nothing when a window opened in the top of her screen:

TARGET E/7 ON 7046/V TO FR.AMB KSA

This told her that Bourrat's office phone in the *Elysée* was being used for voice communication (rather than fax or data) with the phone belonging to the French ambassador in Saudi Arabia. This was a lucky strike indeed – the call was bound to be highly encrypted as soon as it left the *TONNANT* system and raced up to a satellite. Quickly she selected Bourrat's line.

'*C'est Marmont sur l'appareil,*' the ambassador announced haughtily. She was in on the very beginning of the call – one of the prime advantages of telling the computer to keep tabs on certain lines.

'It's Bernard – how are you?'

'Very well, very well,' the ambassador sounded impatient with the smalltalk.

'You're not hungover again are you?' Bourrat teased him. Margaret sipped her coffee and smiled. She liked Bourrat's voice – he spoke a highly educated but entirely unpompous French.

'Bernard. Enough! OK?'

'I went shopping with the Prince on Saturday – he spent 600,000 francs on a First Empire bed – I hope he's not expecting us to provide a Josephine for it . . .'

'Did you talk to him about the contract?'

'Of course, Marmont,' Bourrat's warm voice momentarily took a chillier 'what kind of fool do you take me for?' tone.

'Anything I should feed into the negotiating team?'

'Well, he doesn't seem to think much of the British support contract offer on the first seventy-two aircraft.'

Margaret was pleased she had started recording early in the conversation.

'He argues their figures are misleading and that they're only offering it so cheap because they think they can sell a lot more parts through it than the kind of arrangement we've offered.'

When the conversation was over, Margaret prepared a priority TOP SECRET POLYP report for London. Although she had been trained by Dan Birnbaum in the use of the E-mail system, she felt a little awkward about it. How could something so secret be entrusted to the medium used for office smalltalk? Before she had even finished the short account of the French negotiating strategy, another window popped open:

TARGET E/7 ON 7046/V TO U/K FR P

Bourrat had picked up the phone again to an unknown French party. Margaret was inclined to ignore it – she could easily spend her whole day listening to this one presidential adviser if she wasn't careful. The Wasp software was not yet offering keyword filtering of calls. Then she reflected that it might also be about the Saudi arms deal, coming as soon as it did after the last one. She routed the call to her headset.

'Jacques, how are you doing?' It was Bourrat's voice. The tone was relaxed, loving.

'We're both fine, Papa. Looking forward to seeing you at the weekend.'

'Yes, the weekend, that's why I rang.' Bourrat's voice betrayed guilt.

'You're going to cancel, aren't you?'

Margaret decided she should not listen to a family call like this. It was the normal GCHQ procedure, mainly because listening to personal conversations, often long and rambling, was generally unrewarding in intelligence terms. She moved her hand to the mouse on her desk, directing the pointer on screen to an icon which said DISCONNECT.

'I've got to work, Jacques, I'm sorry.'

'We'd lined up someone for you to meet.'

'Matchmaking again?' Bourrat said, bemused.

Margaret let her finger hover in the air over the button she had to double-click to stop listening. Her other hand toyed with her hair.

'Not exactly. . .'

'My son, I'm touched, really. You've been to some trouble on my behalf and I'm going to have to let you down.'

Jacques answered with a flash of annoyance, 'It's been long enough, surely! If you moved on it wouldn't be a betrayal of *Maman* – you know we don't think that.'

'I know, I know. We've had this conversation enough times before.' Bourrat sounded weary. 'I've got my memories. I'm just not ready for anything more.'

Margaret felt a profound sense of guilt at the remark she had made to Colette when they were watching

Bourrat on television: 'I bet he cheats on his wife.' The words rung in her head. It wasn't like anybody else had heard it, but she felt crass and ashamed.

'Yeah, well listen, Dad, have a nice weekend whatever you're doing. We'll be thinking of you, and if you change your mind . . .'

'Thanks son. Listen . . .' Bourrat struggled to find the words, 'maybe one day I'll just meet someone – it's not good to plan these things, it just makes me too nervous.'

'I know, I know,' said Jacques

'Bye son.'

'Bye.'

Margaret's screen flashed up:

TARGET E/7 ON 7046/V HAS CLEARED

She double-clicked to get rid of the window. Before she could think what to do next, one of her worst memories had pushed to the front of her mind.

She was sitting at the kitchen table in Ascot with her brother, spreading bright red strawberry jam on sliced white bread. Her A level mocks had been coming up; her mind had been full of French irregular verbs. Suddenly he was shouting excitedly, 'It's the police! It's the police!' They had both pressed their noses to the window, as the village bobby leaned his bicycle against the Cotswold stone wall, removed his helmet and walked up the garden path.

They could hear their father going to the front door and the mumble of grave male voices. It was indistinct until they saw the policeman turn to leave and say the words, 'I'm so very sorry, Mr Reynolds.' Nothing could ever erase from her mind the look of complete shock on her father's face as he had walked into the kitchen.

Their mother had been killed when her Morris 1100 was in a head-on collision with a lorry.

Margaret's memories of the days which had followed this tragedy were quite indistinct. She could remember only the sketchiest details of the funeral itself. Her father's face, moments after he had heard the news, was, however, burned into her mind like some awful hologram – as real and as three-dimensional now as it had been all those years ago. She found herself snuffling, and quickly doffed her headset, making her way through the two rows of analysts immersed in their own private worlds to the loo on the landing.

As she sat on the closed lavatory blowing her nose, she had a powerful desire, a craving almost, to see her father again. She wondered whether Ted Lofting might let her go home one weekend. Margaret felt a sense of suffocation – she didn't want to go back to that small room full of tense analysts. She just wanted some fresh air.

Two floors below, the familiar figures of Tom, Fergus, John and Martin were once more in the garage. A ringing bell announced the descent of the car lift, bringing Ray Skinner in one of the Mercs with five bags of Blue Circle in the boot. Large amounts of cement were being mixed in the corner: preparations to start back-filling the heading. Ray Skinner had been to the front of the tunnel with Roger the boffin to make sure the two pods were securely anchored and powered before the Ulstermen started filling around them with cement.

Skinner emerged from the heading and called, 'Tom, get a fry on, mate! I'm so hungry I could eat the crotch out of a low-flying duck!'

'You'll have to wait, Ray – work to do.' Tom looked

around. 'Where are my wellies? I can't work in these.' He examined a pair of trendy walking boots with disgust.

Ray smiled knowingly: 'It's operational, mate. Don't ask me to explain further. Don't worry, they're your size.'

Tom sat down and began fiddling with the laces. 'They're an awful job getting on and off.'

Ray knew this was a final protest intended for nobody in particular. Sure enough, within fifteen minutes the big Ulsterman was shuffling down the tunnel to begin a shift pouring cement at its front. Each time the front of his right foot pressed into the wet clay it left a tiny indentation of Hebrew letters, 'Made in Israel'. In due course Skinner would ensure that an Israeli snack wrapper and a chisel, unmarked but made on a kibbutz on the Golan Heights, would also be deposited in the setting cement.

It was about an hour later, when Ray was making himself a cup of instant coffee in the area behind the showroom, that he noticed Margaret Reynolds walking in off the street. She was wearing a long navy blue wool coat and looking tall and striking.

'Been somewhere?' he asked.

'Out,' she said tersely.

'I can see that. Did you tell anyone where you were going?'

'Don't be daft, Ray.' She was still upset about the memories Bourrat's call had triggered and in no mood to be cross-examined.

Skinner felt empowered by the morning's events, so he answered, 'You know it's the rule that we can't just go walking around the streets of Paris on our own.'

'Don't tell me the rules, Ray,' she said as she began

mounting the stairs to the first floor. 'You're just Grade 9. Remember?'

Skinner was shocked by her aggression. It was not a side he had seen to Margaret before. Anger welled up inside him as she raced away.

'Bitch!' he suddenly said aloud and wondered how he could take his revenge.

Chapter Twenty-Three

The next morning Margaret had gone into work in a terrible rush. She was coming down with a cold, she could feel it. Her throat was getting sore and her body nagged her with strange aches. She had arrived to glimpse Ray Skinner scurrying down to the basement. He had not seen her, and for a moment she tried to convince herself that her anger of the previous day had been justified. In her heart of hearts though she knew she had been rude and would have to apologise. While she pondered this unappealing prospect she opened a steaming cup of coffee and a bag containing an almond croissant.

'Max?' she asked her American opposite number.

'Uh-huh.'

'Sorry to bother you, but I've forgotten that stuff that we were shown at Cheltenham about how to set up keyword recognition on the computer.'

The bow-tied NSA man swivelled his chair round to face her computer screen. 'Allrighty – you go to "TOOLS" like this . . .' he clicked away with the mouse, 'and then to K/R – you remember Keyword Recognition?'

'Yes – I may be hopeless, but that I remember!'

'OK – now create new K/R protocol.'

'Right,' she had taken over control now.

'Now Margaret, you just type in the name.'

Her fingers tapped in B-O-U-R-R-A-T.

'The *Elysée* guy?' The computer, unprompted, produced a list of numbers associated with Bourrat, and Max confirmed that the K/R check referred to the man normally using those numbers.

'Yes,' she replied, hoping to sound as nonchalant as possible and noticing that there was also an E-mail address on the screen. 'A lot of interest from our people in Franco–Saudi relations.'

Kampfner knew that his bosses had also been on to him about the huge fighter jet contract: there was an American firm in the running as well as British and French. He did not let on. 'Now you need to get some samples of someone saying his name – preferably including the man himself.'

'I got one yesterday.'

They went to the recording of the conversation with the ambassador in Saudi Arabia and, with dizzying speed, Kampfner marked the name and copied it into the new K/R file. After that, he went to the corner of the office in which a microphone was kept for this express purpose and recorded another couple of pronunciations of the same name. Five minutes later the computer was set up to search any call passing through for Bourrat's name.

The Bourrat K/R had been in action for no more than forty minutes when it yielded something of interest. It was a call from the French company hoping to sell fighters to the Saudi Arabians. The executive did not speak to Bourrat himself but to an assistant. The conversation allowed Margaret to type up a new E-mail for London with the price of France's tender for the upkeep of the fighters they were planning to sell. 'Could you ask Monsieur Bourrat whether he thinks they'd wear it?' the corporate type had asked of a contract priced at more than two billion pounds. For a moment Margaret marvelled at the way they discussed astronomical sums in the manner of used car salesmen. Then she remembered that years of listening to the affairs of foreign governments had taught her that the seriousness with which money was discussed seemed in inverse proportion to the size of the sum: two bureaucrats could natter away for an hour about the purchase of a couple of new limousines for their ministry, but a frigate could get funded with the briefest of exchanges. It was only towards the end of the conversation that a tone of hesitancy crept into the businessman's voice. 'Could he call me back about the . . . er . . . the commission for the . . . er . . . distinguished guest.'

For the Defence Export Sales Organisation in London, this of course went to the heart of the matter: how much did the French intend to pay as bribes and to whom. Margaret surmised from the call though that, even on a channel of communications allegedly as secure as *TONNANT*, she would be very lucky to get that information. Still, there was an implication that the businessman expected Bourrat to discuss the matter on the phone, so she was able to enter the company's number into the Wasp database so that it would detect the call as soon as the President's adviser made it.

She looked at her watch: it was already past 1 p.m. Margaret popped out to buy a baguette stuffed with brie and grapes, and while she was gone Wasp automatically recorded Bourrat's return call. When she put her password into the computer, a window opened to flag the recording performed in her absence. She fed herself lunch with her left hand while the right worked the mouse beside her keyboard. As she put her headset on, Margaret wondered for a moment about Bourrat's involvement in largescale bribery. She had learned enough about government during her years at GCHQ not to be surprised that an otherwise honourable man could be doing such a thing. Still she recognised that, whatever the reasons, she was developing a protective feeling towards him.

'Michel, forgive me. *Le Patron* needed urgent advice about his speech tonight for the Prince's banquet. You know how keen he is to strike the right note of humour and learning.'

'*Pas de problème.* Do you expect to tie up this commission business before he goes back to Jeddah?'

'There's no hurry. They know we'll be generous. Perhaps it's best discussed by you on your next visit.'

'Shouldn't you mention it tonight, at the banquet? Good to crown a successful visit with a little . . . promise of something?'

Bourrat clearly found the executive's approach irritating: 'Michel, be serious – you want us to do it in the *Elysée*?'

'A fine meal, good wine – maybe after the cognac a word in his ear.'

'He won't drink at an official banquet!' Bourrat's temper was close to going.

'Of course, of course, I'm sorry. Maybe you're right. Maybe best left for our next visit.'

'I think so. By the way, we mentioned the support contract figure and they didn't bat an eyelid.'

'Good – fine. Bernard – sorry for being pushy about that commission business.'

'Don't be silly! Forget it.'

'By the way,' Michel the planemaker was now trying to restore the atmosphere, 'did you give the boss some pearls of wisdom for his speech?'

'Nothing very inspired. The obligatory allusion to Voltaire. He's going to say too many people in France regard him as Papambo – you know, Candide's Peruvian servant?'

'Yes, most amusing.'

'Too many people think of him as the man who can lead them to an Eldorado of streets paved with gold and untold personal riches. It's being polite to the Prince – suggestion that they don't just fall over themselves to give their money away to the right foreigner.'

'Thank heaven they do!'

'Indeed, Michel, indeed.'

Margaret moved straight to the E-mail which she had started earlier for London but decided not to send, because she was expecting Bourrat's return call. It had been worth waiting – now they knew the Saudis had accepted the French maintenance contract bid – a sum of money not that much smaller than the purchase price of the seventy-two aircraft themselves. Something, an element of doubt, gnawed away at her while she was typing the message.

After she had finished it and sent the E-mail, she listened again to the recording. 'Too many people in France regard him as Papambo – you know, Candide's Peruvian servant?' That's what it was. She listened again. Not right. She thought of turning over her shoulder and asking Colette about it. If she'd been at home she could have just checked her own student's edition of *Candide*, which had sat unopened on its shelf for at least fifteen years.

'Philippa,' she turned to the GCHQ linguist beside her, 'I'm nipping out for a moment to get something for this cold, I'll be back in about fifteen minutes.'

Margaret raced to the small bookshop just by the metro at La Madeleine. It was crammed with those nondescript cream-covered volumes with plain typed titles – the sort of books sold in France which proudly declare their inaccessibility to all but the most self-confident intellectual. She knew she would find *Candide* there – otherwise it would be like a British bookshop without *Pride and Prejudice* or *Oliver Twist*. She flicked through until she saw the chapter heading 'What They Saw in the Land of Eldorado'. Almost as soon as she triumphantly confirmed that the servant's name was Cacambo not Papambo, her pride at spotting the mistake gave way to a strange foreboding. She felt a pang of protectiveness towards Bourrat. If he had given the President the wrong name for his speech, then he would be humiliated in front of an audience of France's great and good, many of whom would surely know their literature.

As she walked back to the office, stopping to buy some sachets of cold remedy, she found herself struggling to make sense of her feelings. Of course she couldn't save Bourrat from this gaffe – and anyway, he might have only got the name wrong when talking on the phone, not when he was with the President. Even if he had, maybe one of the President's other aides would spot the mistake. There must be all sorts of people in a government office who might look at a president's speech – one would notice. Was there any hope the President himself would spot it? Again she found herself thinking that there was no way she could warn Bourrat.

Of course there wasn't. How could you disobey a more basic rule of signals intelligence than to ring him up and say 'By the way, you're all wrong about *Candide*'? If he had only made that mistake in his conversation with Michel it would pinpoint exactly what was being intercepted – the whole operation would be compromised. She smiled at her own stupidity. No way. Silly.

While Margaret stood at the kettle in the kitchenette behind the showroom, Ray Skinner appeared.

'Would you like a coffee or something, Ray?' she asked pleasantly.

'Oh, so you're not biting my head off today?'

'No. I'm sorry, Ray. It was really rude of me. I'm just not feeling myself.'

He thought but did not say 'I know you're not: I saw that bite on your neck!' but confined himself instead to a conciliatory 'No worries'. Ray had perked up in his hope-springs-eternal womaniser's way. 'Maybe I'll drop round this evening and we can drink a toast to peace!'

'Fine,' she said, without meaning it.

Ray concluded that she couldn't seem to be too keen and looked forward to dropping in on Margaret's flat.

Margaret surveyed her steaming Lemsip as she sat back at her desk. She was feeling hot and cold, running a fever. Her fingers began clicking away on her keyboard:

BB@ely. gov.fr

Bourrat's E-mail address. BB at the *Elysée* had a strange ring to it. BB meant Brigitte Bardot to most French

214

people. She tried to come up with the best translation –
it was like a reflex for a linguist. The British equivalent
would be an E-mail address which suggested Diana Dors
at Downing Street. She selected 'write E-mail' and put
Bourrat's electronic address in the top box. What was
she doing? If they ever found out she'd be dismissed in
an instant – on the first train back to London and
probably never allowed through the gates at Cheltenham
again. How likely was it they would find out? If a French
minister or president's speech was like a British one, it
would go to all sorts of government departments to
make sure he wasn't putting his foot in it one way or
another. As it found its way around the central
government machine, surely there must be a chance
someone would notice, so therefore why not her? She
pressed 'tab' and put the word 'Candide' into the subject
box. Then she wrote in French:

> BB,
> Could a man like you possibly forget,
> That Cacambo was Candide's scout,
> Tell the boss: that's your best bet,
> Or else your shame will come about.

Even this simple verse took her several minutes in
another language and she found herself repeatedly
checking that nobody was watching her. She did not
sign it. It would arrive simply with her E-Mail address
of '108476@ezlink.com'. As Dan Birnbaum had
explained, this would simply identify it as coming from
one of several million subscribers with a huge global
Internet provider. The best efforts of any intelligence
service in the world would never reveal more than that
this subscriber paid his or her bills through a standing

order in a Caribbean tax haven. Margaret felt strangely invulnerable as she moved the mouse to the 'send' icon and clicked it. The window opened telling her it had been sent and for the rest of the afternoon she worked away on matters entirely unrelated to the President's special adviser.

Margaret had forgotten about her agreement to Ray's offer of a drink. It only came back to her when he banged on the door of her flat just after nine that evening. She was wearing a grey cotton tracksuit and was just about to take to her bed with a Lemsip.

'All right there, darling?' he asked as she opened the door.

'Oh, Ray . . .'

'Thought I'd come round and tend to the patient.' He held up a bottle of Scotch as he eased past her into the flat.

'Ray, I'm afraid I'm going to have to be rather inhospitable—'

'Nonsense, my dear, I'm known for my toddies! I won't stay long.'

For a moment Margaret felt powerless and angry as Ray began to busy himself in the kitchen.

'I'm sorry about the business yesterday too,' he called out. 'I didn't mean to overstep the mark or anything but Ted Lofting asked me to keep an eye on everything and everyone in his absence.'

'Really?' She was disgusted at the idea of Ray feeling he had the right to know her comings and goings but instead decided to be conciliatory. 'Well, we've both said sorry now, so let's forget it eh?' She stood in the kitchen doorway and cocked her head, inviting an answer.

'Sure! I don't want no more ructions, Christ no!' He handed her a hot mug of whisky, honey, lemon juice and assorted herbs.

She took a sip – it was delicious. 'Thanks Ray, that's very nice.' Margaret began to relax a little. 'Another thing you learned in the Navy?'

'It was in fact, yes.'

They said nothing for a few moments. Until Margaret dashed his hopes once again by saying, 'Well if you'll excuse me . . .'

'You turfing me out already?'

'I'm sorry, I'm just so knackered.'

'I'll tell you something else I learned in the Navy.' He was looking down at his feet: 'It was that no matter how many airs and graces a girl gives herself, she'll always want servicing in the end.'

'Sorry?' Margaret really wasn't sure she had heard him right.

'I got a run ashore in the Bahamas once and I'd heard about this place where you could find women who'd go for it at the drop of a hat.'

'Really?' She was getting angrier now.

'Some shipmates told me about it. It was a place in Nassau where the American birds went to find some rough – local boys, visiting matelots and the like. They'd walk up and down and you'd exchange glances. They'd start the conversation and then in a surprisingly short amount of time they'd say – well the one I met came out with the immortal phrase "I like you, I'm clean and I want to fuck" – pardon my French.'

'Ray, I'm just not in the mood for your reminiscences.'

'Well, there's a moral here, Magsie: I know you think I'm thick and you're so smart you'd never learn a thing from me. But these women they were all thirty- and forty-something. They were high-powered women – from New York mainly. Some were divorced but I think most had never had a regular fella. That's what they'd been reduced to. Picking up blokes like us.' Now Ray was looking straight at Margaret, but her eyes were averted. 'I quite liked the girl I spent my hour with. She probably would have been quite happy settling down somewhere in the suburbs. But instead she got a petty officer full of Bacardi and a one-night stand. It was passionate though – I remember leaving her with a fearsome lovebite just here,' he touched a spot on his neck which corresponded exactly to the place he had seen Margaret's mark.

She could not bear to follow his fingers. 'Could you go now please?'

'I'll go, of course I will,' he put down his drink. 'But just remember two things. One: you're no better than me, despite your airs and graces. Two: in the interests of the security of this operation, I have to do what I have to do.' He walked past her and banged the front door behind him.

As Skinner was leaving, the President had not yet begun his speech at the banquet in honour of the distinguished Saudi guest. Bernard Bourrat sat in his Balmain dinner jacket with a Saudi air force colonel who spoke no French on one side and the wife of a former French ambassador in Riyadh on the other. He caught the eye of one of the President's aides and summoned him over. He whispered into the younger man's ear and some notes were produced from his inside pocket. Bourrat unclipped a Mont Blanc pen from his jacket and made an alteration to the text. He felt intense relief and gratitude, wondering for the tenth or eleventh time that evening who might have sent the E-mail which had saved him from humiliation.

Chapter Twenty-Four

It was the last day of January and the tunnellers had already back-filled twenty feet from the point where GCHQ's two pods now sat astride France's most sensitive communications artery. Tom and his men had adopted a shift system again and were carrying along their work with all the seriousness that a one-thousand-pound bonus for ontime completion could generate. Tom and John were at the front of the heading, positioning the hose which was being used to pump cement.

'Have you looked upstairs since we've been back?' John asked.

'We've no business poking our noses up there, son,' the older man replied as he wrestled the cement pipe into position.

'I went up there just before we started our shift last night – it's like Computers R Us up there! Have they ever told you what they're all for?'

'Well, you don't need the brains of an archbishop to know they're listening in on Frenchie do you?'

'I suppose not . . .' John answered a little disconsolately.

Margaret came into work hoping desperately she could avoid her tormentor and that there would be a reply E-Mail from Bourrat. She had gone to sleep in turmoil after Skinner's little speech. He had made her cry and she would never forgive him for that. As she had lain there in the darkness she had longed to be transported from the attentions of idiots like Ray Skinner. Was that all that would be left for her as she got older?

Her entry into the Hamsin office had gone to plan: no sign of that ghastly man. She said her friendly hellos to the other analysts and logged in to her computer. A small sign came up: 'You've Got Post'. She looked around her to make sure nobody had spotted it. Part of her wanted to wait until some time when there were fewer people in the office before reading it, but her pulse had quickened and she could not stop herself taking the risk. Bourrat had replied in the same way she had written, French verse.

> From: BB@ely.gov.fr
> Who are you? My unknown friend,
> Last night you did me proud,
> So my sincerest thanks I send,
> Let us meet so I can say it out loud.

Margaret felt a tingle of pleasure. Of course she had anticipated that he would be curious about who had sent the message, but she knew that meeting Bourrat was out of the question. Still it had put her in an excellent mood. There was hope, not all men were morons.

At coffee time, Margaret had joined a conclave of the British and French analysts in the kitchenette. Early on in their presence, Colette had revolted against the jars of instant coffee which had fuelled the diggers, gone out and bought a filter system. They stood chatting while the machine spat and bubbled ten cups' worth into its clear glass flask.

'This time next week I could be home,' Philippa said.

'Oh, I wouldn't be so sure,' Margaret countered a little nervously.

The others deferred to her in such matters because she was a manager but the relationship was informal enough for Colette to say, 'I understand you, Margaret . . . but I miss my kids. I never thought I'd hear myself say that. I'll be happy to go home.'

'Why do you think we could be longer?' Philippa asked.

'Well . . . the analytical phase of the operation still has a way to go . . . I suppose it's not likely to be much more than two weeks though,' and as she said it, Margaret realised she regarded that prospect with dread.

Bert, a rotund NSA linguist in his late forties and the only man in this coffee conclave, suddenly said, 'I find this really stressful. Maybe guys with our kind of specialism just aren't used to being in enemy territory . . . but I don't draw much comfort from this Canadian ID,' he patted his pocket for emphasis. 'I haven't been sleeping too good.'

'You too?' a woman with a soft Virginia accent who Margaret hardly knew spoke up.

'You betcha! I kind of get this waking dream of being stopped just before I get on the plane home—'

'Bert! Don't be so melodramatic!' Margaret knew she had to cut short this kind of alarmist conversation.

'You're going to put down roots here I suppose! Make sure you get some of that nice fabric that's on sale at BHV for your cell curtains!'

Margaret didn't know whether to let this remark ride,

as an example of the gallows humour of people 'in enemy territory', or whether to stamp on it. 'Let's not get carried away, eh? We're probably halfway through our stay here and there's absolutely no reason to suppose we're going to do anything other than go home when the time comes.' She took her mug of coffee and strolled back towards the office wondering whether she had convinced her colleagues.

Bourrat's desk in the *Elysée* was a suitably splendid Louis XVI affair. He confined his papers to a small area of its large expanse immediately in front of him. Beyond the working space were framed photos of his daughter, two sons and a black and white image of a family ski trip to Les Arcs back in the seventies in which his late wife looked particularly happy. The large table lamp and inkwells were furnished by the state, but he had placed a handsome bust of the writer Balzac there too. Bourrat was no technophobe, but he would not have a computer on this handsome desk. Instead it stood on a modern metal trolley to his side and he had to turn to face it. From time to time he found himself glancing across to see if any more E-mail had arrived. Twice he saw with excitement that it had, only to read mundane stuff about a defence technology seminar from some bore down the corridor.

Just before he was due to go to lunch, Guy Marechal, the man who had been carrying the President's speech the night before, dropped in to ask Bourrat about a forthcoming state visit to Gabon. The older man allowed the conversation to run its course before asking, 'Guy, who do you think would have seen the President's speaking notes before I made that correction?'

'Well, me . . . you . . . Madame Morel, who typed

them up from the President's notes . . . I can't really think of anyone else.'

'Mmm,' Bourrat closed his eyes in concentration. He could not think of anyone else either and he didn't buy the idea that it was Madame Morel since she was a battle-axe of fifty-eight who would never have had the imagination to send the E-mail. 'We didn't send it out to the Foreign Ministry or Defence?'

'No, no – not on a private visit like the Prince's.'

'You didn't put the notes down on your desk or anything?'

The young civil servant looked a little guilty: 'Well . . . I did leave them on my desk, as a matter of fact, while I was changing into my tux. Has there been some . . . irregularity?'

'No, no, nothing serious – it would take too long to explain. Had Claudette gone home at that hour?'

'Claudette?'

'You share an office with her don't you?'

'Yes . . . She might have been there, yes.'

'There's no problem, Guy – someone left a remark about the speech on my desk and I couldn't read their writing.'

'Let me see it, I know Claudette's writing.'

'It's OK, don't worry, I think I've thrown it away.'

Bourrat thought about it. Claudette was a more promising suspect: she was a bright enough civil servant in her early forties. He had never thought of her as being particularly attractive, so he felt a slight sense of anticlimax. But it could definitely be her. Who else could possibly have seen it? There was a small possibility someone might have popped into Guy's office while he was changing. No sooner had he wondered about Claudette and the mystery passer-by than he had to rule them out. The E-mail had arrived in the late afternoon. That would have been before Guy was out of the office changing. The idea began to dawn on Bourrat that his office might be bugged.

During a reception that evening for the Tunisian Foreign Minister's delegation, Bourrat was distracted. As he mouthed platitudes about the cordial relations between France and its former possession, his mind kept wandering back to the issue of the E-mail. Everybody had heard rumours about different factions using the intelligence services to keep tabs on their opponents. But he wasn't a political figure, so he doubted the boss was doing it against him.

Bourrat didn't think the internal security boys, the DST, would do it either. He had connections there and nobody there would do something so amateurish as send him an E-mail revealing what was going on. The President's special adviser smiled pleasantly at the Tunisian minister, who was offering him the use of an official residence for a couple of weeks' holiday. 'You're so kind, I've heard it's ravishing there!' Bourrat exclaimed. 'If only I had the time, my children always tell me I neglect them. I'm a grandfather you know.' Bourrat batted back the offer. Barely a week passed by without some company or foreign government offering its hospitality in compromising ways.

Later, as the official Citroën swept him home, Bourrat peered out, numbed in a three-Martini haze. The driver did not attempt to make conversation. Bernard noticed the eyes surveying him in the rearview mirror occasionally. What lay behind the Tunisian's offer? Simple Maghreb hospitality? He smiled weakly, wondering why the minister might think that he, as an *Elysée* adviser, held such clout. Bernard remembered how much he had thought he might do with the job while he was campaigning for it, and what it had actually amounted to in reality. A role in foreign policy, to be sure, but rarely a place at the centre of events.

He was home. Bourrat had said his goodnight to the driver, fumbled his way into his apartment and plunged into its stillness. He looked across at his desk and a photo of his late wife. Work suddenly seemed very trivial.

About lunchtime Mike McPhee returned from a couple of days back in the UK. Nobody asked him whether it was work or personal time. The friendly reception he received from Ray Skinner soon turned into an anxious one.

'I've seen two water board surveyors messing about on the Faubourg just a couple of yards from the interception point,' McPhee announced.

'I thought they'd finished the mains repair?'

'Well they had. But there were two blokes with a *Général des Eaux* van and some plans.'

'Are they still there?'

'They were two minutes ago.'

'Let's get Zeke from the tunnel, clean him up and send him out to stroll past the two water board men – he might be able to see what they're doing.'

'We ought to send a French speaker with him, Zeke's a zero in that department.'

While McPhee went to get Zeke, Skinner went up to the analysts' room and put his hand on Margaret's shoulder. She turned to face him and blushed slightly. 'Yes?'

'Can I have a quick word outside?'

Margaret was wondering, 'What crap is he going to spring on me this time?' and found herself pleasantly surprised that Skinner's request was purely professional.

Within ten minutes, big Zeke and statuesque Margaret were playing an unlikely looking tourist couple walking up the street. As they neared the two water board men it became clear they were indeed surveyors of some sort. They had spread a map out on the bonnet of their van and seemed deep in discussion. Zeke and Margaret knew they could only make one pass and that he would have to concentrate on the diagram and she on overhearing what they were saying about it. Margaret felt her heart thumping as they came within a few feet and she began picking up words.

'. . . the last problem . . . investigate . . . further damage' – there were just fragments.

Zeke and Margaret walked past them and were about to turn right off the Faubourg and begin their roundabout return to the showroom when a commotion caught their attention. Outriders with wailing sirens heralded the launching of armoured Citroëns from the *Elysée*. Margaret heard a passer-by say, '*Le patron est partie pour une casse-croûte*' – the boss's going out for a snack. As the black cars zoomed by, she saw the handsome man sitting beside the President and felt a warm pang of excitement. It was the same man she'd seen on television – yes, that was Bourrat sitting beside the President himself.

When they got back to Hamsin there was a conclave in the kitchenette.

'It was fragmentary,' Margaret began, 'they seemed to be concerned about the risk of further damage from the thaw – the possibility that another section of main might have been cracked or something.'

'I'll tell you one thing,' Zeke said in a melodramatic

voice, 'they had the *TONNANT* heading marked on that plan of theirs and make no mistake.'

'Well, they would, wouldn't they?' McPhee countered. 'They don't want to dig it up by mistake.'

'Well, that's secret stuff – what's their need to know on something thirty feet down?' Zeke asked portentously.

'I'm not sure we can draw any conclusions from this,' Skinner announced, a little uncertainly.

McPhee responded, 'I think we've got to tell the bosses PDQ, maybe get them over . . .'

'I think that would be sensible,' Margaret concurred as one of the most senior officers on the ground.

As they were nodding their agreement, George the salesman appeared from around the side of the wall separating them from the showroom.

'Good news *hamdilullah*! I have sold the Aston Martin.'

'That's all I fucking need, Georgie-boy!' Skinner replied. 'I'll have to bring in another motor now!'

Margaret believed Bourrat must have been involved in a heavy round of appointments, because he did not appear to have used his phone all day. She had busied herself with other traffic analysis tasks, while enjoying the afterglow of seeing him earlier. Just before five, when the streets were already in a dark gloom, her computer told her:

TARGET E/7 ON 7046/V TO DST 3042

She felt panic as she put on her headset. Bourrat was on the phone to a French security service extension. Was he about to report worries about eavesdropping?

'Jules?'

'Bernard! Are you fit?'

'Tolerably – too many official banquets are slowing me down a bit. Listen, I got your message.'

'Can you make it?' the DST man asked.

'Sure, I've got to get my 500 francs back, haven't I?'

'Don't be so sure, old man.'

'I'm quietly confident.'

'You've played at that court before, haven't you?'

Margaret was begining to feel relieved – was Bourrat fixing up a tennis or squash game?

'Yes, yes, it's two minutes from the Pont de Neuilly metro.'

'Exactly.'

'I'll take the metro I think, the traffic's just ridiculous at that sort of time.'

'See you at six thirty then?' Jules confirmed.

The call ended. Margaret found herself feeling ecstatic. For the moment, she did not consider that someone worried about eavesdropping would hardly use the phone to report it. Instead she thought 'Bernard's going to relax, how nice!' Then she considered that he must be quite fit and began to think about what sort of legs he had. And then she wondered what time he would leave the *Elysée* in order to get to Pont de Neuilly in time for the game.

The other analysts thinned out quite early that evening and Margaret found herself longing to send Bourrat another E-mail. She wasn't going to wish him luck for his contest with Jules – that would be stupidly obvious. What could she say then? It couldn't be in verse either: it took too long to compose those, danger time when the message would be on her screen. She began:

I'm not going to be bothered with verse this time.
I'm so glad everything went well the other night. Of
course I can't tell you who I am, for reasons too
difficult to explain. Just think of me as someone who
watches over you but whom you can never meet.

Like her first message, it was in flawless French, only
this time the words she chose and use of the first person
had forced her to declare her feminine gender. She
worried for a moment about ending on 'never meet' –
wasn't it guaranteed to make him want to even more?
She directed the mouse to 'send' and clicked. So what if
it was? As she gathered her things and got ready to
leave, she couldn't remember when she had last felt so
excited.

Chapter Twenty-Five

Ted Lofting and Dan Birnbaum arrived in Paris that morning on the same British Midland flight. They gave one another no signs of recognition on the journey and took separate cabs into town. The American arrived first in the Hamsin office, just after 8.30 a.m. and his British partner shortly afterwards. Both of them thought the reappearance of the water board men did not in itself constitute a reason for ending or suspending the operation. Equally they knew they had to honour their orders on the subject of 'maximum deniability' and that, if they had been discovered, there were likely to be few or no warnings before the building was raided.

Mike McPhee was ready to meet them on their arrival. He talked through what Zeke and Margaret had seen and heard. One by one, Birnbaum and Lofting strolled up the Faubourg – but there was nothing for them to see.

When Ted returned, he found Ray Skinner had made a large flask of coffee and spread out fresh croissants on a platter.

'I'm reasonably confident that there was nothing untoward in what you saw yesterday,' Lofting announced, 'although we could start trying to move faster to Phase Two and get people out of here.'

'It's a very tight plan, Ted, and if we cut people, we make it harder not easier to meet the Phase Two targets,' Birnbaum responded.

'Point taken, Dan. Perhaps what I'm saying is that we need to look again at our targets for Phase Two: how much do we really need to know before we close down this operation and move out?'

'The boys reckon they'll finish back-filling the tunnel in about forty-eight hours,' Skinner chipped in.

'No no!' Birnbaum said emphatically. 'We need seven or eight days' worth of traffic sorted into Wasp before we can turn her live and bug out of here.'

Ted was toying with his unlit pipe: 'I defer to your knowledge of the traffic analysis system, Dan.'

'We'll just have to make sure we don't get too nervy then,' McPhee said, smiling a little uncertainly.

Margaret Reynolds stood in front of the mirrored door of her bedroom wardrobe. She had put on some beige trousers and a navy guernsey sweater and was pacing about in an agitated way. She piled her hair on top of her head, looked at the effect, changed her mind, went to the cupboard and fished out the navy skirt she had worn on her first blind date to Bristol. Jonathan the officer hardly registered in her thoughts; he seemed to belong to another century. Eventually she could not stand her indecision any longer. 'Colette!'

Her flatmate came into the bedroom, '*Oui?*'

'I can't decide between these trousers and the skirt . . . It's so hopeless! I can barely go on the street with all these gorgeous Parisian women making me feel like a tramp!'

Colette was thrown. She had always regarded

Margaret as one of those intellectual English roses for whom looking glamorous is an act of treason against some kind of unspoken code of ordinariness. 'It looks very nice with the trousers . . .' she said, a little unconvincingly.

'I wish I could go out and spend a fortune on clothes!'

'The French woman does not spend a fortune, Margaret – she would wear the same as you are wearing, but she would add a Hermès silk scarf, some earrings and perhaps a new handbag – as they say in the American magazines: Accessorize!'

'You're right, but I haven't got time . . . It would be such fun if we could go shopping, wouldn't it?'

'I'd love to . . .' Colette was taken aback for the second time that morning, 'but I'm not sure Max will let me – you know we're not allowed to.' She felt awkward reminding her superior of the rules.

It was not long after Margaret had arrived in the office (in the end she had changed into her skirt and boots, despite Colette's advice) when there was consternation on the American side of the monitoring room. One of the analysts had found something of interest; Max Kampfner had been summoned and had donned a headset; someone had then gone to get Dan Birnbaum from the basement, and finally Ted Lofting had been fetched across the line. Kampfner decided to put a recorder on the line, and it was left running for much of the morning. Margaret of course was desperately curious to know what was going on, and kept straining to see her colleagues' screens.

Eventually, Lofting removed his headset, grave-faced, and approached her. 'Quite extraordinary . . . this operation really has been an eye-opener . . . amazing.'

'What exactly have they found, Ted?' Margaret's patience had given out at last.

'There's no doubt about the voice . . . It's Terry Donald.'

'The Cabinet minister?'

'Yes, Secretary of State for Health.'

'What sort of line is it?'

'Well, that's the remarkable thing – it's a direct feed from a special facility into the DGSE headquarters in Paris.'

'They're bugging his house?'

Lofting seemed impatient with her: 'No, no! He's obviously on a skiing holiday in France somewhere – we just heard him and his wife getting the kids organised to go to ski school.'

'They've wired his chalet and they're linking it back to DGSE headquarters in Paris,' Margaret observed to herself. 'Enterprising of them.'

'Enterprising? Bloody cowboys, the DGSE,' Lofting remarked with evident distaste.

'I'm not sure we're in a position to get angry with them, Ted,' she could not suppress a giggle.

Lofting did not seem to see the funny side of it at all. He walked away, saying to nobody in particular, 'I'll have to notify the Cabinet Secretary as a matter of extreme urgency,' and then went over to Dan Birnbaum, tapping him on the shoulder.

The American removed his headphones and said, smiling, 'Well, how about that?'

'Indeed . . . well I think this firmly scuppers the idea that this operation might be compromised,' Lofting announced with a mixture of annoyance at the breach of a British minister's security and relief that they had discovered it.

'I guess it does.'

Throughout the morning an idea which had been lurking somewhere in Maragret's subconscious since she heard Bourrat arrange his squash game the previous day began to dominate her thoughts. What would the harm be in watching him leave for his game? She wanted to see him. It would cheer her up no end if she did. As she tried to suppress this idea for the umpteenth time, the E-mail sign appeared on her screen. After a quick glance around she clicked it open.

> Guardian Angel,
> If we can never meet, are you just trying to torture me? You hold all the cards. Have we ever met in the past? Tell me more about yourself. BB

Margaret was thrilled to get it, but there was also a slight unease. Was he doing the E-mail equivalent of getting the anonymous caller to keep talking so he could trace her? She knew from the lectures they had received in Cheltenham before coming to Paris that the NSA had a very high degree of confidence in the re-mailing system. The intelligence reports sent back via the same means had to be untraceable after all. Margaret tried to dismiss her anxiety. She knew Bourrat was lonely: perhaps he was hoping that she was some glamorous French woman that he had his eye on but did not feel able to ask directly – hence the 'have we met?' question.

She opened a blank E-mail to send back to him and reasoned that if she told him a little more about herself, at least she would not be revealing more of what she knew about him.

BB,
We haven't met. What can I tell you about myself? I cannot send you a series of clichés. I am just the right side of forty, and have picked up the amount of emotional wear and tear you would expect from a woman of that age. I am not married and never have been. Work has been an alibi for too much of my life – too much has been sacrificed to it. I could go on and on, but both of us are too busy for that. Thinking of you.

She did not want to sign off 'Angel'. It was sweet if he wanted to call her that, but she couldn't do so herself. Margaret re-read her message and was shocked that she had written the line about work being an alibi. It was the kind of thing she would say to Bella Crewe, her best friend, but now she was saying it to this stranger. And then it seemed obvious to her – of course she could say it, it was like telling someone you'd just met on the train about your deepest anxiety and doing it all the more succinctly because they knew nothing about you. Margaret was very surprised when a reply to her message popped up on the screen less than an hour later. It took a while before she felt she could read it: Max Kampfner kept swivelling around on his chair to talk to one of the British analysts. At long last he shuffled out towards the loo.

Angel,
How pleasurable it was to read your E-mail. You are beginning to crack! The few things you say about yourself simply make me want to ask you so many more questions. You are obviously a young and successful woman, whereas I am the wrong side of

fifty. Of course I would like to know what you look like too . . . If we have never met, how do you know me? What do you know about me?
BB

Margaret was thrilled to get an answer so quickly but was nagged by the sense that this was madness. One part of her felt things would be OK so long as she and Bernard did not meet. After all, what harm was there in sharing their feelings? At other times though she recognised that she was in the grip of a romantic fantasy which could be disastrous for her and everyone working with her. She wondered whether it would be possible to resign from GCHQ a few months after getting back to England and come and meet Bourrat. That was stupid, she thought as she prepared a reply to the latest message: she would always know about the tunnel under the Faubourg. And while her mind almost seized up with doubt, her fingers galloped across the keyboard.

BB,
Describe myself! Typical Frenchman—

She caught herself. 'Frenchman' would suggest she was foreign. Margaret started again:

Typical man! You care about the looks of a woman you can't meet. Well, what can I say? I'm tall – probably about four centimetres shorter than you. I am slim – I don't want to be smug but I am content with my figure. My hair is blonde – I should say was – there are streaks of grey now. Very fitting for an old maid. I mustn't go on. We're both too busy for long correspondence. You ask how I know about you. You are a public figure, Bernard, a man of some importance. People know about you – one gleans details here and there! Bye for now.

Bourrat read the message in the solitude of his office. He glanced at his watch – mustn't be late for squash. There was still time. He smiled as he read Margaret's description of her looks. He had to meet her, that would resolve everything – what she looked like, how she knew about his mistake in the president's speech. He had to get a meeting, but he didn't want to scare her off. He wanted his reply to match her candour but not to be so direct as to cause problems.

Angel,
You are obviously an impressive woman but how diffident you are about your looks! You cannot be French! I suppose you must have been hurt by a man. Is that why it is so hard for us to meet? Please think about it. I already admire you for your kindness in saving me from my gaffe and your candour in writing to me. How nice it would be to meet. Nothing serious – maybe a spot of lunch one Saturday?

Margaret had spent much of the afternoon in a meeting with Max Kampfner trying to trim the list of things they needed to do in order to complete Phase One. Throughout she found he was being typically 'can-do' and she was raising all sorts of reasons why it might take longer rather than less than the expected time. When she finally escaped the meeting, it was already past five thirty. Bourrat's latest E-mail had not reached her. Re-mailing via the Caribbean and two other servers takes time. She wanted to take a stroll past the

Elysée, but she wondered if she was too late.

'That meeting, honestly!' she exclaimed to Philippa. 'I'm going out for ten minutes to clear my head.'

Margaret felt her heart pounding and her palms becoming sweaty. She had been in a state like this when she went to her first blind date, but she had no intention of speaking to Bourrat.

Bernard knew he should allow an hour for the journey – just to be safe. That would have meant a five thirty departure. Instead he worked through the pile of papers on his desk until five forty-five, longing for Margaret's next reply. At last his secretary walked in.

'I'm off now, if that's all right?'

'Sure, enjoy the cinema,' Bernard said, while allowing his glance to flick to his screen.

'I don't mean to nag – but your squash—'

'I know, I know – you're right.'

He picked up his sports bag and went out through the door at about five forty-seven.

Margaret knew she could not loiter around the gates of the Presidential residence. It was a very secure place – or at least the French thought it so. The guards could notice someone making repeat passes back and forth. She found herself by the last shop window on the opposite side of the street which would allow her to view the pedestrian exit. It was an upmarket children's clothes shop – full of sugar-and-spice creations for little French horrors. Margaret felt censorious – she wouldn't buy any child of hers clothes like that even if she did have the money. Sixty pounds for an outfit: what a waste for something they could only wear a couple of times! She glanced at her watch: five fifty. He'd gone, it was pointless waiting any longer. As she was turning to head back to Hamsin, Bourrat sauntered out of the front gate. He marched quickly towards the Rue de L'Elysée, which ran beside the building, connecting the Faubourg with the parallel Champs Elysées. She knew he was heading for the Clemenceau metro: it was on the same line as Pont de Neuilly, his destination. Watching his confident stride and his handsome head she felt giddy. She wanted to follow, but he had been saluted by a couple of formidable Gendarmes who stood in the road and she did not have the nerve to follow him past them. So she watched Bourrat disappear behind a grey police bus with mesh on its windows, sighed and turned to walk back into the office.

That was when she collided with the man she least wanted to see. 'Ray?'

Chapter Twenty-Six

Ray and Margaret parted after their one-word exchange and walked back to the office by separate routes. The tradecraft of pretending not to know one another had quickly reasserted itself. She had initially been in a state of turmoil. There was one brief moment when she had thought of heading for the Gare du Nord and taking a train home rather than give an explanation. She was able to compose herself during the time it took to go back to Hamsin, where the inevitable cross-examination would follow. What had Ray seen after all? It's not like she'd been kissing Bourrat in the street. More's the pity!

Skinner was in fact surprisingly wary when she saw him lurking in the showroom.

'I hope nobody picked up on your signs of recognition,' he began.

'I don't expect they did; anyway, sorry about that, you gave me a shock.'

Having launched into the conversation, Ray began to shift towards what really interested him: 'Thinking of having kids?'

'No,' replied Margaret, trying to hide her hurt.

'You spent a long time looking in that window . . .'

'I was thinking of getting something for my brother's kids, if you must know.'

'We're not here to go shopping – you should know

241

that, it's not allowed. What's more, it's not very secure to do it outside the *Elysée*.'

Margaret decided to counterattack. 'What were you doing there anyway? Were you following me?'

'No, I wasn't, although being in charge of security I have—'

'Don't be so pompous, Ray, it doesn't suit you.'

'I'm not being pompous, and I am in charge of security,' he said firmly. 'You know the worries about this operation – the water board men we saw last week. I make periodic checks just to make sure nobody's conducting fresh excavations or getting ready to clap us all in irons.'

'I understand, Ray,' she adopted a conciliatory tone, 'honestly I do. I was in a fug after that meeting – I still haven't got that cold out of my system. I wanted to clear my head.'

'I see.'

Ray seemed satisfied, nodded and walked towards the spiral stairs down to the basement.

As their conversation finished, Bourrat was meeting his old university friend Jules Lacroix at the squash club. Jules was number two in the French security service, a bear of a man from Alsace. His squash game was based on power: almighty lobs and smashes – he was always in trouble when he had to move quickly. The two men were still doing their stretching warmups when Bernard told him about the mystery E-mails.

'I want you to write down exactly what you did on the day of the speech: when you wrote it, who you saw.' Lacroix put a big arm behind his head and flexed over sideways. 'We'll sweep the office, make one or two other checks, keep her sending messages and we'll probably find out soon enough what's going on. I expect you'll find it's one of the sad palace secretaries, you old goat!'

'I know.' Bernard pushed his fingers down towards his toes and suddenly felt profoundly guilty about what he had done – he was probably going to get some lonely middle-aged woman put through the security mangle when all she'd done was help him.

'I'm sure we'll find it was nothing.' Lacroix turned and by way of further warmup hammered a ball at the back of the court with an earsplitting crash.

The game had barely begun as Margaret went upstairs at the Hamsin office. The number of people sitting up there was already down to three. She decided to log into her computer.

You Have Post

She double-clicked the mail icon. 'How diffident you are about your looks! You cannot be French!' Margaret blushed, a deep warm rush to her cheeks, her mouth dried up. Was it so obvious from so few words she had written Bernard? Instead of worrying that he might guess her real nationality, she marvelled at his intuition. Then she read his proposal of lunch. How delightful! How impossible. She was amazed that he had moved so quickly into asking her out, brushing aside her 'we can never meet' line like the flimsiest of defences. Perhaps things would be all right if she could hold the line until the team had been withdrawn from Paris. Then she could think hard about her future – whether it might be worth leaving GCHQ and trying to make a go of it with Bernard. What would happen when her former employers discovered she was consorting with the man she'd been listening to? It was all too awful to contemplate. Still, she wanted to send him a message so there would be one waiting for him the next morning.

BB,
You are too forward! You know I can't see you although, heaven knows, I'd like to. How can I best explain? Let's just say I'm not ready for it yet. I think you will understand that. Anyway, we should get to know one another a bit better. Tell me about your kids . . .

After sending the message, she went to her file of recent E-mails and erased the copy. Margaret knew she would have to be extra-careful after the incident with Skinner. It was almost 7 p.m. She knew there was a sale on at Max Mara in Les Halles: they wouldn't be closed for another hour. She packed up her things and raced downstairs. As she was about to leave, Margaret spotted Skinner talking to George.

'Ray, I'm going to take a stroll – but I should be at the flat before nine.'

'I see.' He didn't though. Her cheerfulness surprised him.

She bounded through the door with all the joy of someone falling in love.

Ray went down to the basement and found Ted Lofting emerging from the heading. He removed an overall and then used a damp cloth – first on his glasses and then, somewhat comically, to take the dust off his balding head.

'Everything OK up front, skipper?'

'Yes, they've back-filled more than half of the tunnel.

I was just checking the fibre optic and power lines – everything looks perfect.'

'Can I have a quick word?' Ray looked around slightly furtively. The two men stepped into one of the corners of the cold, concrete space. Their heads dipped close to each other so they could hear one another without raising their voices to compete with the cement pump.

'It's a bit embarrassing to have to tell you something about a senior officer,' Ray began, in fact savouring his power.

'Yes?'

'There's been something rather odd about Margaret Reynolds's behaviour on this operation.'

'Go on.' Lofting's face was a picture of almost paternal concern.

'I saw her acting very suspiciously outside the *Elysée* about an hour ago. She was loitering outside this shop, but she seemed to be looking across at the Palace the whole time.'

'I see . . . How long was she there for?'

'Well, I watched her for a few minutes. When I approached her she almost jumped out of her skin. She looked very guilty if you follow my drift, Mr Lofting.'

'Indeed,' Ted rubbed his furrowed brow, 'have you noticed anything else?'

'It's a bit intimate really . . .'

'Well, you've started now, Ray, so let's not be embarrassed.'

'As far as we know, she finished with her boyfriend a couple of months back, right? Well, she definitely had this ruddy great lovebite on her neck – I noticed it about ten days ago.'

'Well, she might have found someone else in England,' Lofting said as if acting as her advocate.

'It's possible of course. She's very resentful about the orders concerning letting someone know her whereabouts. I just wonder . . . Well, I was thinking . . .'

'Yes?'

'Whether she might have found someone out here . . . '

'Would she really have the time to be carrying on with someone?'

'I don't know . . .'

Lofting reflected in an almost pained way on what he had been told.

'OK, Ray. Thanks for telling me this. I think my concerns are twofold. If she's picked up a local chap, then we can send her back to UK immediately and deal with it quietly. If what you saw was something more ominous . . . contact with French officials or something, well then . . .' He shook his head slowly as if to shut out this possibility. 'I'm going to have a word with SIS and see if they can lend us a couple of people to keep an eye on her – I'm telling you this because some eagle-eyed person may notice them and come to you thinking they're the opposition – but for Christ's sake, Ray! Don't tell anyone about this – especially the Americans.'

'Right, chief.'

'I'm sure there could be a perfectly innocent explanation . . . After all, it's not as if you've seen her actually with someone else?'

'Indeed not.'

Lofting patted Skinner's shoulder and walked off upstairs, deep in contemplation.

As Ray and Ted held their conclave in Paris, Terence Jennings, the Foreign Office PUS, made his way into the Cabinet Secretary's outer office in Downing Street.

'Sir Peter will be with you in a moment,' his PA said with a slightly flirty smile. Jennings stood looking at a painting of eighteenth-century Whitehall as he waited.

The PA's phone purred. 'Can you go through?'

Peter Scarlett greeted Jennings at the door. It was intended as a gesture of intimacy by the higher-ranking man, but it made Jennings uncomfortable since he towered over his boss. 'Never trust a short-arse,' Jennings's tutor at Marlborough had told him: 'they always resent taller chaps like you and me.' They sat in the armchairs in front of Scarlett's desk. The PA poked her head through the door without prompting and raised a quizzical eyebrow.

'Will you take some Lapsang, Terence?'

'I'll stick to Ceylonese or whatever with a spot of milk.'

The PA disappeared obediently.

'PM is jumping up and down for some more dirt on the French: I don't suppose you cave dwellers have delivered any?'

'Alas not. You know what the hush-hush boys are like. Keep telling me to be patient. They have struck a rather rich vein on the Saudi business.'

'Oh yes?'

'Yes. They've pinned down a lot of details of the French bid.'

'I have to say,' Scarlett nodded slowly, 'a five billion export order would be very useful for PM to pull out of the hat. We're tailoring our bid accordingly?'

'Of course, and our commissions,' Jennings adopted the arms trade euphemism for bribes.

'How much in commissions?'

'It's around the three hundred million mark.'

'Christ!'

Both men said nothing for a moment as the tea arrived. Once the PA had retreated and banged the door, Scarlett poured himself a cup of almost black brew which he drank without milk or sugar.

'Well, it all comes out of the Saudi government coffers one way or the other. The King doesn't come cheap, Peter.'

'I'll say!'

'The Frogs are wasting too much money on the minor princes again. Same mistake as last time. Anyway,' Jennings said with some emphasis, 'there's something else that has come out of this Paris thing.'

Scarlett nodded and then sipped his tea.

'Terry Donald is being bugged.'

'He's on holiday, isn't he?'

'Yes, in Val d'Isère. The French foreign intelligence service are bugging him. He's due to stay out there for another six days and clearly we've got to get him out.'

'Have we?'

'Yes, he's ringing his backbench mates every day making mischief for the PM – and carrying on his anti-Mandelson thing again. Obviously the French are getting all of this.'

'Did you ring the PUS at Health?'

'I did, but I couldn't explain about Operation POLYP, obviously. I had to be vague and he more or less told me to sod off. Said he wasn't going to ruin S of S's ski trip.'

'I'll have to cook up some sort of cover story,' the Cabinet Secretary observed in a 'Do I have to do everything myself?' sort of way.

'Yes, we could always use the old terrorist threat.'

'We could . . . A little tricky what with the IRA taking an extended break of their own. Even bloody Abu Nidal's gone into retirement.'

'We could work up something on the animal lib front. You know, 'three known nutters sighted with bags of paint heading for Val d'Isère', let him know they're planning to make him the victim of some anti-vivisection protest.'

'Yes, that's got possibilities.'

The two men smiled in their complicity and then began to gossip about how the Tory party might ever make itself fit for government again.

Ted had been deeply troubled and decided to get to the root of the allegations about Margaret as quickly as he could. When he returned to the flats he left a note in Margaret's flat:

If you're not feeling too tired, perhaps you'd like to join me for a spot of dinner? I'm in Flat 278.
Yours, T.L.

It was around eight thirty when his doorbell sounded. Margaret had deposited her three Max Mara bags in her own flat and picked up the note.

'Oh hello, Margaret, do you approve of my plan or are you too tired?'

'No, it's a good idea. I've not been out once for dinner.'

They took a taxi to a small place across the Seine in Neuilly which offered Provençal specialities. Ted had no difficulty steering them into a corner table where they would not be overheard. Margaret was tucking into a tomato and goat's cheese salad when Ted shifted from smalltalk to his real business.

'Margaret, Ray told me about this business this afternoon.'

'Yes, I'd gone out for a stroll, gone to clear my head,' she tried to respond as calmly as possible.

'Ray's taken it into his head that you might be seeing someone – here in Paris.'

Margaret could not stop herself blushing. Then she ran a hand through her hair and took a quaff of wine. 'Well, Ray must be off his trolley then.'

'You must forgive him his professional suspicion – we all have our nightmares about what could happen if this all went wrong.'

'It's not just professional suspicion, Ted.' She had decided it was time to counter-attack. 'Ray has been making passes at me and I've told him I'm just not interested.'

'I see.' Lofting felt intense relief. He did not want to believe that she was doing something so stupid as seeing a Frenchman, let alone betraying the operation. 'I have your assurance then that there's no substance to his charge?'

'Of course!'

Lofting reached into his jacket pocket and passed an air ticket across to her. 'Margaret, this is a ticket for Air France to Geneva tomorrow morning at eight twenty-five, you're booked from there Swissair to London under your British cover name: it's a pre-paid ticket.'

Margaret felt suddenly overwhelmed – she was off the operation. Within hours they would probably be searching her things, checking her computer and the phones she used. How would she ever contact BB again? She felt her self-control slipping and tears begin to surge over her eyelids.

'For God's sake, Mags! Don't take it like that!'

She tossed her head to one side, trying stupidly to hide her emotion: 'I'm finished I suppose . . .'

'No, no,' Lofting countered a little half-heartedly. 'You're tired – you've been giving 110 per cent for months now. I want you to have a rest. Go home: visit your dad, see your friends. Come back in forty-eight hours or seventy-two hours – I'll tell you when the coast is clear. I'll be going back to Blighty myself tomorrow or the day after.'

'I can come back?'

'Let's just wait and see – there's only a week or so of the analytical phase left; there may be no point in you coming back.'

'Ted, don't insult my intelligence.'

'I'm sorry, my dear.' Lofting looked down slightly ashamed. 'It's best to just let things blow over. It'll probably be all right for you to come back in two or three days. Nobody except you, me and Ray knows about this, but now he's made an accusation I have to take it seriously. I know it's rough on you, but you have no idea of the sort of pressures that this operation generates – it all boils down to maximum deniability.' Ted found the possibility that she might have been carrying on an affair truly horrifying – if their investigation discovered it, they would have to get her out of the way, and keep her out of the way for as long as POLYP continued. They couldn't put her in jail. He had heard tell of one or two employees who were considered security risks in the past being posted to remote outstations. He wondered about whether they could send Margaret to the new GCHQ station in the middle of a desert in northern Australia. They would have to keep her there for years. The thought that he might have to send her into this kind of exile chilled him, but he knew there might be no other way of protecting the operation.

* * *

Margaret excused herself from any more dinner and
said she wanted to walk back to the flat. Ted politely but
firmly insisted on accompanying her. When she fell into
her bed it was a wretched, sleepless night before she
had to get up at six thirty. Time and again the same
thoughts bounced around her head: Ray Skinner, that
little shit . . . Why did I have to work for GCHQ? . . .
I'm going to resign as soon as I decently can . . . Why
can't I just have Bernard's love and be done with all of
these bastards?

Chapter Twenty-Seven

Things moved very swiftly in Paris that next morning. As Margaret sat in the departure lounge at Charles de Gaulle clutching her Spanish passport in the name of Pilar Carrizosa, a man from MI6's Security Department was on his way into town in a taxi.

Ray Skinner met the SIS man, Philip, at Flat 273 in the block at La Defense. Philip was a hawkish-looking, scarily thin Security Officer in his mid-thirties who brushed aside all of Ray's attempts to make small-talk.

'Look, there's just one of me, so I'm not going to take the place apart, understand?' His manner was public school and if Margaret would have approved of one thing as the molehunter donned his surgeon's gloves and began going through all her things, it was the way Philip talked to Ray Skinner as a complete inferior. The MI6 man was observant enough to spot Skinner's interest in Margaret's knicker drawer, so he turned and said, 'This is going to take a couple of hours, so be a good chap and make us both some coffee, eh?'

By the time Margaret had reached Geneva she had a plan. It was vital that she stop BB sending her any messages, since she could only assume that they would log into her desktop in her absence. An answer had presented itself in her in-flight magazine – a new Nokia gizmo which was a mobile phone mated with a personal organiser which allowed Internet access. The manufacturers called it a Communicator. It worked anywhere in Europe – the only problem was that if Bourrat did get the French authorities to try and trace her, it would be much less secure than the re-mailing system used at Hamsin. She didn't care any more: she would take the risk. Buying herself this piece of high tech might take hours – or rather learning how to use it would – and Bourrat would arrive in his office any minute, she was used to his routine. Something swifter was needed to stop him sending her a message. Margaret eyed a phone box. She knew his direct-line number by heart. Could she risk it? One thing was sure – the Swiss had always been bloody uncooperative when she had wanted GCHQ favours in the past. The greater risk was allowing Bourrat to reply to her come-on message: 'Tell me about your kids'.

'Bourrat,' he said smoothly as he picked up the phone.

'It's me, the Voltaire fan.'

Bernard's eyes shot towards his computer – he had only come in a few moments ago and hadn't even turned it on. His voice however betrayed nothing but a suitably muted desire: 'You've decided to accept my lunch invitation!'

'I haven't – not just yet. I just rang to ask a favour.'

Bourrat thought to himself: 'She isn't French!' – the grammar might be flawless but there was definitely some accent: 'Of course, I owe you a big one.'

'Don't send me any messages at the old E-mail address: I'll contact you from a new one soon.'

Until then his tone had been friendly, playful, but now he could sense desperation in her voice. 'Of course, that's no favour! I'll wait for you to contact me. Are you in some sort of trouble?'

'Just a minor drama at the office.'

Bourrat could hear the echoing ambience of the phone box: 'Where are you?'

'Never you mind,' she said in a cheeky way. 'Take care of yourself, goodbye.'

Before he could say another word the line was dead. Bourrat often recorded calls, but cursed his stupidity at not recording this one. He had been too flustered to think of it. Jules hadn't mentioned putting a bug on his phone either. Bourrat replayed it all in his head. Her accent – was it German, Scandinavian perhaps? Could it have been English? She knew his direct-line number. Enough people knew that, he reflected. It wasn't like her knowing the details of the President's speech. Did she sound neurotic? Nervous – but still she had shown a certain humour at the end of the call. Throughout the morning he would think of little other than the call, the message which he then promptly read from his screen, and returned to the central question of the past week: who on earth was this woman?

A little later that day a pair of experts from the DST came over to sweep Bourrat's office for bugs. The two DST-types appeared in rather comical jumpsuits and para boots while BB was out at an appointment. They spent a couple of hours checking for electronic emissions, taking apart various bits of office furniture and poking endoscopes into various nooks and crannies. Bernard saw the team leader briefly as they were packing up their paraphernalia. 'You're all clear, nothing suspicious,' the moustachioed DST-type announced.

'Could there be something on the line?'

'*C'est impossible, Monsieur Bourrat*, the line is ultra-secure. All of the exchanges on the new system are checked every month for interference. You probably know about *TONNANT*: it's fibre optic, impossible to tap – it's the best system in the world!'

'Very reassuring, thank you.'

As Bourrat made himself comfortable at his desk and arranged the yellow sticky message labels in order of which calls he would return first, he overheard voices in the corridor outside. Eventually he detected the gruff, Alsatian-accented Jules Lacroix. There was a tap on the door. He shouted, 'Come in, Jules.'

'Everything is clear.'

'Yes, they told me. I suppose there's some innocent explanation.'

Bourrat was becoming uncomfortable with this whole business and his role in it. To his consternation he saw that his friend looked more worried not less.

'Maybe. Maybe not. We've tried to trace that E-mail address. Our experts think the message went through a re-mailer, maybe more than one. The last address is a big commercial server, the billing information tells us nothing. It's a little suspicious.'

'So you won't find her through messages?'

'No, you need to get her to a meeting.'

Margaret went into Bayswater to browse among the electronic stores before heading for Paddington and the train home. She bought one of the new Nokia gizmos with her own credit card – being slightly surprised when the company authorised it. The machine came with a free Internet connection offer – one month in which she could use up to ten hours. A kind sales assistant also provided her with another company's free introductory offer. Margaret did not envisage that she would need more than one month using this new connection – therefore she would never be billed. If she had to carry on using it, she could simply switch to the second free offer and notify BB of another new E-Mail address.

Her first call was to Bella Crewe. Happily her old friend was willing and able to come and see her that evening in Cheltenham. Above all, Margaret wanted to stay busy so she did not worry too much.

When they met, Bella was full of beans as usual and managed to deflect Margaret's anxiety until well after they had repaired to the Rajput.

'I didn't tell you! I've got myself a new fella,' Bella announced.

'We've been talking for over an hour and you tell me this now?'

Bella adopted a husky *femme fatale* voice: 'So many foolish creatures are drawn into my web of seduction, dear.'

'Vital stats?'

'Micky. Toyboy. Very energetic!'

'Tell me more!'

'Magsie, he made my eyes water.'

'No!' Margaret spluttered into her beer.

'He's just a sweet boy, really. Came around to put in my new carpet, and ended up laying both of us. Twenty-seven, married young, no kids. It's just a bit of fun really.'

Margaret wanted to tell her friend about Jonathan, the Tank. She didn't though: she didn't feel able to share toyboy confessions, even with her best friend. Especially with her best friend: Bella might have died of shock. Anyway, she felt recounting her night of lust in a cheap hotel would be disloyal to Bernard.

Bella could see her deep in thought. 'Confession of

your own coming up, my dear Magserella?'

'You read me too easily.' She smiled self-consciously, a lover's smile with her head tilted forward and eyes looking up.

'Dooooo tell Auntie Bella!'

'I'm in love.'

'Good start!' Bella was almost beside herself: 'I'm so excited for you!'

'It's very early days, Bella.'

'Tell me everything.'

'It's tricky because it's connected with work . . .'

'Oh God! Don't tease! Tell and then kill me afterwards if you have to!'

'No, it's all tricky. His wife died. He's an older man, but very attractive,' Mags seemed to be going through a mental list of things she felt it was OK to tell Bella, 'good SOH, understanding . . .'

'Does he have a brother?'

'It's not at all simple though.'

'Why not, darling?'

'He's foreign, that makes it tricky with work.'

'Tell them to fuck off!'

'It's not like that, Bella.'

'Have you . . .'

'No! I said, it's very early days.'

'How many dates?'

Margaret was tempted to invent a fabulous evening on the town with Bernard but didn't want to deceive her friend. 'We haven't met.'

'Darling?' Bella's tone betrayed her concern.

'We've talked on the phone; we exchange a lot of E-mails . . . You must think I've gone potty!'

'No.'

'I haven't gone potty. I know we're right for one

another. I don't want to say any more for the moment.'

'OK. I'm very excited and I hope it all works out – but please, Mags, don't get yourself hurt, because you're not a rough old bruiser like me.'

Margaret smiled. Inside her head she struggled to suppress the heresy that kept gnawing away at her – that Bernard might only be communicating with her to try and smoke her out for the French spooks.

Colette, Margaret's flatmate, knew nothing of her sudden return to the UK as she spent her day working at Hamsin. Margaret had left a note on the kitchen table when she went out, but her American colleaue had not seen it. Colette's day proved to be a miserable one. Just before lunch George summoned her downstairs to see Pierre Moutet, the young salesman for the printing firm, and this made her intensely nervous.

'How are you?' Moutet asked self-confidently. 'I just thought I'd drop in a rate card for our spring promotion – we're open now, have you seen our shop?'

'I haven't, no,' Colette replied gravely.

'Drop in, we'd love to show you our operation.'

'Yes, of course, but I'm afraid I don't see us making any orders.'

'The Aston Martin's gone then?'

Colette was struck silent. She didn't even know what an Aston Martin was.

'What a beautiful machine!'

'Yes, yes, I'm afraid I don't know much about the cars themselves.'

'Is there any chance I could have a look around some time? Maybe go down to the underground garage, see some of the other cars – just as a favour?' Moutet looked up at her with imploring eyes.

'Yes, well . . . perhaps . . . it won't be possible today, but perhaps another time.'

When Moutet left, there was another nervous meeting with Birnbaum and Lofting about whether the salesman was a French spy. Birnbaum insisted the background checks on his firm had all gone OK. They all tried to convince themselves there was no reason to suspect he was anything more than an energetic salesman with in interest in cars.

Early that evening, when Max Kampfner and another American analyst were the only people left in the Hamsin offices, Ted Lofting, Ray Skinner and an MI6 Technical Officer called Derek went into the working room and logged into Margaret's computer. The MI6 man spent an hour meandering around her files and looking for traces of anything untoward. Ted and Ray retired to the kitchenette, where some cans of McCaffrey's had been secreted in the fridge. Eventually Derek came down and joined them.

'Looks clean to me.' He popped a beer and took a long draw straight from the can. Derek was on a very different wavelength to Philip – much more Skinner's wavelength.

'Could she have erased anything compromising?' Ray asked.

'Yes, she could have. You gents probably know we have means of looking at residual energy on hard disks, but it requires us to take the disk unit out. We send it up to your CESG boys at Cheltenham as a matter of fact.'

'That's not possible,' Lofting said firmly. 'We don't want Uncle Sam picking up on that kind of thing: it's out of the question.'

'Absolutely, boss – it's your call. It would take a few

days anyway and it's not 100 per cent reliable.'

'No, Derek, thank you, we won't do that. I didn't see this as a completely exhaustive search, it's just a check for signs of anything suspicious. She's too valuable to us for me to give her the ninth degree on the basis of the evidence we've got.'

'I had to report suspicious activity,' Ray countered defensively.

'Of course you did, Ray. No reproach intended.' This wasn't quite true. Ted felt sorry for putting Margaret through it, even though he knew he had to.

'There was one odd thing . . .' Derek observed.

'Yes?'

'She seems to spend a lot of time listening to a target called E/7 on her interception log.'

'Really?' Skinner said almost hopefully.

'Yes, well she would do,' Lofting checked him, knowing that Skinner and Derek could not be told who E/7 was. 'That target is someone of particular interest to this operation – our customers regard him as a very high priority target.'

Derek drained his beer and made his excuses, leaving Ray and Ted together.

'I hope you don't think I've made a plonker of myself.'

'No. You saw something suspicious. We had a duty to investigate.'

'That's how I feel too.'

'One thing I must say,' Lofting fixed Skinner in his stare, 'is that Ms Reynolds believed your action was connected with her refusal of advances she alleges you made—'

'She should be so—'

'Bear with me, Ray. I consider Margaret an honourable woman. I expect a pretty girl like her doesn't have

261

to make up stories of advances. Whatever did or did not happen is entirely between the two of you – you're both single; I see no security risk. I am going to ask Margaret to come back onto this operation and I expect you to behave with complete professionalism about everything that's happened.'

'I never asked her to—'

'Ray! Save it! Just don't let this thing build into a feud between you.'

'Fair enough,' Ray replied through gritted teeth and downed another swig of bitter.

It was past 11 p.m. when Dan Birnbaum sauntered into the analysts' room on the first floor for one of his occasional late-night chats with Max Kampfner. The two men reserved these meetings for the discussion of matters which they didn't want their British colleagues to overhear and they knew, Brits being Brits, that they would never usually be working after 7 or 8 p.m.

'I've done an E-mail for Meade with the latest bid information on the Saudi order.'

'Uh-huh,' Birnbaum nodded seriously.

'The Brits were ahead of us in finding Bourrat's lines, but of course it's irrelevant with this software.' Birnbaum smiled nervously at the compliment as Kampfner got into his stride: 'We've got a pretty complete picture now, we might as well move onto the other bilaterally sensitive targets before we go to Phase Two.'

'Good work, Max.' Birnbaum leaned back in his office chair and rubbed his eyes. 'I'm bushed, I'm going back to the apartments if that's all.'

'There was something else, Dan.'

'Yeah?'

'It's the darndest thing! I don't know what to think about it.'

'What have you got?'

'I put two and two together, but I just can't believe it adds up.' Kampfner handed Birnbaum a set of head-phones and tapped away on the screen. 'This is a call Bourrat made to an old friend of his, another high ranking *fonctionnaire* called Rémy.'

Birnbaum heard some smalltalk about plans for the weekend, Rémy's children's school studies. He could only pick up about half of it, since his French was of the basic conversational variety. Then the question:

'Any more from your mystery admirer?'

'Yes. A call this morning . . .' Bourrat sounded uneasy. 'It's all turned into a security thing now.'

'Oh?'

'Yes, so we've got—'

'Sure, sure.'

'Nothing concrete yet, and they reckon the phone's OK.'

'Right.' Rémy sounded relieved.

'She's foreign, that's pretty clear. So they're a bit worried, Jules's lot. I just sort of feel guilty for dropping her in it, whoever it is, but I suppose it's suspicious that she knew so much about me.'

'Well it's probably best that it's checked out. I'm sure there'll be an innocent—'

'Yes, so am I.'

As Birnbaum removed the headset, Kampfner looked at him with an air of intense expectancy. Eventually, the NSA boss shrugged and said, 'So?'

'So?' Kampfner seemed almost disgusted that Birnbaum was not following his hunch: 'So I checked the log of incoming calls that came through on Bourrat's private line. There was one just after nine thirty this morning, from a box at Geneva airport. It was his first call of the day. He spent most of the morning with the President. There were only two others between that one and his conversation with Rémy and we know exactly who both of those were.'

Birnbaum still could not see what Kampfner was driving at and was becoming a little irritable. 'So you're saying the mystery woman made the call from Geneva.'

'*Tochno!*' Kampfner used the Russian for 'exactly'.

'Max, it's late, and whatever you're driving at, I'm too tired to get it.'

'OK, add in two other things,' Kampfner's eyes were burning with a scary intensity. 'First: this morning my UK opposite number had to make a short-notice return trip to Cheltenham; I heard the Brit analysts saying they don't know when she'll be back. Second: Lofting, Skinner and some guy I've never seen before were in here earlier going through her computer files and E-mails.'

Birnbaum shook his head and stood up from his office chair, 'Max, you must have done some real bad acid at Stanford if you're saying what I think you're saying.'

'It's not conclusive I grant—'

'Max, it's paranoia. How many women in Paris do you think might fall into the category of foreign, flew via Geneva this morning and have access to E-mails? Ten thousand? Five thousand?'

Kampfner was not cowed by his boss's scorn – almost the opposite. 'How many of them would know a lot about the presidential adviser's life? One, two?'

'You didn't record the call from Geneva?'

'No, you know it's not possible to do that: we haven't got the people to listen to everything and the Geneva number wasn't one of the ones programmed into Wasp for automatic recording.'

'So what the fuck am I meant to do about this?' Birnbaum thought aloud.

'Ask the Brits if there's a problem with her?'

'I can't ask the Brits! Bourrat is their responsibility. Remember the I Plan!' Birnbaum began shaking his head again: 'It's too kooky, Max – you're saying Margaret has fallen for this guy just through listening to him?'

'Who knows? I just think that if it's coincidence, it's the strangest coincidence imaginable.'

'OK, leave it with me.' Birnbaum seemed to have decided on something. 'You know something, Max?'

'What?'

'You've got some weird Goddamned head on your shoulders.'

Chapter Twenty-Eight

As Margaret drove her Fiat down towards Clifton the following morning she at last allowed herself to think about the three letters from the nursing home which had been among the pile of correspondence jamming her front door when she came home. She hadn't even opened them until late the previous evening when, after several stiff drinks with Bella, she had summoned up the courage.

The first of the letters was a reminder about overdue nursing fees. The second contained a number of re-commendations of homes which provided cheaper residential care. The final one had been the nursing equivalent of a gas board disconnection notice beginning with the ominous words, 'Since no reply has been forthcoming to our letters of . . .'

She had decided to write the home a cheque for £1,000. It was all she could afford for the moment and it would cover only a small proportion of the debt which had already run up, but she thought it was best to show willing. For a moment she wondered whether Bernard had money. She felt utter disgust at herself for that, but she just yearned for something which might provide an answer to all her problems.

When Margaret saw her father sitting alone in one of

the home's great panoramic windows it was like she had been recharged with energy.

'Hello, Dad!' she said, flinging her arms around his shoulders and kissing his cheek fervently.

This triggered a vivid memory in him, of picking Margaret up when she was a toddler – she always threw her arms around his neck. 'Ooh, you're getting heavy!' he said.

'I am,' she sniffed back a tear and laughed, 'I am. I'm sorry I've left it so long.'

'Oh, what a heavy bag of potatoes you are.'

Margaret soon realised that he would be trapped in the memory of her hug for the rest of the visit, probably for the rest of the day. The nurses had told her that the memories their Alzheimer patients recovered could be far more vivid than those of people not afflicted. They were moved to laughter, tears – sometimes abject terror – by something which might have happened fifty, sixty years earlier.

The conversation therefore consisted of Margaret, holding her father's soft hand, telling him in general detail about the last few weeks, while he continued to talk about her as a three-year-old. Eventually she said, 'I think I may have met someone new on the romance front . . .' Margaret hoped against hope that he would take this in – just as he had experienced that moment of lucidity a few months before about Peter. Instead though he said nothing and just stared ahead.

'Excuse me, Miss Reynolds?'

Margaret looked up and saw a middle-aged woman in a suit.

'Val Middleton, I'm the business manager here.'

'Yes, I expect you want to talk about money.'

★ ★ ★

The conversation took place in an office at the back of the home. Margaret was surprised when Val was reluctant to take her cheque. She had said, 'Let's be realistic – you can't really afford to maintain his care all on your own, can you?' Margaret had insisted Val take it, as settlement of some of the debt which had built up. They had agreed that Margaret would give her written instructions on which home she wished her father to be transferred to by 5th April, which was the last day of the financial year.

When she got home from Clifton, Margaret found there was a single message on her answerphone. It was the middle of the day but she felt so wretched she just wanted to curl up and go to sleep on her bed. She pressed 'play'.

'Margaret, it's Ted. I'm back at the office, got in this morning. Director issued three-line whip for his address to the troops this afternoon, so I expect I'll see you there. No problems about the operation by the way, you're free to go back after the boss's spiel if you like. Sorry about all that nonsense.'

Margaret smiled, but she was dropping. She drew the curtains, set the alarm for just after lunch and fell onto her bed. She need not have worried about the alarm because she slept for a mere fifteen minutes. She decided to switch on her new mobile phone/computer gizmo. Margaret had managed to work out how to use her free Internet offer the previous day and had sent Bernard her new electronic address. As she tapped away she was pleased to see that, sure enough, a message awaited her on the small screen.

Angel,
You asked about my children. Jacques, my oldest boy is 27 and married with a baby daughter. Gerard, 24, single and rather wild. Last seen backpacking in Indonesia! I also have a daughter, Sophie, who is 19 and still studying in Strasbourg. Of course she's the apple of my eye! Tell me about the drama when you called the other day. You know you can call any time if you want. My home number is 43-84-62-63. I live alone (do you know that?) and won't resent it, even in the early hours.
BB

Margaret smiled when she read about BB's daughter and then glanced at her watch. There was time to write a quick note back and still get to Oakley in time for the Director's big pitch on the future of GCHQ.

BB,
Nice to hear about your kids. I have got to a point in life where I don't expect to have them, although of course I'd like to be proven wrong.

Margaret paused. Was this too clumsy? Who cared! She pressed on:

There was a big flap in the office and I had to leave Paris for a few days. I think I'll be back soon. You're very sweet to be concerned, but it's just one of those things I have to muddle through. I'm at my wit's end with this job. I wish I could just resign and come and work for someone nice. Like you.

The main canteen at Oakley was packed with hundreds

of employees by the time the Director came to the front, nudging his way through the dozens who could not find chairs or tables to sit on. All of the GCHQ archetypes were there: engineers in their dirty old pullovers; cryptanalysts winking and twitching behind their specs as they battled with some mathematical conundrum; salt of the earth secretaries who had handled the most sensitive of state secrets for years without remembering any of them, and of course the linguists like Margaret and the group she stood among – generally quite well dressed for civil servants, bantering self-confidently among themselves.

The Director's presentation included vu-foils projected on a large screen. He had already run through it two or three times for senior officers and certain selected outsiders, so his patter was reasonably smooth.

'Our funding problem is shown on this graph here,' he used an extendable metal pointer for emphasis, 'given the steady reduction of our funding from the Joint Intelligence Machinery we would face a shortfall of around £70m by 1998/9 if we maintained our operations at the current level. Our task therefore is to rationalise.'

'To give us the chop,' an engineer called Paddy who was standing near the front said in a stage-whisper. Paddy had a Transport and General badge on the lapel of his jacket. He'd been one of the first to take the opportunity to join when the new government came in.

The Director heard the comment but was no ad-libber so he ploughed on with his presentation. 'We can do a lot of this with natural wastage, investment in IT and sound management practice. I have called my strategy for the next three years, Smaller but Better.'

'Smaller but Bitter more like,' Paddy chipped in and savoured the sniggers of his colleagues.

'Really! Please pay attention – this is important.'

As the speech wore on, Ted Lofting, who had arrived late and was standing near the back, strained to hear. He had missed the Heads of Division presentation because of Operation POLYP. He knew of course that the Director would be announcing the 'contractorisation' of various bits of the empire – outsiders were cheaper. He knew also that the staff would hear for the first time about the planned move to a new site, where the sprawling blocks of Oakley and Benhall could be brought together. His ears pricked up however when he saw the vu-foil marked 'Projected Reductions' appear.

'We believe we can reduce our engineering support by 176 personnel, secretarial by 214, general clerical and managerial by around 100. I would stress a number of points here: no cuts in our frontline of linguists, cryptanalysts – there may even be a modest increase. There'll be a generous redundancy package for those who do have to go and a regrading exercise to increase the pay of those who take on greater duties.'

Margaret and Brenda Skuse exchanged worried smiles across the room.

'The other thing I would say is that any pain will be borne all the way up the organisation. I envisage streamlining two heads of division posts and quite a few in the sections.'

When he got back to his block, Ted called Brenda in from her cramped outer office. 'Brenda, I want to ask you something. It's all a bit sensitive but, please, take my word for it, it concerns a matter which I cannot fully explain to you.'

'I see.' She did not appear at all fazed.

'How much do you know about Margaret Reynolds's private life?'

Brenda was clearly uncomfortable. Her reply was a noncommittal, 'This and that, you know.'

'Do you know if she has a boyfriend?'

'Oh no! Not since things broke up with Peter a few months back. I think that hit her very hard. She should have the pick of the field really – she's such a lovely girl, you know. I don't just mean looking.'

'Indeed. Does she have any financial worries?'

'Not that she discusses with me.' Brenda seemed to warm a bit, suspecting that her boss was simply worried about her friend's welfare. 'She has hinted about concerns about her father's nursing care. You know he's got—'

'Alzheimer's, yes I know. Where is he? Do you know?'

'It's a place down near Bristol – Clifton I think.'

'Thanks, Brenda – keep mum, won't you?'

Ted went home to a cold house with nothing in the fridge. During the previous few days, Emma had been fending for herself or getting fed at friends' houses. Sara had been only an intermittent presence, and had told Emma she was staying several nights with a friend in Gloucester. This was what she had said anyway, to explain the fact that she had packed a suitcase and removed a good many of her clothes.

Ted had just resolved to get a take-away curry when the phone went.

'Ted, it's Dan.'

'Dear chap! You're back in the UK I take it?'

'Yeah, I'm in my usual crummy hotel. Are you busy tonight?'

Ted felt so tired, but he didn't want to be rude. 'I'm

not as a matter of fact. Sara's gone off God knows where, so we can have a bachelor evening!'

'OK, I'll be there in about an hour.'

Birnbaum was initially reluctant to go along with a curry, but Ted managed to convince him it would be 'an edifying cross-cultural experience'. They had rustled up some cans of Carlsberg and the Englishman had been totally surprised when Dan had said, 'You reckon we got time for a frigate fight?'

'Certainly,' he smiled, 'certainly.'

Birnbaum was not a good loser. Since their last tabletop scrap, he had got his secretary in Maryland to Fedex a book about nineteenth-century naval warfare to him. He had also devoured a couple of Patrick O'Brians he had picked up during his many passages through Heathrow. He wanted to beat Lofting, but he also wanted to get him as relaxed and unsuspecting as possible.

They had chosen to re-fight *Serapis* versus *Bonhomme Richard* – an engagement from the Revolutionary War which the American had won within sight of the English coast. Despite the historical outcome, Ted felt reasonably confident. At an early stage, though, Birnbaum had managed to push between *Serapis* and the wind; he had then come bearing down on the British ship, prompting Lofting to discharge a rather ineffective opening broadside at long range.

'That's what you get from pressed men!' Birnbaum said triumphantly. 'At least we only ever used volunteer crews.'

'Um? Oh yes,' Lofting was lost in thought about his next move.

Dan inched the *Bonhomme Richard* towards its quarry.

'Are we going to be seeing Margaret back in Paris soon?'

'Margaret?' Lofting tapped the variable into the computer for his second broadside. 'You've got a damaged foretop and five casualties. Margaret, yes she's going back tomorrow I think.'

'Sexy lady.'

'Yes, very bright too.'

'Does she have a regular guy?'

'You're not tall enough,' Ted teased while registering Birnbaum's interest and wondering why, if he really fancied her, he had left it to such a late stage of the operation to declare his hand. 'Anyway, she is a little old for you.'

'She's real charming,' Birnbaum slewed his frigate around to present its broadside to the *Serapis* at alarmingly close range, 'but you never have any idea what's really going on in her head.'

Lofting now strongly suspected Dan's motives for beginning this line of conversation. 'Oh, I think she probably just wants what most of us want really.'

Birnbaum's head was buried in the rulebook. 'OK, so I get the modifier for double shotted, first broadside . . .' He entered the figures into the computer: 'Well, I make that twenty-four casualties, four guns taken out – let's just check for mast damage,' he tapped in more figures, 'and your mizzen's come down.'

Lofting blanched. The real affair had been a three-and-a-half-hour slugging match – he was worried that his defeat would take considerably less time. Ted realised that grapeshot would be most effective at such close range, but he had loaded cannonballs, not realising how quickly the *Bonhomme Richard* would come down on him. Inwardly, he cursed his error. 'You've been swotting up, haven't you, Dan?'

'Knowledge is power, my friend!'

The next broadside from Birnbaum's ship knocked out the *Serapis*'s rudder, which was bad luck, really bad luck. It was then only a matter of time before the American turned across Lofting's bows and delivered a crushing rake along the length of the floundering British vessel. Ted shook his head: 'Have you been swotting up on Margaret too?'

'Me? No way!'

Lofting found the denial a little too forceful for someone who might really harbour a romantic interest. About ten minutes later, following a second rake, the *Serapis* struck its colours, the game was over. The two men parted and Lofting went upstairs, pained with worry.

As he brushed his teeth he wondered whether he had been right to put Margaret back on the operation. She already had her tickets – she was going back early the next morning. Dan had definitely been probing, and if the Americans had their own reasons to be suspicious then there really was something wrong. Ted tried to comfort himself with the thought that he might simply have been trying to discover why she had gone away for two days at such a critical time in the operation. He even said aloud, 'Yes, that's probably it.' He could not suppress his anxiety though. Did the Americans have evidence of their own? If they thought Margaret might compromise this hugely expensive operation, why weren't they sharing it?

As Ted brushed his teeth, he could little suspect that his wife was less than a mile away, meeting Oscar in their usual spot by the football fields behind GCHQ Oakley.

She had driven over from Gloucester in a state of

some excitement. It was the night she and Oscar would leave Cheltenham together and start a new life. She began to suspect something was amiss when she saw him arrive by car. They had arranged that he would come by taxi and they would leave in Ted and Sara's Rover. As he climbed into it she looked at Oscar's rather grim expression and asked, 'Something wrong?'

'No.'

'Are you sure?'

'Oh, I don't know, I'm just a bit worried about Steven.'

'You're saying you're not going to come away, aren't you?'

'He's got his A level retakes this summer – I just don't want to be the reason for him to fail.'

'Oscar, you shit!' Her head snapped forward and she stared at the dark hill behind the sports fields.

'When the exams are over—'

'Oh, don't be absurd! You haven't the courage to leave her, have you?' Her eyes were filling with tears.

'Trust me, I'll tell Monica I want a divorce as soon as Steven's—'

'No you won't! What have you done to me? I've told Ted about us, I've burned my bridges, Oscar!'

He looked suddenly more concerned, 'You said you hadn't told him specifically about me . . .'

'What difference does it make for me? I've asked him for a divorce!'

'I'm sorry . . . I just feel hopeless now.'

'Why are you talking about yourself? I'm the one with no way back!'

'I'm sure we can—'

'—Oh forget it, Oscar! Let's just forget it, I've made my bed so now I'll have to lie in it.'

'You still want to meet, don't you?' His voice had assumed an almost childish tone.

'Oh, don't be pathetic, Oscar!'

A few moments later, he got out of the car and strolled the short distance to his own vehicle. Sara drove back to Gloucester, stopping only to buy a bottle of Gordon's on the way, and downed one gin after another until she passed out in an armchair at 3 a.m.

Chapter Twenty-Nine

The following day began in typically miserable winter's fashion. Margaret, Ted and Dan all had to start journeys back to Paris by different routes. It might have been her lower rank or it might have been coincidence, but Margaret's route was the most roundabout and time consuming. She had to get up at 5 a.m. to make a train to London, then Gatwick, flight to Basel followed by TGV to Paris. Still she was happy. It was raining, her mouth tasted awful, her head was groggy, her limbs felt heavy from weeks without the exercise to which they had grown accustomed, she faced hours in airports and trains – but she was high on hope. For one thing, she was going back to Paris, close to Bernard and for another, when she had switched on her mobile on the blustery platform of Cheltenham station she had found an E-mail from him.

Angel,
Yes! Come and work for me! Wait a moment. How could you work for me when we seem to share such feelings? It's so strange. You have almost all the cards. You know what I look like, what I do, even a lot about my family. And what do I know about you? Sometimes I find it so frustrating that you can't tell me more that it hurts. I was so happy after your call, so I know it

won't always be E-mails. Maybe you could send me a picture? You've got to tell me more about yourself too. Where are you from, where do you work – if not the name of the company, at least what business you're in. I don't want to be pushy, but you know a boy could die of old age!
BB

It was only once she read it for the third or fourth time that a germ of doubt which had shown itself before reappeared. Was BB trying to home in on her so she could be caught? The questions about nationality and her job seemed very suspicious. 'Where are you from?' was just a slightly disguised way of letting her know he had picked up on her foreign accent during the call from Geneva. It all seemed so dangerous now. Then again she wondered as the first glimmer of dawn touched the Oxfordshire countryside rushing past the window and lifted her spirits, wasn't everything he said true? He didn't know anything about her and what person would allow themselves to fall in love with someone who they weren't even sure they were attracted to? A different kind of doubt took over – that one day they would meet and that she would see disappointment in his eyes.

Ted Lofting managed to leave home two hours later than Margaret. It was just before seven when the phone went.

'Ted, it's Dan, I was worried you'd left already.'

'Yes, well, the driver is waiting outside.'

'Something hit me like a freight train during the night, I need to talk to you.'

'Not something about simulating the effects of naval muzzle-loaders I take it?'

'No,' Birnbaum brusquely deflected Lofting's attempt at humour, 'I thought maybe if we shared the car down to Heathrow...'

'Well, I suppose it's unlikely that DST surveillance will be watching the dropping-off points at London airport. Of course!'

As they motored down towards the M4, Birnbaum waited a surprisingly long time before sharing his worries with Lofting and only did so after he had written a note saying 'Is the driver OK?'. Lofting had simply smiled benignly and nodded.

'What hit me during the night, Ted, was that intercept of the Terry Donald material.'

'Ah yes, our ski-mad Health Secretary.'

'Would you route a live bug like that through to DGSE HQ? It's a strange way of working, don't you think?'

Lofting contemplated the proposition for a moment. 'Well, we wouldn't necessarily do things that way ... but equally there might be operational reasons for it which we're not aware of.'

'What if the only operational reason for doing it was to test the integrity of the *TONNANT* link?'

'You're suggesting a barium meal ...' Lofting's head dipped and he began rubbing his temples with his index fingers, 'which they fed to us deliberately, to see if they could detect any traces of leakage.'

'Which we provided by getting Donald to move out of his chalet,' Birnbaum was speaking in staccato bursts. 'Not that I'm implying any criticism of what you guys did. Hell no! We would have done the same.'

Lofting's only immediate response was, 'Interesting.'

'Interesting! What if they've got us by the *cojones* and

now they know it? They could be feeding us seven different shades of bullshit through that line – the whole operation could be compromised, with the geeky printing salesman coming in from time to time to make sure we're still hanging on in there digesting that crap!'

Lofting wanted to say 'calm down' but he knew this would be patronising. Birnbaum was a fearsomely bright man. His concerns had to be thrashed out. 'What are you suggesting we do about it?'

'Get everybody out within the next twenty-four hours.'

'That's a bit precipitate, isn't it? Last time we talked this through, you gave us all the good reasons why Phase One couldn't be hurried.'

'Damn it, Ted, you know the possible consequences of us getting GCHQ and NSA personnel caught there! We've got enough in Wasp now to turn the machine live. And what if the POLYP product has been disinformation from the start?'

'Let's work this through. Bugging Terry Donald's chalet is not a very efficient way of feeding us a barium meal. I can think of two ways we could have become aware of the bugging without tapping into the fibre optic cable. We could have found special facilities in the property itself, we could have—'

'I know that! But they had to do something they were sure we'd respond to.'

'Just hear me through, Dan. You imply a connection between the printing salesman and a disinformation operation, but sending him in to see us would suggest that they know almost everything – most importantly where our operational HQ is. I think if they had all that we would have been raided or received a strongly-worded diplomatic protest by now.'

'Why? Why not watch us waste our money on a compromised operation? We have to stop disseminating the POLYP product while we work this out. We may just be providing them with confirmation that it's all working.'

Stop dissemination? What was the point of POLYP if the already very small circle of people who were in on its product was reduced to zero? Although he thought Dan was panicking, Ted knew he had to tread carefully – the NSA was an equal partner in this and they could afford to junk even the most expensive operations. 'All right, let's have a temporary halt to dissemination. Let's give ourselves four days instead of eight to clear everybody out of the Hamsin office. How does that sound?'

'OK,' Birnbaum said firmly. 'You know I'd like immediate withdrawal, but OK.'

Bernard returned from a meeting with the President to find Jules Lacroix sitting in his office. The big secret policeman was wearing a shirt which was too small. It made his neck looked like someone had their hand around it. Lacroix looked up and gave a businesslike half-smile. 'Any reply yet?'

'No, no, they don't come for a day or two sometimes.' Bourrat sat behind his great desk and fussed a little with the papers he had just had signed by the chief of state. There was a part of him that hoped she would not reply since this whole business made him feel such a sneak. 'There's probably some completely innocent explanation . . .'

'Probably. But the messages are coming via one or more re-mailers, which means whoever is sending them knows how to protect their identity. We can't trace her through the messages.'

This made Bourrat feel almost relieved. 'Maybe it's just someone playing a joke.'

'Maybe. But Bernard, you know Elysée security is Elysée security. It's best that we follow this through.'

Nobody expected Margaret in the office that afternoon – it was almost 5 p.m. when she came to the end of her long journey. Still, she decided she wanted to go in and have a look around. Her arrival was greeted with insipid smiles from those beneath their headsets.

Within minutes of her logging on to her computer it had flagged up:

TARGET E/7 ON 7046/V TO FR/A26

Bernard was ringing someone in the company which was hoping to clinch the Saudi order. She immediately clicked the recording facility.

'I need to be quick, we've got a telegram going to the embassy in Riyadh tonight,' he began.

'Go ahead, no problem.'

'It's about commissions.'

'Uh huh.'

'You know I would rather talk about it face to face, but there isn't time so forgive me.' Bourrat sounded stressed, uncomfortable.

'I'm listening.'

'We've already promised our friend who left yesterday 113, yes?'

'Yes.'

'His friend, the Syrian go-between, gets forty-two?'

'*Exacte.*'

Margaret knew enough about the order to guess who the individuals were and to know that the sums being mentioned were in hundreds of millions of dollars. She felt intensely sorry for BB. He was obviously an honourable man, but he had got himself mixed up in this vast plan of bribery.

'You say we have to transfer 10 per cent of the money for the Syrian and Prince M. before we know whether we've won the order, yes?'

'Their necessary expenses . . . in lobbying for us,' the man from the aircraft company said blithely.

'Eight million? That's a lot of wining and dining . . .'

'That's life – the British and Americans will be doing the same.'

'Yes well, let's just hope it works. I'll get the bank to send it on Monday.'

'Good. I'm confident.'

As the call ended Ted Lofting appeared in the analysts' room. Margaret looked up at him and gave him a broad smile. He looked strangely uncomfortable and distracted.

As he came nearer, she said in a hushed voice, 'Ted, I've just got a brilliant intercept – the entire payoff list for that Saudi order: amounts, who gets them, the works! I should E-mail MoD straightaway, they'll be cock-a-hoop.'

'Margaret, step into the corridor with me for a moment, will you?'

She followed him into the stairwell which led down to the showroom. Her pulse had begun to quicken – he wasn't going to send her home again, was he? She tried to hide her consternation and simply said, 'What's up?'

'You're not to send anything to London. The Americans have asked for a halt to all dissemination—'

'That's crazy! We've got the crown jewels we need to win the Saudi order, we can stuff them!'

'I know, I know, it's a mess,' Lofting had never seen her so animated, 'but they're very worried that we've been compromised.'

She felt anxiety welling up within her: 'Is this to do with me?'

'No, no,' Lofting regarded his denial as only slightly wide of the mark. 'They're worried about that Terry Donald ski chalet business. They think it may have been a barium meal.'

'But that would mean everything we'd done here was compromised?'

'It would, Mags, and I personally don't believe Dan's hypothesis on this stands up. But the decision has been made to stop all dissemination at least until Tuesday, by which time we hope to have gone to Phase Two.'

Tuesday? It was Friday now. She just had a few days left. She tried to sort out her feelings – she had to say something to Ted. 'Well, we'll have to work like billyo to get things done by then.'

'Indeed we will.' Lofting smiled a weak smile.

Margaret was flagging, so she fetched a cup of coffee from the kitchenette. It was time to brief her analysts to get a move on: there would be long days ahead for all of them. In the garage below the tunnel had already been sealed and the four Ulstermen were in their last few hours on the site. They had chopped the power supply and intercept lines into the wall, taking them up to street level. The second cover business, *Radio Télé Outre Mer*, would soon take over. Nobody at Hamsin had been briefed about RTOM, since they had no need to know. It would operate from a premises a few hundred metres away and was far more of a real business than the car showroom – its trade would be relaying French

TV and radio to ex-pats in the UK and elsewhere. The key intercepts, selected by the Wasp computer concealed in its offices would be sent to England as the digital 'watermark' inside the stream of information which made up its TV pictures. The watermark was meant as a protection against piracy, but in this case it allowed RTOM to send over a considerable amount of information within the relayed TV signals. Birnbaum and Lofting were very proud of the ingenuity of this scheme – or at least they had been until the poison of doubt began undermining their faith in the whole operation.

Margaret returned to her PC to find that it had recorded another of Bourrat's conversations in her absence. She felt briefly frightened – why had this happened? Then she realised that she had left the recording facility engaged when Ted summoned her onto the landing. She clicked on a button which said 'Review'.

Bourrat was speaking to a woman called Véronique who, it soon became clear, was a close relative, presumably his sister. They mainly chatted about her children until she asked him, 'What have you got planned for the weekend?'

'I'm staying in the city. I'll do what I usually do on the anniversary,' he replied grimly.

'Of course, I'm sorry I didn't remember.'

'Don't be silly: it's so many years now, why should you?'

'Well, we'll be thinking of you tomorrow evening.'

'Thanks.'

'Lots of love, Bernard.'

'Bye.'

Margaret decided it was some kind of pilgrimage in memory of his wife. Was it the anniversary of their meeting, marriage, her death? It was a deeply romantic and moving idea, whichever it was. She wanted to be with him. She checked herself: that would be the last thing he'd want if he was remembering his wife. Her mind went around again: why couldn't she help him through such a miserable weekend? She tried hard to drive the idea away. Margaret picked up her handbag and went out to the loo. She sat down, placed the little machine on her lap and started tapping away on its tiny keys.

BB,
Back in Paris, still holding all the cards! You want to know something really sad? I've become frightened to tell you more about myself or see you in case you don't like me. Maybe I'll post you a picture. I'll be thinking about you over the weekend, what will you be doing?
Your Angel.

Bourrat was working late that Friday, so he was there when Margaret's message flashed up on his screen at 7.45 p.m. Just after he had put the phone down to the executive at the aircraft company, the coin had finally dropped about the President's speech. For days he had simply forgotten about the conversation with Michel, the other man working on the Saudi contract. He had mentioned the reference to Voltaire during that conversation. Bernard couldn't remember whether he had got the name of Cacambo right or wrong, but he assumed he had made a mistake and cursed his stupidity in not making the connection sooner. The sweep of his office had been clear, which meant the British, the Americans – who knew who else – might be bugging the aircraft company. There was so much of this industrial espionage these days and so much at stake in the Saudi order. He turned to his computer and clicked on the mouse to send a return message. He wanted to tell her to piss off, but he stopped himself. What if she was genuine? Really! A young woman flattering a powerful man – it was the oldest ploy. But, he reflected, if her aim was to ensnare him, why didn't she just get on with it? She was the one who never wanted to meet. The Saudi order was so close to being announced, it could come any day. If seduction was on the cards it should have happened a long time ago. Bernard turned away from the computer momentarily and looked at his wife's photo. If the woman sending the messages was listening to him but afraid of getting caught by her own people, that would explain everything. Bourrat decided not to tell Lacroix about his hunch that the leak might be at the aircraft company, the DST could do their own detective work. If he was going to protect her, though, he couldn't use his own E-mail access. Bourrat got up and padded down the corridor. He saw that the secretary to the transport adviser's door was unlocked and that her computer was on. He flicked the mouse and her Orangina screen saver disappeared. 'Send E-mail'.

Angel,
Send the picture, don't be frightened. What can go so wrong? If things are meant to be, they will be. As for me, I shall do my usual things – read a little, squash on Sunday, perhaps see some friends on Sunday evening. Tomorrow I shall do something I do once a year and drink a toast to my late wife at *Wagrams*. It's important not to forget. It's also important not to get trapped in the past as I think I

did for a few years. What of your plans?
BB

By the time the message came through, Margaret was
already in bed and about to turn off the light. She had
decided to switch on the Nokia one more time, just in
case he had replied. She didn't even notice it didn't
have the usual address 'BB@ely' on it. As she called up
the E-mail, she snuggled up under her duvet feeling like
a child the night before Christmas. She was so touched
with his candour that a tear raced down her face as she
turned out the light. Perhaps tomorrow they would
meet.

Chapter Thirty

Margaret knew she had taken a risk. There was a *Wagrams* café on the Boulevard Saint Germain on the Left Bank and there was a *Wagram* restaurant in the 17th Arrondissement. She had positioned herself across the Boulevard from the café in a bookshop. She could not see all of the tables, which were wrapped around the building and into a side street, but could see most of them. After forty minutes of standing there, the owner closed up and shooed her out. As she stepped onto the broad street she felt exposed, insignificant, vulnerable. The cool air and anticipation sent a shiver through her. She had spent the day at the office and told Colette she was going window-shopping on her way back to the flat. Throughout the time she had spent trying to complete the files of which phone numbers should or should not be intercepted when the computer was left to its own devices, she had been in an unbearable state of apprehension.

She made her way to a crossing where the tide of traffic had temporarily been halted and went over to the same side of the street as the café. As she was approaching a phone booth she had spotted, Bourrat appeared. He was going through the doors and being shown to a table – she didn't know where he had come from, she'd missed his arrival.

Bourrat was parked inside the warmth of the café but with a fine view of the Boulevard through its plate-glass windows.

A middle-aged waiter in a black jacket with a caricature Frenchman's moustache approached, '*Oui, monsieur?*'

'A glass of Chablis and a kir please.'

For a moment the waiter looked as if he might ask a question, but he had been working at *Wagrams* for over fifteen years and he suddenly remembered the man who would order two drinks and leave one of them untouched. '*Oui, monsieur!*' he said emphatically.

Margaret stood in the phone booth no more than twenty feet from Bourrat as the Chablis was placed in front of him and the kir by the empty chair opposite. She felt overwhelmed by sympathy for him and began cursing herself. You can't start crying again! Not here on the Saint Germain! Margaret felt as unwanted and as conspicuous as a guest at a séance. She decided to head for the metro. Moving from the phone booth, she passed right in front of Bourrat; only the glass separated them. He did not immediately notice her; he was lost in thought. She stopped – her handbag was open for some reason. She closed the clasp. Her eyes flicked up to him. He was looking at her. Recognition. It gave her a feeling in her stomach like a fast trip over the world's biggest hump-backed bridge. She broke eye contact almost immediately and began to march once more towards the metro. As Margaret disappeared into the evening throng, Bourrat's hand reached out and touched the cold glass.

After seeing Margaret, Bourrat had felt awash with adrenalin. He had drained his glass and asked the waiter for twenty Gitanes. He hadn't smoked for more than twenty years. He took a long drag of the heavy tobacco and felt good. What was so striking about her? She was striking, that was certain, but it was something in her stare – the intense vulnerability and loneliness in her eyes. He wanted desperately to talk, but the only way to do that was via bloody messages. If he went to the office, his arrival on a Saturday night would be highly suspicious; the whole place would be locked up so he couldn't use someone else's screen again. Anyway, she might not get the message until Monday. He didn't care, he had to write.

Bernard had paid up and was walking down the Saint Germain, drawing on his second cigarette, when he had a brainwave. There was a café called *Micro-Monde* where computer nerds hung out. It was one of those cybercafés full of PCs. He flagged down a taxi.

Margaret had just emerged from a long hot bath when a message arrived. She had a large towel wrapped around her midriff and a smaller one piled on her head like a turban. This time she noticed the E-mail had a weird address on it. For a moment she wondered whether she could actually bear the emotional jarring that reading it might give her, but then her desire reasserted itself.

Angel,
It was you wasn't it, fastening your handbag? These E-mails take so long I can't bear it. Ring me tonight, you beautiful woman. Don't use my home number, call my mobile.
BB
P.S. I sent this from somewhere different for reasons I'll explain when we meet.

She felt faint. For a moment she tried to tell herself it was the hot bath. Then Margaret smiled the biggest smile she had in months. What did the PS mean? She really wanted to know. Was he under some sort of suspicion too? She closed the screen part of her mobile and punched his number into the phone.

'*Oui.*'

'I got your message.'

'I'm so glad you've rung.' Bourrat's voice was mellow and joyful. 'I wanted to go chasing you down the Saint Germain!'

'It didn't feel right staying – I felt I was intruding . . .'

'Don't worry. The moment I saw you, it was a revelation . . . I realised I was ready . . .'

'Good. Why did you send the message from somewhere new? Couldn't you get into the office?'

'I'll tell you when I see you.'

'Tease!' she laughed.

'I should have realised much earlier that I could play you back at the mystery game. Will you have lunch with me tomorrow?'

'Yes I will,' she struggled to keep her voice from showing her emotion.

'Fantastic!' Bourrat gave her directions to a restaurant overlooking the Bois de Boulogne.

Margaret felt a surge of panic and said without thinking, 'You will come alone, won't you?'

'Of course,' Bernard's voice betrayed irritation for a moment and then changed tone. 'You will come alone too?'

'Yes, yes, I feel so stupid for saying that.'

'I think I understand why you did.'

So, he knew, or thought he did – she felt a cold shiver run through her. 'Christ, this is mad!'

'We can talk about everything tomorrow.'

'Yes.'

'OK, one o'clock?'

'Yes . . . Bernard?'

'Yes.'

'I'm so glad you liked me.' Margaret felt like a fool again.

He chuckled. 'Of course I did. Listen, I'll see you tomorrow?'

'Fine, at one.'

'*Soi sage.*'

She switched off her phone. 'Be good,' he had said at the end. It was paternal without being patronising. For hours she was far too excited to sleep.

On Sunday morning, Margaret woke at 8 a.m. She struggled into the kitchen and got the coffee going. It was typical, she had only really fallen asleep a couple of hours earlier after the previous night's excitement and needed to get into Hamsin early, so that disappearing at lunchtime wouldn't seem such a crime. After showering and washing her hair, she dressed decisively – but only because it was one of the things she had spent half the night worrying about. Before the hour was up she had banged the front door and was heading for the metro with her navy blue woollen coat covering the suit she had bought the previous week. It had sleek trousers – she didn't normally like wearing them but they were so nicely tailored, showing off her long legs to perfection.

When she arrived at the office, she noted that a letter had been pasted up in the window. It informed customers that the company had stopped trading on Friday and would shortly be going into liquidation. Margaret had to tap on the glass door until Mike McPhee, the MI6 man, appeared and let her in.

'Thanks. I see we've gone bust, Mike.'

'What?' Then he remembered the notice behind her: 'Oh yeah, funny thing is, we sold seven cars in a few weeks – we've actually made a profit on the cover business, the accountants at the office don't know what to do!'

Margaret smiled and headed for the stairs. Down below she could hear machinery being moved with much grunting and swearing.

McPhee descended the spiral stairs and watched as the Ulstermen loaded one of the water pumps, the last significant piece of equipment, into his van. Ray Skinner was leaning on a broom, taking a break from sweeping up the refuse. There was no other sign that the garage had ever been used for anything other than storing cars.

Margaret found Max Kampfner was already at his screen in the analysts' room and gave her a casual 'good morning'. She had grown to dislike him – not least because of the ridiculous hours that he seemed to spend in the office.

The morning passed quickly enough with Margaret's mind rarely leaving the topic of lunch: how would people respond when she said she was going out? What would happen when she got to the restaurant? She began to worry that she would never be able to go back to the office, to Cheltenham, to England. By the time she had to leave several other analysts were there too. Margaret decided to tell Philippa that she was going out 'for a good long walk to clear my head. Don't be surprised if I take an hour or more.' She walked through the door without being challenged and wondered whether Lofting or Birnbaum would even notice her absence.

The next couple of hours had an unreal quality for Margaret. When she walked into the restaurant, caught sight of Bernard, watched him smile and stand up to greet her, it was like they were old friends. He was wearing a navy-blue polo neck with a brown tweed jacket. He seemed so relaxed, she couldn't believe it. She had feared the conversation would be one of those 'so here we are'-type affairs, pregnant with awkward silences. It wasn't of course, because their impatience to talk face to face carried them through the opening pleasantries with ease.

Bernard had been sure she was English and became convinced of it when he was able to watch her manner and listen more carefully to the signs of it in her language which of course was still French. 'I'm so glad you could come,' were his first words, followed by, 'now would you mind telling me your name?' They both laughed.

In fantasising about this moment, she had wondered whether she would give a pseudonym, but instead settled for, 'It's Margaret, although my friends call me Mags or Magsie – there's something too formal and old-fashioned about Margaret.'

'Not at all. Although perhaps I think that because I'm getting old.'

'You're not old at all,' she replied with an intensity which left them both feeling self-conscious.

As a glass of white wine was placed in front of her, she felt this overwhelming desire to explain herself. 'I know you probably think what I've done is crazy, but there you are, there's no point living in the information age without taking advantage of its benefits. I just knew I wanted to get in touch with you – you probably think that makes me weak—'

'Of course not—'

'Yes well, neither do I.'

'You don't have to explain.'

'I do have to explain some things because you have to promise me something.'

'Yes?'

'That you mustn't ever try to get me to say why I came here, to Paris. I don't care about my work any more – I didn't believe in my job when I was given it and I don't believe in it now. I do feel a certain loyalty to the people I was working with though. I just want to finish working as quickly as possible and then if there's any future . . . take things from there.'

'It's not important to me.'

'Promise, Bernard!'

'I promise.'

'You may also have to protect me from people on your side who want to find out what I've been doing here – it's nothing the average person would regard as a crime.'

That hit him hard. Bernard had been enjoying things so much he would have preferred never to think about the DST and their investigation again. What was worse, it was he who'd set Lacroix's blood-hounds off in the first place. How was he going to get them off the scent? 'Look, Margaret, let's talk about something else. I'm afraid you'll try to get me to sign a pre-nuptial agreement before the *hors d'oeuvre*.'

She smiled and they ordered the food. As the meal progressed the atmosphere lightened. Bernard talked about his kids a lot – managing to do so in a wry, amusing way. She allowed him to find out about her past in a general sort of way, including all of the painful stuff about her parents.

'Margaret,' BB asked as he was about to begin his rib of beef, 'did you ever have the chance to get married?'

'Well, there was someone who asked when I was in my late twenties – I must have been twenty-eight. I was a fool, I said no, I was too busy enjoying my career. He was a nice man but not one of life's great trailblazers – I thought I might find better than him. The last few years, I wasted with a loser who would never have made me happy . . . it's just one of those things.' It was like the E-mails: she felt amazed by her ability to make sense of years of emotional turmoil now she was sitting opposite BB.

'I can't believe you don't have suitors falling at your feet.'

She smiled shyly, looking down at her plate, and then said at last, 'Frenchmen!'

'English Roses!' he replied, winking at her.

By the time she made it back to Hamsin, it was almost 3 p.m. Her timings had been hopelessly wrong: she'd been out for three hours. She didn't care though: she was blissfully happy and the two glasses of wine had very little to do with it.

Ted Lofting caught sight of her in the terminal room and seemed to give her a slightly suspicious look. He was working away at the other end of the room, packing up the first of the PCs with Ray Skinner. In her happy blur, Margaret nipped out to the loo without following the usual precaution of taking her handbag with her. Worse, its top gaped open, and as Ray walked past with a coil of fibre optic cable, the Nokia nestling within it caught his eye.

'Take a look in her handbag,' he whispered into Lofting's ear.

Ted strolled between the two aisles of analysts and

298

peered in. Then, without hesitation, he leaned down and opened up the machine, switched it on and tried to select the last-number-dialled function. This yielded nothing – Margaret had set it that way. He worked the menu again to select the 'Own Number' function. This had been left blank. Ted began to worry that she might return. The phone was back in her handbag well before he resumed his walk out of the room and Margaret was back at her desk.

Having found the phone, Ted was intent on action. He felt such a strong wave of concern that it made his neck and palms prickle with cold sweat. He needed to call the GCHQ Security Department in Cheltenham immediately, but it wasn't possible from Hamsin. It would be possible to make a secure call from the embassy, but this could only be done as a last resort. He would just have to use E-mail. Ted found himself a terminal and tapped away, keeping an eye on Margaret as he did so:

I have developed security concerns about Margaret Reynolds and believe the entire operation may have been endangered. I need you as a matter of extreme urgency to trace a Nokia Communicator 9000. I have examined it briefly and it is on UK settings, I believe she may have acquired it on a visit to the UK between the 23rd and 26th. It is critical that you intercept any voice or data transmissions. Call me either at the operational HQ or accommodation – the lines are insecure of course, but time is of the essence.

When he had sent the E-mail, Ted tried to calm himself by getting busy again with packing up the office. Time and again, though, thoughts of how he was going to deal with Margaret came back to him. It was absolutely clear from the pre-operational briefings in Cheltenham that items like mobile phones were not allowed in Paris – if lost or traced they could reveal to the opposition exactly who you were. Margaret had broken procedures in an unacceptable way. But that was just the beginning of it. He had asked whether she was seeing someone; she had said no. So she was probably lying to her head of division too. Unacceptable. An insult to him personally. Whatever was going on was continuing despite the fact that she had come under suspicion before, which meant she was being impelled by some force so powerful that she no longer cared about her job or the fate of everyone on the operation. Ted hated confrontation; he hated being the management hard man, but no other options were left with Ms Reynolds. Could she be sent home and then immediately to the Australian outback? And successfully confined there, for years if necessary, until the operation was over? That was probably the best he could do for her: Ted knew there would be those who would favour putting her in an Army psychiatric ward instead. He knew he had to get her out of Paris immediately, but he wanted the Security Department to find out more about who she was in contact with if they possibly could.

Chapter Thirty-One

It was about eight on that Sunday evening when Dan
Birnbaum finally decided he had to speak to Ted. He
had been reluctant to have Margaret followed, but had
eventually brought in help – a couple of Agency guys
trained in surveillance had been put on the case the
previous day. It was never going to be easy though to
tell his partner that suspicion had fallen on a British
member of the team. It was doubly hard because it had
happened when the Americans were listening to
Bourrat's conversations – something they weren't meant
to do.

Dan lured Ted to the kitchenette behind the showroom where he suggested they have a beer. Ted agreed,
if a little distractedly.

'Ted, we've got a little problem we need to talk over.'

Lofting thought 'God! What now?' but replied, 'Oh
yes?'

'We need to speak to Margaret – do you know where
she was at lunchtime today?'

Ted was aware of the excuse she had given to
Philippa. 'She said she was going out to clear her head
for a while.'

'She was having lunch with a man, at some fancy
restaurant out near the Bois de Boulogne.'

Ted's heart sank. She had lied to him again. 'Really?'

He wondered what kind of tabs the Americans had been keeping on her.

'Yeah, it was a weird coincidence, an Agency guy noticed her in there.'

'A weird coincidence indeed . . .'

'Yeah well, what can I say?'

'I might ask why exactly your people were following her around in the first place, but it's clearly too late for all that. Can you perchance tell me where my Chief Analyst/Linguist is now?'

'She's at the flat,' Birnbaum almost mumbled. 'Went back not long ago.'

Lofting's head tilted back and he examined the brass ceiling lamps for a moment. 'I suppose she might have fallen in love with someone totally innocent.'

'Yes, she might. The people, the person who saw her at the restaurant didn't know who the guy was – but they're new to Paris, not fully briefed.'

If it was a straightforward love affair, why hadn't she told him? Surely she'd been in the business long enough to be grown up about it? There was a small chance, if it was completely innocent, that they might not even have tried to stop it. Anyway, it was too late for all that: she had betrayed his trust. Ted turned to Birnbaum: 'OK, we'll get her out of here tonight – I suppose you realise this has finished her career at GCHQ?'

'Yeah well,' the American looked back coldly, 'we call it sleeping with the enemy. I hope it'll do more than finish her career.'

'Meaning?'

'Get her out the way somewhere. Some base or maybe some kind of institution.'

'Institution? Dan, my dear fellow, what are you suggesting?'

'Put her away.' Birnbaum looked down at his shoes. 'Hell, we've done it before and you guys have done it – you know, the funny farm, the rubber Ramada.'

'I'd have thought you had more integrity than that, Dan.'

'Listen, there's too much at stake here for us to have loose cannons jeopardising everything – you of all people should know the damage one of those can do in a storm. You guys don't want the NSA losing faith in the partnership. There's a lot to be said for a short spell in a mental hospital. If she ever feels like blabbing about what happened, nobody will ever believe a word.'

'Yes, well, thanks, Dan. Invaluable guidance.'

It was no more than fifty minutes later when Lofting appeared at the flats with his posse. Skinner and McPhee had been joined by another SIS type. Their plan was to spirit her out of the city in one of the Hamsin Mercs – McPhee would drive her to Brussels and put her on a plane home, where she would be met by a couple of Special Branch officers pending a proper investigation. Ted would confiscate her mobile phone and see what they could get out of it. They did not anticipate any resistance – after all, why should there be? All that seemed to have happened was that she had fallen for a foreigner, presumed French, while working on a deeply sensitive operation. In his heart of hearts Ted knew that they might be delivering Margaret to some remote base in Australia or Canada or, worse still, a mental hospital if the Americans had anything to do with it. Given that this operation was meant to last for years, so might her incarceration.

As they sped across the Pont de Neuilly, into La Défense, Ted was lost in anxiety. How on earth would she have had time to meet someone in Paris on the operation? Did that mean she knew them from before, in which case the lover could know her real identity and probably what she did?

It took three rings on the doorbell to get Colette to open up. She stood there in her stockinged feet holding an open paperback. 'Yes?' The sight of the four men alarmed her even though she knew who they were.

Ted asked, 'Is Margaret in?'

'No, she just went . . .' Colette glanced at her watch and began to look really worried. 'She just went out to buy something to read, that's what she said.'

Ray Skinner butted in: 'How long ago?'

'Maybe half an hour.'

Skinner and McPhee pushed past Colette and went into Margaret's bedroom.

'Her kit's still there, Mr L.,' McPhee reported.

Ted was working through the possibilities like some chess player – but there were still too many unknowns. 'Right.'

McPhee spoke again. 'Neil and I can have a quick patrol around the neighbourhood – see if we spot her – meanwhile Ray can pack her things up.'

'Yes, good idea.' Lofting slumped down in the big leather sofa. He suddenly found himself wishing he could talk to his wife and wondered where she might be. He tried hard to keep his weariness and depression at bay while Skinner crashed around in the bedroom, gathering Margaret's things with the finesse of a burglar.

It was easy enough to find Bourrat's apartment. The address had been in one of the operational databases and in moments of quiet longing during the previous weeks she had found herself looking it up in the streetfinder, checking the nearest metro, trying to paint a mental picture of what it might be like. It was in the 17th Arrondissement, not so far from her flat, or indeed the club where Bernard had met his friend for squash. All of these places were on the western side of the city, sandwiched on the one side by the soaring glass towers of La Défense and on the other by the Arc de Triomphe, with the heart of the city, further east, beyond it.

Margaret only went a couple of stops on the metro before getting off at the Porte Maillot. She didn't have the patience to go further into town, change and then head west again on another line. It was a nice evening: she could walk. So she struck up a brisk pace along the Boulevard Periere heading for the address she had memorised. Being a quiet Sunday evening, the American who had followed her onto the metro began to have doubts as the crowds around Porte Maillot thinned out and his quarry headed into quieter streets.

He broke off the chase, telling himself it simply wasn't possible to conduct a proper surveillance without backup, and those cheap bums in Langley should recognise that. This woman did not seem particularly surveillance-aware, but he couldn't carry on following her into these residential roads without her noticing eventually. Anyway, it was Sunday; it was late; the hotel adult video channel awaited.

As she stood outside the solid 1920s mansion block where BB kept his home, Margaret felt a last pang of doubt and foolishness. Bourrat stood out from the serried ranks of French names beside the smart brass buzzers. Her finger hovered about it. What if he wasn't in? What if he had some girlfriend there? Then the strange calm which she had felt throughout the evening reasserted itself. If he was out she would find a bar and drink coffee. If he had a girlfriend with him, too bad. It was like a terminal diagnosis – might as well find out as soon as possible. She stepped up to the entrance and rang the bell.

'*Oui?*' The voice seemed slightly puzzled – who would be buzzing up at this time on a Sunday evening?

'*C'est moi.*'

The electric doorlook buzzed and she was inside the hallway before hearing the words 'fourth floor', disembodied in the distance behind her.

Bourrat opened the front door. Margaret stood there, not smiling, not frowning but somehow conveying the emotional tumult inside her. There were no words. She took one step forward. He began to open his mouth, as if to speak. She shook her head slightly and kissed him deeply, stifling any words he might have prepared. Their heads came apart for a moment as they surveyed one another, each wondering the same thing – was this real? Bernard raised his right hand, almost like a gesture of surrender – half a surrender perhaps. She grabbed it and squeezed it hard as she dipped her head back towards his and pushed her tongue into his mouth once again.

They shuffled into the flat, and she kicked the front door shut with her heel. She quickly surveyed the large, dimly lit living room she had walked into as Bernard drew her back towards the sofa. On the other side of the room, marooned in the light of a table lamp were a half-drunk glass of whisky and an open Victor Hugo beside his armchair. Mozart's *Magic Flute* burbled away on the CD player.

As they kissed, Bernard noticed she was wearing jeans. His hands went to the button flies and began popping them one by one; hers stayed on his shoulders.

She allowed a little moan of pleasure to escape as Bernard pushed his fingers down between the soft cotton of her knickers and the heat of her body to begin toying with her. The smell of her seemed to invade his nostrils and Bernard suddenly surrendered to his passion. He slipped the tip of one finger and then a second into her wetness and she began unbuttoning his shirt.

A moment later, Bernard sat her on the sofa and knelt on the floor in front of her. He pulled off her boots and then her jeans, looked up, smiled and then tipped her back into the deep cushions as she smiled back at him. Taking her left heel in the palm of his hand, he straightened her long leg and began planting small kisses on the sole of her foot. As his head inched along her foot followed by her ankle and calf Margaret's head arched over the back of the sofa; she began to moan softly as he said, 'Such beautiful legs.' By the time his mouth reached the top of her thigh she was so aroused that she was seeping onto the patterned red brocade beneath her. He let his tongue move so softly over her that initially it was almost imperceptible, but slowly its strokes became harder, more determined. She wanted to prolong her pleasure but she couldn't stop herself. Bernard felt the little tremors in her thighs building as she began to come.

Only a few minutes elapsed before Margaret said, 'Take me to the bedroom,' and they stumbled towards the darkness in their dishevelled clothes.

'I think you're too fit for an old man like me,' Bernard said, only half in jest.

She smiled and kissed his cheek: 'If the rest of your body works half as well as your mouth, there'll be no problems.'

As she lay down on the bed, the smell of his aftershave from the pillow pricked her nostrils. She had worried about another woman, but realised that this flat was almost like a bachelor pad: there was no trace of the feminine touch. His shoulders and handsome head were silhouetted above her as she said, 'Come inside me, Bernard'.

When they had made love, he lay beside her, stroking her brow and occasionally planting little kisses on her cheek and forehead. Eventually he said, in English, 'Why do I admire you so deeply when I know so little about you?'

For a moment she felt panic – she had never heard him use her language. In the darkness it seemed almost as if someone else might be lying beside her, not the man she had fallen so hopelessly in love with. Of course she knew that he had guessed her birth – but something about it made her nervous, like it was a trap.

She replied teasingly, in French, 'Well, knowing someone is crazy about you always makes a good start.'

'You don't want to talk English?'

'No, not at the moment – you speak it very well, it's just a bit of a shock to me.'

'No problem,' he answered in his own language: 'would you like something to drink?'

'Yes, I would,' she smiled into the darkness.

'Champagne?'

'Don't open a bottle—'

'Really! I want to celebrate!'

'That would be lovely.' As he padded out of the room she saw him silhouetted in the doorway. His broad shoulders and trim stomach were impressive for a man of his age. She felt a pang of pride that he was in such good shape and turned her head onto the pillow so she could rub her cheek on the expensive Egyptian cotton. There was a great pop from the kitchen as he opened the bottle. Margaret began to feel vulnerable. She wondered whether she should turn the light on: she'd never even seen this room.

Bernard was back before she could act on her impulse. She sat up as he handed her the drink and they clinked their glasses together.

'To us!'

'Us!' She took a sip and then asked him, 'Put your arm around me, Bernard.' As he obliged, she said, 'We haven't done something crazy, have we?'

'Of course we have, but do you think love is logical?'

She felt a tingle at hearing him use the word *amour* but knew it was a little different in French. 'I don't want to go back to my flat.'

'That's fine because I wasn't going to let you.'

'But if I don't go back, they'll find out about us and that will be the end of my job, of everything.'

Bernard was intensely curious, of course, but knew he couldn't ask her explicit questions since he'd promised not to. 'Maybe it's not that bad?'

'Of course it's bad! I work for the government – surely you'd realised that?'

'Actually, no.' Bernard had assumed she was involved in industrial espionage.

She felt wretched. 'Christ, I've been a fool!'

'I'll give you the bad news and the good news.' Bernard reached across and switched on the bedside light so that suddenly their faces were bathed in light. Margaret lifted her head and looked towards him. 'The bad news is, if you work for your government, then you've probably ruined both our careers, since I can

309

hardly remain in my job when I tell them about you.'

'Bernard, I'm so—'

'The good news is that I don't really care! When I think of what's been going on since you sent that E-mail, I realise it's the best thing that's happened to me in years. Really!'

Margaret smiled weakly. 'It might not work out.'

'Of course – and one day we will be old, but let's live for the moment, Margaret, because there's too much pain and suffering out there. Anyway,' he added matter of factly, 'there's already a security investigation going on in the *Elysée*, that's why I added the PS to my message.'

'Oh my God, what are we going to do?'

'I think we'll be all right. They couldn't trace your E-mails and they don't know about your mobile. They haven't got a tap on my mobile, that's why I told you to ring it.'

She felt suddenly overwhelmed with the selfishness of what she had done. She climbed over him and began picking clothes off the floor. 'It's not too late for me to leave – you don't have to give up your work, there's no reason why I should lay all this on you: you're an important man for heaven's sake!'

'Where are you going?'

'I'm going back to face the music, or to walk the streets . . . I don't know.'

He was panic-stricken – if she walked out he would never find her. Bernard vaulted out of the bed and blocked the door: 'For God's sake! I need you!'

She fell into his arms and they clenched one another tightly until they began to kiss and to make love again.

They slept little that night. Margaret told him nothing

about the operation and the team in Paris but much about her early life and her concerns for her father. Bernard listened mostly and at 7 a.m. he went out to buy toiletries from a list she had prepared and to fetch fresh croissants for them. Margaret had not even packed an overnight bag. She had a Spanish credit card in her false name and 230 francs in her purse. She reckoned they probably wouldn't cancel the card immediately since it would give clues as to her movements. As she padded around Bernard's flat in his dressing gown waiting for him to return, she realised that she didn't have the keys to her flat in Cheltenham with her. Was she mad? She began to wonder whether she would ever see her flat again. Would she see England? More importantly, would she see her father?

After breakfast Bernard went to work. It took fifteen minutes for him to get through the front door – each time he said goodbye he would turn around and give her more kisses.

He had told her that he would have to face the music in the office. He still knew little of course of why she was in Paris – only that she was a foreign spy who had eavesdropped on him and who, it could only be presumed, worked for the British. He was already preoccupied with how he was going to try and get the DST off Margaret's trail. He hadn't shared his anxiety with her, since he was ashamed to admit to her that his tip-off had started Lacroix's whole security sweep.

She had felt so happy when he left that she cursed herself as her nervousness began to burn away at her. What exactly would they say at the *Elysée* when they heard he was resigning? Would he come under pressure to turn her in? Would the Gendarmes arrive at the flat before Bernard could even warn her?

She got dressed. She needed time to think, somewhere away from the flat. She would buy herself some clothes with her Banco de Bilbao credit card and then use it to check into a hotel.

It was while she was shopping for underwear in a busy department store in Les Halles that the phone in her handbag went. It was probably a mistake. She had not given Bernard the number. 'Hello?'

'Margaret, it's Ted Lofting here.'

She felt sick; she couldn't think of anything to say.

'Hello?' Ted was standing in the Hamsin office, where moments before, his friend in GCHQ Security had rung him with the number for the Nokia. All around him, people were packing things up as fast as they could.

'Yes,' she replied.

'Margaret, I think we should meet up.' Lofting's voice was deliberate, careful, like that of a man defusing a bomb.

'Ted, I'm sorry about walking out like that . . .'

'That's in the past. What we need to do now is make sure nothing untoward happens in the near future. Have you knowingly done anything or said anything which puts us at risk?'

She was annoyed by his use of the word 'knowingly', so she said 'no', a little tersely.

'Good. Thank you. We need to get you home.'

'No—'

'We can't leave you behind, my dear,' his tone had softened to the paternal. 'Come home, we'll sort everything out and you can always come back once we've got to the bottom of everything.'

'No!' She switched off the phone and wondered whether there was anyone she could trust.

Bernard found his office locked when he arrived at the *Elysée*. Moments after he appeared Jules Lacroix rested his big paw on Bourrat's shoulder, giving him a start.

'We're having your office properly "cleaned". Let's go have a chat, *mon ami*.'

Lacroix led the way to a small kitchen which the secretaries used to prepare coffee and biscuits for the high-ups. There was some DST goon there who moved into position, blocking the door, after Bourrat and Lacroix had entered.

'I was very annoyed with the office this morning,' Lacroix said, turning his head uncomfortably within his chafing collar: 'they told me someone rang you on Saturday night, a number we have no record of. Well, being a weekend, the cretins didn't ring me at home.'

Bourrat was panic-stricken. If they knew she'd rung his mobile, what else did they know? 'What time?'

'Maybe ten o'clock.'

'I don't remember anyone ringing me at home.'

'I didn't say they rang you at home.' Lacroix looked down at the filter coffee machine and then poured himself a cup without offering one to his old friend.

'You mean my mobile?'

Lacroix shrugged and gave a sort of sickly half-smile.

'Were you intercepting my mobile?'

'Bernard, my old friend. There is no higher duty for our directorate than the security of the *Elysée*, of the President and those who surround him. You understand that, don't you? Do you think that's her number? It was an English-registered mobile, although that doesn't mean anything in itself . . .'

Bernard wondered for a moment. If they knew that Margaret had actually been to his flat, why not cut to the chase? Perhaps they had logged the call on his mobile without recording its contents.

Lacroix broke into his thoughts: 'You don't have any more precise information about who we're looking for, do you?'

Well, time to call his bluff. 'No, of course not! Now you mention it, someone did ring me on Saturday night and hung up.'

'We can get a fix on it if she keeps it switched on long enough. The phone locks its position by three cellular points. That means we can determine where she is to within about 100 metres, so get her talking.'

'I see.' Bourrat felt some relief at last. Lacroix would hardly be telling him this if they knew who Margaret was and where she had spent the last night. Still, they had been monitoring his mobile and the man whom he had thought was his friend had made it perfectly clear that he would put duty first. Bernard forced out a weak smile. 'Well, if you'll excuse me, Jules, I have to get to the bank to authorise something.'

Chapter Thirty-Two

It was meant to be business as usual for Phil Keitel and his deputy, Jim MacTernan, that morning on the A6 just south of the capital. The two men had gone to one of the super-cheap commercial travellers' hotels alongside the motorway where you slid your credit card into a machine to get in, were assigned a room and never saw another person until you left the next day. Phil was able to overcome his aesthetic repugnance for these places with their plastic fitted bathrooms and lousy coffee because they were very good for the spying business. The heavy motorway traffic on the edge of Paris made it hard for anyone to keep tabs on them, there were no staff, and Agency credit cards allowed them to maintain anonymity.

Phil had not seen Thierry Dupré, their man in France Telecom, for a few months – not since Lyon in fact. There was no question of course of letting the agent know that his information had launched a $100m operation in the centre of Paris, but it made Phil a little better disposed towards someone he had little liking for. When Dupré rapped on the door of the room Keitel had taken, the American greeted him with a fulsome smile and a firm handshake. Dupré was wearing a black leather jacket over his shirt and tie and carrying a briefcase. His manner seemed a little odd. He smiled at

315

Keitel a little uneasily, then broke eye contact and began gabbling about his family.

MacTernan was prowling outside, keeping an eye on the car park. At that time of the morning there were only departures. He became bored and decided to have a look around the back of the motel. As he strolled around one of the bright red corners of the plastic-clad building he was alarmed to see four men making their way down a steep embankment from a sliproad. Two unmarked Renault 25s were parked above them. MacTernan ducked back behind the wall, pulled the mobile from his mac pocket and punched Keitel's number.

'Yes?' Keitel said, throwing a half-smile at Dupré.

'Go home, go home.'

Keitel replied, 'Roger,' for reasons he didn't entirely understand, and looked over at his agent. 'Time to leave, my friend.' He picked up the briefcase containing Dupré's payment and headed for the door. As he opened it, he came face to face with two of the Frenchmen. 'DST,' one of them said, producing a badge like an enamel keyfob on the end of a chain from his pocket.

MacTernan had already manouevred the car around in preparation to leave when he looked in his rearview mirror and saw another of the DST men approaching. He did not have the room keycard, so he knew there was no quick way through the barrier across the road leading out of the motel. Well, there was one way. He gunned the engine, the car raced forward, crashing through the barrier and out towards the motorway.

It was turning into the worst day of Ted Lofting's life. Security Department had sent him a secure E-mail to say that they had intercepted Margaret's mail. It contained a packet of responses to her lonely hearts ad and a further reminder from the nursing home about her father's bills. Worse, he had received another E-mail from his secretary telling him the Director would be in Paris to coincide with the switching to Phase Two of Operation POLYP. Ted was to go to a hotel in the Rue de Washington and brief him personally that evening. Having read these two messages, he was confronted by Birnbaum, who took him to one side and told him that Margaret had 'been seen' in the vicinity of Porte Maillot the previous evening around the time they had gone to her flat. He knew of course that there were ways to track a cellular phone but they could hardly go to the French authorities for help. It was then that word began to filter in from the Americans about Phil Keitel's arrest.

'Ted, we have a problem,' Birnbaum had almost whispered to him.

'Another one? Trying to liven up an otherwise tedious operation?' He shook his head in disbelief.

'The agency guy who got us the *TONNANT* information? He's been arrested meeting the source who gave it to him.'

'Shall we go downstairs?'

The two men made their way to the basement where there were now no signs of the tunnelling operation.

'You realise what this means?' Birnbaum had been bursting to talk as they had made their way down.

'I'm not sure – it's tricky.'

'The fuck it is! We've been played along – either the French now know what our agent in Telecom told us, or they knew the whole time and Keitel was entrapped. Either way this whole goddamned operation has to be scrubbed!'

'I was thinking rather the opposite,' Lofting replied with complete calm, fishing the pipe from his pocket.

'The last thing you'd do, if the whole *TONNANT* thing was a sting operation, is tell us you'd done it. Don't you think?'

'Maybe they've just got bored with cooking up hundreds of fake phonecalls – they know we've been suckered. Now we know we've been suckered so it's time to end the charade.'

'Put yourself in their shoes,' Lofting lit up: 'if this is a disinformation operation, would you end it when it's going this well? By the way, this might also knock down your theory about the Terry Donald surveillance being a barium meal – after all, if they knew they'd given your chaps the secret of *TONNANT* they would know that you and possibly we were listening to them so it would be quite unnecessary for them to plant that kind of information. These different theories can't all be right.'

Birnbaum's face was screwed up in concentration. He began biting at his thumbnail. Eventually he said, 'Maybe.'

'Probably. Let's keep our heads.'

'Christ! Damascus and Moscow were child's play compared to this!'

'Dan, old boy – it's much harder when you do this to your friends. With the Russians or Syrians you're cock-a-hoop because after years of famine you're bingeing on good material. With these people, we know too much about them: we're bound to get stuff which simply ignites the embers of suspicion.' Lofting's words heralded his next action: lighting up his pipe.

Birnbaum could see Lofting's argument but he was beginning to find his tone patronising. 'I guess next you'll say you never wanted to do this operation, huh?'

'I won't say that.'

'You'll think it.'

'Whatever. Do you think it's been an easy experience for me? My wife's left home; my senior operational officer has disappeared – presumably with her French boyfriend; now you tell me the CIA man who set all this going in the first place has been clapped in irons!' He shook his head.

'Yeah well, let's just get the hell out of here: Keitel might say something in custody.'

'Most unlikely if he's a professional,' said Ted, a little dismissively.

'I'm sorry . . . but you think Margaret's love affair fits in with good operational security?'

Lofting did not speak, but shook his head and then walked up the spiral stairs. When he reached the analysts' room he found Ray Skinner, Roger, the OREGANO engineer and a couple of analysts helping to pack up screens.

'Mr Skinner, it's time for all of these people to go.'

Ray was manhandling a large monitor into its cardboard box: 'In a mo.'

'Now, Mr Skinner!' Lofting beckoned his security officer with his finger and went out onto the landing. 'Go back to the flats and get them to clear out all of their things. I want this place and the flats cleared within the hour and I want these people back in UK as fast as you can do it.'

Skinner thought to himself that it was unusual to see the old man flapping like this. 'Well, we'll have to follow the exfiltration plan—'

'Don't follow the plan: get them back across the water as quickly as you can.'

'How would you propose—'

'Hire a fucking minibus from Hertz and drive them to Calais yourself if you have to!'

Bernard Bourrat had gone to the church at La Madeleine after his little session with Lacroix. Unbeknown to him, it was just a couple of hundred metres from where GCHQ and the NSA had dug their tunnel. It was the big collonaded place which Ray Skinner had admired from afar and which Bernard now sat within, looking high above the altar at the fresco. Bourrat had gone in there to find some kind of truth, but instead he couldn't help smiling at the absurdity of the painting. It pictured Napoleon, that Corsican megalomaniac, sitting at God's right hand. Yes, there was plenty of absurdity in the system he served too – its pompous rituals, self-important phrases and its corruption. It was rotten.

Half an hour later Bourrat found himself in the baroque splendour of the General Manager's office at the Levantine Bank, just off the Champs Elysées.

'So if you'll just check the figures, Monsieur Bourrat,' the elderly banker chirped happily, setting an impressive-looking document in front of him.

'Oh no, there's been an error.'

'Monsieur?' There was horror in the manager's expression.

'No, it's not eight million US to Monsieur Sayed. It's eight hundred thousand.'

'I'm so sorry, sir, we'll get another order made up,' the manager turned and clicked his fingers for a clerk.

'The balance, seven million two hundred thousand US should go to this account.' Bourrat wrote the number on the back of one of his own business cards.

'Of course, monsieur,' the manager peered down through his half-moons.

The presidential adviser stood up to leave. 'Before

the close of business today? Both transactions?'

'As always, monsieur, as always.'

Bernard went to a phone box next. He tried his flat for about the tenth time. What was she playing at? Had she run off forever? He felt panic-stricken and fished into his mac pocket for the pack of Gitanes. He could call her mobile. The DST would be monitoring it, of course, but if he called from a box it wasn't quite so incriminating. He laughed aloud. He had just transferred $7,200,000 into an account in Cyprus in his own name and he was worried about incriminating himself? He lit up and dialled. The phone was switched off: it diverted to voice mail.

'My love, I'm worried, where are you? All of my phones are insecure, so don't ring them. If you're not at my apartment, don't go there, it's not safe. I have resigned and I think we should just go somewhere and sort our lives out. Just meet me at 9 a.m. at the place where we had that meal. I'm thinking of you. I love you.'

By mid-afternoon Margaret had checked into a small hotel in the 6ème. She had decided to keep her phone switched off. She knew well enough from work that there were ways of tracking them. Thankfully the little old lady in reception had taken an impression of her credit card without phoning in its number. It might therefore be a couple of days before GCHQ knew where she was staying and she hadn't told BB anything about her Spanish alias. She sat on her lumpy single bed and surveyed the shopping bags which carried her purchases. How had she got herself into the position where she trusted nobody? How would Bernard react if he couldn't find her? She decided she was being unfair on him and headed out for a stroll so that she could switch on her phone some distance away from the hotel and call his mobile.

As she was about to dial, the machine squeaked at her, 'Message Received.' She dialled her own number and heard Bernard's words, his precious words.

Margaret switched off her Nokia. It was incredible. Bernard had resigned to be with her. It was like the deepest, most intoxicating fantasy she could ever have imagined. She felt such emotion she wanted to scream out and frighten the Parisians who walked their fancy dogs and shopping past her. And then the germ of doubt began to grow once more. Would a presidential adviser really be giving it all up on the basis of one night of passion? Perhaps this was their last chance to entice her into a trap.

By the time Margaret had got up from the bench where she had heard this bombshell, Ted Lofting was walking up the Champs Elysées towards his appointment with the Director. As he nudged his way through the throng, Lofting decided to make one last call to Security Department in Cheltenham: there might still be someone there. He went into an ordinary phone box and rang the number. Sure enough, a man called Ron Spears answered.

'We're very glad you called, we've got something very good for you.'

'Oh yes, Ron? Fire away.'

'We've monitored a conversation, a message I should say, to the person you're interested in. Happily the voice mail server for her phone is in the UK so it was easy really.'

'Go on.'

'There's a clear implication from his message that

he's in as much trouble with his side as she is with us.'

'Yes?' Lofting's flat tone disguised his intense curiosity.

'And he's suggested that she meet him tomorrow morning at 9 a.m. – "at the place where we had that meal" was what he said.'

'Very good, Ron, thank you.'

'Clearly we've got to pass this up.'

Lofting didn't like this idea. 'Oddly enough, I'm about to see the boss, I'll tell him myself. Hopefully we can see her when she comes to the meet.'

'Can I say I'm leaving it with you then?' Spears asked in a covering of back sort of way.

'Indeed you can. Good work, Ron. Call me at the flat tonight if you find any more.'

'Will do.'

Lofting replaced the receiver and dialled Ray Skinner's mobile. 'Ray? How goes it?'

'I'm on my way back to the smoke. Everyone's off.'

'We've got a chance to find the straggler.'

'Oh yes?'

'Get two or three friends: we need to be in go mode at 8 a.m. tomorrow.'

'Understood.'

Lofting rang off without even saying goodbye. Next he dialled Birnbaum's number. The American should still be in town because he was checking the computer at the relay cover business the following day.

'Hallo?' The familiar New York accent.

'I need to find out where your friend saw our missing colleague yesterday lunchtime.'

'Do you—'

'It's not a secure means, Dan. Just call me back with the name of the place. It's vital.'

'OK, give me fifteen minutes.'

Lofting walked into the swish lobby of the hotel and proceeded to the lifts. He had been told to go to room 486. He arrived on the fourth floor wondering what to suggest about Margaret. He supposed they could get an SIS or MI5 surveillance team in, stake out Bourrat's flat and lift her. He couldn't stop feeling some sense of sympathy for Margaret though.

Lofting rapped on the door and the Director's senior staff officer opened it. 'Evening Ted.'

'Hello, Rita.'

The Director greeted him with a sort of sickly grin and they sat in armchairs. 'Just over on a European cooperation meeting – new Foreign Secretary's idea, it'll never catch on,' he announced. 'I wanted to have a chat about something on the personnel side.' The Director then leaned forward and wrote on a pad in front of them, 'Write Anything Operational.'

Lofting was flummoxed by this. The Director was clearly in town with the knowledge of the French authorities, so he assumed the room was bugged. Why on earth would they have any kind of operational discussion under these circumstances when they could do so securely in a few days' time in Cheltenham? Lofting wrote on the pad, 'We've an operational problem you need to know about.'

The Director nodded but seemed uninterested. 'In a moment, if that's OK. I'm off to the States on Wednesday and then I've got some leave booked and I realised this would be the only chance I'd have to chat to you for a couple of weeks. Whisky?'

Before Ted could reply, Rita fixed him one from the minibar and placed it in front of him. Lofting's confusion deepened. What on earth was this all about? 'Going anywhere nice?' he asked, noticing the Director's staff officer disappearing into the neighbouring room as he did so.

The Director ignored the question. 'You know, Ted, that under the Smaller but Better strategy we have to take steps at all levels of the organisation.'

'Yes.' A rising chord of alarm was sounding in Lofting's brain.

'Well, I would very much like you to be one of the two heads of division to take advantage of the early redundancy terms.'

'Me?' Lofting's right hand ran over his pate in despair.

'I know you've given sterling service to the office, but I can assure you the terms will be generous.'

'But what about the . . . the current operation?' Lofting thought he might throw up: 'I led the whole . . .'

'It was teamwork, Ted, and you did a good job in the development phase, but I have to say questions have been flying about your management throughout the operational phase – notably from our Cousins.'

Ted's head sank low. He took a deep gulp of the Scotch. At last he said, 'I've still got seven years.'

The Director produced an envelope from his pocket. 'These are the terms, Ted: there'll be a payoff of £113,000, which I think you'll agree is generous – a chance to settle up the mortgage or buy that yacht you've been dreaming about.'

Lofting opened the paper and shook his head in despair.

'We have all been very grateful for your work – really we have, you've made an outstanding contribution over the last twenty-three years.'

Lofting looked up – the anger had crystallised now.

'This operation has been run in the tightest possible way. For the record, I reject any criticism—'

'Forget the record! There's no point having recriminations here. Surely this hasn't been entirely unexpected for you? Things have been building for some time, didn't you see that?'

Lofting thought of the Director's little chats about working with the Americans and Emma's accident – presumably that's what he had in mind.

'Forget it. I'm too tired. I'll go quietly.'

'All right, Ted. Thank you. No need to come in for a few days when you get back. There'll be a handover of your division, but you can do that in Megan Trelawney's office.'

'A very good choice.' Lofting finished the Scotch.

The silence was broken by a mobile phone ringing in Lofting's coat pocket. 'Yes?' He reached for a pad and, fumbling a biro out of his jacket, took down a name and address. 'Thanks, Dan.' He snapped the phone shut.

The Director did not enquire about the call but picked up where he had left off. 'Your office is being cleared this week.'

'Right. To be expected, I suppose.' Lofting's anger had hardened into a grim mask now.

'Anything else?' The Director pointed at the notepad where Lofting had mentioned his 'operational problem'.

'What?'

'Anything else?' He pointed again.

Lofting thought about Margaret Reynolds. She was hiding somewhere in that city feeling as lonely and confused as he was. 'No, don't worry, I'll deal with it. It can be my last operational decision.'

326

Chapter Thirty-Three

Ted had meandered through some backstreets before settling in a bar. He sat forlornly among the noisy French clientèle and downed two Scotches in quick succession. I'll be good company for Sara, he thought, as the alcoholic numbness engulfed him. He wondered where his wife was, what she was doing. Ted tried to decide where it had all gone wrong: how far was he to blame for their growing apart? He spent so long at work and then as soon as he got home he retired to the attic to potter around with his sailing ships. Could he really blame her for seeking love elsewhere when it had been years since he could bear to talk to her properly? And these last few months – he hadn't slept more than a couple of nights in a row at home. What was all that time at the office for? He had just been sacked, damn it! It had hardly saved him from that.

He headed for the door, surprised that the booze made him wobble a little as he went – he was not a practised drinker. As he bumbled along the street Lofting's hand drifted into his pocket where it found a phonecard. He wasn't meant to call home, even from boxes. Fuck it. He dialled the number, expecting Emma to answer if anyone was in at all.

'Hello, Cheltenham 460734,' she answered.

Ted smiled. Hardly anybody answered the phone like that any more. 'Sara, it's me.'

'Ted?'

'Yes. I miss you.'

'Ted? . . . Have you been drinking?'

'As a matter of fact I have.' He felt doubly intoxicated now with the strangeness of this conversation. 'Why do you ask?'

'You never ring when you're away for work.' Her tone had become harsher: 'You always say it's for security reasons.'

'Pax, darling.'

'What?'

'Peace. Let's just have peace.'

'Are you all right?'

'I'm taking early retirement. Well . . . no point lying to you . . . I've just been sacked.'

'I . . . I'm sorry.'

'The funny thing is, I really don't give a monkey's. They're giving me a decent payoff . . . I wondered,' Ted suddenly felt as awkward and as frightened of rejection as the day he had asked her to marry him: 'I wondered, maybe you'd like to sail around the world with me.'

There was no reply.

'Sara?' Ted's tone was slightly panic-stricken, but then he heard the sniffing of someone trying to stifle tears.

'I've been a bloody fool, Ted . . . I've ruined everything, haven't I?'

'Let's just forget the past. Let's just sail away and try and have some good autumn years, eh?'

'Let's talk when you get home. I'm just so tired I don't know if it can work. Anyway, I'm sorry about your job.'

* * *

That night Ted also found himself staying in a small Parisian hotel. He had his appointment with Margaret the next morning and then he was meant to drop in to the Phase Two site at the TV company – if indeed there was to be a Phase Two. Having checked in he had gone upstairs, wrenched off his tie and perused some trashy magazines full of ads for shops. He was too restless and troubled to sleep, too annoyed with the way GCHQ had just dispensed with his services to be able to bear thinking about the operation and what might become of it and too tired to read. He tried to switch on the television with a remote control which was attached to his bedside table by a piece of flex. It wasn't long enough to reach the bed. Nothing seemed to work – he pushed the 'standby' button, a couple of the channel switches. Ted took the batteries out, gripped them in the palm of his hand for a while and then popped them back in. The 'standby' button worked this time. 'Flat batteries, bloody typical,' he muttered aloud.

'*Coming up,* World Business Today,' portentous music . . . '*CNN: the world trusts us to get it right.*'

Lofting looked over at the printed card on his bedside table to see what other channels were available.

'*Our top story – the United States has won a six billion-dollar order to supply fighter aircraft to Saudi Arabia.*'

Ted fumbled with the volume control.

'*Deborah Cacciatore has the story . . . Board members at General Defence, the Florida plane builder, say the order for seventy-two F-24s was won in the face of intense competition from Britain and France.*'

Ted was so stunned at this disaster, coming on top of everything else which had happened that day, that he actually let out a laugh. He knew he would have to watch the headlines the following hour just to make sure he wasn't dreaming. So began his rotten night.

Neither Lofting nor Reynolds found anything resembling peace in their lonely Parisian cells that night. Both were up before 7 a.m. Ted popped out of the hotel to buy *Le Monde* to see what their take on the Saudi business was. Margaret went for a stroll in Saint Germain, watching the green-clad men from the municipality washing down the streets with great hoses. She switched on her Nokia. Another voice mail.

'I haven't heard from you. Please be where I said at 9 a.m. I . . . I really need you. Bye.'

Ted could not find what he was looking for in *Le Monde*, but when she bought a copy Margaret found something she hadn't even known about. She had made her way to a bench beside the Seine, where the river ran in front of the Palais de Justice. The edition had gone to press too late for the Saudi contract announcement, but the paper did carry a story on the diplomatic scandal caused by the DST catching some American spies red-handed. Her eyes picked out the third paragraph:

> It is believed they were meeting a source who was a middle-ranking manager at France Telecom. Interior Ministry sources suggest the man had been co-operating with the DST for more than a year, feeding selected information to the CIA.

Margaret did not know for sure that this was the man who had revealed the *TONNANT* secret, but she had picked up enough on the grapevine to suspect it. Had the whole operation been the result of the French planting the information? She simply did not have the whole picture. It had been a long and uncomfortable night, she had woken tired and faced a meeting in a couple of hours which could change everything in her life. Margaret got up from the bench and gazed down into the waters of the river below. Once again she felt the flood of uncontrollable anxiety welling up inside her. She could not go back – not because she feared GCHQ with its security types and shrinks, but because her life there was really too wretched and lonely to carry on with. But if she ran away from them, how could she ever see her father again? She felt a cold sweat surge down her – she had already turned her back on them by leaving the flat two nights before, by hanging up on Ted. For the briefest moment Margaret thought of suicide. Jumping into the river? . . . not certain to kill her. Going into the metro and throwing herself under a train? . . . she had read of the trauma caused to drivers and she didn't want to do that to someone. She got her Nokia out and inspected it. Should she call him back? Should she switch it back on and see how long it would take someone to track it and clap her in irons? What if GCHQ had intercepted his messages on her voice mail? What if the French had? There might be rather a lot of men in raincoats waiting at that restaurant near the Bois de Boulogne at 9 a.m. If Bourrat was for real, then nobody else would know where the rendezvous was. Equally it might be a clever way of fixing a meeting point which Bourrat would bring the French secret service to.

She looked down at the lifeless phone: 'He loves me . . .' She switched it on: 'He loves me not . . .' Off again: 'He loves me . . .'

The klaxon sounded on a large tourist cruiser lumbering up the river. She had burned her boats like

331

Caesar invading Britain – or was it Norman the Conquerer? She didn't know any more. Her uncertainty made her smile and then she realised that she couldn't kill herself and that there was a way she might still be able to play everything to her advantage.

When Margaret turned up in the Rue Poniatowski near the Bois de Boulogne she was fifteen minutes early, which by her standards was playing things very cool. The restaurant where they had met for lunch just three days before looked the deadest of morning dead. There were people leaving their classy apartments, heading off to work in their chauffeur-driven Citroëns. She wondered where Bernard would appear from. She wondered whether some of the people she could spy were French secret service who had already gone into place. People leaving home again. A roadsweeper making his way up the road. He was an old man with a droopy, greying moustache. He seemed almost entranced by his work. He was no spook, too bloody old and doddery. Three or four sweeps of the broom, reach for the shovel, turn, dump the rubbish into the bin he was wheeling along. Yes, she thought, he'll do, but not yet.

Although Margaret decided she had chosen her position well, in a small alley beside a rather stylish 1920s building across from the restaurant, Lofting, Skinner and MacPhee and one of his MI6 colleagues spotted her arrival almost immediately.

The Brits had parked a French-registered hire car, a red BMW 325, in a sidestreet. Skinner was at the wheel. 'Right,' said Lofting decisively, looking over his shoulder from the front passenger seat, 'I would like to have a word with this lady to see if we can sort this all out with the minimum of fuss. We have to be aware of the possibility that the French may have turned her and be using her to try and entrap us.' Philip, the MI6 man, looked at McPhee, betraying his apprehension. Not something they had thought of.

'Boss,' Skinner cut in, 'if that's right, shouldn't I go and do the business? If you got lifted, the damage to the office would be much greater, you're a head of division, for Christ's sake!'

Lofting had to shut him down. 'Ray, I wish I could spare your feelings, but we haven't got time. She's not going to be happy to see you, is she?'

'I've no—'

'I'll go and speak to her. If you chaps could position yourselves to block any attempt to run for it, I think that would be best.' Philip nodded his assent.

'We've no comms, Mr L.,' MacPhee began, 'so can we just have a straightforward signal agreed?'

Lofting looked around for a moment and spotted a rolled-up copy of *France Soir* in the footwell. 'If we have to scrub everything and run for it, I'll drop the paper. If I need your help to get her to the car I shall wave you in with the paper. If it's all gone like a dream I will simply put my hand on her shoulder in a friendly sort of way and walk her to the car.'

'We might as well get on with it: Romeo will be here in a moment.' He opened the door and began walking to take up a position up the street.

Philip, who Margaret didn't know, would stand much closer to her. As the doors banged shut, a moment before Lofting was going to get out, Skinner said, 'She's moving, boss.'

Margaret walked out from the alleyway, put her hand

333

into her handbag, and switched on her mobile. Her eyes remained on the old roadsweeper as he dumped a shovel-load of rubbish into the bin, turned, set the shovel beside his cart and did his first sweep. Before he had started his second she dropped her phone into the bin, without looking down, and walked across the road to stand close to the restaurant.

'Good morning, Margaret.' Ted Lofting appeared behind her, standing with his hands buried in his raincoat pockets.

Her nervous reply betrayed the shock. 'Ted, you've got to let me go.'

'Margaret, let's all go home.'

'Why did you come?'

'Because I wanted to make sure that you would do nothing that would harm the operation and put your colleagues – or for that matter yourself – in danger.'

'I haven't told them anything.'

'You could come under a lot of pressure to do so.' Ted had remained rooted to the spot. 'They could arrest you. Your Spanish alias would be blown. HMG would never acknowledge your real identity. You could . . . disappear.'

'You think I haven't worried about that?' Her eyes began to fill with tears. 'I just have to trust this man.'

'It's not too late to come home.'

'I can't.'

'You can. Why not?'

'Because home doesn't exist. It stopped existing when my father stopped recognising me. It stopped existing when I understood I was spying on people whom I admired. It stopped existing when I realised I didn't care about this sodding job any more. So I'm sorry, Ted,

334

because you were always one of the better ones, but you can take GCHQ and stuff it.'

'Well, I have actually – or rather they've stuffed me. I'm leaving. Early retirement they call it. The sack you might call it—'

'I'm sorry—'

'Hear me out, Mags. I'm here because I don't want the French to get their hands on those OREGANO pods. This op may have been a bloody fiasco but we'll need that technology soon against some Saddam Hussein, some tyrant somewhere. I'm also here, you might say . . .' Lofting's stance finally shifted, his shoulders dropped and he ran a hand over his chin, '*in loco parentis*, because I brought you here: you're my responsibility. I don't want you going into a French jail or . . . whatever.'

Margaret smiled at him. 'Ted, I'd feel patronised if I didn't think you were being so sweet.' She took a step forward and took his dangling hand between hers and squeezed it, as if for emphasis. 'I know I was stupid to get into a relationship with a Frenchman – particularly one I was meant to be spying on! It's happened. That's history. I have told him that I can never explain what I was doing here and he's resigned his job.' For a moment she paused, thinking, 'Please God let it all be true: where are you, Bernard?' 'I will never tell him how we did listen to him – I promise you that, Ted. I believe in Bernard and I hope we can get away from here, from all the questions. I just have to hope and trust.'

'Trust has been in rather short supply on this operation.'

Margaret saw that the roadsweeper had already moved almost ten metres up the road from where their paths had crossed. She looked back at Ted: 'Isn't that always the case in espionage?'

'One doesn't usually expect one's partners to do the dirty. That request for us not to disseminate your . . . friend's message about the Saudi bribes?'

'Yes?'

'The Americans, Birnbaum, only did it so they could win the order. Which they have. And to think the Director says I was fired because I didn't work closely enough with them . . .'

'I'm sorry, Ted, and I know what I've done won't exactly help you.' She looked down at her watch. Christ! It was already 9.04. Where was he?

Ted noticed her gesture. 'I'm past helping – in the GCHQ sense anyway! That's why you have to believe me when I say we must ensure that the French don't find those taps. Are you wondering where your beau has got to?'

Margaret turned away from him: 'I'm not going back to Cheltenham with you whatever happens.' They stood silently for a moment. 'Was that Mike McPhee I spotted down the road there? In the blue reefer coat?'

'Yes.'

'In case I don't come quietly?'

'You're not going to be forced—'

'No, I'm not. You'll all be in danger if you stay here much longer.'

'Really.' Ted made the mistake of sounding incredulous.

'Yes, really. I switched my mobile on about ten minutes ago.'

Lofting's expression changed. He took the newspaper from under his arm and held it ready. 'They'd have to be rather hot to track it any quicker than that. Even twenty minutes would be doing quite well in a built-up area.'

'Do you want to put them to the test? End up like our American friends picked up yesterday? Only none of us have diplomatic immunity, Ted.'

It was Philip who noticed first. The trained eye of the surveillance expert. A Renault van had pulled in a hundred yards up the road. What was it that made him suspicious? Two men in the front, not very economic for deliveries. They were a bit too smartly dressed too. The clincher though was the aerial. It wasn't the factory-fitted one. It came up from the same bracket just above the windscreen, but it was a bit longer and thicker. The MI6 man managed to catch Lofting's eye and nodded towards the van. Lofting wasn't sure what he meant, another problem with not having their own communications. But he thought he could guess.

'Do you think they know what you look like?' he asked Margaret.

'Who?'

'The DST, the French security people.'

'I . . . not if Bernard's to be trusted.'

'Ah yes, where is he I wonder?'

She looked at her watch. 'He'll come.'

An unmarked Renault 25 saloon appeared next. Four men inside. This really set Philip flapping.

Margaret took Ted's hand again. 'I'll keep the secret. I promise.'

'Good luck then.' Ted smiled grimly.

This was so entirely unexpected that it brought her instantly to tears. 'Thanks, thanks a lot, Ted, for being so good to me.'

'Bye now,' he turned and nodded towards Philip and then back towards the BMW. In his own mind, Ted wasn't sure whether to believe her about the mobile phone. He just found himself hoping she was right to trust Bourrat for her own sake even more than he hoped the precious things he had buried under the Faubourg St Honoré would never be discovered.

As Ted climbed into the car, Skinner asked, 'Are you letting her go to her Frog fancyman? Just like that?'

Philip climbed in. 'There's French security arriving like it's Bastille Day. We should fuck off.'

Skinner looked over his shoulder. 'Bollocks!'

'Ray, shut up and let's get going!'

'Are you just going to let her ruin this whole operation?' Skinner fired up the engine and pulled forward, swerving left with a screech of tyres.

'Where are you going?' asked Ted. 'It's right!'

'I'm going to deal with her.' He floored the accelerator and aimed the car at Margaret who was still standing there with her small bag on the pavement beside her. McPhee shouted from the back, 'Forget it, Skins, you crazy fucker!'

Lofting reached over and grabbed the wheel. The BMW lurched into a row of parked cars and bounced off them in a shower of broken glass.

'Jesus!' someone shouted from the back.

The collision had caught the attention of the DST men further up the street. Jules Lacroix barked into a walkie talkie, 'The fix is wrong, they're 150 metres back – in the direction of the Pont de Neuilly!'

Margaret grabbed her bag and wanted to run. But where to? She could see half a dozen men running up from the direction of the roadsweeper. Then she heard the noise. At first it was like something in her head, then she heard it for what it was, a car horn. She looked around desperately. A taxi. Bernard in the back. She ran for it.

Big Lacroix came thumping up the street with his heavies. He had seen the woman getting into a taxi and he could see a couple of men who'd been in the BMW running down the road. His men looked to him. Who should they pursue? 'Did anyone get the number on that taxi?' he shouted, breathless. Nobody answered.

Margaret and Bourrat did not do what the pursuing DST men expected them to and head for the airport. They left the taxi ten minutes later and took a metro to the Gare de Lyon. From there it was a TGV to Geneva. Once in Switzerland they booked their plane tickets, Margaret travelling under her Spanish passport in the name of Pillar Carrizosa.

In the weeks which followed, Lofting never let on to his colleagues in Cheltenham that he had allowed Margaret to walk away before the chaos had broken loose that last morning. Operation POLYP continued, and its carefully designed deniability measures all seemed to be working. There was of course a loose end. A human loose end.

Margaret's disappearance caused considerable comment and concern at Cheltenham, but it was one of those things which the minions like Brenda Skuse could only guess about, drawing mysterious connections with Ted's sudden retirement.

In the *Elysée* a full-scale investigation was launched into what had become of Bourrat. An investigation of the abandonned BMW revealed nothing – the credit card used to pay for it and identity documents produced by the hirer all led them to dead ends. Lacroix reported to his superiors that the woman who Bourrat met must have been a high-grade foreign intelligence operator to have hit on the idea of leading them astray with her mobile phone. It had bought her and Bourrat the vital minutes they needed to get the better of Paris traffic.

GCHQ Security and MI6 knew Bourrat had dropped out of view, of course, but the French government was never going to admit that he had done so with $7,200,000 of bribe money for their Saudi fixer. Despite the efforts of the Security Department, it was only when Ted suggested they ring the Nazareth home in Clifton that they found out Mr Reynolds had left in March – driven away by a foreign gentleman. Further enquiries by GCHQ Security established that Margaret Reynolds's flat had been sold after power of attorney had been vested in one Bella Crewe. They were not authorised to find out more about who she was and where the money from the sale had gone.

The POLYP Production Committee, a joint GCHQ/NSA group met at Benhall in May and ruled that there was no decisive proof that the operation had been compromised. Despite the expulsion of Phil Keitel, despite Margaret's disappearance, the taps remained in place, feeding through to the TV company where the best material selected by the computer was sent back to Britain. Monsieur Moutet, the printing company sales-man, came out of it with a clean bill of health. There was no reason to suppose the tunnel had ever been discovered. Dan Birnbaum, chairing the POLYP com-mittee, decided, however, that there was sufficient doubt about the operation for the information coming over from Paris never to be disseminated outside GCHQ and NSA.

* * *

In June, Ted made his final break with GCHQ – colleagues had conspired to keep the handovers and debriefs going weeks longer than the Director had wanted. He had bought himself a thirty-five-foot ketch and he was convinced that Sara would come around to the idea of a world cruise. She had not moved back in though. Sara had got a job in Gloucester working in an estate agent. They had met up a few times for dinner and she had told him they'd 'take things slowly'. Ted still didn't know whether that meant getting back together or breaking the final ties between them.

Emma had agreed to go on holiday with him. They would take the yacht as far as Spain together and then she would fly home. He was then planning to cruise around the Med a bit, see places like Minorca and Gibraltar where great sea battles had taken place. That morning, Lofting was rushing around making final preparations to pick up his yacht. He rushed into the house from an early trip to the supermarket and stepped on the post. He looked down and saw a postcard among the bills and circulars. Ted raced into the living room to give everything a last check before leaving. The light was blinking on his answerphone. Maybe Sara wanted to come after all, it would be just like her to change her mind on the morning he was heading off. He pressed play.

'Hello, Ted, it's Norman.' Ted groaned aloud. Norman was the most boring of the crowd at the GCHQ wargames club. 'Just thought I'd let you know, we tried the spreadsheet the other night at the club and there's something odd about it. I should say! If you press F4 after putting in your variables, you do considerably more damage – it boosts the result. It's a cheat code. Anyway, just thought you'd want to know.'

Ted turned around, trying to go through his mental checklist of things to do before he left so that he wouldn't pick up the phone to Dan Birnbaum and shout at him.

'I'm going, I'm going,' he said to himself. As he stood at the door, getting his keys ready, Ted noticed the card on the mat. It was a picture of an Airbus in the colours of Swissair. He didn't want to read it, it would be like the answerphone, another bloody annoying message from someone somewhere. Curiosity got the better of him. It had been posted in Geneva.

Dear Ted,
Just to let you know that my father died last week. It was sudden, but I think it was a release and take some comfort from that. Before he died, he was able to see me married – he smiled throughout! Forgive me for not inviting you, because I will always remember your kindness that last morning in Paris. Forgive me also for exposing you to the risk of capture. All I can say is that it was the only way I could make sense of everything. I hope you'll understand also if I do not give you my address. A stewardess agreed to post this for me. Just rest assured that I am still very much alive and at liberty and that you are the only thing I miss about Cheltenham.
Lots of love, The Linguist.

Cat and Mouse

James Patterson

Psychopath Gary Soneji is back – filled with hatred and obsessed with gaining revenge on detective Alex Cross. Soneji seems determined to go down in a blaze of glory and he wants Alex Cross to be there. Will this be the final showdown?

Two powerful and exciting thrillers packed into one, with the electrifying page-turning quality that is the hallmark of James Patterson's writing, CAT AND MOUSE is the most original and audacious of the internationally bestselling Alex Cross novels.

'Patterson's action-packed story keeps the pages flicking by' *The Sunday Times*

'Patterson, among the best novelists of crime stories ever, has reached his pinnacle' *USA Today*

'Packed with white-knuckle twists' *Daily Mail*

'Patterson has a way with plot twists that freshens the material and keeps the adrenalin level high' *Publishing News*

0 7472 5788 4

Dead Headers

James H. Jackson

Officially the British Intelligence organisation known as Executive Support doesn't exist. But for its far-from-innocent victims it is all too real. Its aim: to terrorize the terrorists, to eliminate them before they can act. Its nickname: the Dead Headers.

When a sadistic mortar attack turns the streets of Paris into a charnel house, no group claims responsibility and there are no clues to the killers' motives. But the attack is only the first piece of a terrifying jigsaw that leads the Dead Headers from a secretive German pharmaceuticals company to an Iraqi biological weapons base in the Libyan desert, from a gruesome sex-murder in London's Hammersmith to a power struggle at the heart of the Iranian revolutionary regime. And by the time the final piece is in place, the fate of millions will have been decided . . .

'Tense, well researched, fast-paced and hard-nosed' Frederick Forsyth

'Hair-raising' *Guardian*

0 7472 5771 X